Dedication

Frank Stanton

*A wonderful friend. The big brother I
never had, but always wanted.*

SPEAK NOTHING OF THE DEAD BUT GOOD
A Prophecy

By

WILLIAM C. HARRIS JR.

TABLE OF CONTENTS

FOREWORD

THE NEAR FUTURE

As the second decade of the twenty-first century ended, the world was a much different place than it had been at the dawn of the New Millennium. Debt had crushed governments all around the globe. While the United States had not been crushed, it had been greatly humbled, and goods and services always taken for granted were now scarce and expensive.

When it was available, gasoline was over twenty dollars a gallon at the pump and the public's anxiety level was even higher as unemployment had hovered between 15 and 20 percent for more than five years. Private schools were forced to close while public schools were staggered by ever-increasing populations and draconian budget cuts.

While the rate of inflation in the U.S. was nowhere as high as that in Germany's Weimar Republic of the 1920s, it was significant and painful. Due to those pressures, a flourishing barter economy emerged, one that could not be taxed. The modicum of exchange came not to be gold, but rather things of utilitarian value. Guns and ammunition soon became the new gold standard.

But it was the political landscape in America that had taken the sharpest turn. When the government money finally evaporated, so did the politics that had driven it. The overwhelming political attitude had evolved into fiscal conservatism and social libertarianism People of all races and backgrounds who still had something left were attracted to movements that promised to keep taxes low and expenditures lower. State and local governments scrambled to find alternative sources of income that could help sustain cash-starved services such as fire and police protection.

In the twentieth and twenty-first centuries, a long litany of American presidents had vowed to win the "war on drugs" and they had all lost abysmally, with nothing more to show for their efforts other than huge budget deficits and even larger prison populations. Illegal drugs and the crime that accompanied them were a major burden on the taxpayers. This was the driving force that caused the individual states to call for change from the federal government. It was a sweeping demand set forth by the states, with the federal government having no alternative other than to submit to their will.

The Drug Enforcement Administration was disbanded and each state had the right to decide what drugs were legal within its borders. Almost immediately, marijuana use, possession, and production were legalized throughout the country, and the states began to realize substantial tax revenues. Then crime caused by drugs such as methamphetamines and crack cocaine came under close review.

Almost 85 percent of the inmate population in Georgia's prisons was incarcerated due to drug activity. Most of it was from crimes committed while attempting to find money to buy the drugs or those committed while high on them. The state of Georgia had decided to embark on a unique solution to that problem.

The countries of Europe had been ahead of the drug curve for several years, and a few politicians in Georgia had been keeping track. When the European statistics started showing that limited legalization of all types of addictive substances decreased the crime rate and the cost to the taxpayers, those politicians took note. They were particularly interested in the idea of what were referred to as "drug colonies."

The European drug colonies were not a capitulation to drug addiction, but rather an acceptance of the fact that a certain number of people were going to be drug addicts, no matter what governments or societies tried to do. The drug colonies were an attempt to minimize the impact of such behavior. Their data showed that crimes involving drugs producing violent behavior plummeted when addicts were offered the option of a drug colony. Within a year after the colony idea had been adopted, prison populations dropped precipitously.

In Georgia, it was Robert Roy "Big Dog" McFarland, state senator from Gwinnett County, who first had the courage to bring the idea to the public's attention. In the beginning, there was horror and revulsion, but, as Georgia's prisons passed their bursting point and new taxes were the only way to pay for more prison beds, the voters quieted down and began to listen.

Robert Roy McFarland was descended from a long line of Georgia politicians and University of Georgia alumni. He'd been an outstanding football player in high school and an even more successful player for the Georgia Bulldogs, where he was the starting quarterback from his first year through his last. When he entered law school at Georgia, he'd already been crowned with the nickname "Big Dog," and it was the perfect fit.

When Big Dog finished law school, he was offered a position at the prestigious Atlanta firm of King and Spaulding. Just about everybody wanted to meet him, and his practice took off quickly. Before too long, he was elected to the Georgia House of Representatives and then the Senate. Twelve years after he'd been elected to the House, Big Dog ran for governor. One of the main planks in his campaign was lessening the impact of drugs on the populace. He advocated doing so by the institution of drug colonies modeled after those in Europe. He won by a landslide.

Governor McFarland's idea was straightforward and simple. Georgia would start with one colony, isolated and secure. Anyone who was a citizen of the state could check into the facility and he would be provided with any drug of his choice, as much as he wanted. The residents would be fed, clothed, and housed. But, once they were in the facility, they could never leave. Big Dog liked to joke that it was like the old "Roach Motel" ads. You could check in, but you couldn't check out.

CHAPTER ONE

SIGNS OF THE TIMES

He answered and said unto them, "When it is evening, ye say, 'it will be fair weather; for the sky is red.' And in the morning, 'It will be foul weather today; for the sky is red and lowering.' O ye hypocrites, ye can discern the face of the sky; but can ye not discern the signs of the times?"

—*The Holy Bible*, King James Version, Matthew 16:2-4

"At least it's not raining and the wind isn't blowing," thought John-Morgan Hartman as he walked down his dock and looked out over the Skidaway River that wound south past his house on the Isle of Hope. The marsh was the color of straw, bleached of its lustrous, lively green by the sparseness of the winter sun. The sky was a clear robin's egg blue without the hint of a cloud. Its only marks were the streaks of jet contrails leading from New York to Miami. His boat rested gently at the dock, washed by the bright morning sun, its lines and curves sinuous and appealing. She was his other lover.

When he heard voices, he turned back toward his house and saw his three friends making their way down the long dock, framed by the six massive columns of Driscoll House. Any other time he would have looked forward to their boat trip, but now he had something of a knot in his stomach, almost a sense of dread about what they had agreed to do.

"How did all this happen?" he wondered as he climbed aboard the thirty-one-foot *Admiral Graf Spee* and went about the necessary ritual of turning knobs, throwing switches and checking gauges before he could fire off the boat's twin engines. He didn't think things would change so quickly, but he knew he'd seen it coming. "There's only so much people can take," he thought, "before the shit hits the fan." He zipped his leather bomber jacket all the way to his neck and put on his red baseball cap with the bold gold letters "USMC" embroidered across the front.

"Must be in the twenties," said Lloyd Bryan as he stepped aboard and looked at John-Morgan with half a smile.

"The sun'll warm things up some," replied John-Morgan, "if we don't freeze our butts off on the way to the island."

Next aboard was Will McQueen, who held tightly to the grab rails as he eased himself into the cockpit and let go with a long "Sheeeit! I hope you've got something strong to drink for the ride back, I think we're gonna' need it!"

"Have I ever let you down?" answered John-Morgan, shaking Will's hand.

"No sir, not even once," said Will, slapping John-Morgan on the shoulder and laughing.

Last aboard was Judah Benjamin, who said to no one in particular, "This is Yankee weather." He took a pair of gloves out of his coat pocket and began to pull them on while he looked at the houses lining Bluff Drive.

"What's the running time to the island, John-Morgan?" he asked as he sought a place in the sun to keep warm.

"About fifty minutes, maybe a little less. Nobody pays attention to the 'No Wake' zones anymore since there isn't any law enforcement to back it up," answered John-Morgan before he turned the key on his starboard engine.

"Whole lotta things different now," injected Lloyd in his baritone voice, shaking his head in a sign of disgust.

"Where's Big Dog?" asked Judah, checking his watch.

"Late as usual," said Will, just before they all heard a booming voice from up on the lawn yell out, "Hey, y'all, damn it, don't leave the Dog, I'm the governor, remember?"

With easy grace and surprising speed, Big Dog came running down the dock with members of his security following, trying hard to keep up with the boss. His breath frosted as he jumped into the boat's cockpit and began to shake hands. His two bodyguards stood on the floating dock, awaiting orders. Big Dog looked up at them and said, "Y'all take the day off; I want to be with my friends. I'll call y'all when we start back."

"No can do, boss," said the big black agent. "You know the drill, sir. We'll lose our jobs if we do that."

Big Dog looked down at the deck for a second and the bright light bouncing off the white hurt his eyes. Then he looked up at his bodyguards and said, "Ah, hell, can't I get by with just one of you two bruisers?"

The black agent looked at his white counterpart and nodded to him. Then he turned to Big Dog and said, "I'll go with you, Governor. Under these circumstances, I think one cover'll be enough."

"Well, hell, Luke," said Big Dog, "get your butt in here before it freezes off."

Big Dog was actually glad Luke Butts wanted to go. He liked Luke a lot. He was another athlete, played pro ball once, for the Falcons.

Big Dog put his arm around Luke's shoulder and said, "I want to introduce you to my friends, Luke." Then he went down the line, first to John-Morgan, then Judah and Will, telling little anecdotes about each one, all perfectly constructed to be both funny and complimentary. Big Dog was as smooth and skillful as a politician can get. When he got to Lloyd Bryan, the governor rolled out the red carpet.

"Luke," said Big Dog in a mid-Georgia twang, "this here is my all-time hero. He played pro ball just like you and was damn good at it, too, I might add. But kickin' jocks' butts wasn't enough of a challenge for him, so he decided he'd take on the devil himself, and now, he's the Bishop of Savannah and has Lucifer on the run. Lloyd, meet my right-hand man, Agent Luke Butts."

Luke didn't need any history on Lloyd Bryan. He was a legend in Georgia, particularly among the black population, and Luke smiled broadly as Lloyd firmly took his hand and said, "I watched you play many times, and I'm glad you weren't comin' for me across the line, Luke."

Luke replied, "I never coulda laid a hand on you, Bishop, you were too fast for me."

John-Morgan eased *Graf Spee* away from the dock, into the middle of the river. He steered south past the most beautiful houses in Savannah and toward what some thought was insanity. Easily, he brought his boat onto a plane, then pushed her hard for the Skidaway Narrows and what the locals called "Butterbean Beach."

After *Graf Spee* passed under the bridge at the narrows, all aboard were taken aback. Butterbean Beach had changed. It was now enclosed in high fences with razor wire atop and gates that blocked the entrance and the exit. There were no more picnic tables, the little concession stand at the boat ramp was gone, and several large and beautiful oaks had been removed. The whole place looked like a giant holding area for prisoners.

"This is the embarkation area," said Will as John-Morgan pulled back on the throttle and brought the boat to idle speed.

"Looks like a concentration camp," replied Judah, his eyes following the fences all the way up to their beginning on the Diamond Causeway. The causeway led to The Landings on Skidaway Island, a high-end gated community.

"This must put a chill up the asses of such a privileged class of folks as they pass by here each day," said Lloyd.

"Actually," replied Will, "they were some of the biggest supporters of the project. It makes them feel safer."

Big Dog was stone-faced when he said, "It makes a whole lot of people feel safer."

John-Morgan pressed the throttle forward and brought *Graf Spee* to 3600 rpm's, leaving Butterbean Beach in its wake. After the boat passed Pidgin Island, some of the larger houses on The Landings came into view. The "For Sale by Foreclosure" signs on several of the homes caused Judah to sigh and say, "Those are multimillion-dollar homes. I never thought we'd ever see anything like this in America."

"Neither did the people who borrowed the money to build them or the ones who paid cash and lost their butts in the market," added Will, "but it is what it is. So now, we deal with it."

"We've got two right now on Bluff Drive," John-Morgan said as he pointed his boat to starboard and saw Burnside Island visible in the distance. Then his right leg started to ache. It always did when the weather grew cold. It had since he returned with battle wounds from Vietnam almost fifty years ago. Every once in a while, it would almost get the better of him, but he'd shake it off and no one would be the wiser.

It always seemed to surprise John-Morgan when somebody would say or imply how much they envied him and the life he had. He came from an old Savannah family, had been decorated with the Navy Cross, had married a beautiful girl and lived in Driscoll House. He knew he'd been lucky, blessed by God as his mother use to say, but nobody, sometimes not even Ann-Marie, knew what he carried around inside himself. It was true he'd had a successful medical practice, made serious money, married well, but now he was scared in a way he'd never been before. He told himself he was too old to put up with the bullshit that was emerging. His leg hurt more. Then he glanced at Lloyd in the seat next to him.

Lloyd knew what it was like to feel different. Not just different because of the color of his skin at an all-white boys' Catholic military school, but different about the way he felt inside. He'd grown up in a single-parent home when it was uncommon even in the black community. All the other children he played with had daddies at home to teach them how to be a man. But Lloyd's daddy was rarely at home. He was a gambler, a moonshiner, a gigolo. His mother had thrown him out after he infected her with a venereal disease.

Lloyd's mother had been a devout Roman Catholic from birth. She had been strict in his upbringing and tolerated nothing but the best from her only child. Daily morning Mass had been a ritual for her and her son.

In the spring of 1960, things were changing in Savannah and all around the South. The Bishop had decided to integrate the Catholic schools in his diocese and had chosen Lloyd as the first black student to attend an all-white Catholic institution. He had been selected for his grades, his deportment and his mother, who the Bishop knew was a woman of character.

What sealed Lloyd's fate and good standing among the corps of cadets was his athletic prowess. His talent in football had propelled the small school to the state championship. It also won him a scholarship to the University of Notre Dame and then a first-round draft pick by the Washington Redskins. The world was at his feet for several years and all the adulation, the women, the money, and eventually cocaine, overwhelmed him.

Lloyd's mother knew her son was not on the right path and told him so many times. Lloyd knew this, but the allure of his earthly pleasures was more than he could resist until one cold, early morning on a deserted street in Washington. High on coke and sharing it with a woman he'd known only for hours, he witnessed the shooting of a teenage black boy over a small amount of drugs.

Overcome by what he'd seen and smeared with the guilt of his own behavior, Lloyd rushed back to his apartment alone, where he fell to his knees and begged for God's forgiveness. Not long after, he quit professional football, sold all that he had, gave the proceeds to the poor, and entered into the priesthood. It had been a long, arduous journey, but one he had never regretted.

Lloyd was eventually elevated by the Pope to be the first black bishop of the Diocese of Savannah. After many years of work and sacrifice, he thought he could see the end of that journey. He even allowed himself to dream of retirement and enjoying life with his friends. Then he was called upon once more. This time, it was by what would happen on a barrier island along Georgia's coast.

When *Graf Spee* entered into the Forest River, the swells of an incoming tide gently lifted her bows in a slow, rocking motion as the sound of rushing water filled the boat's cockpit. The morning sun was bright and warm.

William Wallace McQueen had been born into a family of money and privilege. His ancestors were Scottish Highlanders, among the first to settle the Colony of Georgia. Will had been brought up hearing the stories of his Colonial, Revolutionary and Confederate predecessors.

With almost everything any reasonable person could want, Will McQueen still knew the deep cut of pain. It was a pain that was difficult to erase, particularly from the face of a child, a child who had grown into an adolescent ashamed of the way he looked.

Will had been blessed with a head of thick dark hair, large and soft brown eyes and a strong chin. But he had also been born with a cleft palate, a hare lip. As a youngster it had cowered Will, made him so self-conscious that he couldn't wait until he was old enough to grow a mustache to somewhat hide his disfigurement, even though his parents had taken him to Atlanta where the best plastic surgeon in the state was able to repair part of the deformity.

But Will found he was made of sterner stuff. After graduating from The Citadel, he accepted a commission in the Navy and shipped out to Vietnam a year later. There, he commanded a river patrol boat in the Mekong Delta and actually enjoyed what he did. But everything changed when his vessel was furiously attacked and, as a result of his injuries, Will lost both legs below the knee.

After that, Will fell into a deep depression that ended only after a long period of earnest soul-searching followed by religious inspiration. A successful political career ensued, master- minded by Judah Benjamin. Under Judah's guidance, Will was elected to the United States House of Representatives and climbed to a position of leadership.

Judah Benjamin stood in the stern of *Graf Spee* and watched his friends as they huddled behind the windshield to protect themselves from the cold. He chose to expose his face to the wind as a means of sobering himself to what lay just beyond the horizon. When he saw the marker for Hell Gate passage come into view he dropped his head and watched the spray from the boat's bow as it fanned the waves and he listened to its watery whisper. "Hell Gate," he thought, "what an appropriate name for the way to this island."

Judah Paul Benjamin had been born and raised in Savannah. His father was from New Orleans, a lineal descendant of the famous Judah P. Benjamin, the first Jewish United States senator and an unrepentant son of the Confederate States of America. His mother was a native Savannahian, and her ancestors had also served the Confederacy with its blood and fortune. His father had met his mother in Savannah during World War II when he had accepted a commission in the Army Air Corps.

Judah had made millions in politics. Not by being elected to office, but rather by getting others elected. He had successfully served multiple congressmen and senators and two presidents. His name was golden in Washington, the *sine quo non* of political consultants, the go-to guy when the going got rough.

When Judah returned to Savannah from his career in Washington, he felt as if he'd escaped from a pressure cooker. Then, somehow, he managed to connect again with the one woman he'd loved all his life, and things had been good. Now, even his happiness with Hannah seemed threatened by the craziness in the world. He worried deeply about where things were going. It gnawed at him so, he had reluctantly agreed to try to find a solution to the madness.

CHAPTER TWO

PARADISE LOST

There was a time when meadow, grove, and stream,
The earth, and every common sight,
To me did seem
Apparelled in celestial light,
The glory and freshness of a dream.
It is not now as it hath been of yore;
Turn wheresoe'er I may,
By night or day,
The things which I have seen I now can see no more.
—Wordsworth, *The Prel*

Georgia's barrier islands are the most pristine along the entire Atlantic Coast. Only four have been developed, while the others remain almost untouched by human hands. Ossabaw is one of those cherished few.

Ossabaw is the third island in Georgia's chain which starts on the north Georgia coast with Tybee. It is Ossabaw that best embodies the combination of the beauty, allure, and history that make Georgia's sea islands so special and unique.

The island of Ossabaw is about 20,000 years old and has known human habitation for perhaps 4,000 to 5,000 years. It's the third largest of the barrier islands, encompassing about 9,000 acres of maritime forest with freshwater ponds and around 16,000 acres of marshlands interlaced with tidal creeks. It is almost ten miles long and about two miles at its widest point. The high ground is Y-shaped with the stem of the Y being the south beach. The two upper parts are in the north, and they are divided by a large area of salt marsh and creeks. The main landing is on the northwestern stem of the Y while to the east is Bradley Point. Almost nine miles of beaches abut the Atlantic. The western side of the island is separated from the mainland by large expanses of marsh dotted with small islands referred to as hammocks.

Ossabaw is an ecosystem unique unto itself and replete with all manner of wildlife. Deer proliferate on the island as do feral hogs and even donkeys introduced by early European settlers. It is a place of deep, full, and vibrant growth. If it could be held on the tongue, the taste would be succulent.

The first humans of note on Ossabaw were the Guale, a distinct cultural group of American Indians related to the Muskogeans. In the early 1500s the Spanish were the first Europeans to explore the island and attempt to convert the indigenous people to Christianity. By the mid-1700s, British control of this part of the coast was firmly established.

In the early twentieth century, ownership of the island finally began to take its final shape under the control of wealthy Northerners who purchased it as a winter hunting retreat and playground.

The Torrey family of Detroit, Michigan, acquired the island in 1924 and built the Main House, a Spanish Colonial Revival mansion on the north end of the island, overlooking Ossabaw Sound. For most of the next fifty years, the Torrey family enjoyed and protected its unique retreat until commercial pressure to develop the property and tax burdens from the State of Georgia forced the heirs to make a choice about the future of Ossabaw.

In 1978, Ossabaw was sold by the West family to the state with the proviso that the surviving descendants could retain ownership of a small part of the island and its buildings until death. When Eleanor Torrey West passed away at an age in excess of one hundred years, the State of Georgia became the sole owner of Ossabaw Island and all it comprised.

The Great Recession of the twenty-first century and all that ensued from it finally forced Georgia's hand. The state could no longer afford the luxury of letting such a large piece of prime real estate lie fallow.

Several ideas were kicked around in Atlanta about how to make money from the island. But they all fell short of what the state was able to spend in up-front money and willing to put up with in bureaucratic nonsense.

So, for the time being, Ossabaw would exist as it had been for centuries: radiant, ravishing, and resplendent until the new social paradigm arose and Ossabaw was changed.

CHAPTER THREE

THE NEW PARADIGM

A single death is a tragedy, a million deaths is a statistic.
—Joseph Stalin

"Sweet Mother of Mercy," whispered Lloyd while John-Morgan maneuvered *Graf Spee* into position at Ossabaw's dock. His eyes traced it from beginning to end, and all he could see was razor wire covering the whole length. He shook his head in disbelief when two men in black battle dress uniforms carrying submachine guns slung over their shoulders moved down the gangway to the floating dock.

"You are Doctor Hartman?" asked the larger one with a German accent. John-Morgan nestled his boat against the dock while Will and Judah tossed the men his mooring lines.

"Yes, I am," replied John-Morgan, "and these gentlemen are part of my party." The men on the dock pulled hard on the lines and soon *Graf Spee* was secured.

"I am Oberst Claus Schwarz, Dr. Hartman," said the man, displaying a rock-hard body. Both guards stood at attention while John-Morgan and the others climbed out of the boat.

"Oberst is German for Colonel, isn't it," responded John-Morgan as he looked at Schwarz.

"Quite correct, sir. I am Dr. Hoorst's executive officer," said Schwarz, "and he has instructed me to direct you to his quarters and to give you and your party a brief overview of what you will encounter on the way there."

"Career military," whispered John-Morgan to Judah, acknowledging the colonel with a crisp nod of his head and starting up the gangway.

While he walked, a growing feeling of coldness seeped into Judah as he thought about the people who would soon come this way and enter into a maddening world of their own making. He looked to his right and watched the plume from Lloyd's breath as his great barrel chest inhaled and exhaled the frigid Atlantic air. Judah caught Lloyd's eye for a moment and both knew they shared the same misgivings. Agent Butts was a step behind the governor, his eyes scanning for any threat. The submachine guns made him nervous.

Colonel Schwarz walked next to John-Morgan and, about halfway up the dock, he said, "Dr. Hartman, I understand you were awarded two Purple Hearts and the Navy Cross for your actions in the Vietnam War, sir?"

John-Morgan trudged ahead, his sinuses feeling the bite of the harsh dry air, and replied, "Yeah, the Marine Corps. A lifetime ago, Colonel Schwarz, and you?"

Schwarz shrugged, smiled and looked at John-Morgan, saying, "Nothing as heroic as yourself, sir, but I served in the *Bundeswehr*, did my time, and then joined the French Foreign Legion. I've always liked the military, it's my home, and the Legion just seemed like a natural fit. I was in their special operations group, you know, those things I can't tell about, but

WILLIAM C. HARRIS JR. | 26

the things we both know go on all the time?"

"And what brings you to Ossabaw Island, Colonel?" asked John-Morgan, eyes searching ahead.

Schwarz's head cocked back and he snorted, "The money, what else? After I became too old for duty in the Legion, I hired on with Executive Outcomes, and after several other deployments, I find myself here on this beautiful island."

John-Morgan nodded and said, "Yeah, it is beautiful, but for how long?"

When the group reached the end of the walkway, they all stopped. Judah was frozen in place by what he saw. He was speechless as he stared at the wrought iron archway overhead. In block letters four inches high was the Latin phrase, *De mortuis nil nisi bonum*. The others were silent also until Judah turned to Lloyd and asked, "Do you know what that means?"

Lloyd slowly nodded his head in affirmation and said, "Speak nothing of the dead but good." He looked back up at the arch.

"Do you remember the first time we saw this phrase, John-Morgan?" asked Lloyd.

"Yeah, I'll never forget," he replied. "It was in our sophomore year at B.C. and we were doing a little amateur archeology for extra credit in our history class. We'd heard about a tunnel that started at the old Candler Hospital on Drayton Street and went looking for it, and damned if we didn't find it. It went under Drayton and opened up into a big room under Forsyth Park. We found out it dated back to the 1830s and served as the city morgue."

"You've got a good memory, my friend," said Lloyd.

"Yeah, and I also remember how creeped-out I was when we found the entrance," said John-Morgan. "The same the exact Latin phrase we're looking at now was carved into the marble over the entrance. You wrote it down and had Father Damien translate it."

Then Judah spoke.

"Listen, John-Morgan, you talk about being creeped-out, well, let me tell you how creeped-out this archway makes me."

Will looked at Judah and said, "Are you OK? You look like you've seen a ghost or something."

"Oh yeah, I've seen a ghost," answered Judah as the stared at the archway, "not just one ghost, but millions of ghosts. This thing looks exactly like the arch that was at the entrances to the Nazi concentration camps. You know, '*Arbeit macht frei*! Work makes you free!' I'm telling ya'll this is in the exact style of that abomination. This gives me a real bad feelin'."

Colonel Schwarz cleared his throat, then said, "That is the motto of Executive Outcomes, sir."

Big Dog shifted nervously and finally touched Judah's arm, saying, "I'll have it taken down if you want me to."

Judah took another breath, thought for a moment, and said, "Naw, Dog, it might not be bad advice for anybody coming in here, after all. Just leave it up. Let's get moving."

The first large building the group came to was the Club House. It was a wood frame structure and almost seventy-five years old. For most of those years it had housed visiting artists and writers on the island. Now it served as quarters for the officers and families of Executive Outcomes, Incorporated. Parked in front were three Humvees. Next to them were three rows of eleven men each, all dressed in black, all at attention, all carrying submachine guns.

Colonel Schwarz slowed and turned to the group, saying: "Gentleman, Dr. Hoorst has requested that you review one of our shift contingents."

With obvious pride, Schwarz gestured and said, "These are the guards for our three-to-eleven shift. They are thirty-three strong, all very well-trained and all quite professional. If any of you has any questions of these men, please feel at liberty to ask."

John-Morgan glanced at Will and then walked slowly down the first rank of men. His eyes went from head to toe. The men appeared sharp and impressive. Their blouses were military style as were the trousers, both black. Pant legs were tucked into mid-calf black leather boots, well shined and reflecting the morning sun. Insignia of rank were American style, sown to the sleeves. Above the left jacket pocket, embroidered in silver block letters, were the words "Executive Outcomes, Inc." Above that was a diving eagle, talons outstretched. Above the right pocket were the names of the individual men.

As John-Morgan walked down the row, not one man's eye moved or even blinked. The men were taut, hard, and muscled. Haircuts were short and there were no beards or mustaches. The names on their uniforms revealed a hodgepodge of European stock: German, French, Italian, Danish, Irish, Anglo-Saxon, even Russian.

When John-Morgan reached the end of the line, he turned to Colonel Schwarz and said, "So, Colonel, this is an impressive group. How many are your fellow Legionnaires?"

Schwarz tilted his head, a slight smile across his lips, and replied, "More than 75 percent. Dr. Hoorst will provide you with each man's dossier if you require, Dr.Hartman."

John-Morgan glanced at the ground for a moment, then looked up his friends. "OK, guys, so I guess we go to the Main House to meet Dr. Hoorst."

Schwarz motioned to one of the Humvees saying, "We'll ride the rest of the way."

Just before John-Morgan climbed into the Humvee, he remarked to Colonwl Schwarz, "The weapons, they're all MP-40's, Schmeissers, are they not? All from World War II?"

"Good eye, Dr. Hartman," replied Schwarz, "not many people would know that."

"I collect firearms," said John-Morgan. "Why in the world are those men armed with them, they're almost antiques?"

"When you get to know more about Executive Outcomes," said Schwarz with a wry smile, "you'll understand. The company is very frugal. Those weapons were purchased immediately after the war by the company when it was in its fledgling stages. They have been well cared for and are still considered among the best of their kind. They have gotten the job done many times before and will continue to do so. They're a bit like this vehicle we have here, all military surplus. That's how the company does business."

"Gotcha," answered John-Morgan, closing the door to the Humvee.

When the Humvee turned into the driveway of the Main House, two similarly uniformed men stood at attention at the steps of the massive house. As the vehicle stopped, one of them approached and opened the doors much as a chauffeur would.

In an instant, Colonel Schwarz was out of the Humvee and at the steps to the Main House. "Gentlemen, please allow me to escort you into Dr. Hoorst's quarters. He should be here momentarily. There is a large fire lighted inside. Please follow me."

The sound of Schwarz's boot steps echoed as he stepped into the Great Room of the Main House. Completed in 1926, the building was little changed from its first days. The Great Room had a large stone fireplace where logs from the island's fallen oaks burned. The room was two stories high with an exposed-beam wood ceiling, and paneled and plastered walls. On the walls hung hunting trophies as well as oils and water colors depicting life on Ossabaw. Comfortable leather chairs faced the fireplace, the silence of the room occasionally interrupted by the pops and cracks of the burning logs. All the visitors approached the fire and extended their hands, soaking up its heat. Colonel Schwarz cleared his throat to get their attention and was about to offer them something to drink when the muffled sound of horses' hooves striking the soft ground cut him short. Schwarz turned and looked out one of the tall windows filled with the winter sun and said, "Ah, Dr. Hoorst has arrived!"

The men walked to the window and watched as a well-built blond man with blue eyes, about fifty, came galloping up on a large Appaloosa. He was dressed in gray riding britches with red stripes down the sides, brown leather boots, and jacket. Great clouds of steam shot from the horse's nostrils as it pranced and reared back, still feeling the excitement of a spirited run. Deftly, the rider reined in his steed and briskly stepped down from the saddle, handing the reins to one of the men standing guard. Then he reached into his jacket pocket, produced an apple and approached the horse. Very tenderly he stroked the animal's snout until it was calm and then offered it the apple. The horse took it and began to crunch it in its mouth. One more stroke of his mount's neck, and Dr. Hoorst turned, straightened his jacket and climbed the steps of the Main House to greet his guests.

Will's eyes fell on the entrance of the great room as a guard opened the double doors and stood at attention when Dr. Hoorst entered.

"Ah, my dear friend Congressman McQueen," said Dr. Hoorst in an aristocratic Virginia accent with a hint of German. "What a pleasure it is to see you again!"

Hoorst pivoted to face Big Dog. "I'm so glad to see you again, Governor McFarland," he said as the men shook hands.

Without hesitation, Hoorst turned and faced his other guests. Arms outstretched, he said cordially, "Don't tell me, I'll bet I know who each of you are!"

Then he approached Lloyd, took his hand and said, "You can be none other than His Excellency, Bishop Lloyd Bryan!"

Lloyd had a dry and biting wit and replied, "Not a hard call, Dr. Hoorst, there aren't too many black Catholic bishops in this neck of the woods."

Hoorst laughed good-naturedly and said, "Welcome, Your Excellency, welcome indeed."

Hoorst turned to Judah, extending his hand again, saying, "You must be the famous Judah P. Benjamin. I think we may have seen each other in Washington, but we've never been properly introduced. What a pleasure it is to have you here, sir. I know you come from a prominent Southern family and I'm most eager to learn more about you.

"I look forward to knowing you better, too, Dr. Hoorst."

Hoorst smiled at Judah for a long moment and then turned to face John-Morgan. He shook his head and said, "You're the one I've heard the most about, Dr. Hartman! I've truly looked forward to this meeting. We have so much in common."

Turning and walking to the fire, Hoorst said, "I'm chilled to the bone and could use a bit of alcohol. Would any of you choose to join me?"

"Yeah," said Will, "I think we could all use a shot or two, Dr. Hoorst."

Immediately Hoorst held up his right hand, saying, "Please, can we stop with this formality? I'm Rudolph, Rudy for short, please address me as such and, with your permission, I will call you Will, Lloyd, Judah, John-

Morgan and of course, Big Dog, if you wish. Are we in agreement?"

"Dog for short, Rudy, you know that," said the Governor.

Rudy laughed, rubbed his hands together and extended them to the fire. "Of course I do, we've been friends for a couple years, now, haven't we?"

"If you will give me the liberty, gentlemen, I would like to serve you one of my favorite liquors for this time of year. Oberst, bring on the Jagermeister!"

Moments later Schwarz appeared carrying a silver tray with seven filled shot glasses and a bottle of Jagermeister. Each man took a glass and held it until their host had been served. Hoorst stood for a moment and then raised his glass in a toast saying, "Gentlemen, here's to your health and to the State of Georgia!" Hoorst tilted his head back and downed the whole thing.

It had been many years since Judah had had a drink. Alcohol had been a problem in his life and he'd been careful and clean for a long time, but if ever there was a time he needed a drink, this was it. He canted his head back just as Rudy had done and knocked back the shot. It felt good going down, and Judah looked forward to the warm glow he knew would follow. He just hoped he could stop at only one, or maybe just two.

Hoorst moved closer to the fire and gazed into it for several seconds before saying, "We have a lot to talk about today, gentlemen. What the State of Georgia has contracted with my company is serious business and will require a clear understanding between Executive Outcomes and the state. You have been appointed by your state to oversee this operation." Horst glanced at Schwarz, held up his glass and said, "Claus, another round, if you please."

Schwarz filled all the glasses, then stood at attention by the entrance awaiting orders.

"That will be all for now, Claus," said Hoorst. "See to the men."

Hoorst didn't drink this shot in one gulp, but sipped it. Looking up at his guests, he said, "Please, let's be seated, get comfortable and talk for a few moments. Lunch will be served in an hour, and I can give you a broad overview of our operation before we dine."

Each of the men took a seat around the fire and nursed his Jagermeister. "Executive Outcomes and the State of Georgia provided me with rather extensive dossiers on each of you," said Hoorst, "and I must say, you're an impressive lot. You pretty much cover the waterfront, and it's an honor to be working with you." Hoorst took a deep breath, reached for his glass and finished it off.

"The Hunt Master has worked its magic," mused Hoorst, raising his palms to the fire, feeling its warmth.

"So, my friends," he said, settling into his chair, "in turn, you should know as much about me as I do of you. My grandfather happened to have served in the Hermann Goering Division. He was sixteen years old when he was sent to Italy to fight the Allies as they climbed up the boot to the Alps. He fought at Monte Casino and somehow managed to survive. I know it will sound trite, but I doubt he was much of a Nazi. He was way too young and very much involved in saving his own neck rather than that of National Socialism. Yet, because he was in the Waffen SS, and we should draw a distinction between the SS and the Waffen SS, he was branded with that mark by the Allies during their occupation."

"There wasn't much in the way of work for a young man like my grandfather in immediate post-war Germany, so he took what he could find. He somehow fell in with a group of German nationals who had managed to chip out a living for themselves by selling war surplus items. As you can imagine, all of Europe was littered with weapons, uniforms, vehicles, and aircraft of all descriptions. It was the beginning of his career in war surplus and, for lack of a better description, a soldier of fortune. In a few years, he was able to ingratiate himself with the Americans and British occupation forces and helped a number of them make small fortunes from the surplus market. Before too long, he was traveling between Germany and the States and fell in with some fellows who had the right contacts. The Cold War was just getting underway, and the West was looking for well-trained proxies to fight quietly and efficiently against the Soviets in a number of faraway places. That's how Executive Outcomes came to be. My grandfather, Joachim, was its first leader."

"And, what of you, Rudy?" asked Lloyd.

"Well, my father, Rudolph, was born not too many years later, and because of my grandfather's close ties to the U.S., spent a great deal of time in America and went to work for the family business. He was in the Washington area in his early years with E.O. and was able to make the acquaintance of a beautiful young lady from Richmond. She turned out to be my mother, Louise. She was from a well-established Virginia family, a descendent of Stonewall Jackson. I was born in Richmond and attended the Catholic school there run by the Benedictines. Both my parents were Catholics and I was raised in a very strict Catholic home."

John-Morgan laughed and said, "Then you know that three of us here attended a Benedictine military school, too?"

"It was one of the first things that caught my eye when I read your bios, John-Morgan. You, Lloyd, and Judah are all graduates from the same class."

"That's right," said John-Morgan, "and several of the priests who taught us were from Richmond."

"Small world, isn't it?" asked Hoorst. "My father wanted me to go to college in England and I was graduated from Oxford, returned to the U.S. and went to Johns-Hopkins School of Medicine. My area of interest was genetics and pathology. After a number of years, I simply lost interest and decided to take my father up on his offer to be a part of his company. I've been with Executive Outcomes now for ten years, and this is the eighth such facility I've gotten up and running."

Hoorst rubbed the back of his neck, stretching it. Then he called out, "Colonel Schwarz!" Immediately the doors opened and Schwarz was there standing at attention.

"Another round, Claus," ordered Hoorst, sinking back in the soft cushions of his chair.

"One more personal note before we discuss business," added Hoorst. "I'm married and have two sons, ages nine and twelve. My wife, Carolyn, and my sons live here with me. You'll be meeting them when we break for lunch." Hoorst spoke again to Colonel Schwarz: "After you've poured our drinks, prepare the visual presentation of our operation."

Hoorst toyed with his Jagermiester while Schwarz turned on the large flat-screen at the end of the room and inserted a DVD disc into the player. Then he handed the remote control to Hoorst and left the room.

The first image on the screen was a map of Ossabaw's northern end. Hoorst walked over to the screen and pointed to the dock, saying: "You've already seen the security preparations along our dock. Here, at the end of the dock, we'll have a large fenced area where our residents will be thoroughly scrutinized. They will be photographed, undergo a full body scan like the ones TSA uses at airports. This will ensure that no weapons enter the island. The females will be checked for pregnancy, and any who are pregnant will be returned to the mainland. The remaining females will receive a subdermal birth control implant. Naturally, the last thing we want is a pregnant woman in the facility."

Hoorst saw Lloyd's head drop, and added, "Gentlemen, I know this is a difficult and trying thing for anyone to hear about for the first time. I remember how I felt the first time I had everything laid out before me, so I can understand your feelings. But, please keep in mind that what we are doing here is the most humane way of dealing with people like this. The alternative is life on the streets, taking and dealing in drugs, stealing, killing, filling the prisons, and costing the people of Georgia more money than they can afford."

Hoorst continued. "There will be no physical exam. The full body scan will tell us all we need to know. We're not here to treat their health problems. The residents will then be asked to declare what their drug or drugs of choice might be. All the information we have collected will be encoded onto a microchip which will then he inserted into the left forearm of each person. Not only will this microchip have all that data, but it will also give us the ability to track them with our GPS system. We will be able to know who they are and where they are, 24/7, anywhere on this island."

"Naturally," continued Hoorst, "this area will be completely enclosed. Armed guards will be strategically placed, and no disruption of the process will be tolerated. We will try to use non-lethal means of control, which is usually effective, but our staff won't hesitate to use their weapons should the need arise."

Hoorst took a drink from his shot glass. A dead silence had fallen upon the room as he turned back to the screen and continued, "Our population will then be divided into three separate groups based upon observed behavioral characteristics and overall physical condition. Those three groups will be moved into one of three corridors right here," said Hoorst, pointing to the screen with his riding crop, "that will, in turn, lead to the transportation that will take them to their designated living areas."

In a subdued voice, Lloyd asked, "What are those three designated groups composed of, Rudy?"

"Excellent question," responded Hoorst. "As I said before, E.O. has established eight other colonies just like this one and the State of Georgia is the beneficiary of what we've learned along the way. It has been our experience that we will encounter, first, people who aren't very far from death, perhaps weeks, sometimes days. They are easily distinguishable by their overall appearance. Any one of you could pick them out of the crowd with no problem. Some will have terminal illnesses such as AIDS or TB. Some will be at end-stage abuse of narcotics, and all they want to do is to die in relative peace, free of being set upon by other addicts and hoodlums. They have given up. This group, Group One, will be the easiest to control and will require the least amount of scrutiny. They will eat less and move around less. Some will never get out of their cots once they've been settled in."

"Rudy," interrupted Big Dog, "can I say something, here?'

"Of course, Governor, say anything you please."

Big Dog stood and gathered his thoughts for a moment before speaking. It was plain to everyone, he was pained by what they'd heard.

"Fellas," said the Dog, "y'all don't know how bad all of this hurts me, but the times are what they are, and I decided that we, as a people, just had to man up to the issue and stop what drugs were doin' to our country. I've visited E.O.'s colony in England, and what Rudy is sayin' is the truth. I've seen it with my own eyes, and, believe me, there were tears in 'em while I was lookin', but what Rudy is sayin' is no bullshit. So, I guess I'm sayin' I know how disturbin' this stuff is to y'all, but just give it a chance, OK?" Then Big Dog sat down with a sigh.

Hoorst paused, looked at his audience and continued, "Group Two is generally comprised of what we have come to call 'Stoners.' Group Two is at a different level than Group One. You see, there are people who just can't seem to cope with the world. They are the younger ones, people with no self-respect, for whatever reason. They simply want to get high, be taken care of by someone else and enjoy themselves as much as they can for as long as they can. The median age is between twenty-five and thirty-five. About a quarter are females. These individuals aren't necessarily violent, but they are leeches. They breed without discretion and place a great burden on us all when they dump the results of their trifles on the backs of the taxpayers."

Judah closed his eyes tightly as Hoorst went on. "Group Two lives the longest. Their preferred drugs of choice tend to be high-octane marijuana, sedatives such as diazepam when they choose to sleep, mild narcotics like hydrocodone, perhaps some coke and, from time to time, LSD. If they are not taken out by some infectious disease or the effects of their drug use, we're looking at a residency of around six months to a year. This group is the most expensive of the three due to their longevity."

The room was silent as its occupants struggled to absorb what they had been told.

"Group Three is the most difficult to handle, but in some ways it is the easiest, because they tend to thin the herd themselves."

Judah caught John-Morgan's eye and held his gaze for a moment. John-Morgan could see the pain in his friend's eyes.

"This group is made up primarily of young, feral males," said Hoorst. "Average age is between twenty-two and twenty-eight. Most are in good shape due to their youth. For the most part, they are also well-developed. Their drug addictions haven't had enough time to wreak their havoc yet. Almost to a man, or woman, if the case may be, their drugs of choice are very strong stimulants such as crack cocaine and meth. We provide the means with which they can choose to ingest it—by snorting, smoking or mainlining—and yes, we provide the necessary implements for self-administration. For the most part, they do it themselves or have friends help them with it. In the end, they all seem to find a way."

Hoorst seemed uneasy as he walked to the front of the fireplace and put his back to it.

"Group Three, as you might expect, is the most violent. They tend to engage in combat among themselves, often severely wounding and often times killing each other."

"Do you try to stop that kind of stuff?" asked Lloyd.

"No, Bishop, we do not," answered Hoorst, looking directly into Lloyd's eyes. "We offer nothing to our residents but food, water, shelter and the drugs of their choice. They are all fully informed of the circumstances. We have signed, thoroughly legal documents indicating that everyone has been informed of, and consents to, the terms of colony residency. These people know exactly what they're getting into."

"I have just one more question," said Lloyd. "I've noticed that everyone on the staff at the colony is white. Why is that?"

"Not only are they of one race, Bishop, they're all devout Roman Catholics." Rudy paused for effect. "Executive Outcomes took a page from the playbook of J. Edgar Hoover on how he ran the F.B.I. Mr. Hoover liked to have all of his field agents either Catholics or Mormons. It was his belief that these religions instilled a very high regard for the chain of command and a structural hierarchy. It was something he felt was very important in running an effective organization. My company feels the same way. Starting a colony like this is very difficult and we have endeavored to remove any problems that could hamper our success. That's why we have only Caucasians and Catholics. It eliminates a lot of problems and greatly helps our unit cohesion."

Hoorst picked up his shot glass and drank the last of its Jagermeister, then cleared his throat.

"Regarding Group Three, it is the most interesting of the groups. Some will die within days, sometimes hours after their arrival. Death is almost always due to some type of mortal combat. Later, it will mostly be due to cardiac arrest from a cocaine overdose. Many of the residents have known each other from the outside and have some pre-existing grudge, generally involving the drug trade, and are intent on revenge. Interestingly enough, in our other colonies we have had members of Group Three survive for several months. They always turn out to be the strongest, the most cunning, the most ruthless and godless of any of our residents. They are extremely dangerous. Little quarter is granted these individuals by the guard staff, and I would be surprised if we don't have one or two a month who are taken down by my security staff out of necessity."

Hoorst waited for what he had said to sink in. "So, there you have it, gentlemen, in a nutshell. It's the worst of it, I believe, hard to swallow, hard to comprehend, but these are desperate times, and times such as these sadly require equally desperate measures."

Hoorst looked up as the doors to the Great Room opened and Colonel Schwarz reported, "Lunch is served, sir."

CHAPTER FOUR

NATURAL SELECTION

We must, however, acknowledge, as it seems to me,
that man with all his noble qualities, still bears in his
bodily frame the indelible stamp of his lowly origin.
    —Charles Robert Darwin

John-Morgan was relieved when he finally saw the six white columns of Driscoll House come into view. It had been a long and troubling day, worse than he'd thought, and the sight of home made him feel better. Not much had been said on the voyage back to the Isle of Hope. Everyone seemed wrapped in his own thoughts. There had been little eye contact and John-Morgan read the body language as tense. Nobody had even asked for a drink on the ride home. The Jagermiester that followed lunch must have served its purpose.

Two walls of John-Morgan's study were filled with books about the Civil War and World War II. The third was framed by two large windows that overlooked the Intracoastal Waterway, and the fourth was covered in family photographs. A fire had already been laid and the first thing John-Morgan did when he entered the room was to light it. He went to the bookcase on the right side of the chimney, and opened the concealed door to his gun room. Looking over his shoulder he said, "The bar's in here."

"I could use a good strong one," said the governor as he followed John-Morgan into his secret room.

"Damn, John-Morgan," remarked Big Dog, "you've had a few new acquisitions since the last time I was here." Dog's eyes followed the rows of rifles that lined the walls and his hands caressed several of the nicest pieces.

"Firearms are still a good place to put your money," replied John-Morgan while he opened the doors to the liquor cabinet.

"Help yourself, Governor," said John-Morgan, then he called to the rest of the group, "Y'all come on in and fix yourselves something. Then we'll settle down and talk for awhile."

John-Morgan motioned to the chair behind his desk saying, "Governor, why don't you take this seat."

"Naw, Doc, that's your place," protested the Dog.

"I want to sit by the fire," John-Morgan replied, easing himself into the rocker next to the fireplace.

For several moments, everyone was quiet; they just sipped their drinks and thought about the day. It was Will who finally broke the silence.

"OK, y'all, what d'ya think about Rudy Hoorst?"

After a few long seconds, Lloyd replied, "Very handsome man with a beautiful wife and children."

Will looked at Judah and asked, "How about you?"

"I, ah, I just don't know. Yeah, he's got polish, very personable, obviously smart as a whip, but I'm not sure," said Judah, listening to the ice cubes crack in his glass as they melted.

"John-Morgan?"

"Listen, I liked the guy. It's obvious that he knows what he's doin'. He seems to give a damn about how horrible this whole thing is, but he's way ahead of us on the approach. It's gonna take some time for all of us to let this shit sink in. I mean…I'm like, what the fuck with this whole proposition."

Big Dog leaned forward to rest his elbows on the desk, looked at each person in the room and said, "I think the real question here is, what do we think about Executive Outcomes, isn't it, boys? What kind of feelin' do we have in our guts about all this?"

"A little late for that, isn't it, Dog?" answered Judah quickly. "I mean, they've got a contract with the State of Georgia for the next four years. Are you tellin' us you've got second thoughts about them now?'

The Dog held his hands up. "No, not at all. I've seen their operation, they'll do a good job at what the contract calls for. I guess I'm just thinkin' out loud, kinda wonderin' if the people of the state'll have the stomach for this, after all."

"Well, they by God voted for it," said Will.

"Hey, I know, I was the one who first introduced the idea, remember?" said the Dog. "We can stop this thing any time we want, but they'll still get paid. The State of Georgia is on the hook for four hundred million, though, even if we stop this whole thing right now."

Judah stood and walked to the windows. He watched the sun begin to slip behind the trees on Bluff Drive while he nursed his drink.

"I'll tell you somethin', Dog."

"Shoot, Judah, whatcha got on your mind?"

"The numbers don't make sense to me, Governor."

"How so?"

"When Hoorst went over his figures with us, I just didn't get it. I don't see how they're makin' money. Somethin' just ain't right, Dog."

"The state holds a performance bond on E.O. and they had to pay the premium. They don't do right, we get paid. It's that simple. Nobody went into this with their eyes closed."

"I know, I know," said Judah impatiently, "but think about it." He drew a deep breath and continued. "Executive Outcomes tells us they're ramping up to handle two thousand people on the island. It'll take a while, but I don't doubt we'll get that kind of population level. You saw all the men and equipment they've got there already, and you heard what they're plannin' to build as far as housing, fencing, the whole nine yards. The logistics of this whole thing alone just blows my mind. Somethin' just ain't right, Dog!"

"All I can tell ya is that I visited one of their colonies in England," replied the Governor, "and the Brits were pleased with the results, as were the Danes, the Germans, the Russians and everybody else. The Prime Minister of Great Britain himself told me that the amount of money they spent on their prison system was cut almost in half after they brought in EO.

He said the crime rate dropped by 40 percent, too. Those are pretty hard numbers to argue with, as far as this country boy is concerned."

"Look," said John-Morgan, "I invited Rudy and his wife to come and spend some time with Ann-Marie and me next week. Why don't all of you come, too, and we'll get a chance to dig a little deeper."

* * *

Judah lived close to John-Morgan and could have walked home, but instead brought his car with the thought of getting it filled up at the BP station in Sandfly. He'd always been quite fond of automobiles and each year usually traded in the one he had for a new model. But it was different now. Even people as comfortable as Judah were reigning in their spending.

When he got to his car, Judah stopped to admire it. He'd always loved Jaguars and thought this might be his last. The gas tank wasn't low, but he'd made it a habit to keep the fuel gauge close to full ever since the gas shortages had surfaced two years earlier. The month before, no gas could be had in Savannah for four days.

As he turned right onto LaRoche Avenue, Judah noticed the neighborhood watch patrol slowly rolling down the street in a Dodge Ram pickup with four-wheel drive and oversize tires. He waved to the two men in the truck's cab and they waved back. It seemed like everybody on the Isle of Hope knew everybody else. It hadn't been that way seven years before.

Roving gangs of mostly young males from across the racial spectrum of Savannah had terrorized its neighborhoods and, as a result, galvanized them into self-defense groups. The neighborhood watch organizations of this day were nothing like the ones back at the turn of the century. These were armed, aggressive and did not tolerate criminal behavior. Judah liked the sense of security the watch gave him. It would be his turn on the watch in two nights. He and John-Morgan shared a shift together.

With a sigh of relief, Judah pulled into the BP station; they had gas. After he topped off his tank, five gallons for fifty-six dollars, he went inside to pay. Credit cards hadn't been in use for over three years, and retail purchases were all done in cash. A lot of everything else was on the bartering system.

"Hey, Mr. Judah," said the black woman behind the cash register as Judah entered.

"Hey, Ella Mae," answered Judah, slipping his hand into his pants pocket for his wallet. "You doin' all right?"

"You know me, I'm here and my feet is killin' me! I can't afford to be nowhere else. Not with the price of food these days."

Judah looked at Ella Mae and smiled. He'd known her since he'd come back from Washington. Her hair was gray now, she was heavier, and the signs of her age and condition showed on her face. He knew she wasn't exaggerating when she talked about how her feet hurt or about how tired she was. Ella Mae should have been at home, but Judah also knew she was the sole support for her disabled husband, her son and her two grandchildren. Furthermore, he knew she could handle the .38 special pistol she carried on her hip.

"You had to use that thing, yet?" asked Judah, pointing to the pistol while he counted out the cash.

"Thank God, no! I hope I never do, but any trash comin' here better be careful with Ella Mae, Mr. Judah. I ain't takin' nothin' off nobody, black or white!"

"I hear ya." He glanced at the merchandise behind the counter. Stacked next to the Marlboros and Winstons were packs of marijuana cigarettes bearing names like Green Island Gold, Mellow Yellow and Laidback.

"Still sellin' a lot of those?" asked Judah.

"Yes, sir, they help pay the bills. We sell more of that than we do beer. You'd be surprised who buys 'em, too."

"Yeah?"

"Uh-huh. You know old Mister Wright? He come in here 'bout once a week for some. Says they helps his wife keep her dinner down, now that she's on chemo for that cancer she has."

As he started out the door, Judah turned to Ella Mae and asked, "How's De'Shawn?"

"Still can't get no work. Nobody hirin'."

"Tell him to come by my place tomorrow, I could use some help cleaning up after that storm we had last week."

"I'll tell him when I get home. Thank ya and God bless ya, Mr. Judah."

"God bless you, too, Ella Mae."

* * *

Dr. Hoorst stood on the steps of the Main House and watched as Colonel Schwarz returned from taking the visitors back to the dock. Schwarz exited the Humvee, approached Hoorst, and asked, "Is there anything else you require of me, sir?"

Thinking for a moment, Hoorst replied, "Well, there is one more thing, Claus. Bring Blitz back out and get a mount for yourself, I want to take a look at what we've got further into the island."

A few minutes later, Schwarz walked up to the Main House holding horses' reins. He kept Dr. Hoorst's mount steady as the doctor pulled himself into the saddle, then climbed aboard his own ride. Together they trotted side by side in silence toward the road that led to the deep parts of the island.

"What do you think of our little group today, Claus?" asked Hoorst when they were a half mile into the woods.

"They appeared quite uncomfortable, Dr. Hoorst."

"Yes, they did, but nothing out of the ordinary for first-timers. Do you remember that party from Denmark when they finally realized what it was all really about?"

"Yes, sir," answered Schwarz, "one fainted!"

Dr. Hoorst looked over at Schwarz and laughed slightly, replying, "Indeed he did! Not much of a stomach for reality. But, Claus, what about these fellows individually?"

"I think I understood Dr. Hartman, Congressman McQueen and Governor McFarland. I believe they appreciate what must be done. I know they don't like it, but they realize how things must be handled now. It's the Jude and the black that trouble me, Dr. Hoorst. They appear much too weak in the knees for what is too come. They may give the company trouble, especially the Jude."

Hoorst nodded and said, "I agree," then put spurs to his horse and shouted to Schwarz, "Let's have some fun."

The men galloped side by side for more than a quarter of a mile through a tunnel of great oaks framing the dirt road. Long tresses of gray Spanish moss brushed past their faces and large clumps of dirt were thrown up by the hooves of their horses. Finally, Hoorst pulled back on Blitz's reins and both riders came to a trot.

"Great fun, eh, Schwarz?" said Hoorst as Blitz breathed heavily and snorted through his nostrils. "Now, show me how we're coming with the disposal unit."

In the European colonies, the crematoriums were fired with coal which was abundant and readily available. On Ossabaw, they would have to be fueled with natural gas trucked in from the mainland. While trucking in the gas was cumbersome, it had one redeeming quality—there would be no ominous black cloud belching from the smoke stacks.

"Looks like our workers have almost finished," remarked Hoorst, riding up to the crematorium located almost seven miles into the island down the main road. He dismounted and approached the massive castle-like red brick oven. He opened the steel door through which the bodies would be shoved into the furnace and peered inside. Then he stepped back from the oven door and tilted his head up as his eyes followed the forty-foot chimney to its peak.

"Excellent work, as always," said Colonel Schwarz as he approached holding the reins of both horses. "The post-mortem exam building should be finished within two weeks. They will be no different from the others we've constructed, Dr. Hoorst."

WILLIAM C. HARRIS JR. | 44

"What about the lodgings, Claus; how long until they're up and ready?"

"I would say two months, maybe even less."

"And the electronic fencing?"

"Most of it has already been installed. As you know, sir, it's the easiest thing to install."

Hoorst laughed and responded, "Just like invisible fencing for the family dog!"

"Exactly," said Schwarz, "only the shock won't be so mild."

Hoorst directed his attention back to the crematorium, looked again into the oven opening. "How many bodies can be processed a day here?"

Colonel Schwarz pushed his cap back on his head and wiped the sweat off his brow.

"It has been our experience that the bodies we have to dispose of will almost uniformly be quite emaciated. They will have very little body fat and we don't anticipate a long burn-time. This unit can render one corpse of this type to nothing but ash in about thirty minutes at a temperature of two thousand degrees. This particular piece of equipment has been designed to accept at least four, perhaps five or six, bodies at one time. If it is called upon to do that, we project that complete cremation to ash will take about two hours, Dr. Hoorst."

"And, if we need a more efficient disposal system, Claus?"

"As you know, sir, the company has another unit disassembled and sitting on pallets at our European headquarters ready for immediate shipment anywhere we need it. I have seen them up and running a week after they have been ordered."

* * *

On the day Executive Outcomes' Ossabaw colony opened, two more states in the union declared bankruptcy. Georgia had been able to avoid that calamity, but barely. It was one of only seven that had been so fortunate. Governor McFarland pointed to his state's continuing solvency with pride and assured the voters that the new drug colony would serve to lessen the burden on the taxpayers.

When the Governor made his announcement about the colony's opening over a state-wide television hook-up just two months before, no one anticipated the size of the response. That first Saturday in April, more than a thousand souls pressed against the gates of the reception center at Butterbean Beach. The lines stretched halfway to the Moon River bridge. Even Dr. Hoorst was surprised by the turnout and was forced to call his headquarters in Brussels for emergency reinforcements. They were on the ground twenty-four hours later.

John-Morgan, Lloyd, Judah, and Will were present as the State's official observers when the gates to the embarkation point were opened, and a multitude of desperate people flooded into the holding area. A great din, a welter of discordant sounds, arose from those gathered as they pressed their way toward the opening. Many fainted and were held up by friends or relatives, there to help them along. Some of the worst cases died before they could make their way to the gates. If the company's employees had not been so well-prepared by previous experience, the situation would have spiraled completely out of control.

Still, occasionally, shots rang out as several dozen of the most aggressive in the mass were shot by EO's guards as a matter of self-defense. For John-Morgan and his friends, the world had been turned upside-down.

By one in the afternoon, the sun beat down hard, much harder than other April suns. The crowd was pressed closely together, and it sweated profusely. There was no breeze. The stench from the assembled mass became overpowering as it mixed with the smell of vomit, urine and feces. Judah had to cover his nose with a handkerchief while he watched Rudy decide, with the wave of his white-gloved hands, which would go to what group. John-Morgan stood in silence as he witnessed the body scans and the insertion of the computer chips into the left forearms. Lloyd stood on the dock and watched as the bellies of surplus military landing crafts were loaded with one hundred at a time and headed off to Ossabaw Island.

On the Diamond Causeway, distraught family members and devout church groups tried to talk those seeking entry to the colony out of their calamitous decision. Very few were successful.

By sundown of that first day, everyone standing in line when the gates were flung open had been processed and was on Ossabaw awaiting transport to their respective areas. Another five hundred would be waiting at eight the next morning. Fifty lay dead along the road.

It took almost two weeks to bring the situation under control, but, once the first surge had ended, things began to settle into the routine Dr. Hoorst had predicted. The colony was at the maximum population of fifteen hundred. It was what the state had agreed upon and deaths soon reached the same level as admissions, around a hundred a day, and Dr. Hoorst gave the orders for a second crematorium.

When the first week of internment had ended, all four members of the commission gathered at the colony on Ossabaw to inspect the facility and see that it reached the standards required by the state. Lloyd never ventured past the area reserved for Group One. He was completely overwhelmed by the suffering, by the degradation and total capitulation to despair and death in the eyes of each resident.

That first week, Lloyd watched from the sidelines as the resigned shuffled to their tents and then their cots. He looked on as the staff handed out piles of pills, mounds of cocaine and marijuana cigarettes, started IV's and pushed everything from morphine to heroin into the arms of willing and grateful recipients.

Lloyd didn't leave the tents for almost two days, and then only when he knew his body and soul could no longer tolerate the strain. When he returned, the moaning and stench filling the tents and wafting across the compound became more than he could handle, and he retreated back to the Main House and the quiet of his room.

But Lloyd could find no repose in the refinement of the Main House. His senses had been overwhelmed by the misery, and no matter what he did or how hard he prayed, he was drawn back to what he'd witnessed and knew he'd helped set in motion. During the middle of the night, in a fit of mental anguish, he wandered into a wooded area next to the marsh. Falling to his knees under the stark light of a full moon, Lloyd cried for God to hear him. Arms outstretched, he begged for mercy and guidance while his body shook and his heart searched.

Lloyd didn't know how long he'd been prostrate next to the big oak whose limbs lifted across the marsh and the creek filled with the incoming tide. It was early dawn when he pulled himself against its enormous trunk and sat transfixed by the sun beginning to peek from its hiding place behind the distant edge of the Atlantic. His eyes ate the colors of the sky changing from dark purple to gold as the morning stars disappeared in the new sun's rays. A breeze carrying the sweet smell of ocean freshness brushed across his face and he breathed its vapors deeply. He felt something had transformed him during the night; that doubt had been replaced by certainty. That frailty had had been vanquished by courage.

Watching the sun spread itself across the horizon, Lloyd felt its warmth on his face, and remembered his dream. He later told John-Morgan, the only one he truly trusted to understand, he had dreamed of the Virgin Mary.

When Lloyd returned to the Main House, he ate a good breakfast, the first food he'd had in two days. Then, he called his office at the Chancery and spoke to his secretary.

"Lydia, listen carefully. This is a letter I want you to send to Rome immediately, addressed to His Holiness. You know all the proper salutations to use, don't you?"

"Yes, Bishop."

"Your Holiness: Effectively immediately, I hereby submit my resignation as Bishop of the Diocese of Savannah. The circumstances are of a spiritual and personal nature and, I can assure Your Holiness, they will not reflect negatively upon Holy Mother Church. I regret I could not afford Your Holiness any advance notice of this decision, but please be assured that the circumstances driving this action require my full and utmost attention."

There was silence on the other end of the phone, prompting Lloyd to ask, "Lydia, are you there?"

"Oh, Bishop Bryan, what's happened?"

"I'll tell you later, only get that off at once. I won't be talking to anyone for the next few days. You know the procedures to follow if I have been incapacitated, so execute them now."

After speaking with his secretary, Lloyd met Rudy in the dining room just as he was about to have breakfast with his wife.

"Rudy, I'm sorry to interrupt, but I have something I need to tell you."

"It's no interruption at all, why don't you sit down and have something to eat?"

"I've already eaten, thank you."

Rudy looked at Lloyd and remarked, "You seemed refreshed. I was worried that you had overtaxed yourself. You appeared so down and out yesterday."

"I was down and out, Rudy, and yes, I am refreshed.'

Clearing his throat, Lloyd continued, "Rudy, I'm staying on the island. I hope the invitation to stay here in the Main House stands."

"That's wonderful, Lloyd! Of course the invitation stands. It's part of the company's contract with the state. How long will you be with us this time?"

"I'm here to stay, Rudy. I'm joining the colony. I'm one of your residents now. When I die, my body will belong to Executive Outcomes."

* * *

The normal routine was that, after finishing his work at Butterbean Beach, Dr. Hoorst would leave for the entrance gate on Ossabaw where he would once more sort through the residents, grading each of them on how long he thought they would survive.

Lloyd watched as Rudy culled through the pitiful assemblage with what appeared to be genuine compassion. He had something soothing to say to each resident as he assigned their places in the tents and asked what drugs they desired. A member of his staff recorded their requests on an iPad as the resident was led off to his or her bed. Men and women were housed in separate tents unless they requested to be in a mixed dormitory. That seldom happened unless husband and wife committed together.

The second week, Lloyd stayed in the tents for almost sixteen hours watching Rudy and his men. By then, 465 people had died, their bodies efficiently spirited away and taken deep into the interior of the island for cremation. Over and over again, Lloyd told himself these people would have died anyway, dispersed across Georgia in places from Atlanta to Savannah, from Athens to Rome, and every little stop sign in between. As he watched, he kept reassuring himself the existence they had in the colony was infinitely better than anything they could have on the outside.

The next day, after very little sleep, Lloyd walked the aisles past rows of army cots filled with people in different states of consciousness and dying. Some called out to him as he passed, and he would stop, kneel and listen to what they said.

During his priesthood, Lloyd had been present at the bedsides of hundreds of people only inches from death and had ministered to them in their last moments. As Bishop, he had often remarked to his younger priests how deathbeds were like foxholes; there were no atheists in them.

"Bless me Father, for I have sinned," pleaded a man in his forties who appeared to be well past a hard-lived sixty. Lloyd placed the purple stole of the confessional rite around his neck and leaned in close enough to the man so only he could hear the man's words. Lloyd drew back immediately from the rotten stench of the man's breath, regained control, turned his ear to the confessor's mouth and listened.

"I don't think I've been to confession since I was a teenager," he wheezed. "I was raised in a good Catholic family, started fooling around with drugs in college. Started on coke after I got hired to a really good-paying job at Gulfstream." He closed his eyes for a second and continued.

"You know what they say about a coke habit, don't you, Father?" Emitting a shallow breath, he answered for himself with a wry smile, "It's God's way of telling ya you're making too much money!"

When the man touched Lloyd's arm, Lloyd turned and looked into his eyes. Dark rings circled them and tears welled in their redness.

"I threw it all away, Father. I had a nice wife and son, but I couldn't let the coke go. It became my all, my everything, ya know? Two years ago she threw me out. I deserved it. I was so desperate I got into heroin just to ease the pain. I became a male prostitute to feed my habit. I can't begin to tell ya how low that made me feel, but I didn't give a shit. That's the way it's been. Then I saw on TV that there was going to be this drug colony and I said, 'Fuck it, it can't get any worse. I'll go there to die.' I was gonna die soon anyway, ya know? Anyhow, I want to tell somebody I'm sorry. I don't know if there is a God, but just in case, I want to say I'm sorry for what I've done with my life, Father. Do you think He will forgive me? Are you sure He's really there?"

Lloyd had heard thousands of confessions and thousands of sins and, over the years had tucked them away in his heart. Some were light, some heavy. Many were very heavy and unforgettable. But for some reason, Lloyd knew this simple, brief moment of complete clarity and honesty would stay with him forever.

"Do you remember what Jesus said to the good thief while he was dying on the cross?" asked Lloyd.

The man blinked his eyes and something came alive in them.

" 'This day, thou shalt be with me in Paradise,'" he answered.

Lloyd smiled, nodded and said, "That's right. You have done all that God requires for salvation and that's to ask for forgiveness."

Lloyd repeated the ritual prayers of the confessional as he made the sign of the cross. After that, he stood saying, "I'll see you tomorrow."

As Lloyd turned to go to the next person, the man asked for one more favor.

"Will you push another couple of cc's of morphine into the IV, Father?"

* * *

The members of the Governor's Oversight Committee for the Ossabaw Island Colony sat at the dining room table in the Main House. They had been at the colony for two weeks and appeared exhausted from their stay. John-Morgan wondered how Rudy and his wife could possibly be so upbeat. As he ate, he decided the couple had grown used to their surroundings. They were, indeed, far removed from what actually happened there. The gate to Group One was more than a mile from the Main House. Nothing could be seen or heard from what happened in the compound. Earlier, Rudy had told John-Morgan his wife had never seen any parts of the colonies where he had served as director. His whole family lived in relative ignorance of what occurred on the other side of the actual and virtual fences of Executive Outcomes' installations. It was only Rudy who journeyed past the barriers, who went to the embarkation points, who saw, heard, and smelled what happened.

After Lloyd had offered thanks before the meal at Rudy's behest, he said he had a special request of his host.

"I know I've committed to the colony, Rudy, and I can't have any contact with the outside, but there is one thing I need."

Smiling, Rudy replied, "First of all, the rules of residency will not apply to you, Your Excellency. You are free to come and go as you please. But what is it you need?"

"I guess I didn't expect to be staying here, "but I know this is what Our Lord wants from me. On that first day I never thought I'd be staying, and I didn't think to bring the essentials for celebrating the Mass. I don't have a chalice, no hosts, no wine, no nothing, and I need to have them brought here so I can say daily Mass."

Rudy sat back in his chair and answered, "I was wondering when you'd realize you hadn't celebrated the Mass." Putting down his napkin, he stood and called for Colonel Schwarz, who appeared immediately.

"Have the men fetch the chaplain's trunks, will you, Claus?"

Ten minutes later there was a rap on the door and Rudy said, "Enter."

Guards carried two large olive drab trunks to the middle of the room. Stenciled on the tops of both were Nazi eagles, clutching a swastika in their claws. Underneath were the words 'Feld Mass, Roman Catholic.'

Rudy stood beside the trunks and placed a hand on one of them. "As I've said, the company has come upon and purchased many military surplus items over the years. This is one of the items acquired just after the end of the war."

Looking at Lloyd, he said, "Bishop, this is a complete set of everything you will need to celebrate the Mass. It has a chalice, a foldable altar, cruets, candles, vestments for every occasion and even wine and unconsecrated hosts." Rudy opened the trunks to display their contents.

Gesturing to the trunks, Rudy said, "I hope you will find this suitable for your needs, Bishop. If the wine and hosts are not acceptable, I can have replacements here tomorrow."

After Lloyd finished examining the contents of the trunks, he thanked Rudy, walked over to one of the large leather chairs next to the fireplace and collapsed into it.

"I don't remember a time when I've been so tired," he said.

"Me neither," added Judah, sitting in the chair next to him.

Rudy cleared his throat. "Gentlemen, I have to spend some time with my wife and children. Please, excuse me for the evening. More food will be provided if you wish, and you know where the bar is. If there is anything else you would like, one of my men will be waiting outside the door. So, if there is nothing else you need from me, goodnight and sleep well."

"Actually," said John-Morgan quickly, "there is something we'd like, now that you mention it."

Rudy nodded and answered, "Of course, Dr. Hartman. What can we do for you?"

"I think we'd enjoy a nice fire. Even though it was warm today, it's supposed to get into the forties tonight, and a fire would be something we all would enjoy."

John-Morgan opened all the windows in the Great Room, filling it with the chill of the evening air. He knew the cold and the fire would draw his friends in close, and he felt they needed to be close now. They needed to speak in hushed tones, they needed to be honest.

John-Morgan watched as flames licked around the oak in the hearth, gliding smoothly past the chimney stones. He thought about the smoke that curled from its top, and he thought about the crematorium none of them had yet seen. Then he spoke quietly and deliberately, tilting his head toward the fire to let it warm his face.

"Has anybody seen anything that has not been exactly what we were led to believe would happen? Has anybody seen any of the residents mistreated?"

"No," answered Lloyd almost in a whisper. "Everything has been done in a humane manner, exactly as outlined in Hoorst's briefing. I looked hard, but I couldn't see anything I could find fault with. It would be nice if they had more staff to care for those who will never walk again and will die on their cots, but we knew about the staffing levels before the state signed on with EO."

"I want to see the crematoriums," said Judah, as all eyes turned to him. "I want to see what really happens to the bodies."

CHAPTER FIVE
BLOOD

Nothing venture, nothing win-
Blood is thick, but water's thin-
In for a penny, in for a pound-
It's love that makes the world go round!
—William Schwenck Gilbert, *Princess Ida*

"You don't know how my heart is breakin'," sobbed Big Dog, tears running down his cheeks. "She's everything to me. I tried as hard as I could bringin' her up. She was beautiful as a little girl and could wrap me around her little finger."

Big Dog stopped to wipe the tears from his eyes with his large fists, then continued.

"Maybe she had too much. She was gorgeous when she was in high school, looked just like her momma. When she graduated, I was runnin' for governor and won. She was the toast of the Atlanta crowd, made her debut at the Piedmont Driving Club. Then she went to Georgia and was a varsity cheerleader in her sophomore year. I was really proud of her, Lloyd. I never imagined she'd get caught up with coke. Not my little girl," said Big Dog, his thick chest heaving as he tried to gain control of his emotions.

Lloyd put his hand on Big Dog's shoulder, sitting face to face with the Governor of Georgia who was telling him about the fate of his only daughter.

"When was the last time you heard from her, Roy?"

"Oh, hell, that's been a year ago. I thought we'd gotten her straightened out, but she was back with the Columbian marchin' sand, you know, the coke, in less than a month. That's the last time I saw her, Lloyd."

The Dog looked up at Lloyd with pleading eyes and continued, "My people with the G.B.I. told me she was turnin' tricks in Knoxville and Chattanooga for drug money. They said she was a high-class whore. Can you imagine that?"

"I've heard a lot worse, Roy, but I can't begin to feel the way you do. I don't have any children. Tell me what I can do for you right now."

"Pray for Katherine, Lloyd, and pray for me. I've tried to kidnap her and bring her back to Georgia and force her into a rehab place, but nobody can find her. Her mother and I are about to lose our minds over that child."

Lloyd took a deep breath, squeezing Big Dog's shoulder, and looked out the windows of the Main House to hear the heavy spring shower pelting the roof with thick, full drops.

Katherine Agnes McFarland had been blessed with just about every advantage any person could hope for. Family, money, looks, and intelligence had been showered upon her from her first breath and had never stopped coming. She was the latter of the McFarland children, with a brother three years her senior.

Robert Roy McFarland Jr.—Robbie—was the mirror image of his father. He was athletic, outgoing, and politically inclined. Robbie had also been the recipient of marvelous good fortune. He'd followed in his father's footsteps, playing football for Georgia while his sister cheered him on. Robbie was popular and a hit with the girls. He'd graduated from law school and had taken over his father's clients when Big Dog assumed the governor's chair. He'd married well, had small children of his own, and abhorred the humiliating behavior of his little sister. This was to such an extent that Robbie refused even to mention her name.

* * *

While Big Dog spoke with Bishop Bryan, Katherine lay in her bed at the Ritz-Carlton in Buckhead, watching the television. She'd been up most of the night with one of her best customers, a top executive with Delta Airlines whom she had known for almost a month. It was one in the afternoon.

At two that morning, "Larry" had pulled himself out her bed, peeled fifteen hundred-dollar bills from his roll, placed it on the nightstand, and blew her a kiss as he walked out the door. Katie folded the money and stuffed it under the mattress, right next to the .38 special she had for protection. She rose wearily from the bed and went to the bathroom where she kept a bottle of Valium in her makeup case and downed two yellow five-milligram tablets. Barefoot, with only a towel wrapped around her body, she went to the wet bar and took a strong shot of Gray Goose vodka to potentiate the sedative effects of the Valium.

Back in the bed, Katie pulled the covers over her and waited to drift away. It was difficult, because she could smell Larry's cologne on the pillow. It was some kind of Hugo Boss scent and Larry always wore too much. As she waited to slip into nothingness, she thought about Larry and how he enjoyed getting rough with her. He never hit her, he just liked to "fuck her hard," as he would often say during their times in bed together.

But he paid well, had no idea who she was, and felt like a stud when he left. He'd even hooked her up with a couple of his buddies, and they paid well, too. She needed to work only about four hours a day to pull in three to four thousand. She was dropping, on average, five hundred dollars a day for her coke habit and the downers she used for sleep. The deluxe suite at the Ritz was close to another grand, and when all the "extras" were added in, Katie was spending close to two thousand dollars a day while banking another two. She had a plan, though.

Katie might have been a cokehead, but there were still long moments of lucid thought when she'd step back and look at herself. She was fully aware there was no erasing her past; that she'd burned hundreds of bridges behind herself, but still, she had a sliver of hope. That sliver was to save enough money and check herself into one of those high-end rehab facilities somewhere in California and dry out. She'd talked to a couple of her clients she'd grown to trust. One in particular was Sidney.

Sidney was Jewish and wealthy. He was single, from New York City, was nice to Katie, and had kicked a heavy coke and heroin habit five years before he met her. He was in the money management business and could stack cash as high as any of Katie's other clients. He was the one who had told Katie about this place in Oregon where he kicked the habit, and that was what Katie was dreaming about while she sat on the side of her bed on another afternoon, watching the tube. She wasn't prepared for what she saw next.

"I'm Governor Roy McFarland," said the face on the screen, "and behind me is Georgia's answer to the drug problem that plagues the streets of our towns and cities."

Gesturing to Ossabaw Island in the distance, the Governor continued, "This is Georgia's drug colony. It's a place where anyone who is a citizen can check into and get any kind of drug they want."

Katie sat motionless as she watched and listened to her father explain the colony on Ossabaw.

"If you are addicted to any kind of drug, you can come to this place and the state will provide you with anything you want. We'll feed you, clothe you and shelter you, all for nothing."

The camera closed tightly on Big Dog's face as he said, "If you're an addict, you don't have to steal anymore for your drugs. You don't have to sleep under bridges or in crack houses and you don't have to sell your bodies. You can come to his beautiful island and we'll take care of your needs, no questions asked. Only, once you check in, you don't check out."

Big Dog's face faded from the screen as magnificent pictures of Ossabaw's forests and beaches appeared. There were glorious sunsets and sunrises. Then came the graphic which said, "Go to OssabawColony.com or call our toll-free number at 1-877-OSSABAW." No mention was made of Dr. Hoorst's selection process.

Katie didn't budge from her spot on the bed for several long minutes. Then the tears started. She'd cried a lot since the last time she'd seen her father. That was when he'd gotten on his knees before her and begged her to quit while her mother wept in the living room of the Governor's Mansion on West Paces Ferry Road.

The pain became too much and Katie opened the drawer of the end table next to her bed, laid out two long lines of some of the best snort she'd ever had and sucked it into her sinus cavities. The pain went away and Katie started thinking about her dates for that night.

* * *

For three years Robbie McFarland was the only child, showered with attention from a loving mother and a proud father. As a youngster, Big Dog's athletic prowess and political fame had shaped his son's attitude about life. Everywhere he went with his father, Robbie basked in the adulation heaped upon Big Dog by football fans and political supporters. He liked being referred to as "Little Dog," and when the aura of self-awareness began to take hold in Robbie, all the attention he received from being the son of a famous and affable man began to shape his personality.

The governor had been too busy to notice how his son's personality was developing and his mother had been too doting. But Robbie had been shaped by his environment to see himself as important, and this bred arrogance in him. It was an arrogance not tempered by any mental or physical shortcomings. Robbie was a good student and an excellent athlete. He was also handsome and had learned the art of persuasive conversation at his father's knee. If he lacked anything, it was compassion. As he grew older, if he had a weakness, it was his mounting interest in sex.

When his sister was born, some of the attention given to Robbie was, naturally, diverted to Katherine. It was normal for him to be a bit jealous, but he adjusted well and over time, Robbie and his sister formed a bond. As they grew older, both children began to feel a sense of entitlement, but it was not their fault. As was the case with the children of many wealthy and famous people, Robbie and Katherine saw themselves as better than most.

When Robbie took the time to consider what he'd done with his life, he always felt satisfied. He'd accomplished every major task he'd set for himself and then some. His first marriage had failed in divorce, but in this day and age, more than half did. Besides, he argued, it had been her fault, anyway. His second marriage had been a success; he had three lovely, well-mannered children who reflected nicely upon him and his wife. He had a handsome home in northwest Atlanta, a summer cottage on Sea Island, a thriving practice in tort law, and his father was the governor of Georgia. Robbie was satisfied, but he always wanted more. The only thorn in his side was Katherine.

* * *

Rudy stood at his desk and said, "Please, gentlemen, take a seat."

"Is there anything else I can do to make things easier?" he asked, looking at Lloyd.

"Actually, Rudy, there is." They all found chairs.

"Yes?"

"I'd like to recruit some volunteers from Savannah to help me with the people in Group One. I think I could get some very reliable, forthright folks who can help me take care of these people while they die. All I'm lookin' for are people who'd be willing to clean up when somebody soils themselves. Just do the basics. Anything to give a little dignity to their deaths."

Rudy leaned back in his chair, a knowing look on his face, and said, "I was wondering when you'd ask. We've had similar requests in our European colonies and I'll tell you what I told them. No relatives; none at all. You can have volunteers, but the company must pass on them. There can be no more than one volunteer per twenty-five residents, and that volunteer can be here for only eight hours at a time and no more than three days a week. And…nobody after dark."

Lloyd nodded his head in agreement.

Looking at Big Dog, Rudy asked, "And so, Governor, what can Executive Outcomes do for the great State of Georgia?"

The Dog chuckled, shook his head and replied, "Goddamn, Rudy, you're full of more shit than a Christmas turkey!"

Rudy threw his head back and laughed saying, "Nothing like a little folksy, down-home humor. I love it! What do you need, Governor?"

"Only one small thing. You've met my boy, Robbie. You know that I'm turnin' the governor's oversight office over to him?"

"Absolutely," answered Rudy, "Robbie and I met six months ago in Atlanta when we signed the contract with the state. You mentioned that to me then, and I think we could work well together."

"Well, that's a good thing. Believe me, I don't have the time necessary to make sure this place is on the up and up. I want somebody I can trust to tell me the truth. You gotta understand, the state is dealin' with fire here. This place has got to be clean, and I can't think of anybody better than my own son to make sure of that, Rudy."

"I agree, he's an excellent choice."

"Well, Rudy, he's comin' down here this weekend to look things over."

* * *

Dog and Rudy were on the dock when Robbie arrived on Ossabaw. It was Robbie's first time on the island, and Rudy took him, along with his father, on a quick horseback tour of the facilities.

Rudy's words stuck with Robbie when he told him the smell in the tents wasn't so bad when there was a breeze. "But," remarked Rudy, "when it gets hot and the air is still, it can be so overpowering that my men have to wear a type of gasmask in order to function in that sector."

All Robbie wanted to do was leave the tents as quickly as possible. He'd never seen anything like it, and, as he watched Lloyd move from one cot to another wiping feces from the bodies that rested in them, Robbie almost became ill. It was a stark contrast to all he'd ever known, and it made him think about his wife and children who were, at that exact moment, so comfortably enjoying themselves on the beach at Sea Island.

Then Robbie was taken to Group Two. Judah had not been there for two days, but Robbie did watch as three residents were helped by EO staff to inject themselves intravenously with heroin. He stood to the side as staff removed the lifeless body of one resident and placed it on the bed of a pickup truck bound for the island's crematorium.

Big Dog had seen all of this already and had had enough. Outside the enclosure of Group Two, he informed Rudy and Robbie that he needed to leave for Atlanta and would be speaking with them in the next few days.

"You're in charge now," said the governor to his son. Looking at Rudy he continued, "He speaks for me now, Rudy, and for the State of Georgia."

Little Dog and Rudy watched as the governor trotted away with his body guards following close behind.

"How much does he know?" asked Rudy after the governor faded from sight down a long sandy road framed by massive oaks.

"No more than he's seen," answered Little Dog.

"Good," replied Hoorst. "Now, I'll take you to the real show here at the colony."

When Rudy and Robbie arrived at the perimeter of Group Three, Oberst Schwarz was there to greet them.

"You got here just in time, Dr. Hoorst," said Schwarz, "there seems to be a big fight brewing between the skinheads and the black panthers. There'll probably be at least ten dead by nightfall."

Rudy and Robbie entered the control center and immediately Robbie was dumbstruck. Two dozen TV monitors lined the walls of the small building at the entrance to the compound. Two EO guards sat in front of the bank of screens and watched images of men moving around the housing units and the forest that surrounded them.

"Keep your eyes on these two screens," said Schwarz. "This is where the action will probably take place."

Entranced, Little Dog's eyes followed the movement of a group of young white men, heavily tattooed, move through the underbrush. He watched as they stopped and snorted lines of cocaine, seeming to plot among themselves. On the other monitor, a group of young blacks sat close to each other outside one of the enclosures, unaware they were being stalked. Little Dog nearly pressed his face against the screen as the skinheads moved silently toward their prey. He was amazed at how deftly they moved, how organized they seemed, and how totally unaware the blacks appeared to be.

No weapons of any kind had been allowed to enter the island, but that didn't mean weapons could not be manufactured from what resources existed there. Some of the skins held clubs in their hands, large deadly clubs made from oak and embedded with oyster shells on the ends. Others carried well-fashioned spears with sharp points.

Rudy kept his eye on Robbie as the skinheads moved ever closer to springing their trap. In fascination, Robbie focused on the screens. Then, in one sudden movement, the skinheads came screaming out of the woods and descended upon the unaware and unprepared blacks in a devastating assault. In a frenzy of violence that lasted only minutes, the skins bludgeoned and stabbed the blacks. Only one escaped into the brush. Twelve others lay dead as the skins lorded victory over their bloody bodies, screaming and striking their lifeless victims again and again.

Little Dog reeled back from the monitors, saying, "I've never seen anything like that before in my life!"

"If you'd like to see it again," said Hoorst nonchalantly, "I can have it played back for you immediately."

"What the fuck," gasped Robbie as his eyes left the screens and searched Rudy's. "What the fuck, man? You mean you record all this stuff?"

"That's exactly what I mean."

"But, why?" asked Robbie.

Hoorst gave Robbie a condescending glance, then smiled and answered, "For sale and distribution."

"You mean you sell this stuff?" asked Robbie, wide-eyed.

Hoorst chuckled a little. "Not only that, but we have a live internet feed of everything that goes on in the colony. You can log on to our website, select any group you want, pick out any camera site and watch everything that happens, 24/7. We even catalogue events such as you just witnessed for viewing later. It comes, of course, with a steep price."

"Well, how the fuck do you get away with it?"

"Executive Outcomes is a very discreet organization. Most of our viewers are in the Middle East and Asia. Some in Russia, very few in Europe and America, but we do have some. It's all by subscription. We don't divulge the location of our colonies, they're rather non-descript, and we carefully filter our customers. Besides, there's nothing anyone can do about it. It's all spelled out quite clearly, ironclad, in our contract. Executive Outcomes owns the bodies of all who enter our colonies and also all audio and video of everything that happens here. "Believe me, Robbie, we have the very best lawyers money can buy, and the company is on very firm ground. As a matter of fact, a member of your firm was involved in drawing up our international contract. Don't ask me who, I'll never say. Even if the State of Georgia terminated our contract at the end of the proscribed time, EO still owns every bit of what you just saw and the company will edit it, copy it and sell it. It's one part of how we make a place like this profitable."

Robbie was staggered and grabbed one of the chairs to sit in while he processed the information he'd just been given. After a few moments, he began to appreciate the genius behind the idea and nodded his head, asking, "Who thought all this stuff up?"

Rudy smiled smugly and answered, "My father."

* * *

Robbie couldn't help but notice the contrast between what he'd just seen and the overwhelming beauty of Ossabaw Island. The bright green color of new leaves filled the early spring's sky while the cool air felt like peppermint against his cheeks. There was no smell of feces or rotting flesh and no calls of plaintive human cries; only the sound of horses' hooves digging into the ground and the creak of saddle leather. Occasionally the rustle of palmetto fronds or the squawk of some distant birds competed with the easy sound of the trotting horses. He'd been briefed on what to expect by Hoorst, but it was nothing in comparison to seeing the real thing.

When the riders reached an opening in the oaks and the sky was visible, Rudy stopped and looked up, pointing to the dozen or so turkey buzzards circling overhead, saying, "They're waiting for the upward drafts of warm air they can ride to the mainland to feast on road kill," as he watched the large birds fly in easy circles. "Perhaps they're a lot like this island is today; beautiful from a distance, but ugly up close."

Robbie leaned back in his saddle and studied the birds. "I'll bet they're about six feet across."

"Not quite," answered Rudy, "but close."

Rudy lingered for a moment as Robbie watched the buzzards, then said, "We still have one more stop for your inspection, Robbie."

"Yeah, what's that?" asked Robbie, swatting at some gnats buzzing his ears.

"The crematorium complex, it's down that road over there, about a mile from here."

"It's all about burning bodies, isn't it," said Robbie in a tone of voice that indicated to Rudy that he wasn't too keen on visiting the crematoriums.

"Well, yes and no. There's more to it than just disposing of remains. It's like this, Mr. McFarland. Did you ever wonder how Executive Outcomes could afford to discreetly deposit such a handsome amount of money into your numbered Swiss bank account every month?"

Little Dog didn't say anything at first; he just nervously ran his fingers through his hair and stared at the ground. After a second or so he looked Rudy in the eye and answered, "I really don't care to know, Dr. Hoorst. Ignorance is bliss."

Rudy laughed at Robbie's reply and retorted, "Ignorance! That's what so many of the Germans said about the concentration camps. 'Oh, I didn't know what was *really* going on!'"

"What the fuck are you talking about, Rudy?"

Rudy's mount became restless and reared back. He brought the horse under control and moved his ride in close to Little Dog's until they were touching, and said, "Do you think we could pay you what we do just by the internet proceeds from things like that little gladiator event you just witnessed?"

"I don't know, Rudy. I never really thought about it."

"Well, you're about to begin to think about it," said Hoorst as his ride bucked once more, causing Robbie's horse to stir.

"You've taken EO's money to protect the company, and it is imperative that you know just what it is you are protecting. Follow me."

Robbie was a good horseman and when Rudy put his spurs to his horse and galloped quickly away, Robbie did the same. For more than a mile they ran surrounded by a primeval maritime forest so thick that it reminded Robbie of a triple canopy jungle. Ahead, Robbie could see open space where the sun shone through on cleared ground. Rudy was waiting for him at the entrance to the clearing.

For a perimeter of almost a hundred yards, the forest had been cleared and laid bare. In its center were two large wooden buildings, one with twin smokestacks by its side. Surrounding the compound was chain-link fencing with concertina wire on top. Two armed guards stood at the entrance, and Robbie watched as a Humvee passed through and stopped in front of one of the buildings. Men with elbow-length gloves removed half a dozen bodies.

When they reached the gate, the two EO guards stood at attention. What greeted Robbie were a couple of buildings of about five thousand square feet each, connected by an enclosed walkway. The building to his left had two brick chimneys, forty feet tall. Robbie's eyes followed the chimneys all the way to their tops.

When Robbie entered the first building, he was taken aback by more than fifty naked bodies lying on gurneys. EO men dressed in hazmat suits moved from one body to the next as they scanned the micro-chips implanted into the left forearm of each corpse. Occasionally one of the men raised his hand and two others would go to that gurney and push it into the causeway that led to the crematoriums. With other bodies, some were moved into another area where other EO employees began to surgically remove what Robbie clearly could tell were artificial hip or knee joints.

Transfixed, Little Dog watched as these men deftly incised hips, knees, shoulders and spines, sometimes using power surgical saws to accomplish their work. He saw power-driven screwdrivers back out titanium screws and bone plates from vertebrae, ankles, hands and just about every bone in the human body. Eyes wide, Little Dog watched as these artificial joints were collected by another set of EO men, taken to a scrub area, cleaned of tissue, then placed into an autoclave to be sterilized. Following that, they were processed, packaged and scanned into a computer bank. When all that could be salvaged from those bodies was accomplished, other EO employees came and rolled them to the crematoriums only fifty feet away.

Bodies adorned with tattoos were given special attention—great care was taken to remove them without damaging the skin. Rudy mentioned to Robbie, as they watched technicians meticulously remove the hides, that human tattoos were particularly sought-after in places like Thailand and parts of the Philippines. After removal, the skins were soaked in glycerin and then shrink-wrapped.

"For some reason, Robbie," said Rudy, "they seem to like dragon tattoos in Indonesia the most, followed by Nazi insignias like swastikas and SS runes. Quite frankly," he added, "we do a surprising business in tattoos. Who would have thought it?"

"Are those the bodies of the blacks we just saw killed and hacked up in Group Three?" asked Robbie.

"As a matter of fact, they are," said Rudy, looking on as his men scanned the microchips in the arms of the dead men.

"Your men are quite on the money," remarked Robbie. "They were only killed about an hour ago."

"Indeed. These residents are far too young to have much of value implanted in them. And, blacks who are tattooed have very little value. Not enough contrast. Most of the time, we don't even bother to harvest anything from them."

Rudy turned to Robbie and said, "However, there is one thing we've found to be of value from these residents."

"Really, what?"

"Watch and see."

EO men moved from one corpse to the next, inspecting their mouths. Robbie watched as gold teeth were extracted and dropped into a container.

"These blacks," commented Rudy, "they like to flash their gold teeth. I think they refer to them as 'grills.'"

Fifteen minutes into this chamber of horrors, Little Dog began to puke his guts out as he groped for the exit. Rudy followed closely behind while his men immediately came with buckets and mops to clean up the mess Little Dog had made.

Little Dog stood hunched over, hands on his knees as he retched the last of his stomach's contents outside the processing center. Rudy waited a few feet away until Robbie had regained control of himself.

With a coolness that chilled Robbie, Rudy said, "You must have guessed that, after what you've witnessed, we sell all of this stuff."

"Ah, yeah, that did cross my mind."

"Resale of implants is illegal in the States," said Rudy, "but it's not that way elsewhere. There's a huge market for them in India. Needless to say, gold is fungible and the tattooed hides are a niche market. We try not to waste anything."

Hands on his hips, Rudy continued, "So, now you know just a little more about the company you have agreed to represent, don't you?"

"Yeah! Shit, yeah!"

"OK, Mister Governor's son, be aware that what you have just seen is all completely legal. Do you understand, Little Dog?"

That was the first time Rudy had ever addressed Robbie as "Mister Governor's son" or "Little Dog," and it stung. The sound of Rudy's voice and his entire demeanor had changed and Robbie felt as though Rudy no longer respected him.

"You will keep what you have seen a complete secret," admonished Hoorst. "If this got out, it could become a public relations problem for the company…Do you understand me, Robbie?"

For the first time in his life, Robert Roy McFarland, Jr. was intimated and afraid. His mind raced and he wondered if his life might be in danger if this secret were to become public knowledge. He wondered if his father knew about what he'd seen, and he leaned over again with the dry heaves.

Rudy walked to Robbie's side and rested his hand on his back, saying, "Just in case you're wondering, you're the only person outside the company who knows the full truth about the Ossabaw project."

Patting Robbie on the back, Rudy continued, "Now you know how Executive Outcomes can afford an attorney of your stature. If you'd like, we can terminate our contract immediately and nothing will be said. As you can well imagine, with what we're paying, we'll be able to find a replacement within days."

Wiping his mouth on his shirtsleeve, Robbie stood erect, looked Dr. Hoorst in the eye and said, "That won't be necessary."

A sardonic smile crossed Rudy's face. "Excellent, most excellent, Robbie. Now we have only two more learning sessions for you today. As you might expect, I want you to see exactly how efficiently we dispose of the remains. Dead men tell no tales, as they say. Come with me."

Rudy led a very pallid Robbie McFarland through the doors of the crematorium. Inside the building, the first thing that struck Robbie was the roar of the ovens and the way they sucked air into them through the vents in the ceiling. Then, it was the heat.

There were two crematoriums, side by side, and the iron doors glowed red from the intense heat inside them. Even from twenty feet away, with large fans blowing across them, the heat from the ovens was enough to cause Robbie's face to grow ruddy. Silently, Robbie watched as men gloved and wearing masks pushed gurneys next to sliding stretchers that fed into the oven doors. Without blinking, he saw these men roll a body onto a stretcher and wait.

"What are they waiting for?" shouted Robbie above the noise.

"They're waiting for another three bodies," answered Rudy. "These corpses are so emaciated, four at a time can be fitted into one oven. It's quite an efficient way of disposal."

With all his might, Robbie forced himself to watch as one of the oven doors was opened and a worker thrust a rake in to cull through the remaining bones as they dropped through a grate and into a small wagon below, to be carted deeper into the woods and buried in shallow pits.

Once outside, Robbie had regained all his composure and asked Rudy, "How long does it take to reduce a body to ash?"

"With bodies like these, the way they're emaciated, not more than an hour at 2,000 degrees," answered Rudy, matter-of-factly.

"When we're forced to place four at a time into one oven," continued Rudy, "it can take a little longer, but we're still able to keep up the pace of around a hundred bodies every twenty-four hours. And, of course, we use highly efficient ovens invented by the experts."

Without thinking Robbie asked, "What experts?"

Smiling, Rudy answered. "These ovens are built from the same plans used by the Nazis. They were available on the internet and had no copyright law hindering our use of them. It was all for free, Robbie. Executive Outcomes is always looking for a good deal."

As the two men walked their horses back to the tree line toward the cool tunnel through the woods, Rudy sensed that Little Dog had hardened to the reality of the Ossabaw project.

Just before they climbed onto their mounts, Rudy looked at Little Dog and said, "Robbie, I know I was hard on you back there. It was because I had to be. This isn't something for the faint of heart, but if a man is tough enough, there's a lot of money to be made."

Rudy had a very disarming way and a smile that could melt a glacier. "Forgive me, Robbie. I just had to know if you had what it takes to be in this business."

Robbie cleared his throat, looked back at the crematoriums and then at Rudy.

"I have to tell you, Rudy, you kind of pissed me off. Look, I'm no pussy, OK? But I've never seen anything like that before, and it made me sick."

"I know. You're not the first I've seen that way, believe me, but I had to know if you had the right stuff."

Rudy offered his hand to Robbie and Little Dog took it, but not before saying, "Just don't call me Mister Governor's son again. Little Dog is fine, most of my friends call me that, but none of that other shit."

Rudy laughed good-naturedly and pumped Little Dog's hand. "By this time next year, I will have made enough money to get completely away from this place and out of the business. I'll be able to retire with a very comfortable income. You stick with me, and you'll be able to do the same, I promise."

Little Dog pulled himself onto his saddle. Just before Rudy mounted his horse, he said, "The last place I want show you is the central command center up by the Main House."

Central command was located in a double-wide trailer about a hundred yards from the Main House. When he entered the building, the first thing Little Dog noticed was the number of video monitors filling the walls. Little Dog quickly estimated at least fifty of them. He counted eighteen EO men seated all around the room, each responsible for constantly keeping track of what happened on the screens before them.

Hoorst guided Robbie around the room, speaking to his men sometimes in English, sometimes in German, sometimes in French. The command center was divided the same way the island was. There were videos monitoring all three groups.

Stopping at the area for Group One, Rudy placed his hand on the shoulder of his man and said, "Willy, take us on a tour of what you're responsible for."

"Yes sir," replied the seated officer. With a series of clicks, Robbie was shown the entire area of Group One. He watched Lloyd Bryan moving from one bed to the next, often stopping to pray with the person who lay there, sometimes simply covering what he had found to be another dead body. He also watched as EO men came to the cots of the dead and removed them from the area.

"As you might guess, we have little problems identifying the dead in Group One. For the most part, they are not dispersed in a wide area. But still, we can detect when one of our one residents elsewhere in the colony has succumbed, almost within minutes. We also can be given early notice when one of them is getting close to death."

"Show our guest, Willy."

Hoorst's man lit up his screens with identification numbers and locations of every resident in his sector.

"Now, show Mr. McFarland the information on resident number 459," instructed Hoorst as he pointed to a spot on one of the monitors. With click, all pertinent information on that resident appeared on the screen..

"So, as you can see, Robbie, this resident has a Zimmer total knee and a DePuy total hip. When he surrenders to his addiction, the company will know within minutes of his death, collect his remains, harvest the artificial joints, and dispose of his remains all within about an hour."

Hoorst stood back from the screen, well satisfied , and said, "Quite a remarkable system, isn't it?"

"Kinda scares the shit out of me," answered Little Dog in a quiet voice. "I never imagined anything like this in my whole life. It's like you've got a fuckin' death factory here."

"That's why Executive Outcomes pays you so much damn money, Little Dog. The company has the utmost faith in your ability to handle our public relations."

Little Dog swallowed hard and watched the video screen. Pointing to another monitor he asked, "What's this flashing number mean?"

"Excellent question," answered Hoorst, "That means the body temperature of the owner of that micro-chip has dropped below that which is required to sustain life. It means that resident has died."

"Bring up the body scan on this individual, Willy," ordered Hoorst, Instantly, the full body scan taken of the resident upon being processed at Butterbean Beach appeared.

"So, you can see from this scan, Robbie, the company has nothing to harvest from these remains," said Hoorst who turned again to his operator. "Show us the real time images of this resident, Willy, and alert our disposal team of his demise."

"As you can see from the information we have about the deceased, he was forty-two, infected with HIV, a homosexual who was addicted to cocaine and had been in the colony three weeks; nothing to harvest from his remains. Not a money-making situation for the company, but we do stand by our word to take people like this into the colony."

Hoorst looked at Little Dog with what the Dog thought was a smirk and said, "A humanitarian gesture, wouldn't you agree, Mr. McFarland?"

Little Dog had definitely been blown away by all he'd seen this day, and even more so by the absolute precision with which the colony was run and how it actually made a profit. But still, he was Little Dog McFarland and there was only so much shit he'd take before responding.

Drawing his six-foot-two, 270-pound frame erect, Little Dog looked Hoorst straight in the eye and said, "Don't think you can fuck with me either, Rudy. I'll play along with you, but don't you dare fuck with me. I can bring this whole shit-hole operation down on your fuckin' head with one phone call, so don't go fuckin' with me, ya hear?"

With stone-cold emotion, Hoorst returned the Dog's remarks and replied, "I'm not fucking with you. I'm simply stating the obvious."

Hoorst waited a moment and continued, "Also, don't threaten me or this company. It could cause very serious repercussions. You're a part of this operation, now. I thought we'd had that understanding an hour ago."

Robbie didn't say anything for several seconds. He felt like popping the living shit out of Hoorst, but didn't.

"OK," said Little Dog.

"Fine, we have an absolute understanding. I won't fuck with you, and you won't fuck with my company. Now, I have one more small detail to inform you about."

Little Dog shifted on his feet and asked, "What now?"

"In two weeks," said Hoorst, "when one of our surgical specialists arrives at the colony, the company will begin harvesting organs from our newly-deceased residents. They will be sold on the foreign market just like the artificial joints."

"You mean like kidneys and livers," said Little Dog, this time not so surprised.

"That's exactly what I mean. Few will come from Group One, they're too debilitated and with too many infectious diseases. But, there are a number of residents in Groups Two and Three who are infection-free and in remarkably good health, considering the amount of drugs they've ingested. We'll monitor them closely from this control room and when they die, our team will retrieve their bodies and take them to a new surgical suite that will be flown in next week. Appropriate organs will be harvested, which have been typed with waiting recipients overseas, and shipped out the same day. It will greatly increase the company's bottom line."

CHAPTER SIX

THE PAIN

"Sweet is true love though given in vain,
In vain;
And sweet is death who puts an end to
pain."
—Alfred, Lord Tennyson, *The Last Tournament*

Even though Katie was a cokehead, she was able to keep her physical appearances up. She might take a little snort before her five-mile run, but she still made the run. And she still worked out two hours in the gym. She didn't have much of an appetite, but she forced herself to eat well. Katie was what some people referred to as a "Hollywood Head." They were functional addicts, movie star types who could pull off a job while high, with very few people knowing they had a habit. Like these "Heads," Katie kept telling herself she'd straighten out next month or next year or whenever. Whenever the pain stopped. But Katie had gone way too far to come back around to a normal life and she knew it.

In her lucid moments, and they were far more than she cared to endure, she'd stand in front of a mirror, look at her perfect face and body and call herself a whore. Because that was what she was.

For some reason, Katie hadn't gotten into heroin or other narcotics. She smoked a lot of strong weed with her "boyfriends," but the only downers she did were the sleeping pills she'd swallow. Her nasal passages might have been for shit because of the coke, but Katie looked like she'd never even had a beer before. She'd dyed her hair black, changed the style, and wore makeup that had, so far, been enough to keep her anonymity safe. She didn't have any clients who might recognize her for who she was, and as long as that was the case, she'd stay in the Buckhead area of Atlanta and exist…from one day to the next…whatever it took to survive. She earned enough money to live in the style she'd been accustomed to, and then some. And, always, there was her plan to straighten out. She thought about that a lot, but she always got stuck on the part about what she'd do after she'd gone straight. There was no way Katie could ever be a part of the life she'd once had; no way her family would ever accept her after what she'd done.

Somewhere along the line, Katie had started watching religious programs on TV in the afternoons. When she jogged down Peachtree Street, occasionally she'd stop at the Cathedral of Christ the King and sit for a few minutes and think about her life. It was cool and dark there, and often the choir would be rehearsing. She'd listen, stare at the gold crucifix on the altar, and things might feel better. Then she'd get that deep, terrible feeling that only a little snort could take care of, and she'd exit the church feeling guilty. And then she'd remember why. She'd remember what Robbie had done to her.

* * *

"Welcome again, fans, to *Ultimate Gladiator*! I'm your host, Mel Abbot, and this is your co-host, Buddy Stevens. We're here on The Gladiator Network for another exciting, live broadcast from Gladiator Island. As our premium members know, they can access any of the previous *Ultimate Gladiator* events and download them for only $39.95 a month.

That's hours of the most thrilling battles you'll ever see. And remember, these guys are for real! There's no faking on *Ultimate Gladiator*. These can be battles to the death, and you can see it all right here on The Gladiator Network. Buddy, why don't you give us a rundown on what to expect today?"

"Thanks, Mel, and as our fans know, anything can happen. This is not a show for the faint of heart. As you can see on the screen, it looks like things are beginning to happen in the *Ultimate Gladiator* section of Gladiator Island. Things are breaking down along racial lines just like they have from the start of our series. While the skinheads are outnumbered by the Brothas, they're not giving up anything when it comes to brute force."

"Who's that big guy in the center of the screen, Buddy?"

"The one with the big swastika tattooed on his chest?"

"Yeah, he looks bad."

"And he is, Mel. He's new to the colony. This will be his first televised encounter. That's Purvis 'The Exterminator' Newington, a 35-year-old member of Georgia's chapter of Hell's Angels. He's already done ten years' hard time at Reidsville, and when he got out, he vowed never to be taken back alive. He's six-four, 260 pounds of pure muscle. When he joined us here on Gladiator Island, he said all he wanted to do was 'kick nigga ass.' Take a listen to what had to say when he checked in two days ago."

A clip of Newington was played: "All I want to do is kill niggas. They're fuckin' monkeys. I'll snap their fuckin' tiny little heads off."

"Sounds like he means it to me, Buddy."

"Me, too, Mel."

"So, who does it look like he'll be in combat with today?"

"Well, let's take a look at this shot from the area where the 'Brothas' like to marshal their forces. The big guy standing next to his tent is Lucius 'Mad Man' Martin. He's been on the island for almost a month and, if he decides to do battle, this will be his twelfth fight. So far, he's killed every one of his opponents, and it hasn't been too pretty. Mad Man likes to get'em on the ground and then slowly choke the life out, as you can tell by this replay from last week."

"Ouch, Buddy, that looks like it hurts!"

"And it does, Mel! Just to remind our fans, they can see this episode in its entirety, and any other episode, for only $39.95 a month."

"That's quite a deal, Buddy."

"Yeah, Mel, and if you sign up now, you'll get this *Ultimate Gladiators* T-shirt absolutely free, but you have to sign up now."

"That's a great deal, Buddy! OK, fans, looks like things may be starting to happen. Call this for us, Buddy."

"Right, Mel. As you can see on your screen, The Exterminator has taken another hit from his pipe and appears to be getting pumped for some heavy action."

"How about Mad Man, Buddy?"

"Take a look at this, Mel. There's Mad Man taking a snort, and it sure looks like he's ready to rumble."

"Give us his stats, Buddy."

"Lucius Martin is thirty, six-two, 270 pounds. He was serving twenty years for voluntary manslaughter and got an early out when he opted to come to Gladiator Island. Jailhouse jive has it that Lucius and Purvis had been trading insults in the slammer for a long time, and this just might be high noon for these two."

"This could really be a fight to the death, Buddy."

"Mel, I don't see how it could be anything else. If we're lucky, some of their buddies may get into it, too, and we could really see some kick-ass gladiator action."

"And that's what to expect from the Gladiator Network. While we watch as these two ultimate gladiators move through the woods on Gladiator Island to their showdown, we'll take a pause to tell you about the full product line of clothing and personal gear you can get from The Gladiator Network."

* * *

Katie thought she could exist in anonymity while working in the Buckhead area of Atlanta. She'd done it for months with great success. But, in the back of her mind, she knew she'd probably be discovered. She'd thought about it several times and wondered what she'd do if it happened. But, with the aid of chemicals, she was able to force those thoughts back into the cracks and crevices. The world came tumbling down one night when she least expected it.

Robbie had many friends in the Atlanta area, particularly in the affluent northwestern part of the city. Many of them had known both Katie and him since high school and college. As luck would have it, Katie was spotted in the lobby of the Ritz-Carlton in Buckhead by a close friend of Robbie's.

Lyndon Wright knew all about the travails of the McFarland family when it came to Katie and was eager to report his findings to Robbie. After all, he was only a junior partner in the law firm and was always looking for a way to move up.

Robbie was seated in front of his 57-inch flat screen about to watch a CD of *Gone With the Wind*, his favorite movie of all time, when his cell phone went off. He had to put down his fresh mixer of Jack Daniels and ginger-ale and fish the phone out of his pocket.

"This shit pisses me off," he said to his wife, who was nursing her third glass of what Robbie had told her was very expensive wine. "This better be important, 'cause I don't give this number out to just anybody."

Looking at the caller ID, Robbie pressed the talk button, and said, "Talk to me, Lyndon."

"Robbie, I'm sittin' in the bar at the Ritz-Carlton lookin' at your sister Katherine."

"You're doin' what?"

"You heard me, Dog. I've got her in my cross hairs as we speak."

"You sure?"

"Goddamn straight I'm sure. How could I ever forget the hottest cheerleader at Georgia? Only now she's got short black hair, but the tits and ass and those eyes…they're Katherine McFarland, I promise you."

"Don't you take your eyes off her, you hear me Lyndon!"

"I got you, Dog."

"And, if she leaves, you follow her, understand!"

"I'm with my wife and some friends, I can't leave them.!"

"Listen, muthafucka, you want good things to happen at our law firm, you stay on her like stink on shit. I'll be there in ten minutes."

Robbie didn't bother to park his Mercedes in the lot; he just drove it to the main entrance and tossed his keys to the doorman. He also hadn't changed clothes and burst into the hotel lobby wearing jeans, a Bulldog T-shirt and Bass-Weejun loafers with no socks. He was a well-known figure in the Atlanta social scene, and when he blew into the hotel lobby, two people spoke to him as he walked across the Persian rug that covered most of the sitting area. He didn't bother to respond because he was looking for Lyndon. Then he spied Lyndon standing by one of the elevator doors.

"Where is she?"

"She went up to the penthouse level with a guy who looked like some kinda New York City Jew."

"A what?"

"You know what I'm talkin' about, Dog. A fuckin' Yankee Jew. They're easy to spot."

"Did you see them go into a room?"

"I couldn't get to that level. I didn't have a card that would let me."

"OK, go back to your wife and friends. Don't say a word about this and I'll see ya tomorrow."

Little Dog scanned the lobby. He'd been to the Ritz a hundred times and was known on sight by most of the staff. He was always friendly and always a big tipper. In seconds, his eyes fell upon the head bellman, a black man from Mali with whom the Dog had joked around many times.

Little Dog always carried as least five hundred in cash and reached into his pocket as he approached a man he knew only as "Ousmane." He peeled off two crisp hundred-dollar bills and cupped them in his hand.

Passing the cash in a discreet handshake, he said quietly, "I need to get onto the penthouse level and I need to know the room where that hot, black-haired bitch is. You get me, Ous?"

Ousmane smiled, pocketed the bills, and said, "I'll go to the elevators. Follow a few steps behind me. I'll get you what you want, Mr. McFarland."

"Not a word to anybody," said Little Dog as he pulled out another hundred and passed it to the bellman.

* * *

Little Dog stood in front of the penthouse door for maybe thirty seconds, thinking about what to do. Then, in a furious fit of anger, he banged his fists against the door and cried out, "Fire! Fire! You've got to evacuate your room now!"

In moments, the Dog could hear the deadbolt opening and the chain lock being taken off. A small man of about fifty wearing only his Jockey shorts stood wide-eyed before the Dog. Little Dog picked the man up by his arms and forced him back into the suite. When he had reached the bedroom he slammed the man down to the floor and shouted, "Get your fuckin' clothes on and get the fuck outta here."

Katie had been taken completely by surprise. In her fright, she had formed herself into a ball at the head of her bed, covering her naked body with a sheet she'd pulled around her. Little Dog stood at the foot of the bed for a second, then looked to see if her date had left. When he watched the John scurry from the room, he moved quickly to the door, slammed it shut and locked it. Then he returned to Katie. In the seconds he was gone, Katie had pulled on a robe, stood, and placed a chair between herself and her brother.

Like a lion sizing its prey, Robbie eyed his sister and moved in closer. Katie remembered the .38 she kept under her mattress and imagined how much time she had to grab it and fire. She was that frightened.

"Do you know what you've done to our family?" hissed Robbie. The veins in his neck were bulging and his voice was low and menacing. "Do you fuckin' know? Do you fuckin' care, you little whore?"

Robbie moved closer, but Katie stood her ground behind the chair, still judging if she had time to grab the pistol and defend herself.

"Do you know what you've put our parents through, you fuckin' cokehead?"

While Katie was very much afraid, her time on the street had hardened her, and she'd learned to stare down a threat more than once. Now she stood stone solid and stared at Robbie.

"I asked you a goddamn question, you fuckin' piece of shit. Do you know how much pain you've put your mother and father through?"

Katie still didn't move and didn't answer, and Robbie got to within arm's reach of her. Then Katie spoke.

"Do you know how much pain you put me through, Robbie? What do you think the governor and his lovely wife would say if they knew what their wonderful son did to their beautiful daughter?"

Robbie didn't move an inch, but his eyes spoke volumes as Katie continued.

Looking at the phone on the night stand, Katie said, "Maybe I should call the Governor's Mansion right now and tell the governor and Mrs. McFarland how, when I was only nine years old and you were thirteen, you started coming to my room. Remember that, my darling brother? Remember how you started? You were my baby-sitter when our parents were out for the evening, and our father was pumping hands while our mother smiled and made nice with all the snobs at the Piedmont Driving Club. At first I thought you were just playing around when you started to tickle me. Then you started to go further."

Katie took a deep breath as the tears began to flow, her eyeliner forming black streaks down her face.

"Remember the first time you pulled your dick out and told me to touch it? Remember the first time you stuck your finger in me? I do, it was on my tenth birthday! Remember the first time you actually screwed me? I do. I was eleven then. You hurt me that night, Robbie. You told me not to tell anybody about all those things, and I never did because, not only did you screw me that night, you screwed up my life, you miserable dirt bag. You said nobody would believe me, and like the child I was, I thought they wouldn't. But I'll7y8 bet they'll believe me now."

Perspiration formed on Robbie's forehead and trickled into his eyes, causing them to burn. He clenched his teeth, balled his fists and noted that his sister was looking at the telephone again. In a fit of uncontrolled rage, Robbie hit Katie in the face, causing her nose to bleed. She fell to the floor next to her bed and tried to grab her pistol, but Robbie saw what she was up to and stepped on her right arm, taking the pistol from under the mattress.

"You get your fuckin' worthless ass out of this city and this state," shouted Robbie as he stuffed the pistol under his belt. "You dumb fuckin' piece of shit! You're too stupid to know there still isn't anybody who would believe you. You're a goddamn cocaine addict, remember? You try to trash me, and I will bring a world of shit down on your head the likes of which the Roman emperors only dreamed of!"

As Robbie walked out, he stopped at the bathroom and leisurely urinated into Katie's toilet. Then, without haste, he washed and dried his hands. When he left, he didn't bother to close the door to Katie's room.

Katherine McFarland lay next to her bed, blood running from her nose for, well, she didn't know how long. Eventually, she pulled herself up, staggered to the open door and closed it. Then she looked at herself in the bathroom mirror.

* * *

When she woke up the next morning, Katie grabbed the remote and turned on the television. As she stripped for her shower, the words of Big Dog about the Ossabaw project again filled her suite; she almost ran to the set to turn it off, but something stopped her. It was the tone of her father's voice, and it reminded her of how he'd sounded when she was so young and innocent. He'd been good to her and her mother, and she'd loved them both greatly. Naked, Katie fell back on her bed and began to sob. She clasped her hands and raised them above her head. Pleading through the tears, she cried out, asking for God to be real and to help her, swearing on whatever good she had left in her life to remove herself from the decadence that surrounded her.

It was in that moment that Katie felt a peace come over her. Her breathing became less labored and the tightness in her stomach, there most of the time, disappeared. Her body felt warm and good, and she hadn't taken a hit yet that day. It was a distant feeling for Katie, one she hadn't known for years, and for some reason she was happy.

Embarrassed by her nakedness, even alone, she covered herself with a towel as she stepped toward the shower. While the warm water poured over her, she thought and thought. She cried out again to God, if he were real, to help her, but the good, peaceful feeling she'd had was gone. After she got out of the shower, she stood before the mirror, her body dripping wet, and cursed herself once more.

Katie had a very lucrative appointment that evening and should have been getting ready for her date, but instead, she dressed in her jogging shorts and shoes and headed down Peachtree, not know why or where she was going. She just ran and ran. She didn't know how far she'd run until she simply had to stop from sheer fatigue. It was then she knew she'd run over ten miles without stopping. After a minute, she turned around and started running back to the Ritz Carlton.

It was dark when Katie got back to the hotel and her date was pacing in the lobby.

"Where in the hell have you been," asked Larry angrily. "I've been calling your room for almost an hour, and this pisses me off!"

Katie actually liked Larry, but the time had come. Standing by the elevator doors, she wiped the perspiration from her forehead with the back of her hand and said, "It's over, Larry. I know I'm just a high-class hooker, but I'm done. Even high-class hookers get to the point where they can't do it anymore. You're a sweet guy who never abused me, but it's over. I can't live like this anymore. If I have to flip burgers at McDonalds, I'll do it, but I'm done, OK?"

"You're a fuckin' cokehead, how are you gonna get the money to support your habit?...I tell you what, I've got two large in my pocket for the rest of the night. Don't go tellin' me you're turnin' that down."

"I'm turnin' that down, sweetheart."

"You're fulla shit! Where're you gonna go, you silly bitch?"

Katie hadn't really thought about where she was headed until that very moment, and then the idea came to her head and she replied, "I'm going to Ossabaw Island and join my daddy's drug colony. I can have all the nose candy I want and won't have to turn any tricks for it."

* * *

There was a sharp rap on his office door and Hoorst knew from its sound and rhythm exactly who it was.

"Enter, Schwarz," called out Dr. Hoorst. The door was immediately flung open as Oberst Schwarz took three measured steps into his commander's presence. Standing at attention, Schwarz looked straight ahead, his left hand holding his cap in the proper fashion. Hoorst pushed his chair back from the computer screen and swiveled around to face Schwarz.

The early May morning poured through the windows of Hoorst's office while the roses his wife had planted just outside bobbed in the gentle breeze wafting in from the sound. Hoorst looked at his executive officer for a moment before speaking. Schwarz was always the ultimate professional soldier, loyal and obedient, but Dr. Hoorst often wished he could relax a little, that they could become more personal in their dealings."

"Stand at ease, Oberst. You appear to be a bit tense, Claus. Is there something out of sorts on the island?"

"No, Dr. Hoorst, nothing out of sorts, no problems, I mean, but there is something that just happened I thought you should know about."

"Well, thank you, Claus," replied Hoorst, propping his chin on his folded hands. "And what might this thing of such importance be?"

"We have just processed a high-value resident into the colony."

"How high?"

"As high as it gets, Dr. Hoorst."

"Well, there's no news like good news," said Hoorst, leaning back in his chair to glance at the computer screen.

"So, then," said Hoorst, "we must be talking about a healthy resident with good organs and numerous tissue matches, are we not?"

"That is correct, Dr. Hoorst. For someone who has abused cocaine, she is in excellent health. Relatively young, and she matches with ten waiting recipients on the kidney list and five on the liver list. As far as her heart donor status goes, it's almost off the charts. I might add, sir, that all the waiting recipients are on our 'Class A' payers' list."

"That is good news, Claus, and how many residents like that do we have in the colony at present?"

"She's the only one, Dr. Hoorst. I checked the potential recipients, and if we can harvest her kidneys, liver and heart, the company could realize a $900,000 profit. But that's only if the harvest takes place within the next week. Most of our potential recipients are on life support and probably won't live much past that point, Dr. Hoorst. But that doesn't include organs like her corneas or bone stock for grafting. I estimate, perhaps, another $150,000 if we include those things."

"And, what about her joints, Claus? No implants to sell?"

"No sir, she'd much too young for that. She's only twenty-nine."

Hoorst thought for a moment. "Twenty-nine, you say?"

"Yes, sir, twenty-nine."

"What a pity for her and what a windfall for the company.!"

"Yes, sir, I agree, but there's also one more thing."

When Hoorst heard those words, he sat straight up in his chair and asked, "Really, what might that be, Claus?"

"She gives her name as Katherine McFarland, Dr. Hoorst. She lists her next-of-kin as Robert Roy McFarland, the governor of Georgia, along with her mother. She's requested that we contact them and advise them of her admission to the colony."

Dr. Hoorst's legs propelled him to a standing position instantly.

"You are telling me the daughter of the governor of Georgia has checked herself into our colony?"

"Yes, sir, that's exactly what I'm reporting. I've done an identification cross-check on her and it appears that she is, indeed, exactly who she says she is."

"Please tell me, Claus, that you haven't notified the governor about this."

For the first time since Schwarz had been under his command, Hoorst detected a bit of irritation in the voice of his subordinate when Schwarz replied, "Dr. Hoorst, you know me better than that. I'd never do anything of that sort without first checking with you."

"I'm sorry, Claus. I was simply quite taken aback with what you just told me. Where is she now?"

"She's on the island, sir. I had her placed into Group Two, awaiting your inspection."

"Has she taken any coke yet?"

"Yes, sir, but not that much. She appears to be in a very depressed state. The residents I've seen like this before often overdose themselves within three or four days. If that happens, we'll be able to harvest her organs and deliver them to our recipients within thirty-six hours following her demise."

"I don't want anything untoward happening to her, Claus."

Schwarz reflexively assumed attention and answered, "Yes, sir!"

Hoorst looked at his computer screen and asked, "What's her resident number?"

"Zero-four-seven-six-hundred."

Hoorst typed in the code and Katie's photo instantly appeared on the screen.

"My God, she's beautiful," gasped Hoorst. "What in the world is she doing on this island?"

"The short answer, Dr. Hoorst, is that she's a cocaine addict. The long answer is that I don't know, sir."

Hoorst turned to Schwarz and smiled, saying, "You've done a good job, Claus. Take the next weekend in Savannah with your wife, everything on Executive Outcomes."

"Thank you very much, Dr. Hoorst."

CHAPTER SEVEN

REVELATIONS

Every man's work shall be made
Manifest; for the day shall declare it,
Because it shall be revealed by fire; and
The fire shall try every man's work of
What sort it is.
—*The Holy Bible*, King James Version: I Corinthians, 3:13

It had been almost a month since Judah had visited the colony. His contract required that he make monthly visits and he'd put this one off as long as he could.

As the colony's launch pulled away from the marina at Delegal Creek, the only good thing about the trip for Judah was the weather. It was Easter weekend, Good Friday, and the eight o'clock sun caught him in the face as he stood into it, letting it warm him. The wind was from the east, cooled by the ocean as it swept in with its scent. It was well before the heat of the day that would eventually bring large cumulous clouds in the west with thunderstorms and rain.

"Rudy knows how to stroke a person," thought Judah when got to the end of the dock on Ossabaw where a vintage World War II Jeep was waiting for him.

"Dr. Hoorst wants you to enjoy yourself with this," said the guard standing by the mint condition specimen, "and says that he'll catch up with you in a few hours."

Judah couldn't help smiling as he stood next to the Jeep. When he climbed into the driver's seat, he nodded his head approvingly when he noticed the M-1 carbine mounted next to him and the markings of Patton's Third Army on the Jeep's exterior. Every detail was perfect and Judah could hear Rudy telling him how Executive Outcomes had purchased it dirt cheap at the end of the war. It's what he always said. Still, Judah would have fun with this toy until he got to the entrance of Group Two and his inspection began.

The first block of resident housing was a half mile from the entrance. The group now had six hundred residents in three different locations in a six-square-mile area. While it had been a cold winter for Ossabaw, the residents had fared well in the large tents provided for them. Warmth had come from propane heaters centrally located in each of the tents. It may have been only the basics, but it was enough to survive.

As Judah entered the first tent, he heard a distantly familiar voice calling out to him.

"Judah," cried a weak sound from a cot only yards away, "it's me, David."

Judah's head snapped quickly to his right where he saw a skeleton of a man raised on his elbows beckoning to him.

"Oh, my God, David," said Judah as he approached.

"I know, I look like shit," replied David. "I don't have much longer. The coke and the horse have finally got the best of me. From what I've seen happen here, I've got maybe a week at best. But, I haven't been in pain and, I'm not scared about what's going to happen to this world. That's for you to worry about. I'll be long gone and at peace when that shit comes down."

Judah dropped onto the cot across from David and listened as his boyhood friend continued.

"Remember the last time you saw me here, Judah, and I told you about how the world was about to end?"

"Yeah, I remember."

"The signs, Judah, they're all around. The world as we know it is going to end. God has revealed it all to everyone, Jews, Christians, Muslims, everybody. It's going to be bad, Judah. A whole lot of pain, man."

Judah simply nodded, looking into David's wide eyes.

"No, man, it's happening now! That's why I'm here. I don't want to be around when it happens."

"I understand."

David had become very agitated and flailed his arms, ranting about signs concerning the end times. Finally, Judah stood and said, "Here, why don't you take another hit from this heroin," offering the loaded syringe to David.

"Yeah, good idea. Not much longer now for me or anybody else. Maybe you ought to think about checking in here, too. It's gonna be bad, real fuckin' bad, man."

Looking down at his old friend, Judah asked, "Is there anything else I can do for you, David?"

Just after he'd tightened the tourniquet on his left arm and just before he pushed the contents of the syringe into his vein, David looked up and said, "Yeah, there is."

"What?"

"This chick checked into the colony a few days ago. She didn't look like one of the usual suspects, though. She was a kinda young, high-class lookin' shicksa. Liked to snort the shit. Said her name was Katherine McFarland. Claimed her father was the governor of Georgia. I'd like to know if she was just another bullshit artist before I go to the big spirit in the sky."

"Where is she now?" asked Judah.

"A couple of guards came and got her about two hours ago, I think. It could have been more; I don't know. I'm pretty well gone right now."

"Are you sure, David? Are you sure she said her name was Katherine McFarland and her father was he governor?"

"I might be fucked up, but I'm sure about that."

Judah knew Katie. He'd met her several times over the years, before she went over the edge. He also knew about her problems, most political insiders did, but for over a year she'd simply dropped off the radar. A lot of the people who were friends of the governor assumed she'd been checked into a drug rehab program. None but his closest friends dared ask him about

Katie.

Judah's initial impulse was to hunt down Rudy and get to the bottom of David's story. But he decided to dig a little further into it as he continued his inspection of the facilities and residents in the group. He was well aware that all his movements were being monitored, and he tried to act as normally as possible. He just hoped the monitors weren't able to capture the audio of his conversation with David Feldman.

After an hour of observing several hundred people strewn about the compound, some unconscious, some hyperactive, some having sex in the woods, others doing nothing but staring into space, Judah couldn't find anything that contradicted the agreement the State of Georgia had with Executive Outcomes.

When Judah returned to the entrance of Group Two, he noticed thirteen bodies stacked in the back of a Humvee, covered with a bright blue plastic tarp. When he lifted the cover to inspect the bodies he recoiled in horror. On top of the stack was his friend David. He'd died of a heroin overdose only minutes after Judah had told him goodbye.

"I'm sorry, Mr. Benjamin," said Sergeant Feisler, who was standing at the back of the Humvee, "I know he was boyhood chum of yours. He was very proud of that and very proud of you, sir. He told everyone who would listen about you. I spoke with him often, sir. He wasn't an evil person. He was really quite a gentle soul, only very weak of character, Mr. Benjamin."

"Thank you, Sergeant, I appreciate your words."

In a soft voice the sergeant replied, "You're very welcome, sir. Is there anything I can do for you? If not, Mr. Benjamin, these remains are to be taken to the disposal unit immediately, and it is my duty to command the detail."

Judah shook his head as if he were trying to clear his brain, then looked at Feisler.

"This man," motioning to David's body, "was an Orthodox Jew. I'm sure there are others in this pile who also had religions convictions. Is there any kind of religious service conducted before they are cremated?"

"No, Mr. Benjamin. But each week Bishop Bryan goes to the pits where their ashes are buried. He conducts a brief, quite moving, service in memory of the deceased. I have attended that service several times. Members of the company are always present out of respect for the dead."

"When does the Bishop perform this service, Feisler?"

"Every Saturday just before sundown, sir."

"That's tomorrow," said Judah mostly to himself, "at the end of the Sabbath."

For several seconds there was silence. Then softly, Sergeant Feisler asked, "Will you be all right, Mr. Benjamin? Shall I have someone drive you back to the Main House?"

"Thank you Sergeant, I'll be fine…and thank for your concern. And…you said David was a good soul, just weak?"

"Yes, sir. He was indeed a good soul. But his spirit was weak."

Judah watched as Feisler's men pulled the tarp over the bodies and listened as the Humvee roared to life, then trundled across the bumpy dirt road that led to the crematoriums.

While Judah stood watching the Humvee with David's body disappear into a wall of trees, Rudolf Hoorst was seated in front of a bank of computer screens in the Central Command headquarters. He'd watched for an hour as the implanted forearm chips signaled one death after another. In that hour, ten people had succumbed to their addictions or diseases.

"Dr. Hoorst," said Schwarz, "as you requested, sir, here is the printout of the artificial joints in the residents who have died within the last hour."

Handing Hoorst another list, Schwarz continued, "And here, sir, is the printout that involves tissue matches from these bodies with eligible recipients."

Hoorst took the list, looked it over, and said, "What a pity we have to destroy such valuable tissue. I'll be happy when we have our donor harvesting team up and running, Claus."

Before Schwarz could reply, his cell phone rang.

"Dr. Hoorst, it is Sergeant Feisler with a report for you."

"Speak, Sergeant Feisler," said Hoorst, watching the computer screens.

"Dr. Hoorst, I am on the way to the disposal unit with thirteen bodies. When I left, Mr. Benjamin was still there. He had completed his inspection and told me he felt all was in order, sir. Then he spotted the body of his old friend, Feldman, who had died only an hour before. He was demonstrably upset, sir. But I believe he is all right now."

"Does he know anything about the McFarland woman?"

"Not that he said, sir."

"No questions?"

'No, Dr. Hoorst. He only asked about funeral services for the dead and I told him about Bishop Bryan."

"Very good, Sergeant. And what about this McFarland woman?"

"She is well, sir, she is under guard, isolated, comfortable, receiving just enough drugs to keep her happy."

"Be sure nothing happens to her, Sergeant Feisler, and there will be a reward for your service."

"Nothing will happen to her, Dr. Hoorst, unless you order it."

Rudy turned from the computer screen to Schwarz, saying, "I believe she's worth a lot more alive than the sum of her parts."

* * *

The Friday after Easter dawned cool and clear. The humidity was only 26 percent and there was no haze across the marsh to dull John-Morgan's view of Skidaway Island from the front porch of his house. It was eight in the morning, only a light breeze from the south and seventy-two degrees. John-Morgan had chosen to eat his breakfast on the porch, and Judah had joined him.

Judah hadn't smiled during the breakfast, and John-Morgan was about to ask him if anything was wrong when Judah put down his napkin and said, "We need to talk, strictly confidential. Are we safe here?"

"The best place would be on my boat. Is it bad news?"

"Depends on who you are and what the circumstances might be."

As John-Morgan guided *Graf Spee* toward Butterbean Beach, he looked at Judah and asked, "OK, what's up?"

"I've got information that Katherine McFarland is now a resident at Ossabaw."

"How good is the quality of that chatter?"

"One to ten? I'd say a six or seven."

"Who told you?"

"This guy I grew up with was in Group Two. He was into the 'H' pretty heavy. Basically, he told me Katie was on the island. He said he talked with her for a while and she told him who she was. Then he claims some guards came and took her away and says he never saw her again."

"When can I talk to him?"

"You can't, he died only hours after I talked to him."

"You believe him?"

"Yeah. I do."

"Am I the only other person who knows?"

"Yeah, but we gotta tell Lloyd and Will."

John-Morgan nodded, said, "Agreed," and pressed the throttles forward.

All of Green Island Sound looked like a lake as *Graf Spee* plowed across it heading for Hell Gate. In the distance, Ossabaw Island was a half-inch strip of deep green cut across the horizon, pressed between a bright blue sky and olive-colored water.

The monthly meeting of Executive Outcomes' Ossabaw Project was called to order by Rudy precisely at noon in the Great Room of the Main House. Placing his hand on a bound copy resting on the table before him, Hoorst said, "Anyone who wishes can review this report. It goes into infinite detail about how the island has been doing over the last month. As a matter of fact, a copy will be provided to each of you, should you desire."

Hoorst cleared his throat while he looked at the hands of the old grandfather clock across the room.

"However, getting right to the meat of the matter, I'll briefly outline the numbers I'm sure you're all interested in."

Glancing down at a typewritten report, Hoorst began to read the statistics.

"There are currently 1,596 residents living in the Ossabaw Colony. We are now approaching maximum capacity. The pressure on the facility can easily be sustained at this level. We have had an average daily mortality rate of 105 over the past month. So far, the company has been able to dispose of the remains within twenty-four hours. At any one time, there has been an average of 130 people waiting at our Skidaway Narrows facility for immediate acceptance into the colony. They have been on a first come, first served basis.

"As you know, our policy at the embarkation point has been modified slightly. We now provide the first one hundred people on the waiting list with minimal drugs in order to maintain a sense of calm. With our twenty-four-hour turnaround of one hundred residents, give or take a few, these unfortunates won't have to wait more than a day for subsequent admission. Does anyone have any questions?"

Hoorst stood for a second or two, then turned to Little Dog and said, "I'll turn the rest of the meeting over to Mr. McFarland."

Robbie was dressed in a red polo shirt, jeans with a few holes in them, and a pair of alligator cowboy boots. He was relaxed and jovial as he started to talk.

"I imagine the biggest thing y'all want to know about is governmental support. I'm happy to tell ya that the state's support is strong, very strong. It's been hard for our opponents to argue with the results. Over this past month, the most conservative estimates show that, since the start of the Ossabaw colony at the beginning of this year, the State of Georgia has saved $1,356,000,000. Our prison population has been cut almost in half. We just don't have much more street-level crime caused by the drug trade. Not only that, but the rate of violent crimes like armed robbery, aggravated assault, and murder have fallen by almost 40 percent. It's my opinion that, because of the savings realized by the existence of this colony, the State of Georgia will actually show a surplus in the next fiscal year of almost half a billion dollars. And that, gentlemen, is sweet music to the ears of our legislators!"

Robbie's report ended the formal portion of the meeting. The men then wandered into the dining room, where roast beef sandwiches were served. It was during this time that Judah was able to catch a private moment with Lloyd.

Judah was disturbed with how Lloyd looked, but wasn't surprised. Lloyd had lost almost twenty-five pounds, and his eyes appeared sunken and drained of energy.

"You've lost too much weight, Lloyd," said Judah as he watched Lloyd nibble at the sandwich on his plate.

"I know I look like crap," replied Lloyd before he took a bite. "It's my line of work. There's so much to do here. So much suffering, I'm forced to move from the last moment of one person's life to the next. I don't have time to eat like I should. Rudy keeps getting on to me about how I drive myself. But it's not just the work, it's the smell. When I come back here to the Main House to eat and go to bed, the smell of death is in my clothes. It's in my hair. I've gotten into the habit of taking off the clothes I wore in the camp and hanging them outside. I take a long hot shower, and even then I think I can still smell death under my fingernails."

When he felt free to speak, Judah looked at Lloyd and said quietly, "This will be quick. I have information that Katherine McFarland is a resident here and that she has been removed from the general population."

While he chewed and sipped from his glass of iced tea, Lloyd's eyes never left Judah's. Using his napkin to wipe his mouth and also to hide his lips, Lloyd replied, "I've heard the same thing. I was gonna tell ya when I had the chance. We can talk later. Who else knows?"

"John-Morgan and, when I get the chance, Will. I assume everybody else in the colony knows. But I don't think Rudy knows we're in on the secret."

"We need to do our best to keep it that way. There's more I have to tell you, but we've got to be careful."

Judah noticed Rudy approaching and said with a smile to Lloyd, "Here's our host."

Rudy laughed, then turned to Lloyd and asked, "Is there anything more we can do for you in Group One, Bishop?"

"Yeah, stop the dying."

Rudy looked down at the polished toes of his riding boots, then back at Lloyd and said, "No one gets out alive, do they, Bishop? Not from this facility, not from Planet Earth. That is, unless you're present for the Second Coming. Then, according to Roman Catholic doctrine, you'll be swept up into the gracious arms of your Savior. Do I have it right, Bishop?"

Lloyd swallowed the last of his lunch and took a long drink of tea.

"Nobody gets out alive. Nobody at all, Rudy, and that includes you and me."

Composing his thoughts, Lloyd's expressive eyes fell upon Rudy with their full force.

"I remember when I was in grammar school at St. Pius X how the nuns would try to teach us the importance of a happy death. Can you imagine, we little colored children in the fourth grade looking at this white

WILLIAM C. HARRIS JR. | 92

woman dressed in a full habit talking about a happy death! It had us terrified. She was an ultimate authority figure, and she's telling us about having a happy death? That scared the hell out of me then, but as the years have gone by, I've come to understand what she was teaching us."

Rudy pursed his lips as his eyes checked for a moment to Judah's, and replied, "I remember the same thing being taught to me when I was in Catholic school in Richmond. I remember thinking about death as a youngster. It wasn't a taboo subject in Catholic Doctrine. The Church has always confronted death head-on. It is, after all, the Gates to Paradise."

Before Rudy could add another word, Lloyd interjected, "Or the Gates to Hell."

"Well said, Your Excellency."

Rudy looked about the room and said, "Gentlemen, I have work to attend to. If you have any questions not pressing, please save them for dinner tonight."

Looking at Robbie, standing next to the windows attacking his second sandwich and third beer, Rudy said, "When it is convenient, Mr. McFarland, I should like you to join me in my office."

Judah looked at John-Morgan and Lloyd, and said, "I think it would do us all some good to take a tour of the island in that antique Jeep the company has provided. Perhaps we can catch up on old times."

* * *

The temperature was only seventy degrees when Rudy mounted his horse, and he and Schwarz began to trot toward the entrance to the deep woods that ultimately led to the ocean. For the first week of May, it was still cool and even cooler when the sun was blocked by the oaks. Rudy felt relaxed and happy; there was no sight of the camps, no smells, no sounds. When they finally reached the beach house, Rudy stopped to admire the sand dunes and the deep wind-swept oaks that held the dunes in place. He strained to hear the sound of the wind blowing through the sea oats and watched as they bowed to the ocean's breeze.

In Europe, the company had discovered that, inevitably, one or more high profile persons would enter one of their colonies. Sometimes they made no difference on the balance sheets; sometimes these residents were useful in a number of ways. Rudy was of the opinion that Katherine McFarland was one of those useful persons.

When the house wasn't occupied by a high-value resident, Rudy would take his family there for a weekend at the beach. The house was just behind the dunes, elevated and overlooking them with a clear view of the Atlantic. It looked much like any of the old Tybee Island cottages with tall windows, spacious rooms and a large screened porch facing the ocean. The interior was simple, but well-appointed. A sound system was mated to a large screen television served by a satellite dish. Considering the location and accommodations, Executive Outcomes' beach property was quite a comfortable place to be.

An EO guard was waiting when Rudy arrived. Handing the reins to the guard, Rudy asked, "Where is she, Werner?"

"On the screened porch, sir."

"Is she high?"

"Not so much, Dr. Hoorst. I've been surprised. She's done some coke, takes pills at night to sleep, but mostly only wants to drink red wine and look at the ocean."

"And, how does she appear, Lieutenant?"

"Again, sir, a surprise. She is a beautiful woman. When I was told she was a cokehead, I had expected someone completely different. This woman is in good physical condition. Really quite pretty."

Rudy stepped onto the screened porch and paused for Katie to notice him. She was seated at the other end in a lounge chair, watching the breakers from the incoming tide crash on the beach. He was unable to determine if she was ignoring him or if she simply hadn't noticed him. Rudy wasn't accustomed to being ignored and was irritated. It did, however, give him a chance to evaluate his most prized resident.

"Schwarz was right," thought Rudy, "she does favor Marilyn Monroe." Rudy's eyes started at Katie's feet and moved upward. They traveled across her legs and then her thighs. There was nothing he could criticize. Her calf muscles were well formed and strong. Her thighs, also muscular and well-shaped. He couldn't see much of her backside, but he was experienced enough to know that it, too, would be tight. Katie was wearing a pair of red short-shorts and a yellow halter top. Her belly was flat and her breasts full. Rudy could see her nipples making little peaks in the fabric that covered them, and that appealed to him. Katie was letting her hair grow out and turn its natural sandy blonde color. Her chin was strong and her nose petite and well formed. He knew she had blue eyes and imagined how they'd appear when he finally had a full view of her face.

In the finest aristocratic Southern accent he'd heard since leaving Richmond, Katie said, without taking her eyes off the ocean, "I assume you're the famous Dr. Hoorst I've heard so much about."

While Katie's gaze was still on the Atlantic, Rudy approached within ten feet of her, stopped and stood almost at attention.

"You are correct, Miss McFarland, I am Dr. Hoorst."

Slowly, Katie turned her head to Rudy. She put her glass of wine on the end table, then turned her reclining body in Rudy's direction. Rudy was dressed in his favorite riding clothes, knee-high brown leather boots, the grey German general's riding pants he adored, and a military style khaki shirt.

Around his waist was a brown leather belt, the buckle polished brass with SS runes in the center. His father had given it to him on his twelfth birthday.

Katie shifted into a sitting position, bracing both arms on the seat of her chair, forcing her breasts upward and outward. For several seconds she said nothing while she looked Rudy over from head to toe. Then, with a bit of a snicker, Katie said, "I don't know whether to raise my right arm and say 'Seig Heil,' or laugh out loud. You remind me of a wannabe Nazi. But don't get me wrong, Dr. Hoorst, your taste in clothes is really quite good—dashing, as a matter of fact. I particularly like the *Afrika Corps* shirt you're wearing. Something like that would look good on me."

For a second, Rudy felt like a fool, but he quickly recovered and said, "I'm impressed, Miss McFarland, that you would recognize this shirt for what it really is."

"Well, I only dated the biggest international dealer in military collectibles for almost six months." Katie reached for her wine glass and took a sip, her eyes never leaving Rudy's.

"Perhaps I should modify that last sentence," added Katie. "I had sex with him for six months. After a while, he became boring and I became too expensive. But I did enjoy learning all about military collectibles."

Katie stood, approached Rudy and extended her hand, saying, "Forgive me, Dr. Hoorst, for being so rude, but you must realize that this is a stressful time for me and sometimes I lash out."

Rudy shook Katie's hand, bowed slightly, smiling broadly, and said, "I take no offense, Miss McFarland. I'm rather flattered that you would notice such things. Much of my interests go right over my wife's head. She couldn't tell a helmet from a hat rack."

Katie walked to the porch railing and let the wind fill her hair. It was then that Rudy was fully able to appreciate her beauty, and he was smitten, smitten terribly. Katie could read a man like a newspaper and knew that Rudy was immediately attracted to her. Turning to him she said, "You're not a bad looking man, Hoorst. How old are you, early forties?"

Coming closer, Rudy laughed and replied, "Oh, no, I'm in my mid-fifties. But thank you for the compliment."

"Don't go getting your head all pumped up," answered Katie. "When I guess ages, I always guess low. It's fun to see how excited people become when they think they look younger than they actually are."

Rudy tilted his head slightly and said, "You're having fun with me, aren't you, Miss McFarland?"

"Under the circumstances, about as much fun as a girl can have."

Assuming a more formal posture, Rudy said, "I'm here to see that you are well taken care of, Miss McFarland. Is there enough coke for you? Any other drugs that you'd like to try? Are you happy with your accommodations?"

Turning back to the ocean, Katie asked, "Why am I here, why can't I be back in the camp with everybody else?"

"Because it's much safer here. The food is better and you can't argue with the view, Miss McFarland."

"How 'bout you just cut the 'Miss McFarland' crap, OK, Hoorst?"

Unperturbed, Rudy leaned against the railing next to Katie and said, "That's fine. I'll call you Katherine and you may call me Rudy."

"I like Katie, not Katherine."

"Very well, then; it's Katie."

"Have my parents and my darling brother been informed that I'm on this island?"

"We're considering that option, Katie. But no one's been told anything yet."

Katie snapped her head toward Rudy and angrily asked, "Why the hell not?"

"Because, Katie, the company is in charge now. Your life is here, on this island. You no longer have any life and any family on the outside. You signed all that away when you joined the colony, remember?"

Katie instantly softened and looked into Rudy's eyes. He could feel the excitement of her beauty in his stomach, and she could see it on his face.

"Rudy, if you would do me just this little favor, it would mean so much to me. I want my parents to know where I am, and I want my brother to know, too."

"But why, Katie? That would only hurt them more."

She turned back to the ocean and said, "I know all about hurt, Rudy."

Putting on the "help me" look that always melted men, Katie said, "I want my brother to know, and I want proof. You can help me ease some of the pain, Rudy. I know you can."

"I'll see what I can do, but no promises."

Rudy drew himself straight, nodded slightly and said, "I'll visit you again tomorrow. By the way, I've had my men bring in some hashish straight from Afghanistan. You have that at your disposal, as well as a water pipe, so you won't burn your throat. I've been told the hash is quite good. If there is nothing else, Katie, I'll see you tomorrow."

"Actually, Rudy," answered Katie, "there is something else."

"Yes?"

"I like to jog. I want to run on the beach, right now."

"I'll see to it on my way out."

* * *

John-Morgan was behind the wheel of the Jeep as it crossed the open field in front of the Main House. He stopped when he heard a thudding sound in the distance. It was unmistakable to him and he watched as old memories blasted back. A Huey helicopter was coming in low over the tree line. Pensively, John-Morgan followed the craft as it flew in, flared its blades and settled down only a hundred yards away. The sound of that machine was forever imprinted in his mind, and for a few seconds he was back in Vietnam waiting for a Huey to take him from harm's way.

"They have two flights in and out of here a day," shouted Lloyd into John-Morgan's ear.

"For what?" called back John-Morgan as a Humvee approached the Huey, then backed up to its open door.

"For whatever it is they're taking off and putting on, John-Morgan!"

John-Morgan, Judah and Lloyd sat and watched while the Huey's blades slowed, and EO men loaded about a dozen boxes onto the helicopter.

"Whatdaya think that stuff is?" asked Judah.

"No tellin'," answered John-Morgan just before he let the clutch out and pointed the Jeep toward the woods.

Riding at a crawl through the largest trees on the island, John-Morgan looked at Lloyd in the seat next to him and asked, "OK, what do you know?"

Judah was in the back and leaned forward between the seats so Lloyd wouldn't have to shout an answer.

"The camp's been buzzing about Katie McFarland," responded Lloyd. "Word is that she got here sometime last week. Spent a day or so in Group Two, then disappeared in the custody of EO guards. Hasn't been seen since."

Lloyd looked at Judah and waited for his answer.

"Basically the same thing I heard. I've got a feeling it's for real."

Lloyd faced his two friends and said, "I think there's more going on here than meets the eye."

"Like what?" asked Judah."

"I don't know for sure. It just seems as if this whole place is a well-oiled machine. The company has the concept down to a science. It's scary how quickly and cleanly they can turn over the resident population. In three weeks, the population of my group is gone. No old-timers."

Lloyd let his eyes wander across the marsh when the Jeep reached the low areas and started climbing toward the dunes. At the top, John-Morgan peered over the hood, then froze and let the Jeep roll back.

"What's the problem?" asked Judah.

"I think I just spotted Katherine McFarland," answered John-Morgan, raising his head up behind the sand to watched a man and a women running on the beach.

Judah had fallen in next to John-Morgan, and when he saw the runners, he thought the same thing. Lloyd wasn't far behind; when he got to

John-Morgan, he asked, "What's going on?"

"From the times I've seen her, looks like Katherine McFarland to me. That's Katherine, no doubt about it. I've seen her a thousand times. It's hard to mistake that figure, even at this distance."

John-Morgan sat up and asked, "OK, so what does all this mean? Why is Katherine McFarland so important that she rates such treatment?"

Judah snorted and replied, "That's kind of a no-brainer. She's the governor's daughter. What do you think she's worth?"

* * *

Rudy found Katie on the porch again, lying in the same lounge chair, staring at the ocean. Only this time, her shorts were white and she was wearing a black tank top with no bra. Just as before, Rudy waited at the other end of the porch for Katie to notice him.

Without turning her head toward Rudy, Katie remarked, "You said you were coming back the next day, Dr. Hoorst. That was three days ago."

Rudy walked closer, then took a seat in the chair next to Katie. It was the middle of May and the afternoons were beginning to get warmer. This day, the wind was from the east, bringing in the cool ocean air, and it whistled slightly as it passed through the porch screens.

"I'm flattered that you would take such note of my absence, Katie."

"Don't go flattering yourself, Rudy. You're not that grand. It's just that I don't get to see many different faces, living in this gilded cage of yours." Katie sat up and faced Rudy. "Oh, fiddlesticks, Dr. Hoorst, no military dress today! I was so looking forward to another costume."

Rudy was wearing tailored jeans, ostrich-skin cowboy boots, and a tight-fitting black T-shirt with EO's diving eagle logo on the front. He lifted weights three times a week and jogged the other days. The hard work was readily apparent by the size and cut of his arm and chest muscles.

"But," said Katie, "I do like the boots."

"Thank you, they're a gift from my wife."

"So, what brings you to this neck of the woods, Rudy? Slumming?"

"I have responsibilities, things to do…anyway, did you get to try the hash?"

"No, I wasn't interested."

"How has the food been?"

"Certainly better than the other residents are getting, when they care to eat."

"And the entertainment center?"

Frustrated, Katie stood abruptly and walked back into the living room. Rudy followed and once inside, Katie wheeled around to face him.

"Look, Rudy, just cut the crap, OK? You don't give a damn about how I'm doing. So, just what is it that brings you all the way out here? Just wanna exercise your horse, or is it some other type of exercise you're interested in?"

"As I explained before, Katie, you are a very valuable asset for the company. I'm simply trying to insure you stay that way."

"And what else, Hoorst?"

"Well, I had just wondered about you, Katie. I wondered how a young woman like you could wind up here."

Katie nodded her head and said, "You mean how I became a high-priced call girl, don't you, Rudy?"

"That has crossed my mind, yes."

Katie went to the cabinet under the flat screen TV and pulled out the water pipe and hash Rudy had talked about. She placed it on the table in front of Rudy and said, "OK, Rudy, you want to know how I got where I am today?"

Rudy nodded his head.

"Well, then, you're going to have to share some of this with me. Then I'll tell you the whole story, OK?"

Rudy had smoked hash and pot before, but other than alcohol, that was the only drug he'd ever ingested. It had been almost a year since he'd been high. The last time was with his wife when they smoked some grass together and made love the rest of the night. The idea of getting high with Katie intrigued him enormously.

"That sounds like something I'd like to do, Katie," said Rudy with a smile. "It's been a while."

Rudy watched as Katie prepared the bong, first with water, then ice cubes, then the hash. Using a Zippo lighter, Katie set fire to the hash block, and when it glowed, she sucked some of the smoke over the ice and watched as it filled the long tube leading to the mouth piece. When the transparent tube had been filled with thick smoke, Katie inhaled deeply and held her breath. Rudy followed suit, and they both finally exhaled together in mutual laughter. Neither said a word as Katie loaded the bong for another hit and the process was completed once more. Rudy wasn't sure if he'd been at the beach house for twenty minutes or two hours. Whatever…he was feeling good.

Katie was impressed with the hash and she began to think about what she'd say to Hoorst.

"Wanna do another hit, Rudy?"

"Why not?"

After the third hit, Rudy began to become a little paranoid. But he'd had been there before and knew if he were patient, the feeling would pass. It did pass, just as Katie looked at him and asked, "Feel good?"

All kinds of "do not trespass" signs had vanished from Katie's face.

When Rudy looked at her, he knew full well that the hash was working on his brain, but she still was the most beautiful woman he'd ever seen. His wife was beautiful, but she didn't burn with the pure, hard sexuality that Katie had.

"Wanna walk on the beach?" asked Rudy.

Katie and Rudy walked ankle-deep through the surf. Everything was bright and pleasing for Rudy, and he concentrated on how the ocean's waters felt when his feet sank into the wet sand. Katie walked in front of Rudy. He couldn't take his eyes off her legs and her behind. A piece of driftwood lay ahead and, when she came to the log, Katie sat and watched as Rudy approached.

"So what's the long, painful story?" asked Rudy as he settled next to Katie, close, but not touching her.

"How well do you know my brother?"

"Well enough; your father appointed him as his representative. I've spent time with Robbie. He seems bright enough."

"He's the reason I'm here."

"How so?"

Katie breathed deeply, then began to recount, in great detail, how Robbie had molested and raped her.

"I was married to two very nice men, Rudy, and what my brother did to me ruined any sexual relationship I could have had with them. I was hell on earth for those boys. I'm just glad no children came from those marriages. I'm not the kind of woman suited for motherhood."

"But why the drugs and prostitution?"

"The coke made a lot go away for a while. When I was high, I wanted to have sex. I thought it was going to save my second marriage, but my husband got scared about how much we were doing. He was right; of course, we couldn't keep on like that. Then I left for a boyfriend who was richer and wilder than my husband, and well, it just went from there. For what it's worth, I've dated, no, make that screwed, some of the most powerful men in this country. You should see my 'little black book.'"

"So the coke became an anesthetic for your pain and, at the same time, a stimulant for your sexual appetite?"

"Pretty much."

Rudy looked down at his feet digging into the sand, then watched the large waves pushed higher by the wind and tide. There was a long silence, and Rudy tried to comprehend what Katie had just told him. It was a world totally alien to him.

"I never had anything remotely like that happen to me," said Rudy quietly. "It's really easy to understand why you've done the things you have. I did two years of residency in psychiatry before I switched to pathology.

Sometimes the emotional pain is much worse than the physical. At least with physical pain, the patient can point to something and say, 'This hurts me.' With pain of the spirit, it's invisible. People are much less likely to believe you actually are in pain. There's nothing they can put their hands on."

"Maybe you're beginning to understand why I'm here," said Katie. "The pain became so intense, I had serious thoughts about killing myself. But I was too scared for that. I wasn't sure if there was something or nothing when the lights went out. Then, after my brother beat the shit outta me, I begged for something to be bigger than I was; and if there was that something, I begged for help. One day, I saw my father on TV talking about this place. I figured it had to be better than the life I was living."

"I'm sorry for what happened to you, Katie."

"Me, too, Rudy." There was silence for several moments as both watched the waves.

"I want you to do something for me," said Katie.

"Such as?"

"I want to meet the priest, the black bishop."

"Why?"

"I heard he has great karma."

CHAPTER EIGHT

THINGS IN HEAVEN

They have pierced my hands and feet,
They have numbered all my bones.
—*The Holy Bible*, King James Version - Psalms 22, 17 &18

A large tent had been pitched in the woods at the Group One compound. It looked like a circus tent but was actually U.S. Army surplus. It could hold around four hundred beds. The sides had been rolled up to allow the air to circulate, and oil lanterns had been hung from every tent pole. This gave an appealing yellow glow to the interior.

About two hundred residents of Groups One and Two gathered in a semi-circle under the tent to attend the first evening Mass celebrated by Bishop Bryan and hear him speak. Some could walk, some needed wheelchairs, and some lay on their cots.

Rudy had a wooden platform built in front of a large oak and Lloyd had erected the altar given him by Rudy on it. The sun had set and the low light provided by lanterns masked some of the suffering there. A light breeze partially removed the smells.

Off to the left of the crowd stood Rudy. Next to him was Katie, dressed in a black EO uniform with her hair tucked under her hat, trying to be as inconspicuous as possible. Two EO guards stood in front of her providing cover. Everything had the feeling of an old-time tent revival.

At the sound of a small bell, Bishop Bryan entered the tent. He was dressed in blood-red vestments that were eighty years old, a relic from the Latin Mass. When Lloyd reached the front of the platform he stood before the people and let his eyes wander over the assembly. He momentarily dropped his head in prayer, then looked toward the heavens and stretched his arms wide while crying out in a loud voice, "Who knows what are the only man-made things in heaven?"

People looked around for someone with the answer and Lloyd waited. When no answer came, Lloyd's voice rose again saying, "The holes in the hands and feet of Jesus made by the nails when he was hung from the cross! Those are the only things in heaven that man has made! There aren't any Mercedes Benz automobiles, there aren't any fancy diamond rings, there aren't any yachts!"

Smiling in admiration of Lloyd's powerful delivery, Rudy could see that Lloyd was getting into a cadence.

Pointing to the palms of his hands, Lloyd said, "Just those nail holes in His hands and feet. That's all." Lloyd shook his head and repeated, "That's all that made it into Heaven. Just the marks of the pain we all have caused our Holy Savior. How many of us here helped drive those nails? Raise your hands, I want to see 'em."

Every person who was able, put his hand up. Lloyd raised his arms high and shouted, "I helped drive those nails into the hands and feet of Jesus. By my sins, I held that whip in my hand and beat that helpless man tied to a pillar. I tore the flesh from his back, I spit in his face when he passed by me on the way to Calvary, I gambled over his cloak at the foot of the cross."

Katie thought Lloyd sounded like Martin Luther King when he gave his "I have a dream" speech. Then Lloyd let his voice drop, shook his head sorrowfully and said, "The only thing I've done that's gotten to Heaven are the holes in Jesus' hands and feet."

Katie watched Lloyd's eyes as they seemed to connect with every person present. Then she saw him look at her. He was almost thirty feet away, but Katie knew he had seen her and recognized her. Lloyd waited for a moment, and looking at Katie he continued, "I had a woman come to me once in confession, and she said, 'Father, I've sinned terribly. I cheated on my husband and he was good to me. I just couldn't control my sexual desires. Can you and God forgive me?' Yes, I said, you are forgiven! 'But,' she asked, 'will the pain and the scars still be there?'"

Lloyds's voice began to rise to a crescendo as he shouted, "I told her the pain would ease and go away with time if she led a holy life, but that the scars would always be there. I told her about the wounds that Jesus took to Heaven. That His scars are still with him."

With the exception of coughs and wheezing, the tent was quiet and still. Lloyd continued.

"When I looked around this gathering here tonight, I noticed a number of faces that are gone since we last met. They've died and have been judged for their lives."

Just when Rudy was sure Lloyd had reached the peak of his oratorical skills, his voice grew even louder and stronger, more filled with passion. "I'm here before you in the presence of the Holy Eucharist on this altar, the Body and Blood of Jesus Christ, and I'm telling you that those people who asked for forgiveness and died this very day now stand at the right hand of the Lord. That's right, some were horrible sinners, but they asked for God's forgiveness. They told God they were sorry for the hammer blows they struck on those nails. Tomorrow, more of you won't be here, and it'll be the same the next day and the day after that. Soon, you won't feel the pain; soon you'll know the answer to the ultimate question. All I ask is that you humble yourselves and ask for forgiveness. If it hurts you to say you're sorry, or if you don't know how, I'm here to help you. But as you all are aware, you don't have much time left."

Placing his hand on the center of the chasuble, his outer vestment, Lloyd said, "This is blood-red because today is the feast day of a saint who was a martyr. That saint was Dismas. I guess you've all heard the story of Dismas. He was called the 'good thief,' one of the two men who were crucified with Jesus. When the other thief mocked Jesus and told him to call down his angels to take him from the cross, Dismas defended Jesus saying, 'This man has done no wrong. We are guilty of our crimes, but he is innocent.' It was then that Jesus turned to Dismas and said, 'This day thou shalt be with me in Paradise!' Think about that. The only person we know of who Jesus said would actually go with Him to Heaven, was a thief! A criminal!"

Once more Lloyd's eyes found Katie's and he continued, "There is nothing you have done in your lives that can keep you from eternal joy and peace. Just two little words will lift your soul, maybe tonight, maybe tomorrow, past all the pain and sorrow that has brought you here. Those words are, 'I'm sorry.'"

Katie was overcome and quietly said to Rudy, "I want to go back to the cottage. I want to look at the ocean."

* * *

It was late in the afternoon as Katie sat on the same piece of driftwood where she and Rudy had talked only a week before. It was still unseasonably cool for the end of May, and the wind from the ocean was pleasing. Every few seconds Katie looked over her right shoulder toward the cottage high over the dunes. She was waiting for Bishop Bryan. She wasn't sure what she wanted or expected from the meeting, but she knew she had to speak with someone she thought was a spiritual person. After a large wave broke and crashed onto the beach, Katie looked over her shoulder once more and noticed a large black man gingerly walking down the cottage stairs leading to the beach below.

When Lloyd reached the hard-packed beach, he removed his shoes, put his hands on his knees and looked toward Katie almost two hundred yards away. After three deep breaths, he exploded into a run. Lloyd pumped his arms and drove his legs forward, remembering what it was like to run down a football field, seeing the goal line just ahead. He heard himself breathe and felt his heart beat. He saw the evening sun turn the clouds over the ocean pink and tasted the salt air. For those few moments, there was only the run, the beach, the ocean and the sky. There was no pain, no death on Ossabaw.

When Lloyd approached Katie he slowed to a trot, then came to a full halt a few yards away. As he had done when he began his run, he leaned over and rested his hands on his knees while he caught his breath. He stood up, cocked his hands on his hips and quietly looked at Katie for several seconds..

"I've heard you sleep in your priest's collar, Bishop," said Katie.

Laughing, Lloyd replied, "I don't sleep in it, but it's the last thing I take off before I go to bed."

Katie smiled, patted the thick oak trunk she sat on, and said, "Why don't you sit here and rest. Maybe we can talk for a while."

Katie was modestly dressed in jeans, a white long-sleeved shirt, and had a scarf tied over her hair.

"I remember you from your father's early days in politics," said Lloyd. "You were on the fund-raising side of his campaigns. Everybody said that Katherine McFarland could squeeze blood from a turnip when it came to her daddy."

Katie let her head drop, then pulled off the scarf. The wind filled her hair and brushed it back from her face. For many seconds she didn't look at Lloyd and said not a word. Lloyd reached out and placed his hand on Katie's shoulder, asking, "You want to talk?"

Katie still didn't look at Lloyd, but nodded her head and said, "Yeah," just before tears began to fill her eyes and roll down her cheeks.

"What do you know about me?" Katie blurted out.

"All bullshit aside?"

Without speaking, mucous streaming from her nose while she tried to control her sobbing, Katie nodded and managed to say, "Yeah, no bullshit, Bishop."

"It's my understanding you have a coke habit and to support that habit you became a high-priced hooker. Is that correct?"

"Right as rain," coughed Katie, trying hard to control her tears.

"I guess the next question is, why are you here, Katie?"

"To remove myself from this nasty world and to die in peace."

"To get away from a nasty world, Katie? You came to the wrong place. To die in peace, maybe. Only if you die so stoned you really don't know where you are. Perhaps that's peace, I'm not sure yet. But you wanted to talk to me about more than that, didn't you?"

For the first time, Katie faced Lloyd directly and looked into his eyes. Their faces were only two feet apart.

"I heard you speak last night. I want you to tell me about heaven and hell. I want you to tell me about forgiveness. I want you to make me believe there is something good after I die."

Before Lloyd entered the priesthood, he had been with many beautiful women. It was simply one of the benefits that came with being a high-profile professional athlete. When he looked at Katie, he remembered the thrill he used to get the first time he'd take one of those girls to bed. He felt the blood rush to his head and was glad his skin was dark so Katie couldn't see him blush.

"Katie," said Lloyd softly, "why are you really here? What's the real reason? I can understand getting hooked on the coke from being in a party crowd, but from what I hear, you almost drove yourself to it."

Nothing was said for minutes while Katie sat and watched the Atlantic. Then, in almost a fit of fury, Katie turned to Lloyd and cried out, "Because my brother raped me when I was nine years old. It wasn't just once, it was over and over and over again. It didn't stop until he went off to college."

Lloyd liked Robbie, and was staggered by this revelation.

* * *

"We have a number of requests for the Zimmer and DePuy total hip replacements, Dr. Hoorst," said Schwarz, "as well as total knees."

"What kind of inventory do we have?"

"Do you mean harvested or not?"

"Both, Claus."

"None that haven't already been harvested, Dr. Hoorst. But we have twenty hips in twelve residents and sixteen knees in thirteen residents."

"What is the group breakdown, Claus?"

"With the exception of two residents in Group Two, they are all from Group One."

Rudy leaned back in his chair and scanned the monitors arrayed before him. Then he looked at Schwarz and asked, "What value do you place on these stocks upon harvesting?"

Schwarz had been ready for the question and quickly replied, "If we can deliver within the next twenty-four to forty-eight hours, between $300,000 and $350,000. It depends, of course, upon the condition of the hardware."

Rudy swiveled his chair so he could look out the window of his office and watch as his two sons received riding lessons from an EO guard. After a few moments, he turned back to Schwarz and asked, "What are the drugs these residents take?"

"Seventy percent are taking our standard 60-percent heroin, the rest are mixing it with company-grade cocaine, sir."

Rudy nodded. "Increase the percentages of both. We should be able to meet demand within forty-eight hours, don't you think, Claus?"

Schwarz brought himself to attention and answered, "Yes, sir," then did an about-face. Before he could leave the room, Hoorst said, "One more thing, Claus."

Schwarz turned and stood before Rudy's desk once more. Rudy locked his hands behind his head and leaned his chair back. Suppressing a yawn, Rudy asked, "How many people are waiting at the embarkation point?"

"Yesterday there were 163."

And how many did we admit today?"

"One hundred forty."

"Of that number, how many have hardware implanted that can be retrieved?"

"Ninety-eight."

"Estimated value?"

"Close to $600,000."

"Any interesting tattoos?"

Schwarz let himself relax somewhat and even smiled when he answered, "Some of the most interesting renderings I've seen to date, Dr. Hoorst. Several whom you selected for Group Three have the most amazing and colorful pictures of Christ and the Virgin Mary. They are, of course, Hispanics."

"What is the status of the *Klebsiella* project?"

"Very close and quite promising, sir. Our lab in Munich may be ready to ship strains within the month."

Rudy nodded and watched his sons again. He said to Schwarz, "As usual, Claus, you're on top of the situation. Now, go and be with your wife."

* * *

The end of May continued to be surprisingly cool, especially the evenings, and Rudy enjoyed his late afternoon ride to the beach cottage. While his horse trotted down the trail to the beach, Rudy thought about Katie. When he reached the cottage around seven, there were storm clouds in the west and he could see lightening flashing in distant black clouds. The wind picked up as a low-pressure system over Liberty County pulled cool moist air from the Atlantic toward its center, where it would fuel the growing storm.

An EO guard held the reins of Rudy's horse as he dismounted. His name was Liam Collins, a native of County Cork who had spent ten years in the British Army, ten in the French Foreign Legion, and had been with the company for five more. Liam was happy with his assignment and, like the rest of the company's men on the island, liked Rudy because of the respect he showed them and the rewards for good work he liberally dispensed.

"So, Sergeant Collins, how is our guest today?"

"She appears to be doing quite well, Dr. Hoorst. She runs often on the beach and sometimes it's hard for me to keep up."

"What about her drug intake?"

"She'll do a small line of coke before a run and have a glass of wine when she finishes. She'll maybe do another line later, but nothing that is particularly destructive. In the evening she smokes some of the hash you have provided and listens to music or watches movies. Around eleven she takes ten milligrams of diazepam and goes to bed."

"How long was Bishop Bryan's visit?"

"He was here for three hours, sir."

Katie could hear Rudy's footsteps as he climbed the stairs. She went to the cottage's back door and was waiting when Rudy knocked.

"Hello, Rudy," said Katie, flashing her eyes at him and walking into the living room. She was wearing the same pair of red shorts she had the first time Rudy met her. This time she wore them over a black one-piece bathing suit.

Katie melted into the cushions and used the remote to turn down the sound system. Rudy sat in a soft chair opposite her. She was wearing no makeup; the sun had given her all the color she needed.

"Would you care for a glass of company wine?" asked Katie.

"I think I'd much prefer a bottle of beer."

"It's in the fridge," said Katie, "you're a big enough boy to get it yourself. I assume you want to talk about my visit with the Bishop, don't you?"

"Not really, I just thought we'd talk."

"OK, have you told my parents and Robbie that I'm here?"

"The word on the street is that you're on this island, Katie. Both your parents and your brother have contacted me about this. I saw no reason to lie; after all, your father is the governor and your brother is his personal emissary. So, the answer to your question is yes, they know. But they don't know where you are on the island."

"How did they act?"

"You father was stunned and saddened, your brother was enraged."

"What do you mean, enraged?" Katie asked with a wry smile.

"He demanded that I give him access to you. I refused, since I believe there is the potential that he would do you bodily harm."

"It's more than potential."

Rudy finished his beer, then looked at Katie and asked, "How many people know what Robbie did to you?"

Katie broke eye contact with Rudy and looked into the distance. "There's you and there's me. That's two, right?"

"What about Lloyd Bryan?"

Katie was silent for almost a minute. She returned her gaze to Rudy and responded, "I told him everything…everything. I didn't spare any of the lurid details."

"I wish you hadn't have done that, Katie."

"Why, what difference does it make?"

"It limits my options in dealing with Robbie."

The thunder that had been distant was now close and the wind began to pick up from the east, whipping the waves higher and higher as they clawed their way across the sand. Soon, bolts of lightning streaked from angry clouds hanging over Ossabaw, searching for the tallest pines on the island. The power failed and the cottage was filled with almost complete blackness interrupted only by the lightening. It filled the room for milliseconds, but each time it did, Katie and Rudy knew where to find the other's eyes. The thunder claps and lightning flashes became instantaneous as the storm crossed the beach where the cottage stood.

Between the flashes, Katie asked, "You want to make love to me, don't you, Rudy?"

In an instant the next flash illuminated Rudy's face. Katie saw his jaw was tight, his pupils dilated. From what seemed to be nothingness, Rudy answered asking, "Why do you think that?"

Another flash-bang, another snapshot of two people facing each other.

"Don't take me for a fool, Rudy; I can smell it. It's written all over your face. I knew it the first time you were here. You're not any different from the other men I've known."

Rudy and Katie listened as branches beat against the windows and watched as the anger of the storm moved over them and out into the Atlantic. In minutes, the temperature dropped and the only reminder of the storm was the wetness from the rain and the tenseness in the air.

When the sky cleared and the last bit of afternoon light filled the room, Rudy looked at Katie and said, "I find you very attractive. I'm also a normal man who has normal primal instincts, but I will admonish you in the same fashion you have admonished me. Don't flatter yourself, Katie. Remember, you're a prostitute, by your own admission."

Katie rose from her seat and lit several candles. She returned and faced Rudy.

"I know volumes about men, Rudy, and you don't know shit about women. I wouldn't be surprised if you think about screwing me while you jerk off in the shower. There's no doubt in my mind that you'll make your move sooner or later."

Katie turned away from Rudy and watched as the lightning danced in the clouds far over the Atlantic. She turned back to Rudy and continued, "Truth be known, you can have me anytime you want. You can have your guards hold me while you take me, if that's your desire."

"Does this mean you aren't interested in having me visit anymore?"

"No, not at all."

"Then what is it that you want?"

"I screwed guys so I could have money for the coke and life style I wanted. Now, I don't have to do that."

"You do know that you could be back in Group Two tomorrow, under the tents with the rest of the dirt bags."

"Is that a threat?"

"I don't threaten people, Katie, I don't have to."

Katie looked directly into Rudy's eyes and wondered what she'd have to do to stay in the cottage by the sea.

* * *

"Good morning, my name is Chris Wallace and this is *Fox News Sunday*. Today our guest is the First District Congressman from Georgia,

William Wallace McQueen. Congressman McQueen, welcome to *Fox News Sunday*.

"So what about it, Congressman, are you a candidate for president?"

Will sat back in his chair for a moment and exhaled a long breath. "Chris, what I'm gonna tell ya is the God's honest truth."

"I could stand a little God's honest truth for a change."

"It's like this, Chris. I'm sixty-five years old. As you know, I've given a lot to this country; I left large parts of my body on foreign soil, fighting for what I believed was in the best interests of this nation. After that, I served twelve terms in Congress and, to be really honest with you, Chris, I'm gettin' tired. I want to go back home to Savannah, get in my boat, drink a few beers and relax."

Wallace laughed and said, "I can certainly respect your honesty and desires, but, Congressman, we both know the buzz that's going all around the country these days, and it says you're the one who can most likely unseat this president."

"I hope somebody can beat him, Chris."

"Yeah, Congressman, but all the people in the know say you're the hands-down favorite to do just that. So, what do you have to say?"

Will shifted in his chair and answered, "I'm flattered that some people think I'm of the caliber to hold that position. Havin' said that, I also believe the honor should seek the man and not the man the honor."

"So you're not running?"

"Listen to what I just said, Chris. I said I would not seek the honor."

"Well, Congressman, what if you were drafted by your party, would you run as their candidate, then?"

"Chris, as I said from the beginning of this program, there'll be no BS. If my party comes to me with a strong endorsement, if they choose me at the convention in an overwhelming fashion, I will accept the nomination, and I will run my guts out to win the Presidency."

"So, you're declaring your candidacy today."

"No, Chris. I will not scratch and claw my way to my party's nomination. That's simply not gonna happen. What I will do, if they nominate me, is to accept the nomination and run like my pants are on fire."

"I have to tell you, Congressman, it's been a really long time since I've heard any honesty like that."

"I have no intention of changin', Chris."

Wallace was clearly impressed with Will's candor and continued with the interview.

"OK, let's say you are nominated, you've got some baggage, right?"

"I'm sixty-five; I've been a sinner; I guess I do."

"Perhaps the biggest piece of baggage you might have to face is the legislation that did away with the federal Drug Enforcement Administration. That allowed the states to legalize marijuana nationally and a host other drugs that vary from state to state."

"It also allowed most of the states to balance their budgets off the marijuana taxes."

Nodding with respect, Wallace said, "OK, perhaps not many people outside your district know about you. Let me do a rundown of your life, if I may, Congressman."

Will smiled and said, "Just don't talk about the time I got a DUI in Charleston. I was only nineteen."

"Well, actually, I did plan on talking about that, but I'll get to it later."

"I was guilty, Chris. But it was over a girl who had jilted me!"

"I know all about that, too, Congressman, but later, OK?'

"OK, later, Chris."

"Congressman, you were born into one of the finest families in Savannah, actually the entire State of Georgia. Your direct lineage goes back to the founding of the colony in 1733. You have ancestors who fought in the Continental Army during the Revolution. Your great-grandparents on both sides fought for the Confederacy."

Will nodded and said, "That's correct. But, don't forget to add they were also slave owners."

"Yes, they were, and that was the next question I was going to ask. How do you feel about that?"

"I'm not guilty for the sins of my fathers. If I were, we all would be doomed to hell."

"Well put, Congressman, and, if I may continue, you went to The Citadel and, after graduation, accepted a commission in the United States Navy, commanded a river patrol boat in the Mekong Delta in Vietnam, where you lost both legs in a fire fight."

"I believe I remember that, Chris."

"You were awarded four Purple Hearts while in Vietnam as well as the Navy Cross, which, I might add, is second only to the Medal of Honor. When you came back home to Savannah, you were elected by overwhelming majorities to the United States Congress. By some reports, you may even be able to walk, unaided, across the Savannah River."

Will laughed loudly and Chris Wallace joined him. He looked at Will and said, "Many people in Georgia insist that, without your support, the drug colony on Ossabaw Island would never have gotten out of the planning stages. More than a few people scattered across the country are against such an undertaking and think this could hurt you badly in a national election. Your take on that, Congressman?"

"That's nothin' I shy away from, Chris. The Ossabaw colony has resulted in massive decreases in crime and illicit drug use as well as decreases in the prison population and, most important, eased the burden on the taxpayers of Georgia. I'm proud and happy to have helped Governor McFarland pass that legislation and would do it again if necessary."

"You're on the board of directors of the colony, are you not?"

"That's correct, Chris, the governor appointed me and three other Georgians to oversee the project. They're all old friends of mine, and I can attest to their utmost credibility. Our medical director is Dr. John-Morgan Hartman, our spiritual director is the Most Reverend Lloyd Bryan, and our governmental liaison is Judah Benjamin."

"Which brings me to my last question, Congressman. It's all the talk around Washington that Judah Benjamin, perhaps the biggest political kingmaker of the last two decades, is the one who's pushing your name for the nomination. Any comments?"

"It's like I said all along, Chris. If the Republican Party sincerely wants me as their candidate, I'll run and run as hard as I can. I have no control over what Judah Benjamin does."

"Have you spoken with him about this?"

"Yes."

"And what was said?"

"I'll leave the description of that conversation up to Judah."

"OK, fair enough, but let's return to where you are right now. We've known each other for a number of years. You mentioned that you were getting tired of the Washington scene, and I must say that, when I saw you this morning, I was impressed. You'd just come from your workout at the Congressional gym. You are a well-built man for sixty-five. I can't see how you'd be too tired for a run at the Presidency."

"Chris, other than the Civil War, I can't think of another time when this nation was in greater peril. During the first and second World Wars, the threat to the country came from outside our borders. Now, as with the Civil War, the threat to our republic comes from within. Our public debt, both federal and state, is staggering. If we can't come up with a solution and fast, however painful it may be, this country will fragment and perhaps even fail."

CHAPTER NINE

FINAL SOLUTIONS

Every advantage in the past is judged
in the light of the final issue.
—Demosthenes, *First Olynthiac*

Klebsiella is a normal bacterial flora in the human digestive system. It is an organism that, in usual circumstances, is not a human pathogen. However, bacteria mutate, and sometimes those mutations can lead to lethal outcomes. So it was in the bowels of the poorest parts of India during the beginning of the Third Millennium.

Members of international health organizations working with the United Nations began noticing cases of fatal pneumonia appearing in the ghettos of that country around 2003. Attempts to treat the infections with all known antibiotics proved fruitless and people watched in terror as the bacteria, known as *Klebsiella pneumonea,* ate its way across the sub-continent and headed toward Europe. The only good thing about *Klebsiella pneumonea* was that its victims appeared to be those most compromised to fight infections, such as the chronically ill and severe drug addicts.

Executive Outcomes was heavily invested in India and news of the new killer germ soon reached the ears of its headquarters there. It wasn't long after that the company acquired a sample of the lethal strain and shipped it to its laboratories in Germany.

The company learned the strain could kill within seventy-two hours of infection by nasal inhalation when administered to a physically debilitated subject. There was no known antibiotic that could blunt the bacteria's advance. Even in healthy subjects, a lung infected with *K. pneumonea* would generally die within weeks or suffer permanent pulmonary damage. Some in the company identified this as a means to swiftly eliminate residents in their drug colonies who had only weeks left to live or were proving to be a burden to the colonies as a whole.

* * *

The early heat wave of mid-June hit Ossabaw like the Hammer of Thor. Lloyd and John-Morgan weren't surprised, but everyone else who wasn't a native was staggered by its intensity.

Residents in Group One already on the cusp of death succumbed even more quickly. In Group Two, the little respite from the sun provided by the tents proved to be nothing more than ovens, and scores of people died as they tried to find their way to the beaches and a cooling breeze. In Group Three, the heat leached all fighting spirit from its gladiators and they parked themselves in the coolest spots they could find, avoiding all physical exertion.

* * *

Colonel Schwarz was drenched in sweat as he stood at attention before Dr. Hoorst's desk. He welcomed the cool air pouring upon him from the outlet in the ceiling.

"Please, Claus, stand at ease."

"Thank you, sir."

"Sorry I don't have any German beer, Claus, but, down here in the Deep South, we have beer drinking figured out. Southerners like to drink beer all day long during the summer. If it's like German beer, we'd be drunk before noon."

"I've come to like American beer just for that reason, Dr. Hoorst."

Rudy leaned against his desk and let Schwarz take several more sips before asking, "What do you have for me today, Claus?"

"The *Klebsiella* strain has arrived, Dr. Hoorst."

"And, Claus, how much do we have?"

"The company reports enough to liquidate around a thousand on the first administration, sir. They say there will be enough for that same number in about a month."

"What is the means of administration?"

"Via nasal spray. Much like inhalants used for allergies. Simply a squirt in the nose and the company reports problem solution within forty-eight to seventy-two hours. They're saying, based upon the physical status of the resident, a solution could be achieved as early as thirty-six hours. But they advise the utmost caution in administration of this substance. If a mistake were made, sir, we could lose some of our own personnel."

"When would you be ready?"

"It should take our lab here on the island about three days to have the substance processed and in applicator form. Of course, we will have to train our staff, and that could be another two days."

Rudy thought for several seconds, then asked, "Do you have air-conditioning in your quarters, Claus?"

"No, sir, only fans."

"Well, Claus, we have an empty room here in the Main House. Bring your wife and stay here until this heat wave breaks."

"You're most kind, sir. My wife will be very happy."

* * *

Lloyd thought about the residents on Ossabaw as the island's launch took him to John-Morgan's house. He'd seen almost two hundred die in the past twenty-four hours. The suffering on Ossabaw was as intense as he'd ever seen it, and he didn't condemn the ones who had chosen to exit that life as painlessly as possible. He wondered what he'd do in the same situation.

Lloyd was surprised by the security waiting for him when he stepped onto John-Morgan's dock. There were two very professional-appearing members of a larger detail who, even though he'd never seen them before, greeted him by name. One escorted him to the house, while the other stayed on the dock and scanned the river.

Lloyd welcomed the coolness of John-Morgan's living room and wondered again about things on the island.

"That you?" called John-Morgan from the library.

"Yeah, I'm here and it sure feels good."

"Come on back, everybody's here. We been waitin' on ya."

Outside the library door stood another member of the security detail and Lloyd nodded as he entered.

"Come on in and close the door behind you," said John-Morgan, standing to shake Lloyd's hand.

"Sir, we don't like to have the Congressman out of view. We'd prefer to have the door be left open."

Will was already standing, ready to shake Lloyd's hand, and replied to the guard, "It's OK, Dick. I'm safe with these guys."

"Yes, sir, understood." The door closed quietly behind Lloyd as his eyes caught Judah's and both smiled.

"You've lost more weight, Your Excellency," said John-Morgan.

"Not much on Ossabaw to stimulate my appetite, Dr. Hartman."

"As your personal physician, I wouldn't be happy if you dropped any more pounds."

"OK, I'm here for the meeting," said Lloyd, "and I guess all the added security has something to do with it."

"You're the only one who doesn't know yet, Lloyd," said Judah.

"Know what?"

Gesturing toward Will, Judah answered, "There's an excellent chance you're looking at the next President of the United States of America."

Lloyd's eyes caught Will's directly for several moments and in that time he thought he saw something. Finally, Lloyd whispered, "Holy Mother of God. I think you could be right!"

"Lloyd," said Judah, "you're kinda outta the loop on that island. Things have been movin' very fast lately. Everything that calls out to me from my gut tells me that Will can be the Republican nominee. My gut also tells me he'll win the election. I'm not the only one who feels that way. The Speaker of the House is of the same opinion. That's the reason for all this security."

Lloyd smiled broadly at Will and said, "You know you've got my vote!"

Tension in the room lessened for a moment. Judah put on his serious face and said, "I know more about Will McQueen than his wife does, and I don't think there's a viable skeleton in his closet. I also don't think the Ossabaw colony can hurt him. But I am concerned that something about the colony could be out there, lurking in the shadows. Does anybody have any comments about the colony?"

"We've been down this road before, Judah," said John-Morgan, "and we all agreed that the colony was, in fact, what it appears to be."

"I know we did, John-Morgan, but I just want to go over things once more."

Judah looked at Lloyd and said, "There isn't anyone who knows more about the Ossabaw colony than you, Bishop. What's the graveyard truth about the place? Tell me about Dr. Rudolph Hoorst. I understand he attends Mass daily and always receives Communion. I'm also told he gets on his knees before you each Saturday afternoon to confess his sins, is that correct?"

"You're right on all points, Judah, but don't ask what he says in confession."

"I'm a Jew, but I do know about the Seal of the Confessional. What about the man? Is he trustworthy, is there the possibility we might have a ticking time bomb in Rudy Hoorst?"

Lloyd had come to like and respect Dr. Hoorst. Rudy had always done his best to accommodate every request Lloyd had made about the physical and spiritual welfare of the residents. Outwardly, Lloyd couldn't think of anything about Rudy or the colony that would hurt Will.

Bishop Bryan had forgiven thousands of sins poured out from contrite and not so contrite hearts. He thought he knew when someone was going through the motions, doing what they had been trained to do. He knew people so well indoctrinated by priests and nuns that they obeyed the laws of the Church to the letter, while their souls languished in half-truths and the lies they told themselves and convinced themselves to believe. They were Catholics who adhered to the letter of the law and not the spirit of the law.

Lloyd looked at his friends and wished he could tell what he really thought about Rudy. Even then, he still wasn't sure about the man. True enough, Rudy went to daily Mass and Communion, a good habit for a nice Catholic boy, but the things he confessed were, well, rather juvenile.

Rudy confessed, on a weekly basis, about masturbation, about impure thoughts of sex with women other than his wife. He never confessed about anything else. No anger, no hatred, no gluttony, no avarice, no sloth.

"As far as I know," said Lloyd, "there isn't a bogeyman in the closet. I think everything's OK."

* * *

Rudy kept the Main House "meat locker" cold. Only a week ago, Claus and his wife Eva had been dripping with sweat at the officer's mess, wondering when the heat wave would end. Now, Eva felt comfortable in the dining room with a sweater over her shoulders as she spoke with Mrs. Hoorst about her children while Claus and Rudy were at the bar in the Great Room discussing business.

The temperature was topping a hundred by ten in the morning, and Eva didn't want to think about going back to their old quarters. Ossabaw was the hottest, most oppressive place she and Claus had ever been sent to since he'd signed on with Executive Outcomes. She'd made it quite clear to Claus how happy she was with their new accommodations and how much she'd like to remain in them.

"Are we ready with the *Klebsiella*?" asked Rudy as he poured Claus another shot of Scotch.

"In about four days, sir."

"That's excellent work, Claus."

"Thank you, sir."

Rudy leaned on the bar and swirled the ice around in his glass before he swallowed the last of his drink.

"When the order is given, Claus, here is how it will be executed."

Colonel Schwarz placed his glass on the bar and looked at Rudy with undivided attention.

"When the time arrives, a directive will be given, stating a very malignant bacteria has infected the colony and it's mandatory all personnel, other than company men, be evacuated from the island. There will be no exceptions. This includes Bishop Bryan and all his volunteers."

Rudy paused for a moment. "You will have our men serving in Group One dressed out in hazmat garb. They will appear so dressed an hour before the declaration of medical emergency is made. They will make themselves conspicuous to the Bishop and his helpers and will appear to be checking the residents for infection. When I give the order, the Bishop and his apostles will be rounded up and taken to the dock, where they will be transported to the mainland. After that, all dependents of the company will also be removed from the island. Within six hours, the island will be cleared of all non-essentials."

Rudy paused again, looking at Schwarz, and said, "Finish your drink, Claus, things pick up quickly after that.

"When I give the order, your men will enter the confines of Group One and begin spraying the area using hand-held atomizers saturated with *Klebsiella*. They will be certain that each resident receives a full face spray, enough for them to inhale deeply and infect their lungs with the bacteria.

"After your men have completed their task in Group One, they will then move to Group Two. They will inform the residents about the infection and tell them what is in the spray should help guard them against the infection. Our men will then retreat to their quarters, where they will be taking appropriate precautions such as wearing face masks. At no time, with the exception of a direct order from me, will Group Three be infected. They are too important as they are. Do you have any questions, Claus?"

"What about the woman in the beach cottage, sir?"

"You will double the guard and tell her nothing. No visitors will be permitted."

"Sir," replied Schwarz, "the number of subsequent deaths will put a huge strain on our harvesting and disposal units."

"I'm aware of that, Claus. I have decided that, until we can catch up with the crematoriums, excess bodies will be temporarily buried. You will add more men to our harvesting unit as required. Not as neatly done as I'd like, but we'll make do while we must. Think you can handle that problem, Claus?"

"Without a doubt, sir."

"Excellent," said Rudy. He clapped Claus on his shoulder, saying, "Let's put all this business aside and join our lovely wives for dinner."

* * *

Rudy sat in his Hummer H2 while he watched the governor's helicopter approach and gently touch down on the landing zone. After the weather had grown so oppressively hot, he'd stopped traveling the island by horseback and had taken to his Hummer.

When Big Dog's bird came completely to rest, Rudy drove to within yards of it and waited for the Dog to alight. Like a bear, Governor McFarland set his feet on the ground and charged toward the Hummer, his bodyguard close behind carrying two clothing bags.

After Big Dog had climbed into the passenger's seat and slammed the door shut, he exclaimed, "Hotter than a motherfucker!" The bodyguard threw the two bags into the back seat and pulled himself into the cabin.

Gesturing with his left thumb, Big Dog said to Rudy, "This here is my new main man, Bad Leroy Brown. He was one of my men when I had a company of Special Forces troops during Gulf War One. We kicked some serious Iraqi ass, didn't we, Leroy!"

"Governor, you kicked ass," said Leroy, "all I did was stand outta the way!" Rudy smiled while both men erupted in laughter ending with a high-five from Big Dog to Leroy. As Rudy drove toward the Main House, silence fell inside the Hummer. Finally, Big Dog said, "I gotta see my baby girl, Rudy."

Rudy slowed to a stop about a quarter-mile from the Main House, turned to the Dog and said, "This is for your ears only, Governor."

Rudy turned around to Leroy Brown and said, "I hate to do this, Mr. Brown, but Governor MacFarland and I need to speak in private." Leroy nodded, stepped out of the car, and stood in the inadequate shade of a palmetto.

Big Dog said, "I want to see Katie, and I want to see her now."

"I know you do, Dog, but things are a little dicey right now. We've got rules in place that forbid such contact. You even approved and signed the bill into law."

Big Dog shifted his entire body to face Rudy. He was an imposing figure filling the entire side of the Hummer's front seat. With a dead serious look on his face, the Governor responded, "I said I want to see my daughter. I'm the Chief Executive of this fuckin' state and I will have things my way! Do you understand, Hoorst?"

Rudy wasn't fazed by the Dog's show of force and sat impassively while he let cold air coming from one of the vents pass between his fingers

"Do you understand what I'm fuckin' tellin' ya' Hoorst? I'll call in the Georgia National Guard and take this fuckin' place over if I have to."

"I know what you're goin' through, Dog. All I want you to do is take a couple of deep breaths and let me give you the lay of the land, OK?"

"It better be a goddamn good fuckin' lay!"

"First of all, Dog, you're going get to see Katie, so relax. She's safe and in good health. But you have to let me handle this the right way, OK? Everybody on your oversight commission is at the Main House right now waiting for you. You need to go in there with all the humility you can muster and beg them for a chance to see Katie. As I said earlier, we'll be breaking the law you sponsored and signed, so we have to do this thing right. Once we've all settled in and had a few cocktails, I'll break the ice. You just follow my lead. It's important you do what I've suggested, Governor, OK?"

Big Dog rolled back into his seat away from Rudy, looking like a deflated balloon, and said, "I'm sorry, Rudy, but you don't know what I've been through with that child, and you don't know how much I love her."

"Wrong on both points," replied Rudy. "Katie and I have had some long talks and I know a lot. But, you have to trust me on this."
* * *

"Your son, Robbie," said Rudy just before he opened the doors to the Great Room, "is the only player missing tonight, Governor."

When Big Dog entered the Great Room, the first person he saw was Will.

"Governor!" exclaimed Will, putting his arms around the Dog and patting him on the back.

"Hell, Congressman," replied the Dog, "I might be callin' ya Mr. President, from what I hear."

Will pulled back from him, planted both hands firmly on the Dog's shoulders and asked, "If I do it, will ya stand with me, Governor?"

"It hurts me to know you'd think it was necessary to ask. You've got everything that's mine, Will."

The Dog's eyes next found Judah's, and they both knew serious things were afoot.

"So, Judah," asked the Dog, standing with his feet separated in a linesman's stance, "do you think he's got an honest-to-God shot?"

"I know he does, Governor. All the stars are lining up right over his head.   Unless something really bad and tawdry comes out, he'll win the nomination. Hell, the general election is almost a given for anybody but the same-old, same-old."

"Bishop, how the hell are ya?   Or, maybe I better rephrase that question!"

Lloyd and Big Dog shook hands as they exchanged words and nods.

"What's it like for ya here?" asked Big Dog.

"It's the most intense experience of my life.   It's horrible and it's wonderful at the same time. I've seen the worst and the best, and it all has strengthened my belief in God."

For the next ten minutes, the conversation centered mostly on politics and Will's prospects for winning.   For another five, Rudy gave a brief rundown on how things were in the colony.   It was mostly about the numbers. Rudy put it succinctly when he summarized, saying the numbers that mattered most were admissions and departures from the island. Nobody had to ask Rudy what he meant by "a departure."

Rudy went to Big Dog's side and said, "I have a favor to ask of this board."

Rudy let his statement sink in for a moment, then continued, "We all know that Katie McFarland is a resident here."

All the Dog did was look at the floor.

"Our friend here is hurting in a big way. He wants desperately to see his daughter."

The Dog squeezed his eyes shut hoping that would stem the tears, but it didn't, and they soon were dropping to the floor.

"In its charter with the State of Georgia, Executive Outcomes gives this board of directors the ability to suspend the rules concerning visitation prohibitions. I ask that you grant Governor McFarland the ability to see his only daughter."

The air in the room was thick with emotion, and for several moments, no one said anything.   Then, Lloyd spoke up. "I don't have a problem with that, does anybody else?"

"Not at all," said Will.

"Same here," answered John-Morgan and Judah.

With fists the size of ham hocks, Big Dog wiped the tears from his eyes and managed to say, "Thank you," before the tears started to stream again.

"I suggest we leave for the cottage now," said Rudy. He looked at Lloyd, adding, "I'd like you to come with us, Bishop."

* * *

When Big Dog reached the sixty steps that led up to the cottage, he took a deep breath, looked at Lloyd behind him and started the climb. That was the easy part; the meeting at the top would be difficult.

"Let Lloyd go in first," said Rudy as the men stood outside the cottage door. "She has no idea that you're here."

Big Dog nodded and Lloyd stepped forward. Rudy and the Dog moved back from the door so they couldn't be seen. Three sharp raps and Katie opened the door.

"Bishop Bryan, I'm surprised to see you here."

"Let's step inside, Katie, there's something I have to tell you."

Big Dog was so tense he could hardly breathe. When Lloyd finally emerged, the Dog almost called the whole thing off.

"You can go in now, Governor," said Lloyd softly.

Big Dog gently pushed the door open to find Katie standing directly in front of him. Neither made a move or said a word for what seem an eternity to Lloyd and Rudy, then everything started to happen.

Katie was the first. She cried out, "Daddy, Daddy!" and rushed Big Dog, who swept her up in his arms. She wrapped her legs around his waist and her arms around his neck.

Katie continued to wail, "Daddy, Daddy," as she buried her face in her father's neck and kissed him repeatedly. All the Dog could do was hold his daughter as close as he could while he sobbed, repeating her name again and again, saying, "It'll all be OK, my sweet little girl."

Lloyd and Rudy looked at each other for a long time as they listened to the noises from inside the cottage. It wasn't too long before they heard Katie give a loud, terrifying wail; one that Lloyd had heard before. He'd never heard it from Katie, but he had heard that same cry of anguish and relief from people who had, at last, given up their last vestige of pain and shame. He was sure it was what had held them in spiritual bondage.

Big Dog stayed with Katie for almost two hours. They talked about everything, and when he finally climbed into Rudy's Hummer for the ride back to the Main House, he appeared to both Lloyd and Rudy to be a man bereft of his dreams.

The night was terribly hot and humid and the Dog unconsciously welcomed the coolness of Rudy's Hummer as it slowly wound its way over the sandy trails back to the Main House. No one said a word for almost ten minutes. Then the silence became too much, and from the back seat, Lloyd said, "I guess you know about Robbie."

* * *

The central command trailer was so cold, Rudy was surprised his breath didn't frost. But with all the electronics stuffed inside, Rudy knew it had to be kept cool. He was standing in front of the large screen monitor focused on the entrance gate at Butterbean Beach. He estimated between 150 and two hundred people were lined up waiting to be processed for admission with at least another hundred already processed and in the holding areas awaiting transport to the island. Then he heard Oberst Schwarz behind him.

Turning to Schwarz, Rudy said, "Colonel, how are you this fine afternoon?"

"Quite well, sir." Schwarz handed Rudy a sheaf of papers, saying, "These are the latest figures concerning the colony, Dr. Hoorst."

After looking over the stats, Rudy handed the papers back to Schwarz, commenting, "It appears we are at maximum capacity, Claus."

"Actually, sir, we're about 10 percent past that. Unless something is done to alleviate the overcrowding situation here on the island, we can expect things to get rather ugly back on the mainland."

"Ugly?"

"Yes, Dr. Hoorst. I inspected the embarkation point only three hours ago, and things are beginning to get tense. There could be violence. There are relatives of those seeking admission who are threatening such things unless these people are admitted right away or at least provided with the drugs of their choice on site."

Rudy looked at the monitor once more, his hand to his chin, then back at Schwarz.

"It's a bit stuffy in here, Claus. Let's go back to my office at the Main House and discuss this situation in privacy."

Claus enjoyed being in Rudy's private office. It was decorated with all manner of things military. Rudy had edged weapons that went back to the ancient Romans, a complete collection of Civil War Colt pistols, original war art by German artists commissioned by the Third Reich to document their triumphant march across Europe.

"We are ready to use the *Klebsiella* bacteria, are we not, Claus."

"Yes, sir, we are. All you have to do is give the launch order."

"Thank you, Claus," answered Rudy, studying the same picture on his monitor he'd watched earlier at the command center.

"My instincts tell me to let this situation simmer just a little longer. There's not quite the proper amount of pressure on Butterbean Beach for us to begin Operation Mercy."

"Operation Mercy, sir?"

"Oh, yes, Claus, I neglected to tell you it's the code word the company has chosen when referring to the *Klebsiella* bacteria."

Rudy sighed as he looked back at the monitor and added, "I'm waiting for one of our board members to call me saying they're getting complaints about Butterbean Beach from the residents on Skidaway Island. When sufficient weight has been brought to bear, I'll contact you."

Rudy looked at his watch. "It's getting to be dinner time, Claus. My wife informs me the menu tonight contains crab stew."

* * *

The next afternoon Rudy and Claus sat in Rudy's office awaiting the arrival of Robbie McFarland. Robbie hadn't called ahead to let Rudy know he was coming, but he didn't need to. The moment Robbie appeared at the Delegal Creek docks, Rudy was informed of Little Dog's presence. Rudy wasn't at all surprised by Robbie's visit; in fact, he'd expected it much sooner.

Claus stood before an eight-foot scale model of the battleship *Bismarck* admiring the work. The sound of loud voices caught their attention. Rudy looked at Claus. "That must be the Governor's son."

Robbie brushed aside the lone guard at the entrance to the Main House, but when he entered the foyer and started toward the doors to Rudy's office, he was confronted by two well-armed EO men blocking his path.

"I'm Robert McFarland, special representative of Governor McFarland, and I'm here to speak with Dr. Hoorst. I need to see him at once."

Without saying a word, one of the men knocked on the door, then entered. In only moments he stepped back out and said, "Dr. Hoorst will see you now, sir."

Robbie was so angry he almost bulled his way into Rudy's office. Once inside, without even acknowledging Oberst Schwarz, he strode right up to Rudy and said, "What gives you the fuckin' right?"

Rudy glanced toward Schwarz, who moved his hand to the pistol on his hip.

"The right to do what, Robbie?"

"Aw, come on, Rudy! The right to hold my slut sister here and use her as a tool to manipulate my father."

"No one manipulates Governor McFarland!"

"Oh, really! Well, my father called me in the middle of the night to tell me everything she had to say about me. She told him I raped her when she was nine!"

"Well, did you?"

In an instant, Robbie drew his right hand back, his fist clenched, ready to strike Rudy. Rudy didn't flinch at all, staring into Robbie's eyes while Schwarz quickly moved between the two men and faced Robbie, saying, "Mr. McFarland, it would be a terrible mistake to even think about placing your hands on Dr. Hoorst. Such actions could cause you severe harm."

The faces of Robbie and Claus were only inches apart, and it was Robbie who blinked first when he looked at Rudy and said, "Call off your fuckin' Doberman, Hoorst, I'm not gonna' hurt ya."

Rudy leaned against his desk and savored, for a moment, the standoff between Claus and Robbie. Then he stood upright and said, "You can stand down now, Oberst Schwarz, I believe Mr. McFarland understands the ground rules."

Keeping his eyes firmly locked on Robbie, Schwarz moved slowly away.

"So, Little Dog," said Rudy as he walked to the office bar, "you look like you could use a drink. It's Jack Daniels and ginger ale, right?"

"Don't fuckin' play with me, Rudy."

Schwarz tightened up a little, and Robbie caught it out the corner of his eye. Realizing he was being foolish, Robbie softened and replied, "Yeah, make it a double."

"You know why I'm here, don't you, Rudy," said Robbie between long shots of the liquor.

"I suppose it concerns the meeting between your sister and father only a few days ago."

Robbie tilted back his glass and emptied it. He shoved it toward Schwarz without looking at him and said, "Fix me another."

Rudy glanced at Schwarz and smiled saying, "I think that'll be all, Claus. Go and be with your wife."

Robbie watched as Schwarz came to attention and said, "Thank you, sir." Robbie also saw Schwarz's eyes catch his for a moment as he walked toward the door.

Robbie hadn't liked Schwarz from the first moment he'd met him. He regarded Schwarz as a "Nazi mothafucka," but was confident he could easily handle him.

When Schwarz entered the foyer, he dismissed the two guards at the door and stood there himself, listening, ready to act if necessary. He didn't care for Little Dog at all and relished the thought of using his martial arts skills to break Robbie's nose in one lightening blow...or maybe even his neck.

"Relax and get comfortable," said Rudy, waving Robbie to a chair. "I know this has been a trying episode. Let's see what we can do to make things less stressful for you, Little Dog."

"I want to see that fuckin' whore, and I want to see her right now."

Rudy had returned to his desk chair and leaned back in it as he studied the expression on Robbie's face.

"I want you to take me to where she is right now," yelled Robbie, beginning to feel the bravado of his third drink.

"I can't do that, Robbie."

With more aggression in his voice, Robbie asked, "Why the fuck not?"

Outside, Schwarz placed his ear to the door.

"Because I fear you will attempt to do her harm."

"I'd like to choke the livin' shit outta' her."

Rudy thought for a moment, then asked, "Why don't you tell me your side of the story?"

"I don't have to tell you shit!"

Rudy leaned forward and placed his hands on the desk, calmly saying, "You're right, you don't have to tell me shit, Little Dog, but it would help if you really want to see Katie."

Robbie squirmed in his chair, thought a little, then answered, "OK, you want to know the story, I'll tell you what really happened. It was Katie who came on to me."

Taking a deep breath and another sip from his glass, Robbie continued, "She comes into my room one night when our parents were out. She was naked as a jaybird. Katie was a precocious little bitch and I don't just mean in the way she acted. She filled out faster than any of her friends. By the time she was twelve, she already had curves most sixteen-year-olds would envy. She was the aggressor, not me. By the time I knew what was going on, she had my pants down and was jerkin' me off. I ain't gonna lie, it felt good. I thought maybe it was just that one time, but, whenever our parents were gone, it was always the same damn thing. I know I shoulda stopped it, but I was thinkin' with my dick. Finally, I realized how wrong it was and put a stop to all that bullshit. When I told Katie no more of that stuff, she begged me not to tell my parents and I didn't. What was really strange was that when all that stuff stopped, Katie just acted like nothin' ever happened."

Rudy dropped his head, looked at his folded hands and asked, "Did you tell this to your father when he confronted you?"

"Yeah, I told him everything, and he believes me."

"Well," said Rudy, "that's certainly a different story than Katie told me and Lloyd Bryan, to say nothing about what she told your father."

"Yeah," replied Robbie in a rasping voice, "how well I know."

Leaning back in his chair once more, Rudy asked, "Why do you want this meeting with your sister? What do you hope to accomplish?"

"I want her to hear that our father knows the real truth about what happened and that he's not buyin' into her bullshit."

Rudy let out a long breath. "If you act in a proper manner, Robbie, I'll have Katie brought here and the two of you can speak. But you must promise me there will be no physical contact, no threats, nothing. Do I make myself clear?"

* * *

Oberst Schwarz escorted Katie into Rudy's office and stood next to her while Robbie sized her up from across the room. With his eyes firmly on

Robbie, Rudy leaned on the glass case that held the model of the *Bismarck*.

"Our father told me whatcha had to say," spat out Robbie, "but I set him straight. He knows what a sick cokehead you are, so don't think he's believin' a word you said."

"I've never underestimated your power to convince people that the obvious simply wasn't true," answered Katie.

Robbie snorted. "It really doesn't matter anyway. Your worthless life is over. You'll never leave this place. You've got a life sentence, so enjoy all the coke and other shit you like, while I can walk outta here and do whatever I want."

"You did whatever you wanted with me when I was only a child," retorted Katie coolly. "I'm just concerned you'll start doing the same things to your own daughter you did to me."

With that, Robbie completely lost his composure and came at Katie. Schwarz stepped between Katie and her brother and would have dropped Robbie in his tracks if Rudy hadn't stopped Robbie.

Robbie had a snootful of sour mash when he charged his sister. Rudy grabbed him by his collar, nearly lifting him off the ground, shoving him backward and forcing him into a chair at the other end of the room.

"You broke your word to me, Robbie!" shouted Rudy as he pushed Robbie down into the chair.

"She's fuckin' lyin'," screamed Robbie, "and I'm not standin' for it."

Robbie looked at Katie with a face of rage and yelled, "You're done for, you little bitch! I'll pull every string I have to get your ass taken off this island and put back on the streets with all the rest of the niggas and whores, and I got a lotta strings to pull. You fucked with the wrong goddamn person!"

Katie was unfazed and, when her brother had quieted down a bit, she softly said, "Just wait until the video I made about you comes out. You won't be able to serve up French-fries at the Varsity in Atlanta when it hits the tube."

"Jesus Christ," shouted Robbie, trying to rise from the chair and get his hands on Katie, "I'll go to fuckin' Hell for the pleasure of killin' you with my own hands!"

This time, Rudy didn't push Robbie back in his chair, he slammed him into it hard and pushed his face against Robbie's, saying, "That'll be quite enough from you, Little Dog."

Rudy looked at Katie, then to Schwarz and said, "You may take her back now, Oberst Schwarz."

After Katie was gone, Rudy sat at his desk and stared at Robbie, who was breathing hard and still pissed as hell.

"I'll tell you one thing, Hoorst, that video she's talking about, if it comes out, I'll have one of my own that exposes this fuckin' place for what it really is."

Rudy smiled wryly, fiddled with the handle on his desk drawer, then replied, "Oh, but you'll do nothing of the kind. If you do, you'll be cutting off your nose to spite your face. Just think of the handsome income stream you'll be losing."

* * *

Rudy's Hummer crawled along the road that led to the beach cottage through standing water left from the deluge the night before. The month-long heat wave had finally broken. The storm that swept Ossabaw had also dumped six inches of rain on the Okeefanokee Swamp fire, putting it out and ending the clouds of smoke that had hung over Georgia's coast for weeks. The air was fresh, sweet, and cool, and Rudy lowered his windows to smell the scent of the deep, thick forest that pushed against the sides of the Hummer.

The last time Rudy had seen Katie was when Little Dog had confronted her in his office. Rudy had begun thinking about Katie more and more, and he wasn't comfortable with it. He thought infidelity was a sign of weakness as well as a sin in the eyes of the Church.

Rudy knocked gently on the door and when Katie answered, she appeared genuinely happy to see him. She took Rudy by the hand as he stepped inside saying, "I was hoping you'd come, I've missed talking with you."

Katie turned to Rudy and said, "I want to thank you for letting my father visit with me. It meant a lot to me."

With no sign of awkwardness, Katie hugged Rudy, her head resting against his chest, and said once more, "Thank you very much."

"I was glad to help both you and your father."

"Want to smoke some of that hash?" asked Katie.

"I can't stay that long. Besides, I have something important to tell you about."

Katie arched her eyebrows. "Really, what?"

"There's good reason to believe the colony has been infected with a deadly strain of bacteria that could be fatal for hundreds of our residents. That means you must strictly adhere to any rules that may be put in place. You'll be notified if anything happens."

Then Rudy stood, saying, "I've got to go back now."

* * *

Dressed in gold vestments, Lloyd stood before the congregation of more than five hundred, extended both arms and cried out, "Peace be with you!"

Some could say nothing and only blinked as they struggled to hold their heads up, while others replied, "And with your spirit!"

The size of the tent where Lloyd celebrated Mass had been increased twice since the preceding January. Lloyd said in a loud voice, "I want to talk about the Gospel you just heard. It was about a man who was paralyzed and whom Jesus healed."

Lloyd began walking back and forth in front of the altar as he spoke, oftentimes pausing as he looked out over those who listened, and searched for faces yearning to understand. Then he stepped down and walked into the crowd.

"Do you remember what that man said?" he asked as he touched the shoulders and heads of people lying on stretchers.

"That man cried out and said, 'Jesus, Son of David, have mercy on me. I've been paralyzed because of my sins and the sins of my fathers'!"

Placing a finger to his lips, Lloyd paused, then continued, "Jesus went to the man and looked at him. He was lying in a contorted state with his arms and legs drawn up to his body. He had bed sores that oozed with pus and there were maggots in 'em. His beard hadn't been shaved in years and it was caked with the vilest spittle. Flies swarmed around, attracted by the urine and feces that covered him. The only reason he was alive was that people had pity and fed him and tried to care for him."

Pausing for effect, Lloyd asked, "Sound familiar?"

Walking a few steps deeper into the gathering, Bishop Bryan shouted, "You think you got trouble? Think again! That poor man would have loved to be here with you on Ossabaw Island. You don't have to feel the pain he felt. You've got somebody to wipe your butt and feed you and give you the drugs you want!"

Nodding his head, Lloyd walked back to the altar and turned to face the listeners.

"But what happened next is what can happen to you this very second. You see, Jesus knew the man was paralyzed not by some physical disorder, but by the guilt he felt for something he'd done years before. He thought God was punishing him for his sins."

Lloyd took his glasses off and rubbed his eyes. "The Bible reports that Jesus had compassion for that man and said to him, 'Pick up your stretcher, stand and walk, your sins are forgiven.' With that, the man's limbs began to straighten out and he was able to get up and walk. Everybody there was amazed by what Jesus had done. They proclaimed it to be a miracle, an act of God from on high."

Lloyd shook his head, chuckled some and said, "But Jesus knew better. He knew that man's problems weren't because of some disease, they were psychosomatic. They were brought on by his guilt and all Jesus had to do was forgive him!"

Smiling, Lloyd said, "An easy day's work for the Son of God!"

The Bishop saw a number of faces light up and he drove the point home.

"So many of you are here because of guilt. You weren't able to ask for forgiveness and, worse than that, you weren't able to forgive yourselves, and you let yourselves be paralyzed by the chemicals you forced into you bodies."

Rudy glanced at Katie standing only a few feet away, then watched as Lloyd almost exploded. In the rich lights, the gold vestments were contrasted against Lloyd's mahogany face and white beard, his arms flung out as he shouted, "I want everybody here to die in the knowledge that you are forgiven and to unwind your twisted arms and legs and to stand and walk before you die."

* * *

"Here's what I have in mind, Claus," said Rudy as he stood at the bar in his office and mixed drinks. After handing Claus a tumbler, Rudy walked back to his desk. Claus followed and stood in front of one of the chairs facing the desk.

"For goodness sakes, Claus," said Rudy, "sit down and relax. We have some important things to discuss."

Rudy sat in his desk chair and looked at the monitor screen. With the click of his mouse, he moved from Butterbean Beach to Groups One and Two. Then he went to Group Three and watched as a knot of skin heads fought with several blacks. It wasn't particularly intense, and Rudy quickly lost interest.

"I have decided to change the plan for administering *Klebsiella* to our residents, Claus. I've decided to have a multiple-stage infection of the island. This way, the chance of detection will be much less."

Schwarz leaned forward and said, "Yes, sir, I believe that's a good idea."

"I want you to arrange to have six of the incoming residents at Butterbean Beach infected with *Klebsiella* before they are brought to the island. I believe we'll need about eight hours of lead time. These subjects should begin to show signs of the infection within twenty-four hours of admission to the island. The residents you choose for this initial infection must show signs of advanced physical deterioration, Claus, to insure they die within our projected termination time of forty-eight hours."

"That won't be a problem, sir. The men we have at the beach are some of our best and most experienced. They can sort out the sheep from the goats."

"Excellent, Claus," responded Rudy, glancing back to the action in Group Three. "How have the numbers been with our *Ultimate Gladiators* project?"

"They continue to increase each survey period. Last week, we were number two in pay-for-view satellite channels in that category. I think if we can inject a little more drama into the action, we could be number one in a matter of weeks."

Rudy focused on Schwarz, asking, "What do you mean by drama, Claus?"

"My wife likes to watch reality television, things like real housewives of Atlanta and other such drivel, sir, and they all have some kind of personal story behind each of the characters that tends to draw in the audience. If we can work that into the series, I think we could increase our ratings."

Rudy rocked back in his chair and smiled while he finished the last of his drink.

"I'm impressed, Colonel, very impressed. Now, tell me how you plan to administer the bacteria to our first recipients."

"As you know, sir, we have installed a delousing walk-through at the beach. We have canisters of anti-insect powder that thoroughly dust each resident when they are accepted. Switching to the aerosol containing the bacteria will be no problem. The residents selected will be segregated, and when the appropriate time arrives, they will be sprayed with the proper dose when they are deloused."

"What about our men?"

"I had the men ramp up precautions immediately after you first discussed this possibility with me, sir. They now wear masks, gloves and disposable gowns. I feel certain they will not be infected."

Rudy nodded in approval then said, "Let's talk about what happens after these infected residents join us on the island."

"Yes, sir."

"As soon as these people begin to show signs of the infection, which will be profound coughing, wheezing, etcetera, you know, the classic signs of pneumonia, you will notify me and I will contact Dr. Hartman and have them examined. By the time he gets here, some of the infected may have succumbed as well as infecting others in their proximity."

Schwarz nodded knowingly.

"After Dr. Hartman has confirmed the presence of the infection," said Rudy coolly, "we will begin to evacuate the island of all non-essential personnel. That will include my wife and children as well as all dependents of our staff. Have you made arrangements for this, Claus?"

"No, sir."

"That's good; we don't want things appearing to be planned. As soon as the island has been evacuated, you will begin with the dispersal of the bacteria."

* * *

Rudy and Colonel Schwarz were having dinner with their wives at the Main House when Rudy's cell phone rang. Very few people knew the number of that particular phone, and when it rang, he knew it was important. Excusing himself, Rudy walked to the foyer and answered.

"Rudy, this is Judah Benjamin."

"Nice to hear from you, Judah. I've been following Will's election prospects. I even saw you on *Fox News* again last week. How are things?"

"The campaign is looking up, but that's not why I called."

Rudy had been expecting a call from either the governor or the congressman about the situation at Butterbean Beach. He was surprised it hadn't come sooner.

"The congressman's office has been getting a lot of calls from people at The Landings about the conditions at Butterbean Beach. A lot of them are beginning to be afraid of the situation there. They say there're far too many people waiting to be admitted to the colony and want something done about it. Can you help at all, Rudy?"

"As you know, Judah, the colony is maxed out. It's limited by our agreement concerning how many people we can take in. The company has no control over how many people show up seeking admittance to the colony. Control over those people is the responsibility of Chatham County and the State of Georgia."

Rudy almost smiled when he added, "We can't process people any faster than we have spaces available, Judah.."

"I understand," replied Judah, "I just wanted to check with you and see if there was anything more you could do."

"I can well understand, but my hands are tied."

"Thanks, Rudy."

Rudy snapped the cover shut on his cell phone and went to the door of the dining room. He opened it slightly and quietly said, "Claus, may I have a word with you for a moment." Claus rose and joined Rudy in the foyer.

"I just received a call from Mr. Benjamin. It seems our rich friends on Skidaway Island are starting to be uncomfortable with things at Butterbean Beach."

"Do you have any instructions for me?"

"Execute Operation Mercy."

* * *

Thirty-six hours later, just as Rudy had planned, six new residents began to exhibit signs of severe pneumonia. Their coughing was profound and without relief. Sweating was profuse and breathing labored. When they called for morphine or heroin, it was administered. It was the only relief the victims had, but one that served to suppress their breathing even more. They started to expire from their illness in the time frame Rudy had anticipated, but not before John-Morgan had examined them.

"I've taken sputum samples, Rudy," said John-Morgan while he removed his protective clothing, "and had them sent to Memorial Medical Center for a culture and gram stain."

John-Morgan paused, looked at Rudy and said, "I think this is a very virulent strain of pneumonia. If it gets out, it could kill the entire colony in a matter of weeks."

"Should I evacuate all non-essential personnel, John-Morgan?"

"It wouldn't be a bad idea. At the very least, I wouldn't have any of Lloyd Bryan's volunteers around this group. And I'd have your men dressed in hazmat gear. I think this is gonna get nasty."

An hour after the specimen arrived at the hospital's lab, John-Morgan received an urgent call from the lab's director.

"Dr. Hartman," asked a concerned male voice, "I just want to be sure this specimen was from sputum."

"It was," answered John-Morgan, expecting bad news, but nothing like he was about to get.

"Well," said the lab director, "I've got some really alarming results."

There was a pause and John-Morgan listened as the person on the other end took a deep breath before continuing.

"The gram stain shows *Klebsiella*. There's no doubt about it. The cultures will be ready in about forty hours, but it looks like you've got a case of *Klebsiella pneumoniae* on your hands. I've heard about this, but I've never seen a case, and I don't believe a case of pneumonia caused by *Klebsiella* has ever been reported in North America. I did a quick search on the internet and couldn't find anything about it here. All I could find were reports of cases from southeast and central Asia."

There was another pause so long it prompted John-Morgan to ask, "Are you still there Dr. Russell?"

"I'm here," came the hesitant reply. "The quick research I did shows there is no known antibiotic that can touch this thing. The person who has been infected by this organism has a death sentence, and it probably won't be pretty."

"I wish it were only one patient," answered John-Morgan, "but right now it looks like a half-dozen or more. It could climb into the hundreds, maybe many more."

Closing his cell phone, John-Morgan looked at Rudy and Lloyd as they stood together in the Great Room of the Main House.

"It's the worst possible news we could get," said John-Morgan.

"I recommend immediate evacuation of everyone with the exception of the guards and, as we discussed earlier, Rudy, they must have maximum protection."

John-Morgan turned to Lloyd and added, "That means you, too, Lloyd. There's no point in senseless losses."

* * *

"There's been an infection in the colony," said the fully-clad EO guard who entered Group One with a large spray gun in his hands.

"This is a disinfectant that will be able to kill the bacteria before you get infected," he continued as he misted the prostrate, helpless souls who lay on their cots.

"Breathe deeply," instructed the guard. "You must get the decontaminant into your lungs for it to work."

Without question, each of the residents did as instructed. In twenty-four hours they would be delirious; in thirty-six, all would be dead.

The same scenario played out in Group Two, only with a little more resistance. Some of the colony members fled into the forest seeking refuge, only to be tracked by the GPS signals from their microchips. Others forcibly fought back, sensing the sinister motive of the mysterious aerosol spray, but their efforts were futile. One good whiff and it was only a matter of hours. They could, at least, die pain-free. Extra rations of cocaine and heroin were available for the asking.

* * *

The black Huey helicopter Rudy was on touched down just outside the perimeter of Butterbean Beach where the national press was waiting. When Rudy alighted, Oberst Schwarz was at his side.

Rudy walked to a bank of microphones and faced more than thirty print and television journalists. He was calm and immaculate as he waited for the cameras to be focused. After several seconds, he began to speak.

"My name is Dr. Rudolph Hoorst. I'm the commanding officer of the drug colony on Ossabaw."

"This is Colonel Claus Schwarz, my second-in-command. I'm going to make a brief statement about the situation on the island, and then I'll be glad to take any questions you may have."

"A most unfortunate situation has arisen in the colony. A very serious bacterial infection causing pneumonia has taken hold in our resident population. The microbe causing this infection has been identified as *Klebsiella*. It is a normal flora of the human digestive tract and is not considered a pathogen. However, the strain of that bacteria that has infected the colony is a mutated one, and there is no known cure.

"We have experienced more than thirty-two deaths so far due to this disease. I have ordered all non-essential personnel on Ossabaw to be evacuated, and I've been informed this evacuation was completed two hours ago. None of these people demonstrated any signs of this infection. However, the situation on the island is quite grave, and I anticipate there will be further spread of the infection in the colony. All precautions to keep this infection from spreading to the mainland have been taken, and, as a medical doctor, I feel completely at ease telling you the mainland has nothing to fear."

Rudy waited a moment, then said, "I'll now take any questions you might have."

Hands shot up and voices called out. Rudy looked at the young brunette in the front row from CNN and said, "You can go first."

"Dr. Hoorst, what is being done for those with the infection, and what efforts are taking place to control the spread of the infection?"

Because the Ossabaw colony was the first of its kind in the U.S., it had garnered a great deal of national attention and this news conference was being carried live on all the cable channels. Katie was watching it from her cottage.

"As everyone knows, we do not provide any life-saving treatment in the colony. We don't treat cancer, we don't treat infections. All we do is provide the residents with the narcotic drugs of their choice. We do, however, try to prevent situations such as we have now from spreading. We're taking all reasonable precautions to stem the spread of this infection and limit any unnecessary contamination and suffering."

"How many have the infection right now?" asked a reporter from Fox.

Rudy turned to Schwarz and said, "Colonel, I think you can help us with that."

Schwarz approached the microphones and stated quite succinctly, "I inspected Group One just before boarding the helicopter, and it appeared that the entire group was showing signs of pneumonia. That would be 916 residents. As of time of departure, we've had thirty-two deaths due to this infection."

There was an audible gasp from the crowd, then another reported shouted, "What about the rest?"

Schwarz stepped back and let Rudy field the question.

"I don't have much hope for those residents, either."

"There must be terrible suffering on the island," said the reporter who asked the first question.

"On the contrary," said Rudy immediately, "my men are quick to dispense any and all analgesics the moment it appears someone is suffering."

"But won't that kill them?"

Rudy put on a sad face and answered, "All of these people came here to die. They knew full well what they were getting into. It just appears they may be dying a little sooner than expected."

"What does Congressman McQueen know about this situation?" asked a reporter from one of the local TV stations.

"He's been fully briefed," answered Rudy, "but there's nothing he can do that will change anything."

* * *

Dressed in hazmat gear, Rudy entered the Group One area twenty-four hours after the island's evacuation. Schwarz was at his side as they moved down one row of cots to the next. Almost a thousand corpses lay in a variety of contorted positions, each demonstrating what their last breaths had been like.

The odor that engulfed Rudy was one like no other he had ever known. It was thick, heavy, hot, filled with rotting flesh and excrement. While his protective clothing could save him from contamination, it could not spare him from the scenes of death.

"Dr. Hoorst," said Schwarz, "I believe we need to inspect Group Two, then the disposal area. This will be a most taxing time for our personnel, and I thought it might be a good idea if the command structure showed support by its presence in the field."

At the Group Two enclosure, guards were piling bodies next to the entrance, where others hefted them onto the backs of old army trucks.

"How many in this area, Claus?" asked Rudy, only yards away from the guards who held the hands and feet of the dead and, with a one-two-three cadence, tossed them onto the truck beds.

"As of eight this morning, the exact count was 1,098."

"Have they all died from the infection?"

"Some have not, sir, but they are near death as we speak. They will be administered a sufficient quantity of morphine that should ease their suffering and gently bring them to their end."

"When should that be, Claus?"

"I would estimate all should be terminated by five this afternoon."

Schwarz then turned to Rudy and asked, "Would you care to journey further into the compound, Dr. Hoorst?"

Rudy shook his head, then looked at Schwarz and said, "I guess we should inspect the disposal area next."

* * *

Rudy looked first at the crematoriums' chimneys and watched as waves of heat streamed from their tops.

"As you, know, Dr. Hoorst," said Schwarz, "the ovens cannot keep up with the demand and, as we agreed, the surplus is being temporarily buried."

Rudy felt as though he were in a daze and fought to maintain his focus as he answered, "I remember our agreement, Claus."

"As you can see, Dr. Hoorst," said Schwarz when they entered the building where joints and body parts were being harvested, "the company flew in extra men from our special action group to keep up with the demand."

Rudy felt light-headed again and fought it while he watched an EO officer scan the computer chips in the arms of fresh bodies as they were brought into the building. He listened as the officer instructed his technicians about what to look for and where to make their incisions. With revulsion and, at the same time, fascination, Rudy watched the members of the special action group cut into the joints of the bodies before them.

There were several occasions when Rudy thought the subjects of this dissection lab weren't truly dead. The body of one male who was tagged as having a total hip replacement ready for harvesting showed signs of life when the incision was made. Rudy thought he saw the man's eyes open wide and his lungs inhale deeply when the incision was made over his right hip and a bone saw was employed to remove the prosthetic joint. Rudy was only a few feet away and recoiled in horror as he tried to convince himself that the stress of the situation was causing him to imagine what he thought he saw. But, then, there was the women who had her corneas taken who seemed to sense pain as the members of the special action group thrust retractors into her eye orbit and shaved off the cornea of her left eye, before repeating the procedure again on the right eye.

"Dear God," exclaimed Rudy to Schwarz, "some of these people are still alive!"

"I know it appears to be the case in some circumstances, sir, but I can assure you that is not the case, Dr. Hoorst."

"How can you be so sure, Claus?"

"Their computer chips record no signs of life, Dr. Hoorst. Also, they have undergone an examination by our men who are thoroughly trained in detecting signs of life. These are dead bodies and nothing more, sir."

"But I saw them move when the dissections took place. This isn't a normal thing, Claus!"

"Dr. Hoorst, you're a physician, but I am a man who has seen much more death than you can imagine. Every now and then, some of these bodies react as one might expect to see from a snake with its head cut off. They may twitch and turn, but it is only a reaction to an outside stimulus. These people are truly dead in every sense of the word."

Rudy staggered back from the dissection table and felt as if he might vomit.

"But what if they really aren't dead when they're shoved into the ovens? That means they will be burned alive," blurted Rudy, turning away to seek the exit.

Once outside, Schwarz helped Rudy get out of his hazmat suit saying,

"I know this is a trying situation for you, Dr. Hoorst, but I can assure you all these bodies are stone-cold dead when they get to this disposal area."

Rudy nodded and looked blankly at the crematorium chimneys.

"Are you all right, Dr. Hoorst?"

"I'll be just fine, Claus. I suppose our next stop should be the temporary burial pits."

Three miles away, in the deepest, most secluded portion of Ossabaw, truck loads of bodies had been delivered. Rudy watched as they were dumped, while a back hoe racked them into a fresh hole and immediately covered them with the black, rich dirt of Ossabaw. All had the open wounds of dissection and implant harvesting.

That evening, Rudy drove his Hummer to the cottage by the ocean and got stoned with Katie. He simply wanted to be around her. After he was very high, he called the guards to drive him back to the Main House.

Rudy had never had trouble falling asleep, but that night he did. Even with all the hash he'd smoked and the alcohol he'd consumed, he still could not sleep. It was only after he'd taken ten milligrams of diazepam that he finally was able to close his eyes and drift away. But the bliss of nothingness was soon shattered by his dream.

In the dream, Rudy was one of the bodies taken to the disposal area. He tried to move and cry out, but he was paralyzed. He felt himself being heaved onto the dissection table and recognized the coldness on his back and buttocks. He watched in horror as EO technicians picked up their scalpels and saws while they prepared to remove artificial joints from him. He could feel the sharp pain as his knees and hips were cut open and could smell the scent of burning bone as the bone saws threw off hot bone dust. His hips and knees were on fire and the inability to scream only intensified the pain. After all this, he felt himself being placed on a cart with other bodies. He felt the weight of those bodies being stacked on his. He struggled to breathe but the pressure on his chest was too much.

Then, in an instant, Rudy was at the door of a crematorium when an EO guard opened the door to the oven. He could see the flames and he tried to scream again when he was shoved inside and heard the loud sound of metal against metal as the oven door was slammed shut. Then he felt the heat from the flames and, all at once, he was able to move as he threw off the bodies stacked on his and clawed his way to the oven door. With a great cry, Rudy tried to force the door open, and then he found himself wide awake, sitting up in his bed, soaked in perspiration and shaking.

* * *

The morning sun bled through the windows of the dining room at the Main House where Rudy and Schwarz were having breakfast. It was beautiful, cool and bright. Freshly-cut flowers filled the vase in the center of the table and the silver coffee pot off to the side shone brightly. Schwarz had already finished his French toast and sipped his coffee while he watched Rudy play with the scrambled eggs on his plate. It had been almost a week since Operation Mercy had been completed.

"Dr. Hoorst, you appear a bit fatigued, sir, have you been sleeping well?"

"No, Claus. I've had a recurring nightmare and it seems to drain me of all my energy. It's really quite horrible."

"Would you care to tell me about it, sir?"

Rudy sighed, and after several seconds rattled off a brief explanation of his dream.

"I've heard of similar things before, Dr. Hoorst. I've even had dreams very much like that, myself. But they abated after a few weeks. I wouldn't worry too much about them, sir."

"I hope you're correct Claus," answered Rudy in a quiet voice.

Schwarz cleared his throat. "I have the final numbers on Operation Mercy, would you like to hear them, sir?"

"Yes, of course, Claus. Tell me what you have."

"Well, first off, Dr. Hoorst, the colony is empty of all residents except those in Group Three. The areas for both Groups One and Two have been cleaned and are now ready for new residents. I anticipate final disposal of bodies from the overflow of Operation Mercy should be completed in about forty-eight hours."

"What is the bottom line, Claus?"

Schwarz smiled broadly leaning forward to say eagerly, "We've sold and shipped every piece we've harvested, Dr. Hoorst. Last night, I ran the numbers and, after the overhead of flying in extra support personnel and all it entails, the company made a profit of $6,700,000. That's clear profit and all for only one week's work, sir, and that doesn't factor in what we get from the State of Georgia."

"When can we start to re-stock the colony?"

"Immediately, Dr. Hoorst. Simply give the order and I'll have this island filled by the end of the day."

* * *

"I'm very impressed with the way you've brought the colony back up to speed, Claus."

"Thank you, Dr. Hoorst. We now have a full complement of residents with a daily turnover of about one hundred fifty."

Rudy looked over at the fireplace and remarked, "I'll be happy when we can enjoy a big fire here once more."

"So will I, sir. It's been a terribly hot summer."

"It's been the hottest summer on record," said Rudy. He sat in one of the big chairs and gestured for Claus to take a seat as well.

"I received a call today from Congressman McQueen's office," said Rudy, sipping his drink, "and they expressed his gratitude for how promptly the overpopulation at Butterbean Beach was alleviated. Another job well done."

"Thank you, Dr. Hoorst," answered Schwarz. He hesitated a bit before asking, "How have you been feeling, sir? It appears that you've come back to being your old self."

Rudy laughed, saying, "I suppose you were right, Claus. The dreams did stop after a few days."

That evening, after everyone was gone and the boys were fast asleep, Rudy and Carolyn embraced and fell together into their bed. It was a passionate and lively lovemaking and, after an hour, both Rudy and Carolyn were deeply asleep.

* * *

Colonel Schwarz watched from his Humvee as the governor and Congressman McQueen climbed from the Georgia National Guard Blackhawk helicopter and trotted toward him on their way to the monthly meeting of the Ossabaw Colony Drug Commission. Big Dog took the front seat while Will and their security team piled into the back. The governor spoke first.

"If you don't mind, Colonel, I'd like to visit with my daughter before going to the Main House."

"Dr. Hoorst anticipated your request, Governor, and has given me permission to take you to her. As soon as we drop off Congressman McQueen and your staff, I'll drive you to her residence."

"You're number two here, Colonel," said Big Dog as he watched long moss tresses sweep across the top of the Humvee, "so, tell me how my daughter is doin'."

"She's in good health, sir. She never left her compound while the infection was raging in the northern part of the colony. Dr. Hoorst and Bishop Bryan check on her several times a week; she runs daily and she has decreased her drug consumption to about a quarter of what it was when she was admitted."

"What a shame she couldn't do that on the outside," remarked the Dog.

"If you wish, sir, I'll radio ahead and let Miss McFarland know you're coming."

"Naw," answered the Dog, "I'd like to surprise her. I guess she doesn't get many good surprises anymore. Just find out where she is."

When Big Dog reached the beach, he could see Katie running in the distance. He could tell she'd seen him when she picked up her pace. Perhaps twenty feet away from her father, Katie stopped. Big Dog was perplexed and asked, "What's the matter, honey? I thought you'd be glad to see me."

Katie stared down at some shells scattered on the beach, then looked at her father, saying, "I saw Robbie. They took me to him at Hoorst's house. He said he'd talked to you about what I said, and that you don't believe me anymore."

A wind from the south had picked up, and it blew dry sand low across the beach. It stung Katie's ankles and filled her father's shoes. Governor McFarland wiped tears from his eyes with the back of his hand before saying, "Robbie told me you were the one who got things goin'. He was very persuasive. The boy's a damn good trial lawyer, Katie, and can talk a good line."

When she heard what her father said, Katie crumpled to the ground, pulled her knees to her chest and sobbed. Big Dog ran to her and knelt beside her.

"I didn't say I believed him, Katie. I just said he told a good story."

"You believe him, Daddy. I know you do."

"Aw, honey, how many more times do I have to have my heart broken? All I care about is that you're well and gettin' off the drugs."

Big Dog stood and reached down for Katie's hand to pull her up.

"Listen to me, Katie. You keep doin' this well, and I'll get you off this island and give you your life back."

* * *

At the Main House, Will was greeted by Judah, who had good polling news. Will led the entire Republican pack of candidates by more than fifteen points.

"I think you can do this," said Judah, pulling Will into the dining room to rattle off more in-depth numbers. "Everything is moving in our direction, Will. We just don't need any fuck-ups."

"What do you see as a potential fuck-up, Judah?"

"This whole island. This place is radioactive for you, Will. You need to resign. You can say you don't have the time anymore. Get the hell out now, while you still can!"

"I don't know how I can step away from this place now, Judah. Besides, it's worked out better than we hoped, and the press is saying that."

"Listen," replied Judah quietly, "there's more to this than meets the eye, OK? I've been told some very disturbing things about this place and the people who run it. I'm not even going to tell you what I know, but right now, you need to be thinkin' about an exit strategy."

Will nodded, and said, "Tell me about the governor and his son. The Dog told me things weren't too good between the two of them."

In a hushed voice Judah said, "Katie McFarland claims the reason she turned to drugs and prostitution was because Robbie molested her for a number of years when she was nine until about thirteen. She says it screwed up her whole life and is the reason she had two failed marriages and an entire litany of other screwed-up life experiences. She told her father he's the reason she checked into this colony."

"Shit, man," hissed Will as he struggled to comprehend the meaning of what Judah had just said.

"I always thought Robbie was a shithead, Will. I don't know for sure what happened, but at this point, I wouldn't be surprised if Robbie did what his sister said he did."

"Son-of-a-bitch," muttered Will. "What does the governor think?"

"It's hard to say, but something tells me he believes Katie." Judah stopped and drew his breath. "Look, Will, our governor has a lot of pressure on him because of this. I'm standin' here lookin' at this whole thing from a political perspective with your best interest at heart. I'm tellin' ya, as your best friend and closest advisor, to bail right now."

Will thought for a moment and asked, "So, what do you think I should do?"

"Resign tonight, before the meeting even starts."

* * *

Everyone was gathered in the Great Room at the Main House when Big Dog and Colonel Schwarz entered. The Dog scanned the room looking for his son, but he was nowhere to be seen. Then, like magic, the governor turned on his large disarming smile and worked the room.

When he reached Rudy, he leaned in close and whispered, "Where's Robbie?"

"His wife called two hours ago and said they were in the emergency room at Piedmont Hospital. She said the doctors think Robbie is trying to pass a kidney stone. Of course, that means he won't be here tonight."

"Gentlemen," said Rudy, "before we have dinner, I'd like Colonel Schwarz to give you a brief summary of what's happened in the colony since our last meeting."

There was nothing overtly offensive about Schwarz that Judah could discern, but still, for Judah, there was that little "something" that made him apprehensive. He decided it was Schwarz's German accent.

As Schwarz cleared his throat to speak, Will stood and apologized to Schwarz for interrupting. Then he said, "I guess it's only appropriate that those who have been my closest friends should hear this first."

There was a hush in the room.

"I've decided to run for the presidency."

Everyone broke out in smiles, then applause.

"That's the good news. The bad news is, I can't stay any longer.

Judah and I were talking to potential campaign staff just before the governor arrived, and I have to meet with them in Atlanta tonight. I've looked forward to spending the weekend on Ossabaw with such wonderful friends, but, if I'm gonna do this, I'm gonna do this to win, and I've got to start right now."

Turning to John-Morgan, Will asked, "Can you take me back to Isle of Hope?"

* * *

It was the autumnal equinox and it was certain to everyone that the changing of seasons had begun in earnest. After breakfast, the members of the governor's drug colony commission piled into two Humvees and began their inspection of each group.

When the commission members arrived back at the Main House, everyone seemed to be drained with the exception of Judah, who appeared agitated to John-Morgan.

Once inside, John-Morgan put his arm around Judah's shoulder and said, "Lemme buy you a beer, you look like you could use one."

"I sure as hell could," answered Judah as they pulled two bottles from the fridge in the kitchen and stepped into the garden out back.

"I knew I shouldn't have taken this fuckin' job, said Judah. "My life was so completely care-free. I was happy, had a beautiful wife and a nice home. The country was getting' more fucked up, but I wasn't. Now, I'm up to my nose in some really serious shit, John-Morgan."

"There's some nasty stuff here, but overall, it's been a positive thing for the state."

"What you don't know, and what I'd gonna clue you in on, will cause your hair to stand on end, John-Morgan."

Pulling back a chair, John-Morgan sat and moved close to Judah.

"I've done a lot checkin' on this bunch runnin' the island. One of the things I found out was that they have a satellite channel, pay-for-view, where the fights and killings in Group Three are shown. Executive Outcomes is makin' a fortune off that shit. There're other things, too, like who Rudy Hoorst really is."

* * *

Sunday morning arrived bright and clear. The sea and winds were calm, the heat and humidity low. The smell of Ossabaw's pines filled the Main House while members of the governor's commission began to rise and prepare for the day.

Lloyd had been the first to awaken and skipped breakfast as he continued his fast before morning Mass. It would be the first he'd celebrated since the great infection. Before he left his room, Lloyd knelt before the crucifix on his dresser and asked for inspiration in delivering his sermon. Then he quickly left and headed for Group One.

Rudy never missed daily Mass and was there with his wife and sons. John-Morgan sat beside Judah who came, mostly, to hear Lloyd speak. Off to the left sat Big Dog with his arm around his daughter.

Standing before the congregation in the green vestments of Ordinary Time, Lloyd's eyes moved slowly across those gathered. His gaze was intense and his eyes were framed by his white hair and beard.

"My dear brothers and sisters in Christ, the Gospel today deals with the return of the prodigal son. I would imagine most of you know the parable of the prodigal son. It's a famous parable and, really, my favorite Gospel story."

Lloyd began to walk among the people.

"Jesus tells us about a very rich man who had two sons he loved a great deal. One day, the younger son came to his father and demanded his part of the inheritance. As was the custom, the father gave this son what he was due, and the boy left his father's house and went out whoring and drinking and drugging."

Lloyd's eyes shot around the room. The last he looked upon were Katie's.

"It wasn't too long before this boy had snorted all that money up his nose and didn't have a penny left. The Bible says he envied the swine, who at least had garbage to eat. That's how hard up this boy was! Is there anybody in this room who's ever been like that?"

Many heads nodded. Lloyd walked back to the altar and continued, "Finally, the son decided he'd take a chance and go to his daddy and ask to be taken back. This bum, this drunk and drug addict, knew it was a long shot, but it was the only shot he had left in life and he took it."

When Lloyd reached the top step to the altar, he whirled around to face the audience and his vestments followed in a flash of color. Stopping, he looked up and said, "One morning, this broken-hearted old man was sitting on his front porch having coffee with the good son and looked off into the distance, and he saw the figure of a man coming his way. He watched for several minutes as that figure moved closer. Then, in a shout of joy he said to the good son, 'That's your brother! Go get the best suit in the house and put it on him. And get the biggest diamond ring in my jewelry box and slip it on his finger! Have our maids fix the best meal we've ever had!'

"Now the good son, and he was really a good and devoted son to his father, was appalled by what his daddy had told him to do. This boy had never done a thing wrong and had never spoken back to his daddy, but this time it was way too much for him to bear and he challenged his father. 'My brother has disgraced you and our name and now you want to treat him like royalty. I don't understand. I've never disobeyed you. I've worked my butt off for you, and you wouldn't even give me enough money to have my friends over for a Super Bowl party. Why would you treat me that way, Daddy?'

"Can you imagine how the good son felt?" asked Lloyd. "I can. But, you see, he wasn't that prodigal son's father. After the good son rebuked his father for welcoming back his brother, the father looked at that boy and said, 'You have been an excellent child, and I will never forget you for that. But what you don't understand is that my son, your only brother, was dead and is alive again. He was lost and now he's been found!'"

Lloyd looked at Katie and her father, asking, "Is there anybody in here today who can relate to that story? You are the prodigal son in this parable! No matter what despicable, nasty, horrible things you've done to yourself and others, your Father in Heaven will dress you in the finest clothes, put rings on your fingers, and have a great feast when you return to Him in humility."

After Mass, Judah passed the word to the other commission members that he wanted to have a private meeting with them. The cover story was that John-Morgan wanted to take them on his boat and show them the waterways surrounding Ossabaw. The plot was sprung about an hour before lunch, when Judah knew Rudy had already planned his day and could not be with the commission for the boat ride. It worked perfectly.

John-Morgan guided *Graf Spee* into the mouth of the Ogeechee River and then into the Florida Passage. From there, Ossabaw was a thin green tree line miles to the south.

At the entrance to Cane Patch Creek, John-Morgan slowed his boat and cut the engines and everyone looked at Judah.

"I've found out some rather disturbing things about Executive Outcomes," said Judah, reaching for the laptop tucked into the basket that held their lunch. "I have a friend in the Far East who has other friends there, who sent him this video. What it contains are images of scenes of actual fights to the death among people who are most certainly in Group Three on Ossabaw. It appears that Executive Outcomes has a pay-per-view channel where they show these fights with live action commentary."

Judah placed the laptop on the boat's console and let the video tell the story. Nobody said a word as the skinheads and the Brothas fought it out to the death in a most brutal and sadistic fashion. Lloyd and Big Dog were riveted as the announcers joked about the combat and offered specials to those viewers who signed up for another month. Judah folded his laptop, looked at the governor and asked, "So, what do we do?"

"Well, hell," said the Dog, "what *can* we do? Did any of you think this would be the result?"

"I don't believe any of us ever thought it would come to this," said Lloyd as he walked to the stern and looked at the southern end of Ossabaw where Group Three was located. "In the end, I guess it's always about money."

"I have friends in India, too," said Judah as he put the laptop back into the picnic basket, and removed the sandwiches. "These people tell me there's a large after-market business in Asia for used artificial joints like hips and knees. My people tell me Executive Outcomes is a big player in this market. They don't go by that name, but my sources tell me EO, under another name, is one of the leading providers of such devices."

John-Morgan's mind raced forward as he struggled to shed himself of things that were taboo in American culture, things he never imagined would happen; when he had reached that moment of clarity, he said, "Son-of-bitch, they're harvesting joints and God knows what else from those bodies before they're cremated!"

The Dog's mouth dropped open and Lloyd jerked his head toward John-Morgan. Quietly, Judah added, "That's exactly what I've been thinking."

Graf Spee rested gently in Cane Patch Creek as the tide began to sweep her closer to Ossabaw. Finally, Judah broke the silence when he said, "There's also the question about who Rudy Hoorst really is."

By this time Big Dog was really hyped. He could envision the shit storm that would follow if all the stuff about videos and joint harvesting hit the news. He already felt like a damn fool for not picking up on what really was at the center of Executive Outcome's plan. When the question about Rudy was raised, all the Dog could say was, "Shit, now what else?"

"Here's what I've been told," said Judah. "I haven't got absolute confirmation on this stuff, so you'll just have to take this with a grain of salt, but my sources come from way up the food chain, and I'm certain they're reliable."

"My people tell me Rudy's real family name isn't Hoorst, but Höss. That's H-o-s-s with two dots above the 'O'. Rudolph Höss was the commandant of the Auschwitz concentration camp complex. This man was a war criminal of monumental size. It is my understanding that he was Rudy's grandfather."

Big Dog shook his head and looked at Lloyd, then back at the deck. John-Morgan nervously ran his hand through his hair and waited for the rest.

"The records on Rudy's father, Rudolph Conrad Hoorst, all indicate he was an eighteen-year-old member of the Sixth Waffen SS Division. This was the Nazi division which fought the Allies to a stand-still in Italy until the end of the war. Hoorst surrendered along with the rest of the division in May of 1945. After almost a year in a POW camp, he emigrated to Argentina, where he went to work as an agent selling Argentine beef to American and European buyers. On a trip to the States he met his future wife, one Eloise

Lee Jackson, a descendent of both generals Lee and Jackson. In 1955 they married and ultimately the only issue from this union was Rudolph Conrad Hoorst Jr. who was born in Richmond, Virginia, in 1959.

"That's the official line on the Hoorst family and, for many years, it was the one the State Department chose to buy. Rudy's father turned out to be quite well-connected with anti-Communist elements in both East and West Germany. Just as we overlooked the histories of Nazi rocket scientists who proved helpful to our national defense, we did likewise with all manner of other former Nazis who had their own little areas of expertise in fighting the growing threat of the Soviets.

"When it became clear to a number of well-placed Nazis, especially the high-ups in the SS, that Germany would lose the war, they started making plans for the future. They were really quite clever. One of these men was Rudolph Höss. He had a son who was only fifteen in 1944 and a member of the Hitler Youth and who served on one of the flak batteries that guarded Berlin. Right after D-Day, Höss had his son transferred to the Italian front with the Sixth SS, and he assumed the name of a young man who'd been killed in combat—Rudolph Conrad Hoorst. That's Rudy's father."

"OK," asked Big Dog, "so what does all that have to do with us and this colony?"

"In a nutshell, I believe Executive Outcomes was formed and operated initially by hard-core SS men. They had large amounts of stolen cash and hid that money all over occupied Europe as well as deposited in foreign banks, mostly in South America. They used that money to purchase war surplus items and weapons after the war and sell them at a good profit. The business grew and became up-front and respectable. The original members of EO passed the business on to their descendants. As far as I can discern, there are no more living original members."

Lloyd had been quiet and reserved while Judah spoke, but when it appeared Judah was finished, he asked, "I think you've told a most fascinating story, Judah, but what, exactly, does it have to do with Rudy Hoorst? Do you think he's an actual Nazi or something?"

"I don't know what he is other than what he appears to be, Lloyd. And, that's my point. We've already found out about the television program they have on the island and I think John-Morgan hit the nail on the head about selling artificial joints. I guess what I'm tryin' to say is, this is an organization founded by Nazis, the most brutal kind of Nazis. Their descendants run it now. I have a feelin' that simply sellin' joints and makin' snuff movies isn't all that's goin' on here, Bishop."

Judah pointed to Ossabaw and continued, "Maybe you can chalk it up to my *Yiddishen Cup*, you know, my 'Jewish head,' but I think something really ugly is happening on that beautiful island."

* * *

Sunday night dinners at the Main House were slightly more formal than other evening meals. Rudy and Schwarz always appeared in uniform with their wives, also dressed for the occasion. Rudy's sons would be there, too, well-behaved, polite, and well-spoken. Business was never discussed at the table; that would come later.

Rudy was a perceptive observer of body language and tonal inflections of voice. After the board arrived back from their boat trip, he thought he could detect a subtle change in attitude. Nothing big, just little things like lack of eye contact or a stiffer posture. He suspected something unflattering about the company had been discussed on the boat and decided to get to the bottom of it after dinner. He informed Schwarz of his suspicions and plan. Schwarz replied in a low voice, "Beware of the Jude."

After dinner Rudy, Schwarz, and the board members gathered in Rudy's office.

"So, gentlemen, tell me, how was the boat ride," asked Rudy settling into the chair behind his desk.

"We circled the island," said John-Morgan, "and the weather was perfect. I got to blow out my engines."

Big Dog shifted in his chair and said, "I got to see the cottage on the beach where Katie lives. I was hopin' she'd be out runnin', but she wasn't."

"I'll be happy to have Colonel Schwarz take you to her once again," said Rudy looking at Schwarz who nodded in consent.

"I'd appreciate that, very much, Rudy. Maybe we can go in the morning, before I have to leave for Atlanta."

"I will make it so, sir," said Schwarz.

"And you, Bishop," asked Rudy, looking at Lloyd, seated across the room nursing his last Scotch of the evening, "did you enjoy your time away from your ministry?"

"Yeah, yeah, I did, now that you ask. The thing I enjoyed most was the freshness I felt on the water. There was no smell of death."

"It sounds to me as though this outing was quite therapeutic for the board," said Rudy. He leaned forward in his chair and looked at Judah.

"It seems to me, Judah, that you've been awfully quiet this evening. Is there something on your mind? Something you're holding back from the rest of the board? We have these meetings to vent our feelings about the colony. I apologize if I'm wrong, but if there is something you'd like to share with the board, please, do so."

Judah was having none of the passive-aggressive bullshit talk Rudy seemed to enjoy at times. He was loaded, and the hammer was on full cock. All afternoon he'd rehearsed getting to this moment and knew just what he wanted to say. All he had to do was contain himself and control his temper, which was why he hadn't had a drop of alcohol since the boat trip.

Judah was seated across the desk from Rudy. He sat straight up, leaned forward, and focused his glare directly at Rudy.

"Ya know, there's a lot of very sick shit goin' on in this world, Rudy. I just never thought I'd be this close to it." Judah paused for effect.

Rudy's glance shot to Schwarz who gave him an "I told you so" look.

"OK, Judah, please, let us know what you mean."

"I know about the *Ultimate Gladiators* TV show, and I know it originates from right here on this island. I've seen it myself. I've even downloaded it on my laptop and, if you want, we can watch it right now."

Rudy lifted his chin from his hands, leaned back in his chair and gazed at Judah. When Rudy did that, Judah knew instantly that this man was, indeed, the grandson of Rudolph Höss. Judah had seen numerous photos of Höss, and when he watched Rudy's lips tighten and his eyes narrow slightly, he knew who this bastard was. Only, it wasn't wrong to be the grandson of a war criminal. There had to be something more.

After a few moments, Rudy looked over at Schwarz, then back at Judah, saying, "I hope you read the contract between the State of Georgia and Executive Outcomes. I have a copy of it here in my desk. If you'd care to read it, you'll find that Georgia gave this company absolute rights to all video and audio taken on this island. You will also note, Mr. Benjamin, that the State expressly puts no restrictions on how this information can be used and/or sold. What this company is doing with our *Ultimate Gladiators* program is completely legal. It may be distasteful to some, perhaps for many, but it's not illegal. I don't watch it, I never have and don't care to, but it does improve this company's bottom line. A bottom line that makes this colony such a convenient and cost-effective dumping ground for the State of Georgia to deposit its most egregious human garbage."

Rudy leaned forward asking, "Any more questions, Mr. Benjamin?"

Judah really hadn't anticipated such an aggressive answer from Rudy. He was thinking Rudy would try to lie and gloss over the video. Perhaps even deny knowledge of it; so, when Rudy came out swinging, Judah was caught flatfooted.

The most pregnant of pregnant pauses followed Rudy's admission when, to his own surprise, John-Morgan found himself saying in a strong voice, "I got a fuckin' question I'd like to ask, Rudy. I've been told by some really reliable folks that the company is removing artificial joints from the bodies before they're cremated and reselling them on the overseas market. Is that true?"

Rudy didn't really give a shit about Judah. He always thought Judah was an overpaid, Washington-connected, smart-ass little Jew he had to be nice to. But he liked John-Morgan and when John-Morgan looked at Rudy the way he did as he asked his question, Rudy could see that relationship was probably gone.

So he sucked it up, returned John-Morgan's hard stare and replied, "Again, I will refer you all to the contract we have with the State. In it, the contract specifically says the bodies of deceased residents as well as all their earthly possessions are the sole property of the company. This applies to, but is not limited to, such things as surgically implanted artificial joints. So, the answer to your question, Dr. Hartman, is yes. We do harvest whatever useful things these bodies have on or in them."

Judah had regained some of his poise and, when he heard Rudy's reply to John-Morgan's question, the memory of gold teeth being removed from the mouths of dead concentration inmates flashed through his mind.

"What about their gold teeth, Hoorst, do you take those, too?"

The tone of Rudy's voice was definitely condescending when he answered, "Actually, we do, Judah, but there aren't many these days. It simply isn't fashionable anymore to have gold teeth, with the exception of young, feral African-Americans males. When we have residents die with gold in their mouths, we certainly harvest it before cremation."

Lloyd was rendered speechless by Rudy's remarks and quickly swallowed the rest of his Scotch; he decided he was going to need it. Big Dog, however, was anything but at a loss for words and propelled himself from his chair to stride to Rudy's desk. He set both hands on it and leaned over to get in close. Rudy sat impassively and watched the veins in the Dog's neck distend as his face reddened.

"This is the most disgusting shit I've ever heard about in my life," spat out the Dog, "and I will not tolerate it within the confines of this state, not while I'm the governor."

Rudy smiled slightly and asked, "So, what is the alternative, Governor McFarland? What would you have me do?"

"Stop this shit right now, or I'll shut this whole operation down!"

Rudy looked Big Dog right in the eye and said, "I can have my entire staff and all necessary equipment off this island within seventy-two hours. If that's what you want, then you can have it. But, then what would you do, Governor? You'll have almost two thousand drug addicts on your hands with no knowledge of how to handle them. Plus there'll be another thousand at Butterbean Beach clamoring for admission. You want to shut this operation down, go right ahead."

Big Dog dropped his head, then removed his hands from Rudy's desk and stood up straight. The Dog was a damn good poker player and knew when his bluff was called, so he nodded his head, took his glasses off and rubbed his eyes. He said, "OK, I understand the complexities of the situation, but you must also understand the outrage this board feels about what's going on here. We never dreamed you'd be doing such things, Rudy."

"The board may have the luxury to be dreamers, Governor," responded Rudy, "but the company does not. We deal with the harsh realities of life and death." Rudy stood and walked around his desk to face Big Dog.

"I believe it was Otto von Bismarck who said, 'Laws are like sausages, it's better not to see them being made.' Something we all want, but not very pretty in the making. It's the same way in dealing with the problem of drug addiction. Something we all want, but not very pretty up close."

Rudy relaxed his posture and looked individually at Judah, John-Morgan, Lloyd and Big Dog, saying, "I've come to like each one of you and have had the pleasure of enjoying your company. I'm sorry this situation has lessened that relationship, but business is business. We have an agreement, and the company has lived up to its end of the bargain. As a board, you gentlemen are free to do whatever you like. I only suggest you consider all ramifications."

Rudy looked at Schwarz for a moment, then back at the board and said, "Perhaps it would be beneficial and productive if Colonel Schwarz and I retired to the Great Room and left you gentlemen alone to sort things out among yourselves."

Bowing slightly, Rudy said, "Please, take all the time you need." Then, he and Schwarz left the room.

Once Schwarz pulled the door closed and heard the latch snap shut, he whispered, "Excellent job, sir. You'll have no further trouble with that bunch."

There was silence from the members of the Governor's Commission on the Ossabaw Colony. There was no eye contact among them, and no one even moved for what must have been two minutes.

"If there're no objections," said Lloyd, "the Bishop of Savannah is going to have another Scotch, he feels he needs one."

"I'll join ya," echoed John-Morgan, rising to follow Lloyd.

Big Dog hadn't moved from where he stood when Rudy dropped his bomb on the commission members. Finally, the Dog said, almost in a whisper, "That little bastard has us in a squeeze. The fucker's right. We can't stop what his company's up to, and we sure as hell can't run this place ourselves. I don't blame anybody but myself. I should have been more vigilant. I just never dreamed people would be plotting something like this."

Judah let his breath out, smiling sadly. "I still have a very bad feeling about Hoorst and his whole fuckin' company. There's more goin' on here than we know about, I'm sure of that."

"Like what?" asked John-Morgan.

"I don't really have a fix on it right yet, John-Morgan, but I have this feeling. It's just an overall impression. Things here are too perfect. This place runs like a clock. No bumps, no grinds. Just too good, that's all."

"They've done this before in Europe and Asia," replied John-Morgan, "so they've had practice and experience. It's no crime to do a job well, no matter how distasteful. To be honest, I never thought about what happened to joint implants when a person died until now. It's against the law in this country to reuse them, but, when I think about it, it seems to be a great waste. As long as the implant is intact and sterile, why can't it be used again? What's the rationale?"

"Follow the money," said Judah. "It would be my guess that the companies who manufacture these devices would make less money if those implants could be used again. Just think how many new cars GM could sell if it were against the law to buy and drive a used one."

Big Dog was flat-out weary and almost stumbled to the bar where Lloyd and John-Morgan had sought refuge and solace. He really didn't give a shit what he had to drink, so long as it eased him up some. After he'd filled a glass, the Dog turned to Judah.

"All right, Judah, what'dya think Rudy has up his sleeve?"

"It's all about the numbers, Governor. I haven't quite figured it out yet, but these people are number crunchers. They have this place down to an exact science. They're like farmers looking at their crops. They know what they've put into the ground, and they know what the growing time is. The only thing they can't control is the weather. But, guess what, Dog? They don't have to worry about the weather! All they have to be concerned about is how fast they can process the residents. Quicker processing, more money."

What Judah said was like a slap in the face for Lloyd.

"So," said Lloyd, "you think Rudy is running people through here as fast as he can? I'm askin', do you believe the quicker these people die, the better for EO's bottom line?"

"As long as there's a fresh body filled with valuable hardware waiting to be harvested, Lloyd."

John-Morgan set his glass down so hard he thought it would break. "Do you think the company is speeding up the deaths of the residents?"

"After what we now know, would you put something like that past this bunch, John-Morgan?"

"OK, Judah," replied John-Morgan, "but how are they speeding up the process? We've got really good oversight, I'm here several times a week, and Lloyd's here all the time. We haven't seen anything that indicates they're up to no good."

"I'm just lookin' at the numbers, that's all," said Judah.

"And, what do the numbers tell you?" asked Lloyd, who'd wandered back to his chair and allowed himself to relax and think about things he'd rather not.

Judah looked directly at Lloyd and answered, "Damn good coincidence for Executive Outcomes when the pressure is really on at Butterbean Beach, and all those Yankees at the Landings are raisin' hell about the dirt bags lined up on Diamond Causeway, and presto, a fuckin' plague takes down the whole goddamn colony! It took the pressure off the company overnight, didn't it, Lloyd? I'm sorry, but I really believe this whole place is as dirty as the men's room at a bus station."

Lloyd asked, "But what do we do? I mean, what in the hell do we do? How do we really know? What do we look for?"

Again, no one said a word. Finally, Big Dog blurted, "I wonder how much my son knows about all this shit?"

"Knowing Robbie, answered Judah, "probably everything."

The Dog was tired as hell and intoned, "If there isn't anything new, I mean if ya'll don't have anything positive to add, I guess we might as well call Rudy and his sidekick back on in here and tell'em, in so many words, they've got us by the balls."

* * *

Looking over his shoulder at Schwarz, Rudy smiled ever so slightly before he went behind his desk. Still standing, Rudy addressed Big Dog. "What has the board decided to do about the colony?"

"We've decided to leave things alone. You can keep on like before."

"Thank you, Governor, and thanks to the board as a whole. You've made the right decision, a decision truly in the best interest of the State of Georgia. However, I'd like to poll the individual board members, if you have no objection."

Rudy waited a few seconds and when no one said anything, he looked at Lloyd and asked, "Your thoughts on the matter, Bishop?"

Lloyd pulled off his glasses, rubbed his eyes, and replied, "As long as I can be sure nobody's being abused, I'm OK. I don't like it, but I can't stop it. My purpose here is to minister to the suffering, and I'll be here until I die."

Rudy smiled, saying, "Thank you, Bishop, and you are welcome in this colony for as long as you'd like."

Rudy turned to John-Morgan. "What about you, Dr. Hartman?"

John-Morgan's leg had started hurting again. He attributed it to the cool weather and winced a little as he shifted his weight to his good leg.

"From one physician to another, this whole place is an oxymoron. It's gonna' take me a while to digest the whole thing, but I'll stay on."

Leaving Judah for the last, Rudy turned to Big Dog and asked, "Anything more you'd like to add, Governor?"

The Dog shook his head and said in a quiet voice, "No, not really." Then he looked at Schwarz and asked, "Will you still be comin' for me at nine?"

"Yes, sir, nine sharp."

Rudy paused, then spoke to Judah. "Do you have anything else you'd like to add, Judah, before we call it a night?"

"Here's the way I figure this whole thing, Rudy," said Judah in a calm voice. "The State of Georgia is paying you millions of dollars a year to run this place. Just turning the numbers over in my head, I'm thinking Executive Outcomes should be paying the state for the right to run this colony. I'm thinking that, when it comes around to new contract time, the shoe is gonna be on the other foot."

After the board members had all filed out of Rudy's office, he took a seat behind his desk and Colonel Schwarz filled the chair facing him.

"You did quite well this evening, Dr. Hoorst."

The room was quiet as both men ruminated over the events of the evening. It was Rudy who spoke first.

"How much more do you believe the Jude knows, Claus?"

Schwarz answered, "Hard to tell, sir, but, at a guess, I'd say he has divulged the limit of his knowledge. Still, he is typical of his breed, cunning and insightful."

Rudy nodded and asked, "Do you think there may come a time when we have to deal with him harshly?"

"As in *very* harshly, sir?"

Rudy nodded in the affirmative, watching Schwarz's face for a reaction.

Schwarz replied with an ice-cold voice and stare, saying, "I see what you mean, sir. If that time does arrive, only say the word."

Rudy rocked back in his chair and looked at the photos of his wife and sons on his desk. "The Mafia has an old saying, Claus: 'Nothing personal, it's only business.'"

Schwarz allowed a slight smile and nodded in agreement with Rudy.

"Dr. Hoorst," said Schwarz in a hushed tone, "things are running quite well in the colony at present, but I can foresee a time, in the not-too-distant future, when we will again be confronted with overpopulation. Would you care to share with me, sir, how you plan to deal with this eventuality?"

"Of course, Claus," answered Rudy. "The company has been working on a rather malignant and deadly form of virus. I'm informed that it should be ready for deployment within about two months. The company doesn't want to use the *Klebsiella* bacteria again. Our scientists believe this virus has a faster mortality and is easier to infect."

* * *

Big Dog stood at the door to Katie's cottage watching her for a few moments through the windows as she waited for him on the deck. She looked different from the last time they'd visited. She'd gained weight and seemed to have more purpose in her posture. He took a deep breath and said a silent prayer, turned the door knob and announced in a loud voice, "Your daddy's here, Katie!"

Katie greeted her father the same way she had the first time. After a long embrace the Dog stood back to admire her.

"My goodness, baby, you look wonderful!"

"Thank you, Daddy, I feel wonderful."

"I heard you'd quit snorting coke, that you smoke a little weed and take something to sleep at night, is that right?"

Katie nodded, smiled, and took her father by the hand, leading him to the deck outside and its view of the ocean. She looked for a long time at the waves, as did Big Dog. Without taking her eyes off the ocean, Katie said, "I'm different now, Daddy. I'm not the same person I was when I checked in here months ago."

"Oh, my sweet baby, I'm so glad to hear that! Your eyes seem to have a glow, like you did when you were a little girl." The Dog choked up, but managed to get out, "I never forgot that time, honey. When I first heard you'd checked into this place, Katie, I thought for sure you'd come here to die. What happened?"

Katie smiled at her father and said, "I did come here to die. I had every intention of numbing myself completely out and then overdosing. I was bad-off, Daddy."

"What changed for you, baby?"

"I met a man."

"On this island?"

"Yes, and he changed my life."

Katie turned back to her father and continued, "It's not what you think, Daddy."

"Well then, what is it, and who is this man?"

Looking up into her father's face, Katie said, "That man is Bishop Bryan. He took an interest in me and we talked for hours, right here in this cottage. He told me things about spirituality and prayer and forgiveness I'd never heard before in my life. What he said let me drain out the rage and anger I've held inside myself over what Robbie did to me, and about what I've done to myself. Lloyd started me walking down that road to forgiveness. I've forgiven Robbie, and I've forgiven myself. It wasn't an easy road to travel, but I did it. When I got to the end, the anger that had driven me to do all sorts of crazy, nasty things just vanished. Lloyd was with me every step of the way.

"I never dreamed, in all my life, I'd be telling you this stuff."

The Dog had been baptized when he was twelve. He was a deacon in the biggest, most important Baptist church in Atlanta. He had always believed in God but wasn't sure about those miraculous, just in the nick of time, death-bed conversions. He'd heard lots of sermons about having sins taken away by being washed in the Blood of the Lamb, but all that stuff had never quite hit home as it did this day.

"Explain to me how you feel, Katie."

"I feel clean, Daddy. Unless you've felt really dirty the way I felt for years, you can't understand what it feels like to be clean."

CHAPTER TEN

APPEARANCES

Through tatter'd clothes, small vices do appear;
Robes and furr'd gowns hide all. Plate
sin with gold,
And the strong lance of justice hurtles breaks;
Arm it in rags, a pigmy's straw does pierce it.
—William Shakespeare, *King Lear* IV

"Things are beginning to get a little tight at Butterbean Beach," said Colonel Schwarz when he and Rudy gathered for their usual after-dinner meeting in Rudy's office.

"How long do you think it will be until we'll be hearing from Congressman McQueen concerning complaints from the residents of Skidaway Island?"

"It's not at that level yet, sir, but I did want to bring it your attention. I'd guess we have at least a month."

Rudy stood looking out his office windows, his hands clasped behind his back as he watched the orange glow of the sunset.

"The company is prepared to deal with the problem, Claus. I've seen the statistics on what types of hardware we now have in our island inventory, and they are quite satisfying."

"You're right about that, sir, and my men are ready."

"How well are you acquainted with the great Spanish influenza pandemic of the last century, Claus?"

"Do you mean the one at the end of World War I, sir?"

"Spot on, Colonel, that's exactly what I'm talking about. That disease killed about fifteen times more people world-wide than the war in Europe. And it did it in half the time. The Great War killed an estimated four million from 1914 until 1918. The flu started around June of 1918 and lasted until the middle of 1920. It killed an estimated 150 million people, then simply vanished, burned itself out."

"I recall my parents talking about that, sir. Some historians say Germany lost the war because of it," answered Schwarz, listening eagerly.

"Quite right, Claus, I've heard that argument, also."

Rudy smiled. "Do you also know some of the founding members of this company served in the Great War?"

"Yes, sir. I do."

"I thought so, Claus, but I also know something you may not be privy to."

"And, what would that be, sir?"

Rudy leaned in closer to Schwarz and answered, "After World War II, the founders of this company began to scour everywhere for information about biological weapons. They were interested in weapons of every kind, but some had a particular interest in biological warfare. A really select few were given the mission of dissecting the weapon potential of the Spanish flu. Do you know what they found?"

"No, sir."

"That flu was a world-wide phenomenon. It even hit remote islands in the Pacific. There was probably nowhere in the world this virus didn't strike. It even infected Eskimos in Alaska, Claus!"

Rudy paused and watched Schwarz, who looked perplexed.

Rudy took a breath and said, "It seems those Eskimos who died from the flu were buried in the permafrost and their bodies were preserved, as well as the virus that killed them. Through their investigations, EO scientists learned of these frozen specimens and some ten years back they journeyed to Alaska, exhumed the Eskimo bodies and obtained viable tissue samples from their lungs. It was from these samples that our people were able to culture and genetically modify the virus to make it weapons-grade."

Schwarz leaned back in his chair and said quietly, "I think I understand where you are headed, Dr. Hoorst."

"I suspect you do, Claus. The company has refined this virus. I've been told it can cause clinical symptoms within six hours of exposure, and death within twenty-four hours."

* * *

It had been several weeks since Rudy had last visited Katie at the cottage. He'd seen her as she worked with Lloyd, helping with the residents in Group One. They'd spoken briefly, but that had been their only contact.

Rudy had thought often about Katie over the past few days and, against his better judgment, he'd decided to ride his horse to the cottage. As he let his mount follow the path through the woods, he imagined Katie as a pleasant diversion from the starkness of running a drug colony.

In the beginning, Rudy believed he would be able to insulate himself from feelings of doubt and perhaps regret, but he had been wrong. The first inkling he had of this was the nightmares. He was grateful the dreams hadn't recurred, but every night before he went to bed, he prayed that dream would not be visited upon him again.

As he rode, Rudy decided his attraction to Katie was one based on her beauty and sexuality, that he could see her only as something like a *Playboy* centerfold and nothing more. He'd look and imagine, but that would be the extent of his relationship. It was a fine line Rudy had chosen to walk, but he was confident he could walk it.

Katie had never expected the treatment she'd been given on Ossabaw. She thought she'd be just like all the rest and actually, for a time, she wanted to be. Then she was placed in a luxurious house on a pristine beach overlooking the ocean. Then there was Rudy.

Katie had been attracted to Rudy from the first time they'd met. He was polished, well-spoken and had the finest manners. Sometimes she would think about what might have been if things had been different.

Katie had come to appreciate her living conditions at the colony and knew Rudy could change things in an instant. What might she have to do to keep the comforts she enjoyed at the cottage? Even with her newfound spiritual life, Katie doubted she'd have the courage to give up her surroundings if it appeared Rudy wanted more than just conversation. She thought about Rudy's wife and children, and how her relationship with him could affect them. She'd known many men who'd lain in her bed and cheated on their wives, but she'd never been bothered by that until now. But still there was the reality of the moment, of the physical world, of her wants and needs.

Katie was finishing her first glass of wine when Rudy appeared on the deck. He'd walked around to the front of the cottage, and smiled broadly when Katie saw him standing with his back to an angry ocean.

"I've been thinking about you," said Rudy, walking into the kitchen to pour himself a glass.

"I've thought about you a time or two, also, Rudy," replied Katie.

Rudy sat next to Katie on the couch and sipped from his glass. He reached into his pocket, pulled out a machine-rolled joint and lit it, took a long pull and offered it to Katie. She hesitated at first, and, with a smile, took the joint and inhaled deeply. In seconds both could feel the effects of the strongest pot sold at the BP Station in Sandfly.

"Does your wife know you come here, Rudy?"

"She knows I travel this island on a weekly basis, inspecting our facilities. She knows about this cottage, we've stayed here together before you came. She knows you now live here. So, I assume she knows I've visited you here."

"Is she unhappy with your coming here, Rudy?"

"She's never given me any indication that she is.'

"What does she know about me?"

"She's seen you at Mass and knows who you are. She's even talked to your father about you."

Rudy took another draw on the joint and offered it to Katie once more.

"Why do you keep coming back here, Rudy?"

"Because I enjoy it. Being here is very different than being at the Main House. My little trips to this place are a good diversion from the world that lies just over that tree line. I need a diversion every now and then."

The wind picked up and the sun slipped lower. Soon, the only light was from the fireplace and it seemed to make the room smaller, more intimate.

"Your father has asked me to release you, Katie."

"I know, he told me."

"He said you didn't want to leave."

"I have a purpose in life. On the outside, I didn't have anything. Now, I feel as if I can do some good."

Rudy turned his glass up and finished the wine. He let himself fall into the back cushions of the sofa and rolled his head toward Katie.

"You're a beautiful woman, Katie," he said, reaching out to touch her cheek.

In spite of her newly-found religious fervor, Katie was still human. She needed all the normal things any woman might, and Rudy's attention was something that hit the right chord with her.

"I know this sounds silly coming from a prostitute, but I've looked forward to your visits," said Katie.

Rudy pulled Katie to him. Their faces were only inches apart, and Rudy could smell her scent. He looked at her lips and cupped her face in his hands.

"Don't make me do this, Rudy," pleaded Katie, pulling away from him. "Please understand what my life used to be! How horrible it was, and what I feel like now! Don't make me feel like a whore again. Please don't, Rudy."

* * *

The weather on Ossabaw had turned colder and the sky over the island was clear. Robbie watched from the door of the Georgia National Guard Blackhawk helicopter as it descended to the island's landing zone. He'd come because Rudy had said they needed to discuss a new business venture. Robbie's interest had been piqued when Rudy refused to give him any hint what this new venture might be, saying only that they needed to meet face to face.

After dinner, Rudy and Robbie, along with Schwarz, went to Rudy's office. When Rudy was ensconced behind his desk, he looked at Robbie and said, "I have a new business proposal for you. One that will be most lucrative for both you and the company, but it will require your considerable political expertise with the Georgia legislature."

"I'm all ears," responded Robbie, settling back.

"Executive Outcomes has decided it doesn't want to renew its contract to run the Ossabaw colony," said Rudy.

That surprised Robbie. "I don't understand; by the figures I've seen, you're making a hell of a lot of money off this place."

"That's true, Robbie, the money has been good, but this place is a pain in the ass to run. There're headaches at every turn. The company is essentially in the garbage collection business. This is a very labor-intensive operation fraught with manpower issues and all that entails. There's a little more than two years left on the contract. The company is happy with the implant retrieval income, but it's looking to streamline the operation, make it simpler and aboveboard."

"OK," replied Robbie, "and just how do I fit in and what's in it for me?"

"A change in the state laws governing the funeral home business."

"What kind of change?"

"Executive Outcomes has decided it would be profitable to be in the funeral home business. Only the company doesn't want to be a conventional funeral home. The company wants to offer the family of the deceased an opportunity to realize some cash flow from the death of their departed loved ones."

Robbie thought for a moment as he reached for his drink.

"OK, Hoorst, let's cut the bullshit. What are you talking about?"

"The company wants to start a new kind of funeral home where artificial joints and viable organs can be harvested and sold on the international market, just as they are here in this colony, only quite out in the open."

"That shit's against the law, Hoorst," replied Robbie. The gears in his head started to turn, and he began to realize the potential of such a situation.

"That's why you're here today. We want you to use your influence and that of your father to have that law changed."

Robbie knew there had to be more to this scheme and asked, "OK, what else do you have in mind?"

"The company wants to be the sole proprietor of this process," answered Rudy as he bore in on Robbie. "We want the State of Georgia to give the company, and the company alone, the right to run such an enterprise."

Robbie snorted and said, "Yeah, and people in hell want fuckin' ice water! I can see how the law can be changed about selling the body parts, but, what makes you think the state is gonna give your company a monopoly on that business?"

Rudy grinned and said, "A nice piece of the pie to the state, and two million dollars in gold in a Swiss bank account to you."

Robbie sat motionless as he thought, then nodded slightly and answered, "It'll take some work, but I think it could be do-able. Only, it's gonna take more like four million in gold to get the job done."

Rudy looked at Schwarz, then stretched his hand across his desk to shake Robbie's, and said, "I think we have a deal."

* * *

"Claus, things are starting to get crowded again at Butterbean Beach."

"I know we're quickly getting to the saturation point, Dr. Hoorst."

"I've gotten a couple of calls from Congressman McQueen's office about the overcrowding. I'm thinking we may need to take action in a week," said Rudy.

"What kind of inventory is present in the residents, Claus?"

"A rather well-stocked one, Dr. Hoorst."

"So," said Rudy, "if instantly all the residents died and we had one great harvest, how much money would you estimate could be realized?"

"I've been keeping close tabs on that number as the colony began to fill up again, and my best guess is in the neighborhood of around ten million, Dr. Hoorst."

Rudy nodded. "How quickly do you believe we would be able to liquidate these assets?"

"The market is there. My best guess is that we could have everything sold and shipped within five to seven days."

* * *

The next weekend Rudy's wife and children left the island, ostensibly to visit friends in Atlanta. The following Monday, EO guards and all volunteers who worked with Bishop Bryan were informed of a possible contagion in the resident population, and all but essential personnel were to leave the island immediately. Lloyd refused and Rudy reluctantly agreed to let him stay if he wore protective clothing and a breathing mask.

On Tuesday morning, Rudy gave the order to begin infecting incoming residents. That first group of 150 new residents reached the island at three in the afternoon. By midnight, they were beginning to show signs of the infection. By daylight of the next day, their symptoms were full-blown; twelve hours after that, some were unconscious. In another twelve to twenty-four hours, all of the initial group would be dead. Using the same method employed with the *Klebsiella* bacteria, the EO guards had spread the influenza to groups Two and Three, and most of them were dead by the dawn of the following Saturday.

Lloyd was staggered by the scope and rapidity of the infectious process, and after all the residents in his group had died, he sequestered himself in his room at the Main House, refusing Rudy's requests that he join Schwarz and him for meals. Finally, he relented and met with them for supper.

"We were worried about you, Bishop Bryan," said Schwarz.

"You look like you could use a good hot meal, Lloyd," added Rudy passing Lloyd a plate filled with roast beef.

"The work you do here is noble and much needed, Bishop Bryan," said Rudy. "You must eat properly if you want to keep your strength up to continue the fight."

Lloyd blinked and shook his head, trying to throw thoughts from his mind, answering in a distant voice, "You're right, Rudy." He began to fill his fork and nearly shovel food into his mouth. It tasted wonderful, and the feeling of warmth in his stomach was most satisfying. He felt almost guilty about being in a beautiful house eating such delicious food. In the end, that hot meal had a very positive effect—as he pushed back from the table, Lloyd smiled and said, "I feel better, now."

Rudy nodded in approval and reached over to put his hand on Lloyd's shoulder, saying, "Let's go to my office and top this evening off with a good drink and some conversation, shall we?"

Sipping his drink in the office, Lloyd asked, "I don't understand how this infection could be so devastating so quickly, Rudy. Do you have any idea what the organism was that caused it, and how it got onto the island?"

"Did you ever hear about the great influenza of 1918, Lloyd?"

"Yes, I do remember that. I saw something on the TV about it. It said that flu may have killed as many as two hundred million people world-wide."

"Correct, Bishop. That is what I think took this colony out. The funny thing about the Spanish flu was that it took out young and healthy men, soldiers in Europe who had fought in the First World War, young and fit men. Not the kind we see dying from the various flus affecting us today. These young people had healthy immune systems, but the Spanish flu caused what is called in medicine a 'cytokine storm.'"

"I don't understand, Rudy."

"You see, the Spanish flu caused such an overreaction from their immune systems that it killed these young, healthy people and seemed to spare the older and more debilitated ones—the ones whose immune systems couldn't respond with such overwhelming force."

"But we had hundreds and hundreds of debilitated residents in the colony and they died as rapidly as anyone else," answered Lloyd.

"I know, Lloyd. All I can say is that I believe we've seen a new strain of that virus, which takes out everyone. We can take no chances with this virus, Lloyd. That's why I evacuated the island."

"But how did that virus get to this isolated place?" asked Lloyd plaintively.

"All I can say is that one of the new residents brought it here, and it spread just as it did in 1918. Our three groups are in a confined area, one perfect for such communicable diseases," answered Rudy, watching what he'd said sink into Lloyd's mind.

* * *

Judah and John-Morgan were in John-Morgan's study to watch the Neil Cuvato show on the Fox Network.

"One of Will's assistants called me from Washington this morning," said Judah, "and gave me a heads-up about this."

Will was seated across a desk from Cavuto, who began the interview with Will by saying they would first go live to the Ossabaw colony embarkation point just outside of Savannah. To Will's surprise, Rudy appeared on the screen ready to be interviewed by a reporter from the local Fox affiliate.

"Tell us, Dr. Hoorst, just what has happened at the Ossabaw colony," said the reporter.

Fifteen yards behind Rudy was the entrance to Butterbean Beach. A single file line of twenty-five people in various states of health had formed at the entrance and they shuffled forward slowly through the gate, some appearing anxious, some almost oblivious to their surroundings, a few who were obviously high on something.

"We've suffered an overwhelming influenza in the colony, answered Rudy. "It has killed all the residents. Right now, on the island, we're trying to dispose of their remains and decontaminate the living areas in order to receive new residents such as the ones you see here behind me."

"How infectious is this influenza, Dr. Hoorst? Do the people of Savannah have anything to fear?" asked the wide-eyed reporter.

"So far, I'd say there is nothing to worry about off the island, but I don't believe anyone can be certain. Our best guess is that the infection was carried into the colony by one of the new residents. I can't say whether that person has infected anyone on the outside. We'll just have to wait and see."

"Is this a particularly virulent strain of virus, Dr. Hoorst?"

"I think it is quite virulent. About twenty-four hours elapsed from the time our staff first noticed signs of the disease in our residents until they had expired from it."

Rudy could see signs of fear on the reporter's face as she thanked him for his time, then quickly turned to the camera and said, "Back to you in Washington, Neil."

Cavuto turned to Will and said, "So, Congressman, what do you know about all this? Does this trouble you?"

"It troubles me greatly, Neil. But it's a sign of the times we live in. At least we can hope this infection has been confined to Ossabaw Island."

Judah and John-Morgan watched the rest of the interview in silence. When it had ended, Judah said, "I need to tell you about something I've heard, John-Morgan."

"What is it?"

"I have a friend who owns an Irish pub on River Street," responded Judah slowly. "It's a place the single guards from the colony like to go when they have time off. There're girls at this place who like to be around these guys. Apparently the guards always have a pocket full of money. Anyway, my buddy Vic tells me there's this one guard who's got a steady girl who works at his bar, and he sees her whenever he's in town. Vic says this girl told him her boyfriend got real messed up one night and spilled the beans about what really happens out on Ossabaw."

"Just what did this guard say?"

"Now remember, John-Morgan, this is hearsay from my friend Vic who heard it from this girl who works for him who says she heard it from her boyfriend who's a guard on the island, OK?"

"Not the most reliable source of information, I must admit, Judah, but, please, continue!"

"This gal says her boyfriend told her that he and the other guards are instructed to kill certain residents by administering large amounts of whatever drug they're taking in order to overdose them. He told her they do it when a resident has an artificial joint they have a buyer for, or even a tattoo."

John-Morgan slumped in his chair, looked out the window and let his eyes follow the Skidaway River before answering.

"Rudy's already admitted they're harvesting implants and anything else of value. I don't see that it's too much of a leap to think that the company has an unwritten policy of hurrying the residents along to their final destination whenever something of value is to be had at the most opportune time, do you?"

"It fits in with what we already know, and I wouldn't put it past Hoorst for one second."

"So what do you propose we do about it?"

"Right now," said Judah, "nothing, because I believe if they'd kill people with an overdose, they'd kill 'em with an epidemic."

* * *

The morning started clear and cold for the December board meeting of the Ossabaw colony. John-Morgan was waiting aboard *Graf Spee*, engines running and warmed, watching as Judah walked down dock. There was no wind that day and the waters were smooth and calm. The bright sun warmed the boat and helped Judah relax somewhat as he searched for Ossabaw's dock in the distance. When *Graf Spee* had reached Green Island Sound, John-Morgan cut back on the throttles and slowed his boat. He turned to Judah and said, "What have you got in mind for this meeting? Are you planning to confront Rudy over this drug overdose thing?"

"I tossed and turned all night long over this shit," answered Judah, "and I've come to the conclusion that, if all this crap turns out to be true, that fuckin' Hoorst still has us over a barrel!"

"Granted," replied John-Morgan, "but you didn't answer my question. Are you gonna confront Rudy with this stuff?"

"Not directly, no. But, I am gonna make him damn uncomfortable by letting him know I'm suspicious as hell."

"Just remember," said John-Morgan, "Hoorst and his people have been in this business for a long time. They can be ruthless as hell. Just don't go makin' any threats or shit like that, because it might be an unhealthy thing."

"I'm not as stupid as I look."

"Yeah, I know, but I also know you've got a temper and don't like Rudy at all, so just be cool, OK?"

* * *

Judah and John-Morgan were surprised when they reached the Main House. Big Dog and Robbie were there together in the Great Room, talking and joking with each other as if nothing had happened between them.

Rudy had a large fire going, and everyone gathered around it and warmed themselves. Rudy was in a jovial mood and pumped Judah's hand hard when they met. John-Morgan was impressed at how well Judah was hiding his animus for Rudy, watching with fascination as Judah regaled Rudy with stories and quips about politics in Washington.

"Things are beginning to settle down some," said Lloyd. "It helps a lot to have the volunteers back."

"We had three residents pass away during the night," said Lloyd. "They were in the first wave after the last epidemic. I thought they'd last longer, but having AIDS on top of a heavy coke habit doesn't help with longevity."

"Colonel Schwarz will summarize all that's happened in the last month," said Rudy, choosing one of the leather chairs facing the fireplace.

Schwarz was succinct and to the point as he ran down the numbers. "In closing," said Schwarz, "the company has identified the virus that struck this colony as a mutated form of the Spanish influenza of 1918. Our pathologists are sure this strain was introduced by an infected resident. They further report there is little chance the virus can leave the boundaries of this colony, but have added this one caveat. They believe the virus can be spread to humans via birds, as in the avian flu epidemic of several years ago."

Schwarz's words hung in the air for several seconds until Rudy stood and thanked the colonel for his presentation. He turned to the board, saying, "I know you all want to make your inspections of the colony. Just let Colonel Schwarz know where you want to go, and he'll arrange your transportation."

"I'd like to visit the command center," said Judah when Schwarz approached him. "I'd like to review the computer records."

With a nod of his head, Schwarz replied, "Absolutely, sir. I will have you taken there immediately with orders that you are to be given unfettered access to all records."

* * *

Judah was seated in a private room in the command center. He was instructed on how to access the files and left by himself for as long as he wanted. At first, he was frustrated; then, after several hours, Judah began to properly mine the data and found what he'd been looking for. By five in the afternoon, he had a headache, but he knew so much more about the colony than ever before. Finally, he wearily pushed away from the terminal and called for a ride back to the Main House. Dinner was at eight, and he had enough time to shower and take a quick nap. He'd need his strength for what lay ahead.

Everyone seemed to be in a good mood as they met in the Great Room for cocktails and waited to hear the dinner bell.

"Gentlemen," intoned Big Dog, "I have some news I'd like to share with the members of this board."

Everyone grew silent and watched as the Dog eased his way to the front of the fireplace, his back to the flames.

"I'm happy to tell you," said the governor, "all about the progress this state has made with regards to the mortal remains of its citizens. This news is something that dovetails into what's happening here on this island. For some reason beyond my comprehension, it's been against the law in Georgia to reuse an artificial joint that's been in someone's body after they die. These medical devices were simply interred with their remains or destroyed by cremation. By an act of the Georgia legislature, which should take place in this next calendar year, if a person wishes, after their death, to have any implanted devices they may have in their bodies removed and sold on the open market, it will no longer be against Georgia law. This piece of legislation can be of great benefit to their survivors. It will also be a way of offsetting the cost of burial for paupers."

Robbie was leaning on the back of one of the high wing chairs that faced the fire, grinning broadly as his father spoke. "Since this idea is so new and revolutionary, the state feels it should take these first steps with caution and license only a select number of funeral homes to engage in removal of these implants. We all know that Executive Outcomes has a vast knowledge about artificial joint harvesting, and the state is inclined to let this company be the first to operate such an enterprise."

Robbie couldn't help but exchange a glance with Rudy, who nodded slightly in appreciation. It appeared the deal had been done, and Robbie would soon add more to his millions.

John-Morgan gave Judah an I-don't-believe-this-shit look.

As Judah and John-Morgan walked toward the dining room, Judah whispered to John-Morgan, "It's just what I thought it was. They're killing people off for their body parts. We'll talk after dinner."

When the house grew quiet and everyone seemed to be asleep, Rudy and Schwarz met in Rudy's office.

"It took him a while," said Schwarz, "but the Jude found what he wanted in our records. My men were able to trace each and every search Mr. Benjamin made in our records. He was able to piece together orders for implants, tattoos, organs, everything, with the residents who had them and the times they died. Sad to say, sir, it's quite damning if taken as a whole. We might be able to mount a credible defense if taken piece by piece, but not if taken together, sir."

"Did he make any hard copies of this data, Claus?"

"He's much too smart for that, sir. My guess is that he's told, or will tell, Dr. Hartman and Bishop Bryan as soon as he can."

"With no hard copies and after you've erased all computer records of our transactions starting this very evening, what does he have?"

"Only the knowledge he can transfer to the other board members, sir."

"Do you think they know yet, Claus?"

"I watched them very closely during the cocktail hour, at dinner, and afterward. It would be my guess that they don't have the full picture yet. But that will, in all likelihood, change in the morning, Dr. Hoorst."

"But, Claus, with no hard copies and no computer files to examine, it's all speculation, is it not?"

"Quite correct, sir."

"Then, I'm afraid, when he gets back to the mainland, Mr. Benjamin may come down with a bad cold, Claus."

Schwarz looked hard and long at Rudy and quietly said, "I understand completely, sir."

* * *

Sunday morning blossomed like a fresh rosebud. The air was still crisp but not as cold as the day before. The humidity was low and distant tree lines were sharp and clear. Everyone had gathered for morning Mass, and Big Dog stood between Robbie and Katie. Across the room Judah studied their body language, as did John-Morgan.

"Do you believe this shit?" whispered Judah. "You'd think they were cut out of the living section of the Sunday morning paper, the perfect family. A loving father and two well-adjusted siblings."

"I've got a feeling Big Dog had a 'come to Jesus' talk with Robbie about Katie," answered John-Morgan.

With the sound of a bell, Bishop Bryan entered the tent and walked to the front of the altar. With precision and grace, he moved through the rituals of the Latin Mass, and when it came time for the gospel and homily, everyone who knew Lloyd anticipated a stirring sermon. It was the reason Judah attended.

Lloyd stood for several seconds in silence in front of the congregation before he spoke. He took out a handkerchief, wiped his brow and said in a loud voice that carried to the back rows, "You've heard the gospel today about a woman who was a prostitute, a whore. Everybody who lived in her village knew that Mary Magdalene sold her body for money, and she was much reviled. But something changed in her life and she wanted to be clean and feel clean. Is there a soul gathered here today who knows how she felt? Raise your hands!"

Most of the residents responded, but some were so weak they couldn't raise their arms, and others simply stared blankly at Lloyd. Then Lloyd's eyes fell on Katie. Robbie saw it and nervously put his hands into his pockets. Big Dog saw it too, smiled, and put his arm around his daughter.

"Jesus knew what Mary Magdalene was, His apostles had filled Him in on her before He even got to that village. But Jesus knew she was a woman in pain and He knew she would come to Him. While He was meeting with the elders in the temple, she pushed and shoved her way to Jesus and fell on her knees before Him. The elders were appalled and watched in horror as Mary's tears fell on the feet of Jesus, and she dried them with her long beautiful hair, something the men in that village found most attractive. The elders ordered Mary to leave, but Jesus stopped them when he said, 'How many of you offered to wash my feet? Look at this woman, she's washed my feet with her tears and dried them with her hair. I know she's a sinner, and I also know that each one of you is a sinner, too.' Then Jesus looked slyly at the elders. He knew some of them had been her customers."

Bishop Bryan paused and his gaze fell on Robbie. "How many of you here would condemn a person like Mary, who was on her knees begging for forgiveness and salvation. How many of you here might be her customers?"

With no further words, Lloyd climbed up the steps to the altar. At the top he turned and said, "Let he who is without sin, cast the first stone."

"Good shot, Bishop," said Judah under his breath.

CHAPTER ELEVEN

HOWARD

One man in a thousand, Solomon says,
Will stick more close than a brother.
—Rudyard Kipling, *The Thousandth Man*

On Monday afternoon, EO's big Chinook helicopter landed on schedule at the Ossabaw colony. Freshly packaged and newly sold joints, various other body parts, and gold harvested from the residents was loaded onto the craft to be shipped all around the world. Just before the Chinook was about to lift off, two men wearing EO uniforms stepped off the chopper and into a waiting Humvee with Colonel Schwarz behind the wheel. Both were black men in their late twenties, well-developed, with a military bearing. Not a word was exchanged among the men until they pulled up in front of the Main House.

Schwarz turned to the men, saying, "I'm Colonel Claus Schwarz, second in command on this island. You both know why you have been chosen for this job. In a moment you will be meeting Dr. Rudolph Hoorst, the island commandant, who will assess your individual qualifications and brief you on what you'll be tasked to do. Any questions?"

In unison both men replied, "No, sir."

"Enter," said Rudy, leaning back in his chair as Schwarz and the two new men marched to Rudy's desk and stood at attention. With a wave of his hand, Rudy told the men to be at ease and carefully looked them over.

"I've gone over your dossiers, gentlemen," said Rudy, "and it appears you both are qualified and experienced for this mission." Rudy opened a manila folder on his desk, glanced at it and up at the man to his right, asking, "You're William 'Buck' Rogers, originally from Detroit, honorably discharged from the Third Infantry Division after six years of duty and multiple tours in Iraq and Afghanistan, are you not, Sergeant?"

Buck stood at parade rest and stared straight ahead as he barked his reply, "Sir, yes, sir."

Rudy looked at the man next to him and said, "You're Kwame Johnson from New York City with an almost identical background as Sergeant Rogers, is that correct, Staff Sergeant Johnson?"

Mirroring Buck Rogers, Staff Sergeant Johnson roared, "Sir, yes, sir."

Rudy smiled, stood and moved in front of his desk.

"Please, gentlemen, remove your game faces for a second, relax and have a beer with me and Colonel Schwarz. You have some important work to do, and the Colonel and I want to be sure you're up to the job."

Both men instantly loosened up, their arms by their sides, their eyes meeting Rudy's. Schwarz went to the bar and returned with four bottles of Budweiser, and Rudy offered a toast to a successful mission. Then Schwarz began to brief the men on what they had to accomplish.

"You are tasked with permanently neutralizing an individual who has become a threat to the security and well-being of our company." Schwarz reached into his vest pocket and produced a photograph saying, "This is your target. His name is Judah Benjamin. He is one of the board members overseeing this colony. He is also well known in this community and has a high political profile. What we want is a take-down that appears to be an act of random violence. One that can only be construed as such. Do you understand?"

Both men nodded.

"What we have in mind is a robbery of Mr. Benjamin at the gas station where he likes to fuel up his Jaguar," continued Schwarz. "This robbery will go quite sour and result in the termination of Mr. Benjamin. It's imperative that no one suspects this is a professional operation. This man's connections run all the way to the top and fan out from there. If there's any indication to the contrary, it could be a problem for the company."

"We'll do the job properly," said Rogers as he took Judah's picture from Schwarz, studied it, then passed it to his partner.

Rudy leaned against his desk and listened as Schwarz and the two began to discuss the details of the operation. After a few minutes, Rudy interrupted saying, "As the colonel told you, this has to be a very credible scenario. I think it's safe to assume this whole operation will be captured on video surveillance and subject to repeated viewings by the authorities. The two of you must appear to be local thugs out for an easy take-down. Do you know where I'm coming from?"

"Yes, sir, we do," answered Johnson.

"Good," said Rudy, "I'd like to see how you'll act the part."

Rogers looked at Johnson who gave him the "you go first" nod. Instantly, Buck Rogers transformed himself into a young black man filled with anger and hate. He bobbed his head from side to side and gestured menacingly with his hands as he seemed to circle Rudy. His face was contorted and soon words began to spew from his mouth.

"You want to know what I got, you fuckin' crackah mothafucka," said Rogers as he moved in close to Rudy's face, and spittle from his moving lips hit Rudy's cheeks. "Well, I show you what the fuck I got, you fuckin' pasty white boy."

Rogers pulled his uniform blouse up with his left hand to reveal the butt of a 9mm pistol in his waistband. He cocked his head back, put his right hand on the gun, and said, "Maybe after I off that little Jew mothafucka, I be coming after your wife and fuck her in her lily-white ass."

Rogers was right in Rudy's face when Rudy looked at Schwarz, nodded and said, "That's good work, Sergeant Rogers, I'm impressed."

As if flicking a light switch, Buck changed his demeanor in an instant and was once more formal and deferential.

* * *

The next morning Buck and Kwame were stepping off the Ossabaw ferry at Butterbean Beach. They were again dressed in EO uniforms and acted like two guards who'd been granted some liberty time. They were dropped off in downtown Savannah at an apartment the company owned. There they changed into the appropriate street clothes, picked up cash and fake ID's as well as the keys to a white beat-up Chevy Blazer. As soon as they stepped out the door of the apartment, they assumed the demeanor of street thugs intent on stealing something from somebody. The swagger stopped when they got in the Blazer. They were professionals and began to solidify their plan as they drove to Isle of Hope.

Buck and Kwame drove past Judah's house on Bluff Drive and noted his car in the driveway. They circled back around several times wondering when Judah would be leaving. The men realized they stood out in the neighborhood. They also knew the shortest route for Judah to take to the BP station was Skidaway Road and decided to fake engine trouble along the road in front of the gates to Wormslow Plantation.

Buck raised the Blazer's hood while Kwame opened the tailgate and pretended to be looking for tools. For twenty minutes both men had their heads under the hood watching for Judah's car to pass. Finally, their patience was rewarded when they saw Judah drive by in his black Jag. Nonchalantly, Kwame closed the hood while Buck climbed into the driver's seat, started the engine and headed toward Sandfly, a quarter-mile away. When they reached the only traffic light in the little community, they spotted Judah at the BP station. He was outside his car at the gas pump, getting ready to fill it up. The Blazer continued up Skidaway, then quickly cut through the Piggly Wiggly parking lot and circled behind the station. The men had carefully reconnoitered the station and had an agreed-upon plan to take Judah out. They had planned on everything, except Howard.

* * *

Howard was a fixture on Isle of Hope and in Sandfly. He was in his sixties and had been born and raised on Isle of Hope, and everybody in the area knew him. He came from a good family and had a mother who adored him. The only trouble was Howard's behavioral problems, which started at Isle of Hope elementary school.

In the 1950s, no one had ever heard of dyslexia, but Howard knew about it. From his early years in school, he couldn't read, no matter how hard he tried. None of the letters made any sense to him. His classmates began to think of him as stupid and treated him as such. This hurt him greatly, and he internalized that pain until it began to spill out in anger.

While Howard wasn't blessed with the ability to understand the written word, he did have other gifts. He was glib of tongue, ruggedly handsome, possessed of musical ability and built like a prizefighter. When he began to bundle those gifts together, he became somewhat of a celebrity in Savannah. But there was a fly in Howard's ointment.

Alcohol unleashed the anger and resentment that had built up in Howard over the years, and it caused him to become a well-known brawler around town. Howard was somebody no one wanted to mess with, particularly when he was drinking, which was often.

Eventually, Howard's musical abilities drew him away from Savannah to Nashville, where he hooked up with Johnny Cash and his band. For several years, he toured with Johnny and partied with the crew. Somewhere along the line, too much booze, too much pot, and way too much cocaine did a number on Howard's mind, and he found himself back in Savannah living at his mother's house again.

Wearing fringed buckskins and an Indian headdress, Howard walked all over Isle of Hope and Sandfly, carrying a six-foot walking staff topped with eagle feathers. He talked to anyone who would listen and when they did, he'd tell them about the spirit world and revelations he received from God. That was Howard and he'd been like that for the last twenty years.

While he was a little menacing to strangers, to the people of the area, Howard was an odd but gentle soul. As time wore on, he'd often walk to the BP station and sometimes panhandle for cigarette money. Most of the time, he'd sit on the oyster shell mound across from the Driftaway Café, dressed like an Indian, staff in hand and watch the world go by.

Judah had known Howard for years and often gave him a few dollars whenever he'd see him at the gas station and listen patiently as Howard rambled on about Jesus and how He was coming again. Just the day before, Judah had stopped and given him a ride to Sandfly. When Howard got out of the car, he turned to Judah and said, "Jesus has asked me to watch over you, Judah, and I always do what He tells me." Judah thanked him for his concern and chalked it up as another Howard story he'd later tell his friends.

The next morning, Howard was perched on the oyster mound, watching the traffic. He noticed the white Blazer and the two dudes in it; he'd never seen the car or its occupants before. He watched it pass by three more times, always taking the same route past the BP station then across the Pig's parking lot, then through the BP past the gas pumps and back onto Skidaway Road. On the fourth pass, Howard stood, asked for guidance from Jesus and walked to the BP where he sat next to the ice machine in front of the store. Silently he watched as Judah pulled up to the pump and got out of his Jag. Judah didn't see Howard, who was all but hidden behind the ice machine.

Facing the pump, Judah sighed when he saw that premium gas was $28.56 a gallon. With a shrug he inserted the nozzle into his tank and squeezed the handle. He didn't pay attention to the white Blazer when it pulled up to the next pump. His back was to it and he never noticed Kwame and Buck as they quickly exited the Blazer, drew their weapons and moved toward Judah. In an instant they had him pinned against the side of his car. Buck shoved a Colt .45 pistol under his chin while Kwame rifled through Judah's pockets, taking his wallet with over a thousand in cash.

Judah was completely surprised and terrified. All he could say was, "Take whatever you want, just don't shoot me." Then he felt his knees begin to buckle and fold as Buck pushed the pistol barrel harder under his chin.

Howard saw everything and sprang to his feet. He was wearing moccasins and quietly and quickly circled in behind Buck and Kwame. In one great swing of his staff, Howard hit Kwame over the head, then grabbed Buck's pistol and twisted it backward, causing it to fire, at the same time breaking Buck's trigger finger. The bullet cut a furrow across the left side of Judah's neck, nicking the jugular vein, sending out pulses of blood, but missing the carotid artery. For long seconds there was screaming and cursing and blood everywhere as Judah held his neck and crumpled to the ground.

Howard had his staff raised high, ready to rain a crowning blow on Buck, when Kwame regained his senses, pointed his Glock 9mm at the center of Howard's chest and pulled the trigger. Kwame's aim was off, and he hit Howard in the shoulder area. Not feeling a thing, running on the same adrenaline that had seen him through so many fights before, Howard pressed the attack with his staff. But his wound and his age were catching up with him. Somehow, Kwame managed to help Buck to the Blazer, and they were speeding through the light at Montgomery Crossroads before the hysterical cashier inside could stop shaking enough to dial 911.

Judah was sprawled on the pavement, his back against his car, left hand pressed firmly against his neck. As he gasped for air, he could feel the warmth of his blood as it oozed between his fingers and ran down his neck. He wasn't in any pain, just totally stunned. When he looked up, he saw Howard stumble a little, his left arm hanging limply by his side. With his right arm, Howard steadied himself against the gas pump, then eased down next to Judah. In the distance, they could hear the wail of sirens.

"You gonna be OK, Judah," said Howard, "I seen where that bullet just nicked you on the neck. They'll have you in the hospital real soon."

"You saved my life, Howard," panted Judah, gulping for air. "You'll be fine, too."

Judah didn't know how serious Howard's wound was, but Howard did. The bullet had entered through his arm pit, severed the humeral artery and nerve, and shattered his shoulder joint before it exited from his back.

Lumped next to Judah, Howard whispered, "I ain't gonna make it through this one, Judah. They done got me with a good one."

"No, Howard!" cawed Judah, rolling his head toward him. "You're gonna make it, man, you're too tough, you're Howard!"

Howard tilted his head up, looking toward the sky, and he said peacefully, "I can see that light comin' for me, Judah. It's beautiful, man. It's gettin' brighter, I'm tellin' ya, Jesus is comin' for me. I ain't in no pain, I'm happy all over."

With all the strength he could muster, Judah cried out, "Don't give up on me, Howard, don't give up! I need you to tell me about Jesus!"

Howard's head fell to the left and he looked Judah in the eye. "He's comin' for me right now, brotha, that beautiful light is gettin' brighter, and soon I'll be a part of that light. I wish you could see it."

Struggling, Judah was able to pull himself into a sitting position facing Howard.

"The ambulance is only a few blocks away, Howard, just hang on!"

But Judah could see the life quickly ebbing from Howard's body and whispered, "What do you want me to tell your friends?"

"Tell 'em I died in the bosom of Jesus. Tell 'em you saw me go to Heaven."

As Howard bled out, his breathing became very shallow very quickly. His chest began to heave, his mouth wide open as he fought for air. At the end, in one final lucid moment, Howard's eyes focused on Judah and he said with surprising strength, "Them boys was stalking you all mornin', Judah." After that, Howard was gone.

* * *

Rudy sat placidly behind his desk waiting for word from Buck and Kwame, while Schwarz impatiently paced the length of the office. When his cell phone rang, Schwarz quickly flipped it open. His neck became rigid and the muscles in his jaw tightened as he received the bad news from Kwame.

"The news isn't good, sir."

"I gathered that from your expression," replied Rudy, standing.

"They were surprised at the gas station by some man dressed like an Indian," said Schwarz, an incredulous look on his face. "Everything went as planned until this person appeared out of nowhere and struck Johnson over the head with a walking stick, knocking him out. Then this character snatched the pistol from Rogers' hand. Johnson said the Jude was shot in the neck. He doesn't know if the wound was fatal. He also said he shot the Indian in the chest, and he and Rogers were lucky to get away clean."

"I see," answered Rudy, his eyes sweeping across the floor in thought.

"What do we do now, Dr. Hoorst?"

Rudy shook his head in disgust and rubbed his brow. "Nothing other than making sure those two amateurs we thought were professionals aren't caught. We simply wait to hear from the mainland about what's taken place, and then act accordingly. If we're lucky, Benjamin is dead. If that's the case, this mission won't be a complete disaster. I just want you to be sure those two aren't apprehended and interrogated, Claus. Do you understand me?"

* * *

Hannah received a call from Memorial Medical Center only minutes after the ambulance carrying her husband arrived at the hospital's emergency room. She was deeply shaken but had the presence of mind to call John-Morgan. He and Ann-Marie picked up Hannah and went with her to the ER. While Ann-Marie sat with Hannah in the waiting area, John-Morgan found his way to the treatment room where Judah was being examined.

John-Morgan was relieved to find Dr. Carl Boyd, the chief trauma surgeon, inspecting Judah's neck wound. An IV line had already been established, and a quarter grain of morphine had been administered. When John-Morgan approached the treatment table, Dr. Boyd looked up and said, "Good to see you again, Dr. Hartman. I think your buddy is gonna be OK."

Judah's head was turned completely to his right and a sterile drape covered most of it, but John-Morgan could still see his face. Moving in as close as he could, he looked at Judah and saw he was conscious.

"How're you doing, man?" asked John-Morgan, "You in much pain?"

Judah blinked several times before he whispered, "I don't feel shit."

"That's a good thing," said John-Morgan. Then he looked closer at the wound on Judah's neck and asked, "How bad is it, Carl?"

"This is one lucky fella, John-Morgan. Don't see too many that come as close as this one and live to tell about it. My only concern is the amount of tissue damage caused by the muzzle blast and the extent of the burn from the flash. We won't know that for maybe another forty-eight hours or so. Probably the worst case will be that the tissue trauma is bad enough to require some plastic work."

John-Morgan crouched next to the table so his face was level with Judah's. "They're gonna put you to sleep in a few minutes so they can repair your wound. I'll be with you when you wake up, OK?"

"OK," replied Judah weakly. Just before John-Morgan stood to leave, Judah opened his eyes wide and looked at him.

"This wasn't some kinda robbery. Just before he died, Howard told me those guys were stalking me, John-Morgan. They were pros, man. Somebody wants me dead."

* * *

Rudy and Schwarz waited in the Main House for two hours before the call they'd been expecting finally came. It was from John-Morgan, who told Rudy about the shooting.

"Will you tell Lloyd Bryan for me?" asked John-Morgan.

"As soon as I put this phone down, I'll go over to Group One and tell him in person, John-Morgan," answered Rudy in voice filled with fear and anxiety over the bad news he had just been given. "Then I'll come to the hospital. This is absolutely appalling."

Lloyd was hearing confessions when Rudy entered the great tent in Group One.

"Judah's been shot and severely wounded in a robbery. He's at the hospital now and is in surgery. I'm leaving for the mainland immediately."

Lloyd was staggered. He looked up at Rudy, saying, "I'm going to Savannah with you."

* * *

The blades of the black EO Huey cut through the air with giant thuds as it descended to the parking lot in front of the Memorial Hospital emergency room. A small knot of local television reporters watched as the chopper touched down. Rudy and Lloyd climbed out and moved quickly toward the ER entrance. Both men were recognized by the reporters, who shouted unanswered questions at them as they passed by.

John-Morgan shook Rudy's hand and said, "Thanks for being here, Rudy, and thanks for bringing Lloyd with you."

Rudy sputtered a little, seeming at a loss for words, then finally was able to say, "This is terrible, John-Morgan. What can I do to help?"

"Just stay here with Hannah. We won't be long."

Once John-Morgan and Lloyd were in the hallway, John-Morgan leaned close to Lloyd's ear and whispered, "Judah told me he thinks this was a planned hit. He doesn't believe this was some robbery gone bad. I know all this sounds a little crazy, Lloyd, but you need to know what Judah told me on my boat the last time we came back from the island."

Lloyd was motionless as he asked, "And what was that?"

"Bottom line is that Judah went through all the computer records of the colony when he was at our last board meeting. He concentrated on admissions to the island, deaths, implanted hardware in the residents, the whole shootin' match. He thinks Rudy and his boys have been killing people way before they would have died from their drug habits. He also thinks the company engineered those last two epidemics that took out all the residents in one fell swoop, then harvested anything that was valuable from their bodies. He thinks they'll do it again and again. Essentially, Judah believes Ossabaw isn't a drug colony where people come to eventually die from their addictions; he believes it's a death factory where EO matches orders for saleable body parts and kills these people when they've got a buyer."

"And does he believe," asked Lloyd, "that Rudy has tried to have him murdered to keep him silent?"

"He's very suspicious."

CHAPTER TWELVE

SUPERNATURAL

Miracles are propitious accidents, the
natural causes of which are too complicated
to be readily understood.
—George Santayna

The story about Judah's being shot and robbed was the top local news for twenty-four hours before the national networks picked up on it. What had elevated it to national attention was that Will McQueen had suspended his campaign in the New Hampshire primary and returned to Savannah to be with Judah. After that, every major broadcast and cable network had a correspondent in place at Memorial Medical Center, clamoring for a chance to learn more about what had happened to the architect of Congressman McQueen's run for the Presidency.

More than fifty reporters and a dozen TV cameras were packed into a conference room at the hospital when Will and John-Morgan finally entered, and the room fell silent.

"My name is Will McQueen. I'm the Congressman from this District of Georgia. Two days ago, my good friend and trusted adviser, Judah Benjamin, was attacked at a gas station in the little community of Sandfly just outside of Savannah. He was shot and robbed. At this time, that's about all we know. The Savannah metro police have been investigating this horrible crime and have assured me no stone will be left unturned. I now want to introduce you to Dr. John-Morgan Hartman who will brief you on Mr. Benjamin's medical condition."

"I'm John-Morgan Hartman and I'm Judah Benjamin's personal physician. Mr. Benjamin received a gunshot wound to the left side of his neck. Thankfully, this wound does not involve any major structures. Yesterday he underwent repair of that wound and is resting well. No long-term serious damage or impairment to the health of Mr. Benjamin is anticipated. I'm happy to report that, barring any unforeseen circumstances, Mr. Benjamin should be able to return to a normal life in a few months."

* * *

Rudy had stayed at the hospital for six hours, demonstrating apparent sincere concern for Judah and sympathy for Hannah. Just before dark, he flew back to Ossabaw.

Rudy went directly to his office where Colonel Schwarz was waiting. When Rudy entered, he said only, "He's going to live and will be fine in a few months."

Schwarz nodded, waited for Rudy to sit down, and replied, "I have Rogers and Johnson. Would you care to see them now?"

Rudy snorted, "Yes, Colonel, bring them in."

Rogers and Johnson were marched into Rudy's office. Rogers had his right hand wrapped in an Ace bandage and his arm in a sling.

The loudest sound in the room was their breathing. Neither Rudy nor Schwarz said anything for several moments. Finally, Schwarz said, "Perhaps the two of you would like to explain to Dr. Hoorst how you so miserably failed in your mission."

Buck and Kwame remained braced at attention, but the fear in their eyes was quite evident.

"Well," said Rudy softly, "now is the time to speak up and help the Colonel and me make some sense of this disaster."

"For God's sake, you two fools," said Schwarz, "stand at ease and spit it out! This will be your only chance."

"Sir," pleaded Buck as he looked at Rudy, "a civilian dressed like an Indian came from nowhere. We'd reconnoitered the station several times and had the routine down pat. Me and Johnson have been on a bunch of missions for the company. You know the quality of work we do. This guy was almost supernatural in his speed and strength. We were lucky to get away as clean as we did. There just wasn't no way we coulda planned for what came down, sir."

Rudy leaned back in his chair and looked at Kwame.

"Do you have anything else to add, Sergeant Johnson?"

"It's like Sergeant Rogers said, sir. That Indian guy was as quick and strong as anybody I've ever been in a fight with, sir."

Rudy leaned forward in his chair and looked at Schwarz, then at the two men before him. "For the time being, you will be stationed here on the island, assigned to guard duty. You may thank your lucky stars I'm inclined to take into account your past duty to the company. I have no doubt there will be some type of video from that gas station showing this incident. I suggest you pray quite fervently that it backs up your story."

* * *

Martha MacCallum of *Fox News* looked into the camera, blue eyes burning brightly, and said, "We've got this really incredible video from our affiliate in Savannah, Georgia, that we're going to show you, and I have to tell our viewers this is the most remarkable thing I've seen in all my time in television news."

Her co-host, Bill Hemmer, nodded, saying, "I have to agree with you, Martha, this is really something you don't want to miss, folks. But it's pretty rough and gruesome."

"That's right," added Martha, "but it has something in it that has resonated with a lot of folks. Let me set this thing up. We reported several days ago about the robbery and shooting of Congressman Will McQueen's campaign manager at a gas station in the little community of Sandfly, just outside of Savannah. Judah Benjamin's life was saved by a well-known character in Sandfly who is simply called Howard. He thwarted the robbery and, in doing so, was shot and killed by one of the robbers. This video shows the entire incident."

The video was clear and bright as it showed Judah inserting the pump nozzle into his gas tank. A couple of seconds later Buck and Kwame appeared wearing hoodies, ski-masks and gloves. It showed Buck as he pinned Judah against his car with a pistol shoved under his chin while Kwame rifled through Judah's pockets. Then Howard appeared and hit Kweame over the head with his walking staff and pulled Buck's pistol from under Judah's neck. The discharge of the weapon was caught perfectly, as was Howard's getting shot and sitting down next to Judah while he bled to death. The most remarkable thing about the whole video was Howard's face as he told Judah he was dying and that he could see the light coming for him. The sun was at just the right angle and it illuminated Howard's face perfectly. The words he spoke were easily understood and there was a perceptible aura about Howard in his last moments.

"Now that's some incredible video," said Hemmer, looking over at Martha, who had tears in her eyes.

"I'm sorry, Bill, but every time I watch that, I'm overcome. To a lot of people, what we just watched was a person who saw God coming for him. Thousands of people have commented on this piece. It's gone viral now, and we're hearing church leaders from all over the world are using it as a teaching tool."

* * *

Colonel Schwarz was notified by his men at the command and control center that a video of the BP station shooting was being played on national television. In minutes he and Rudy were huddled in front of the TV in the Great Room of the Main House.

As the action unfolded, both men watched intently, then replayed it several more times. Finally, satisfied they'd seen enough, Rudy and Schwarz walked to fireplace and warmed themselves.

"What is your impression, Claus?"

"It appears things happened exactly as Rogers and Johnson described, sir."

"I agree, Claus, that does seem to be the case. However, I have this gnawing feeling there is another shoe yet to fall."

"How do you mean, Dr. Hoorst?"

"Didn't Rogers and Johnson say they had thoroughly reconnoitered the station? I believe they told us they had driven through there several times as they rehearsed their mission, did they not?"

"You're correct, sir."

"My suspicion, Claus, is that the video surveillance system that recorded the attack was also in full operation when our two operatives cased the station. I fear their faces may have been recorded and that there is a possibility they can be identified."

"I see, sir," answered Schwarz. "What would you like me to do for now?"

"Be sure there is no paper or computer trail that links these men to us, Claus."

"That's going to be impossible, Dr. Hoorst."

Rudy looked quickly at Schwarz, asking sharply, "Why is that?"

"When they first signed on with the company, they had just gotten out of the U.S. Army, sir. We used them as private bodyguards in both Iraq and Afghanistan. They had U.S. passports and EO ID's, sir. There's no way we can scrub that record completely clean. All their movements have been recorded by the State Department as well as Defense, Dr. Hoorst."

Rudy nodded and said, "I understand, Claus. What I want you to do is find out if there are any records that tie them to this facility."

"I believe I can tell you now, sir, there are no such records. We flew them in from the UAE on a company plane directly to Hunter Army Airfield. They immediately boarded our chopper and were brought here. They went through no customs along the way, and there is no record these two ever left the Emirates."

"Well, Claus, that makes me feel a little better, but I'm still somewhat on edge about what other apples might fall from this tree."

* * *

Rudy's fears proved to be well-founded. The video showing Buck and Kwame driving through the BP station was aired a little more than twenty-four hours later. There was one sequence that clearly showed a face and it belonged to Buck, who was behind the wheel of the white Blazer. It was freeze-framed and a plea for community support was made every time it was shown.

The Savannah police went to the FBI with the shot and the Feds ran it through their massive data bank. A positive hit came up from both Buck's military photo ID as well as his passport. The hunt was on, and it soon led to Executive Outcomes.

The company gave all appearances of complete cooperation and guided investigators through Buck's record with the company. When he had finally been traced to the UAE, the trail turned ice-cold. The explanation from Executive Outcomes was that Rogers had apparently gone rogue and, from what they could tell, was working for the government of Somalia as a mercenary. Further probing failed to provide any new information and the investigation stopped there.

* * *

"We have a decision to make, Claus," said Rudy as they both stood on Ossabaw's long dock and watched the winter sunset. "What is your opinion about the disposition of Rogers and Johnson?"

"They're good men, sir, and I hate to lose good men, but I believe they've become a serious liability."

"Dead men tell no tales, Colonel."

At breakfast the next morning Schwarz reported to Rudy that the situation "had been sanitized."

CHAPTER THIRTEEN

SUSPICION

Yon Cassius has a lean and hungry
look;
He thinks too much: such men are
dangerous.
—William Shakespeare, *Julius Caesar*

It had been almost a month since Rudy had visited Katie at the beach cottage. So much had been going on, he hadn't had the luxury of fantasizing about her, much less the time to visit with her. As he turned down the trail leading to the beach, Rudy smiled at the thought of seeing Katie.

"I was wondering where you'd been," said Katie as she opened the cottage door.

"Nothing but work," answered Rudy, stepping inside where Katie's fragrance greeted him.

"My goodness, you look pale, Rudy."

"I just finished my monthly inspection of the crematoriums and recovery units. It's nasty."

"You look like you could use a drink."

"I'd like that very much," replied Rudy, walking to the balcony and looking out over the ocean. Moments later Katie was handing him a glass of Glenfiddich, saying, "This should make you feel better."

Rudy accepted it and took a sip as his eyes wandered all over Katie. She gave him that excited feeling.

"I understand you've been a great help to Lloyd Bryan."

Rudy watched Katie's lips as she said, "Strange as it seems, Rudy, I think I gather some kind of inner peace by working there."

"I wish I could find some inner peace by working here," said Rudy, turning back to the ocean. "Truth is, this whole situation is starting to wear me down. I'll be glad when my time here is finished."

"At least you can leave," said Katie, "I can't." She added, "Far too much has happened in my life. I could never live on the outside again."

"Your father asked me to let you go. I can do that, Katie, I have that power. Do you want to leave this place?"

Katie dropped her head for a moment and when she looked back up at Rudy, her eyes were filled with tears that crept down her cheeks. Then Katie completely broke down and began to sob. Rudy put his arms around her and pulled her to him. She did not resist and found great comfort in his embrace. She allowed herself that pleasure for many seconds. But when she felt Rudy's kindness turning into physical arousal, she pushed back from him, saying, "I don't want to go there, Rudy."

* * *

When Rudy returned to the Main House, his wife had a delicious meal waiting for him. For an hour after dinner, he helped his two sons with their homework, and after that watched a movie with his wife. When they went to bed at ten, he made love to her, then drifted to sleep minutes later.

Around two in the morning, Rudy's nightmare returned with great intensity. All at once, Rudy was awake in his bed, drenched in sweat and gasping for breath. Beside him, Carolyn slept quietly as Rudy slipped out of the bed. He went to his dresser where he stripped off the wet T-shirt and pulled a clean one over his head. Still breathing heavily, Rudy staggered a few steps back as he tried to regain control. Then he made his way down to his office, where he closed the doors, went to his bar and fixed himself a strong drink. That one went down quickly, followed by another. He carried his third one to his desk and seated himself. He hoped the alcohol would make him fall asleep again, so he rested his head on the desk and closed his eyes.

When Carolyn awoke the next morning and found Rudy already gone, she thought nothing of it. When she went to the dining room and found only Colonel Schwarz present, she was surprised. After a wait of thirty minutes, she and Schwarz decided to look for Rudy. The first place they looked was Rudy's office, where they found him passed out. Schwarz and Carolyn pulled Rudy into a sitting position. He reeked of alcohol and, when he finally was able to speak, his words were garbled.

Carolyn was horrified; she'd never seen her husband in such a state. "What's wrong, Rudy," she sobbed.

"The dream, the dream again!"

"I think I know what's going on, Mrs. Hoorst," said Schwarz. "Let's get him upstairs and in bed, and I'll explain the problem. It's not his fault; nothing like that at all."

Carolyn sat at the head of the dining room table. She pretended to be eating, but only pushed the scrambled eggs around on her plate as Claus explained Rudy's nightmare while Eva Schwarz and Bishop Bryan listened.

"He's never said a word about this nightmare to me," intoned Carolyn as her eyes welled with tears.

"That's a normal thing for a man of Dr. Hoorst's stature and training," replied Schwarz. "He was raised to place such things aside and soldier on. I know, I was brought up in the same fashion. Dr. Hoorst deals with such anxiety by internalizing it. He will most certainly overcome this present situation."

Carolyn looked at Lloyd pleadingly as Eva placed her hand over Carolyn's and said, "Dr. Hoorst will be fine, he's a strong man."

By noon, Rudy was up, showered, shaved, dressed and seated in the dining room ready for lunch. However, try as he might, the effects of the previous night were clearly visible.

"I guess," said Rudy hesitantly, "all of you know about the terrible night I had. I apologize to everyone, most especially to my wife, Carolyn, for my behavior. That nightmare was the most vivid and terrible dream I've ever experienced. I've had it several times, and it's completely debilitating. Out of fear and desperation I got myself drunk, trying to find some kind of solace. Again, I apologize for my conduct."

There were words of support and consolation from Schwarz and his wife. Lloyd was moved by Rudy's appearance and words and said, "Why don't we talk after lunch?"

Rudy and Lloyd went to Rudy's office and sat facing each other in the chairs in front of Rudy's desk.

"I'm afraid to sleep now, the dream was that real and terrible."

"Why don't you ask John-Morgan about it? Perhaps he can suggest some type of medication that will help."

"I don't want to be dependent on drugs, Lloyd."

"I understand, Rudy, but you have to sleep. Perhaps something mild will block out the nightmare."

"I doubt it, but I'll try just about anything, Lloyd."

There was another long silence as Rudy stared out the window, watching his two sons play. Then he looked back at Lloyd and said, "It's Saturday again. You always hear my confession on Saturdays. Will you hear it now?"

"Of course," answered Lloyd as he reached into his coat pocket and removed the purple stole he wore when performing the sacrament. He kissed it and placed it over his neck, closed his eyes and bowed his head.

"Bless me, Father," said Rudy, "for I have sinned. It's been a week since my last confession. Nothing much has changed. I still masturbate and fantasize about having sex with other women. I lost my temper several days ago with one of the guards and cursed him. I apologized to him, but I could tell he'd been hurt."

Rudy cleared his throat and continued, "Yesterday, I visited Katie McFarland at the cottage, and I...I...was tempted by her beauty. I've even fantasized about having sex with her. For these and all the other sins I cannot remember, I am truly sorry."

Lloyd had rested his head on his folded hands and didn't move at all for almost a minute. Then slowly, he raised his head, opened his eyes and looked into Rudy's.

"You need to avoid the occasion of sin, Rudy. You need to stay away from the cottage and, when you must go there, you should have someone with you at all times. Both you and Katie are in danger when you're alone together. She has come a long way, but she's still weak enough to backslide. For you to take advantage of her would be exceedingly sinful."

"I haven't taken advantage of her at all."

"Not yet, but you may, so stay away from the cottage."

Rudy and Lloyd again sat silent as they looked at each other. Then Lloyd said firmly, "I want to know if you are ordering residents to be killed by overdosing them so their implants can be harvested when you have an immediate sale for the item."

Rudy had already prepared himself for such a question after the confrontation he had with Judah about implant harvesting months ago. He shifted in his chair, let his eyes drop to the floor, then raised them to meet Lloyd's. "You've been here from the beginning. Have you ever seen anything that comes even close to what you're asking me? Have you seen me or my men do anything that approaches such a thing? My answer to you is, no!"

Rudy's back straightened and his eyes tightened a little when he said, "Now, I have a question for you, Lloyd. What proof do you have that residents are dying prematurely so their body parts can be harvested?"

Lloyd watched Rudy transform himself from a wounded and humble penitent back to the strong persona he exhibited the first time they'd met. Lloyd's back also straightened and his eyes narrowed, too, when he shot back at Rudy, "Judah says when he searched the company's records, he found a direct link concerning the time the company got orders for certain parts and when residents who had those parts in them died. Both he and I have also noticed residents we thought should have lived many days, if not weeks, longer, all of a sudden found dead in their beds."

Rudy smiled, relaxed and leaned back in his chair. Then he zeroed in on Lloyd and said, "This colony is a gift from God to the pitiful souls who put themselves here. What you and I do here each day is an act of mercy for these people. The company certainly makes money from this colony, but who will do it for free? While I have realized from the beginning that Judah Benjamin didn't care for me or my leadership style, he is still only a politician, and you are still only a priest. Neither one of you is qualified to make a judgment about how long a resident, any resident, will live. As for Judah's interpretation of the computer data, such data doesn't exist."

Lloyd was cold-faced as he looked back at Rudy and responded, "I don't believe you. I think Judah has your number." Pausing for effect, Lloyd said, "One more thing, Rudy. Was the company responsible for what happened to Judah?"

"You mean the robbery at the gas station? Ha! If it weren't such a serious circumstance, I'd take your question as some kind of bad joke, Bishop! No, the company had nothing to do with what happened to Judah. Don't be ridiculous!"

Without saying word, Lloyd stood, removed the stole from around his neck, neatly folded it and placed it back in his pocket. Then looking at Rudy, he said in a sober voice, "I can't give you absolution, Rudy. I think you're lying to me about this place."

* * *

"You appear to be feeling better, sir," said Schwarz as his horse walked next to Rudy's down the trail to the beach.

"I am feeling better, Claus; at least physically."

Schwarz stopped his horse and turned in his saddle to Rudy.

"Is there another problem, sir?"

"Yes, and unfortunately it involves Bishop Bryan."

"How so, sir?"

The two men were in the thickest part of the forest where there was absolute silence. There was no wind to ruffle the leaves and no bird calls. All was still as Rudy stopped Blitz and looked at Schwarz.

"The Bishop confirmed what we have feared. Judah told him all he knows, and Bishop Bryan confronted me with it when I asked him to hear my confession yesterday afternoon. He refused to grant me absolution because he believes I lied to him about our joint harvesting program."

"Does he know about everything, Dr. Hoorst?"

"If you mean the *Kledsiella* and Spanish flu outbreaks, I don't think so; at least not yet. I have a feeling that Mr. Benjamin hasn't allowed himself to go there yet, but as soon as he is back to full power, he'll probably figure that out, too."

Schwarz took a deep breath and asked, "What course of action do you propose we take, sir?"

"I think any attempt to neutralize the Bishop with extreme measures would only backfire on us. We've seen first-hand what can happen when the hit on Mr. Benjamin went sour."

"But, sir," interjected Schwarz, "Bishop Bryan can be infected with one of our organisms quite easily. It would be impossible to prove any type of foul play."

Rudy nodded, saying, "I've already considered that plan, Claus. But then we'd have to find a way to remove Dr. Hartman, also. I can assure you, he most certainly knows everything the Bishop knows and probably more. Just remember, he's around Mr. Benjamin every day. I suggest we're still in a very favorable position, Claus. If the State of Georgia decides to close this place down, and that would likely be the response from the lawmakers if the whole story of the Ossabaw colony became public, what would the state do?"

"So, sir," asked Schwarz, "what plan of action do you have in mind?"

"First of all, Claus, I want the computer files restored and available for review, but in a reconfigured manner that will not reflect a cause and effect relationship between available materials and time of death. It would be ludicrous to have no records at all. But we must have records that exculpate the company."

Schwarz nodded quickly, stating, "I'll have my best men on it when we return."

Rudy waved his hand in front of his face to shoo away the gnats and continued. "Second, I'll seek to rebuild my friendship with the Bishop. I'll do this by giving up just a little bit. I'll admit that in the case of some residents who are perhaps nearly unconscious and most assuredly at death's door, it is at the discretion of the camp director to put them out of their misery, but only as an act of mercy. I believe I can successfully engage Bishop Bryan on the mercy thing. As you know, Claus, acts of mercy are a big part of the Roman Catholic Church."

"Do you mean to include mercy killings, Dr. Hoorst?"

"Church history is replete with such actions. Only the Church doesn't like to call it that. No just and sane person is going to sit idly by and watch another human, or even an animal for that matter, suffer intense agony when there is no hope of ending it other than death itself. The suffering we see here is often quite intense, and I think I can win Bishop Bryan over with that argument."

"Finally, Claus, I want to turn the Bishop into more of an asset for the company. Do you still have the video from all his religious services and sermons?"

"Yes, sir. We have every one of them. I reviewed several of his best sermons myself only a few weeks ago and shared them with Eva. She was quite moved."

"What I have in mind, Claus, is the sale of this video in the same way we sell our *Ultimate Gladiators* show. Only this is the polar opposite. It will appeal to an entirely different audience."

Rudy nudged Blitz gently and the horse started an easy walk along with Schwarz. A few paces down the trial, Rudy remarked, "I was thinking how interesting it would be to have a show about residents experiencing a religious conversion because of Bishop Bryan's sermons. It would be nice if we could also have a miracle from time to time. You know, the casting out of demons, the lame walking, that sort of thing."

"An excellent idea, sir."

Rudy glanced at Schwarz and added, "I think we can incorporate Miss McFarland into this project, also. What better story is there than a former cokehead and prostitute finding Jesus and salvation in a place like the Ossabaw colony?"

* * *

It would have violated the seal of the confessional if Lloyd had acted differently with Rudy when they were around others. It might cause suspicion in some, thinking Lloyd knew something damning about Rudy. That wasn't the case when they were alone together.

Several days after the ride through the woods with Schwarz, Rudy found himself alone with Lloyd at the breakfast table. Lloyd was quiet and avoided eye contact as the two men sipped their morning coffee. Finally, Rudy put his cup down in its saucer, wiped his mouth, and folded the napkin.

He looked at Lloyd, who appeared to be reading the *Savannah Morning News.*

"I'd like to speak with you again, Lloyd."

Without taking his eyes from the paper, Lloyd asked, "About what?"

"About my last confession, Father."

Lloyd raised his head a little, letting the paper rest on the table, and looked at Rudy.

"What about your last confession, Rudy?"

"You were right, Lloyd, I haven't been completely honest with you, and I'd like to change that, if I may. Can we go to my office where we can talk in complete privacy?"

Rudy and Lloyd sat in front of Rudy's desk as before. Rudy looked refreshed and confident to Lloyd as the two men sized each other up. To Rudy, Lloyd appeared understandably tired and frazzled.

"What I'm going to tell you, Lloyd, comes under the seal of the confessional."

Lloyd nodded in assent and waited for Rudy to speak.

"As the director of this colony, Lloyd, I have very broad discretion granted to me by the EO charter with the State of Georgia. That discretionary power covers just about everything that happens on the island and, among other things, grants me the right to terminate human life when I deem certain residents to be suffering beyond the scope of relief from drugs. It happens when I believe a person is suffering more than this colony can tolerate. Do you understand me?"

Lloyd blinked several times as he looked at Rudy, and replied, "I understand, but that doesn't make what you're about to tell me right."

Rudy leaned forward and asked, "Do you remember the lines from Shakespeare's *The Merchant of Venice* concerning mercy?"

Lloyd nodded, saying "Of course I do. If memory serves me correctly, Portia says, 'The quality of mercy is not strained. It droppeth as the gentle rain from the heaven upon the place beneath; it is twice blessed. It blesseth him that gives and him that takes.'"

Rudy smiled, saying, "I heard you were quite the Shakespearian scholar, Bishop. And I thank you for making my point before I even begin to lay it out for you."

"You're welcome, Rudy. So lay out the rationale for mercy killings."

"I can start with the simple economics of the situation, Bishop," answered Rudy, "but I know you're not interested in the economic side of the equation, so I'll address the human side."

Rudy looked down at his hands for a moment, then back at Lloyd. "There is no way you haven't thought about how much most of our residents suffer, is there?"

"I'm confronted with that every day."

"Do you ever consider how merciful it would be if you could simply facilitate their deaths and relieve their suffering?"

"All the time, Rudy, but that's God's call, not mine."

"Does God call on you to be merciful, Lloyd?"

"That's one of His greatest commandments, Rudy."

"Then why can't you obey that commandment and show mercy for the suffering? Why can't you help them see the face of God a little sooner? I'm not talking days and weeks; I'm talking about hours and minutes earlier. What dignity do those poor souls have as they lie in their own excrement, waiting for you or Katie or whoever to wipe their behinds and change their sheets?"

"No dignity," answered Lloyd, looking directly into Rudy's eyes. "But they do have life. I see them fight for that life every second I'm around them. That life is God's presence in their bodies, and who am I or you to extinguish that presence because they have only a few more hours left? Relieve the suffering, yes! The drugs that render them unconscious do that quite well, but that final push, no—that's God's decision alone."

"I understand your position from a religious standpoint," said Rudy, "but you can afford to be philosophical, I can't. I have to be practical too, Bishop!"

Rudy rested his elbows on the chair arms before continuing, "Do you know how many people are backed up at Butterbean Beach waiting to enter the colony?"

"I don't know the exact number, but I am aware there are sizeable numbers there, why?"

Rudy almost whispered, "Those people are suffering greatly, Lloyd. Their physical and mental anguish is enormous. They have to endure that pain until they can be admitted to this island. We have an agreed-upon maximum number of residents, and we stay at that level all the time. As long as there is someone who is very near death who doesn't succumb for several hours and sometimes days, those people waiting at Butterbean Beach must suffer in torment. I have made the determination that a resident who is near death should be helped along by an overdose. As we both will probably agree, this is a matter of conscience. I'm at peace with the decisions I've made, Lloyd. I feel there is very little difference between me and a general who knowingly sends thousands of young men to certain death in battle for the greater good."

Rudy leaned back for a moment, then added, "I didn't tell you these things before because your knowledge of them wouldn't improve the situation. The company has always operated on a need-to-know basis. What I propose to you now is that we both identify and agree on those residents who appear to have only days left. You will have no say about their disposition, but at least we will have agreed about their longevity, and you will be at ease in knowing they aren't dying for their hip or knee joints."

"In all my years, I never dreamed I'd be having this conversation. I can understand how you're caught in a numbers crunch, Rudy. As we both know, I'm here at your pleasure. You can have me removed from this island today. If this is the best I can do, then so be it."

Rudy reached out and put his hand on Lloyd's shoulder. "I'm on this island for the money. You're here for the souls, Lloyd, and I respect that greatly. Now, I ask that you grant me absolution, Father."

* * *

Just before lunch, Colonel Schwarz met with Rudy in his office.

"Did you discuss things with Bishop Bryan, sir?"

"Yes, I did, Claus."

"What is your take on him now, sir?"

"I believe he is more understanding of the resident population problem."

"Did you speak with him about the television series, Dr. Hoorst?"

"Yes, and he appears to be quite open to the idea, Claus. The company has decided it's time to allow a small number of the press into the colony. These visits will be tightly restricted and controlled, designed to put our best foot forward."

* * *

Rudy decided to begin the company's positive image campaign by posting edited versions of what he thought were Lloyd's best sermons on EO's Facebook page. The results exceeded even Rudy's optimistic hopes, and in a matter of days, they showed up on YouTube, then went viral. Rush Limbaugh began talking about it, and Shawn Hannity showed a clip of Lloyd on his television program. Shortly after that, requests for interviews with Lloyd started flooding EO's American headquarters. Rudy's strategy was to sit back and wait for what he thought was the biggest and best venue. That idea paid off when the *Bill O'Reilly Show* contacted Rudy seeking permission to visit the island and interview Lloyd. Skillfully, Rudy laid out the ground rules and O'Reilly accepted.

* * *

When O'Reilly and his camera crew arrived at the Ossabaw dock, Rudy and Schwarz were there to greet him. First they went to the Main House, where O'Reilly was introduced to Rudy's wife and sons. Then there was a tour of the house followed by lunch, where O'Reilly met Lloyd. After that, O'Reilly was escorted to Group One and then Group Two. He was told he could also visit Group Three, but Rudy advised against it due to security problems. O'Reilly gladly accepted his advice.

O'Reilly and his crew were on the island from Friday morning until Sunday afternoon. They were taken anywhere they wanted to go, but what intrigued O'Reilly was Lloyd's work in Group One. What intrigued him even more was Katie McFarland.

Under the tent in Group One, O'Reilly interviewed Katie for two hours while rows of cots filled with dying people served as a backdrop. Lloyd was at her side most of the time, but would occasionally leave the set to hear a last confession. That evening after dinner, the camera crew set up in the Great Room, where O'Reilly spoke at length with Rudy about the operation of the colony. At the end, Rudy told O'Reilly that Mass in the morning would be something to remember.

* * *

Bill O'Reilly looked into the camera, smiled and said, "Caution, you're about to enter the no spin zone!" Then he described his trip to Ossabaw Island the weekend before, stating the entire program was going to deal with the Ossabaw drug colony. There was video and commentary that started with his meeting Rudy on the dock and continued through his tour of the Main House and groups One and Two. He showed Lloyd and Katie caring for the residents and played segments of Lloyd's sermons. He saved his interview with Lloyd and Katie for last.

"So, tell me, Miss McFarland, why you decided to join this colony. I think by now all of our viewers know your father is the governor of Georgia, and that you had a cocaine addiction and used prostitution to support that habit. What we haven't heard from you personally is, why in the world did you want to come to this place?"

Smiling at O'Reilly, then at Lloyd, Katie answered, "When I came here, it was to die, and die as painlessly and quickly as I could. I had decided I had nothing further to live for. Then I met Bishop Bryan and slowly he helped open my eyes to see and feel the presence of something very much greater than I. The first time he talked to me, he told me my life was as bad as it was going to get. He said if I were willing to put forth the effort and to listen to the spirit that lived inside me, I could be joyful even here in this drug colony."

"OK, so tell me what you think is so special about this guy sitting next to you, Miss McFarland."

Katie looked at Lloyd for a long moment. Then she answered, "It started with the first time I heard him preach. I couldn't turn away, I couldn't shut out what he was saying. When we finally spoke privately and I told him my story, my whole story, I could feel him accepting the pain I had locked up in me. I could feel it draining away from me to him. Then when I began to work with him here in the camps, I saw him do the same thing for hundreds of other people. I saw people, who were in worse shape than I was, be spiritually lightened by his words and presence. I saw those people die a happy death, Bill."

O'Reilly nodded then turned to Lloyd, seeming to consider what he just heard. He asked, "Bishop Bryan, do you believe you have the power to absorb the pain of other people?

"A Catholic like you should know the answer to that question, Bill. My goodness, it's simple, I have the ability to relieve spiritual pain through the power of the confessional. When people believe I have the power to forgive sins, they can't wait to unload on me."

"I understand all the theology involved, Bishop, but from what Katie has told me and from what I witnessed myself as you moved about this massive tent and heard hundreds of confessions, I have to tell you it appeared to me that you were actually absorbing that pain in a physical sense."

Katie nodded, smiled and added, "That's what I think, too, Bill."

"How about that, Bishop Bryan: do you feel you're taking on the pain of their sins, and if you are, how much more can you stand?"

Lloyd looked around the tent, then back at O'Reilly.

"Sin is just another word for evil," said Lloyd. "Some people don't believe in the existence of evil, but I do. I'm protected by the armor of God, just like you and Katie and all believing Christians. If you don't wear the armor of God, Satan will kill you spiritually and physically."

Lloyd paused again, then said, "I believe I can absorb evil into my body. The reason it hasn't killed me yet is that I let it go each morning when I celebrate the Mass."

The picture faded back to O'Reilly in his New York studio, and for a second he said nothing. Then he commented, "As most of you know, I've never taken a drink of alcohol in my life, I've never used any tobacco and certainly have never taken any drugs that weren't prescribed for me by my doctor. Going to the drug colony on Ossabaw Island, Georgia, is the most profound thing I've seen in all my years as a journalist. It's changed my life for the better. If you want to see more about Bishop Lloyd Bryan and his remarkable ministry there, simply go to Ossabawministry.com. He and Katie McFarland have a regularly-scheduled program from the island, and I highly recommend it."

* * *

Rudy and Schwarz watched *The O'Reilly Factor* with their wives in the Great Room. When the program finished, Rudy had a grin on his face. Claus was smiling broadly, too, and was the first to speak.

"A home run, sir! Your idea of bringing in O'Reilly was nothing short of brilliant."

"I believe, Claus, that the company is in a perfect position to ramp up our commitment to our religious network."

"I agree, sir. What do you have in mind?"

"I'm thinking of concentrating more on the confession and redemption side, Claus. We need to show more of the deathbed conversions that are taking place in the colony. What would really be great is if we could video some kind of miracle."

Claus sat up, raised his finger and said, "How about an exorcism? I've watched the Bishop many times when it appeared a resident was resisting to the last, and finally the Bishop unfolded some kind of mystical power that was able to drive out an evil spirit and, at the end, was able to claim that soul for Christ. It was truly great theater, Dr. Hoorst."

"I think you're on to something, Claus. If we can engineer such a situation time and again, this program could be much more profitable than *Ultimate Gladiators*."

Two days after *The O'Reilly Factor* aired, Rudy had several calls concerning Lloyd's ministry. All had to do with televising his sermons. The one from the A&E channel really got Rudy's attention.

A&E wanted to do a reality show about the Ossabaw colony. It would center around Lloyd and Katie, and the initial offer was to start shooting immediately for airing in the summer. They proposed $10 million to start, and if the network was happy with the results, another twenty for the next season. Rudy had to clear the deal all the way to the top, but, in the end, the series would start in June.

* * *

Rudy and Schwarz walked their horses south along Ossabaw's beach. After minutes of silence Claus asked, "What do you think of that apparent exorcism Bishop Bryan preformed last Friday?"

"I thought it was quite convincing. It will certainly spike the ratings. It would be nice if the Bishop could perform one or two a week, but I guess we don't get that many residents who appear possessed by the Devil, do we, Claus?"

"Not that I can discern, sir. Perhaps they're so far gone on drugs that the Devil doesn't see a challenge there."

Both men welcomed the breeze off the ocean and let their horses walk a little farther. Schwarz said, "I have an idea that the Bishop's exorcism started me thinking about."

"What kind of an idea, Claus?"

"About ten years ago, sir, the company was active in experimenting with psilocybin, mushrooms that cause hallucinations. The thinking was that, perhaps, one of these strains could prove useful and be developed and marketed to the pharmaceutical industry. Those experiments took place at our first colony in Russia, and I was stationed there at the time. We had a large resident population upon which to test these mushrooms and, while nothing came about from these tests commercially, there were some very interesting results in the test population."

"What kind of interesting results, Claus?"

"Well, sir, seeing that person who appeared to be possessed very much reminded me of the behavior many of the test subjects manifested once they were dosed with the various mushrooms we tested. They had similar facial contortions and speech patterns; things such as foaming at the mouth and blistering of the skin. They were also highly susceptible to suggestions. Careful records were kept concerning which type of mushroom induced particular characteristics, including how long these behavior patterns lasted. Knowing the company as I do, sir, I believe these records as well as samples of the mushrooms most certainly exist."

Rudy nodded. "So, Claus, are you suggesting we have the company deliver a batch of these mushrooms to this colony, and we use them to induce behavior in a select number of residents that would lead a rational, religious person to believe a demonic possession had taken place in that individual?"

"That's exactly what I'm suggesting, sir. And, even better, the effect of these compounds was rather short-lived. Most of the test subjects were acting normally again within a matter of hours; most within three hours. That would fit perfectly into the time frame Bishop Bryan used when praying over that possessed resident. The apparent effect would be that the Bishop's prayers and incantations had expelled Satan from the resident's body, when, in actuality, their behavior would return to normal anyway. There would be no harm done, and we could manage one or two exorcisms a week."

* * *

The ride to Ossabaw for the meeting of the colony's board of directors was Judah's first time on the water since he'd been shot. The weather was blustery and a threat of rain lay to the west. Once John-Morgan pointed *Graf Spee's* bow into the Forest River and increased speed, spray from waves breaking against the bow occasionally hit Judah in the face. He didn't mind at all; it made him feel alive and well again.

When John-Morgan slowed his boat for its passage through Hell Gate, he looked over at Judah and asked, "You thinkin' about how you're gonna act toward Rudy?"

"Yeah, I was."

"Well, how are you gonna act, and what're you gonna say?"

"I not gonna tip my hand, that's for sure. I believe he has a real good idea that I suspect him, but not much more. I'm going to be friendly, but not too much. I want him to relax his guard."

"For what?" asked John-Morgan, "you got something up your sleeve?"

"No, not really. I'm gonna request to see the computer records again.

If I'm on to something, he's changed a whole lot of things. I can't remember everything I read, but I can remember well enough to tell if the data has been altered."

"Dr. Hoorst and Bishop Bryan are waiting in the Great Room," said Schwarz "We've been notified that Governor McFarland and his son have just taken off from Hunter and should be arriving in about ten minutes.

Rudy was standing just behind Lloyd and reached out to take Judah's hand. "You really came through this thing quite well, Judah. We were all very concerned for you."

"Hannah told me how nice you and the company were to her, Rudy. It meant a lot to me to know she didn't have to worry about anything while I was laid up."

The doors to the Great Room opened and in walked Big Dog and Robbie. Outside, angry, bruise-colored clouds began moving over the island, and soon flashes of lightening filled the sky and the shock of thunder shook the old house. The men moved to the high windows and watched as sheets of rain swept across the island.

Finally, when the storm was no more than a distant rumble out over the Atlantic, Rudy announced that dinner would be served and business discussed over the meal. "If anyone has anywhere special they'd like to go," said Rudy, "just let us know."

Lloyd and John-Morgan went back to Group One, Judah requested to be taken to the command center where he would get back into the company computers, and Big Dog was driven by Schwarz to Katie's cottage. Only Robbie hung back and stayed in the Main House. After the others had left, Robbie approached Rudy saying, "We need to talk."

As soon as Rudy closed and locked the office doors, Robbie was almost in Rudy's face, saying hoarsely, "I checked my account in Switzerland before I came here, and there was still only $2 million in it. You told me once my father signed the funeral home bill into law, I'd get the other $2 million, remember? Well, Hoorst, he signed that bill three days ago. It's the law now. I lived up to my end of the bargain, now it's time for you to do the same!"

Rudy brushed past Robbie, who was nearly blocking his path, and said, "Relax, Little Dog, you'll get your $2 million in gold, just as promised. Let's have a drink first. You're still partial to Jack Daniels and ginger ale, aren't you?" Not waiting for an answer, he poured a stiff shot of Jack and topped it off with a little mixer. Then he filled the other glass with Grey Goose vodka and some tonic for himself. Holding the Jack Daniels out to Robbie, he smiled and said "Come on, Little Dog, let's make a toast to your great legislative and financial success."

Robbie didn't take the glass. Instead, he glared at Rudy and hissed, "I want my fuckin' money, and I want it today, Hoorst."

Rudy smiled slyly, clicked his tongue as if scolding Robbie, and replied, "I wish you wouldn't call me by my last name, Robbie, dear, it hurts my feelings, and I do so want to be your friend."

Robbie's face turned red and his voice rose several octaves. "Cut the fuckin' bullshit, Hoorst. I want my goddamn money!"

Rudy remained very cool as he looked at Robbie, finally saying, "Well, OK, if you have to have it right now before you even taste your drink, then that's the way it'll be."

Still smiling, Rudy walked to the bookcase at the far end of the room and reached behind it. Robbie heard a click and watched as the bookcase opened like a door, revealing a hidden passage. Looking over his shoulder, Rudy said, "Follow me, and grab your drink—I think you're gonna need it."

The passage was narrow, about ten feet long. It led to a concealed room that was twelve by fifteen feet. Rudy waited until Robbie was next to him and then reached for the light switch. What greeted Robbie's eyes was a pallet in the center of the room stacked with gold coins, jewelry and bullion.

"Here's your two million in gold, Little Dog," said Rudy watching the expression on Robbie's face. "Actually," continued Rudy, "it's a whole lot more than two million. Probably more like ten. But, anyway, you're welcome to count out your share however you want. The price of gold as of yesterday was $3,226 an ounce and change. Most of the coins you see here are an ounce. Almost all of them are from European countries and minted when kaisers, kings and czars ruled the continent. For the most part, these coins are in mint condition. I know you're a coin collector, so you should find this grouping most interesting."

Robbie didn't say anything at first as he blinked again and again. He moved into the room for a closer look. Each coin had been placed in an individual clear plastic container to protect its collectable value. Slowly and carefully he started picking up single coins and examining them.

"This is unbelievable," said Robbie as he held one coin after another up to the light for a closer examination. "Almost all appear to be in mint condition."

"Quite right," replied Rudy, "and to show you how much the company appreciates your help, we are going to forget about the collectable value of these coins and go strictly on their weight in gold as payment. The experts tell me their collectable value alone could more than double their gold value. You're free to peruse this collection as long as you like and select whatever coins interest you. As a matter of fact, you may want to pick out a piece or two from the jewelry as a gift for your wife. That will also go for its gold weight. Of course, if you still prefer, the company will be happy to wire another two million in gold to your Swiss account. I just thought you'd be happier with this type of payment."

As Rudy spoke, Robbie began to sink slowly to his knees to examine the treasure pile. He'd never seen anything like it before and was mesmerized, smiling so broadly he thought his face might break. Without taking his eyes off the gold, Robbie slugged back his drink and held the empty glass up to Rudy saying, "You've got a deal and you were right, I did need a drink—as well as another."

"Enjoy yourself Little Dog," answered Rudy, "I'll be right back with a fresh one."

When Rudy returned to the secret room, the wheels had been turning quickly in Robbie's head, and he was full of questions.

"Do I have to take it all right now? It's awfully heavy."

"Take as much as you'd like now or later. These coins aren't going anywhere, Robbie. Perhaps it would be best if you took a little at a time; trying to convert this much gold to cash in a short period of time would bring too much attention."

"You're right," said Robbie who still couldn't take his eyes off the coins. Then he broke his gaze away from the gold and looked at Rudy, asking, "Where did all this stuff come from?"

"Actually, that's a company secret, but since we're partners, so to speak, I'll tell you enough to satisfy your curiosity."

Rudy knelt, as well, and picked out a pair of gold and ruby earrings. Holding them out to Robbie he said, "Here, take these as a gift from me to your lovely wife."

Robbie cupped the earrings in his hands and said, "Thank you very much, she'll be thrilled. But how did the company get all this stuff?"

Rudy shifted to sit on the floor with his back against the wall. He was quiet for several seconds as he looked straight into Robbie's eyes, then said, "When the Third Reich came to absolute power, it began to seize the wealth of German Jews. When the armies of the Reich rolled across Europe and Russia, it did the same thing again. It took everything of value, from gold to precious works of art. A great deal of it was used to finance the war effort. No small amount was taken by those higher up in the regime. When the war ended, vast stores of these valuables were uncovered and returned to their rightful owners. Some of those hiding places were never found and were known only to the founding members of Executive Outcomes, to be used in building the company into what it is today."

Stunned, Robbie looked again at the fortune before him and nodded in understanding.

"I must caution you in the strongest of terms, Robbie, not to speak of this to anyone. Do you understand? If you did, it would hurt only you."

"I understand," answered Robbie. "No one will ever know. I doubt they'd believe me even if I did talk."

* * *

That night, after everyone was asleep, Rudy and Schwarz sat in his office and discussed the day's events.

"How do you plan to deal with the governor's son, sir?"

"He's seen the gold and his greed now drives his behavior. What I've suggested is that he return to the island in the next week or so, in complete secrecy, to begin taking a larger portion of the coins back to Atlanta. He will drive to the town of Forsythe, south of Atlanta. The company owns some farm land there with a small airstrip. He'll meet up with one of our light planes and be flown to the island. Once we have him here, he'll be easy prey."

CHAPTER FOURTEEN

DEMONS

And Jesus rebuked him, saying,
Hold thy peace, and come out of him.
—*The Holy Bible*, King James version, Luke 4:35

Lloyd moved through the big tent in Group One, Katie by his side, stopping frequently to speak with residents who often called out to him asking for his prayers. That was a common occurrence. What happened next wasn't.

There was a man who appeared to be in his mid-thirties lying on a cot near the back of the tent. He watched as Lloyd approached and the closer Lloyd got, the more agitated he became. Finally when Lloyd was only ten feet away, the man began to hiss and his face became contorted as if he were in great pain. Lloyd stopped, stood quietly and watched as the man began to foam at the mouth and his eyes rolled back in his head. Lloyd glanced at Katie, then started to move in closer to the man. As Lloyd approached, suddenly the man recoiled and shrieked, "Get away from me, Priest, this soul is all mine!" He spit at Lloyd, growling in a low and terrifying voice, "He's mine, and all the prayers you can say can't take him from me!"

The camera crew following Lloyd focused on the man's face as Lloyd stood firm and quiet. The man writhed and twisted in his cot, spitting what appeared to be blood-tinged saliva at Lloyd and Katie.

"See you brought your little whore with you, Priest. Did you fuck her this morning?" snarled the man.

Lloyd reached into his pocket and produced a small crucifix, which he held up. In mocking laughter, the man said, "Do you think I'm scared by your Roman mumbo-jumbo? Why don't you stick it up your ass where it would do some good? Maybe it would help that prostate cancer you have." He laughed again before he balled himself into an even tighter knot, staring directly into Lloyd's eyes, growling faintly with each breath.

Lloyd was startled. He had indeed suffered from a low-grade cancer of the prostate which he thought had been treated successfully by radiation and wondered how this complete stranger could know such a thing. Then he closed his eyes and began to pray, invoking the Holy Spirit as he stretched out his arms. Katie stood silently by Lloyd's side and watched the man on the cot.

"I've got nice present for you and your whore, Bishop Bryan," whispered the man. Then he produced a large, wet bowel movement that soiled the entire cot with the foulest odor Lloyd and Katie had ever smelled. They both gagged and retreated several feet while the man laughed in delight. Lloyd regained his composure and moved in even closer, not taking his eyes off the man. Finally, he stopped only feet from the cot and began to pray aloud, invoking the Archangel Michael for help in expelling the demon he now believed possessed the man's body. For the next twenty minutes, Lloyd closed his eyes tightly and repeated almost every prayer and supplication he'd ever learned, while the entire episode was expertly captured by the EO camera crew. Finally, the man appeared to be relaxing a little and Lloyd opened his eyes. Then, he went to the man's cot and pressed the crucifix against his forehead saying, "Leave him!" Instantly, a brief but agonized cry erupted from the man and he went limp, appearing to fall into a deep sleep. Lloyd was completely drained and staggered back from the cot. Katie grabbed his arm to steady him and led him away.

* * *

"That was certainly some excellent video, Claus," remarked Rudy as they sat in the Great Room and watched it on the flat screen.

Schwarz was pleased with his idea and said, "It will air tomorrow night, sir. I can't imagine anything but higher ratings."

"I completely agree. By the way, how is Bishop Bryan doing?"

"He's resting now. It appears that expelling demons takes a physical toll on the Bishop. I would suggest we give him a little time to recuperate."

"I agree, Claus. It would a shame for the Bishop to burn out on us. Perhaps we should give him a week's rest before he's called on again. By the way, how did our subject come to know about the Bishop's prostate problems and Miss McFarland's history of prostitution?"

"If you will recall, sir, I mentioned that when a person is under the influence of these mushrooms, they are highly susceptible to suggestion. That's how we get them to believe they are possessed, and that's when we're able to slip in little tidbits of information that makes the afflicted all the more believable. Bishop Bryan had mentioned his prostate problems, and I passed that information on to the guards who slipped it into their conversations with that resident."

* * *

E.O.'s small plane touched down on Ossabaw at ten o'clock in the morning. The weather was clear and getting warmer as Robbie climbed out of the craft and into the waiting Hummer driven by Colonel Schwarz.

"Dr. Hoorst is waiting for you in his office. Will you be staying long enough to have lunch?"

Robbie looked up at the sky, watching the thick cumulous clouds drift overhead, and said, "I don't know. I've got to be back before sundown, since that little plane can't land in the dark. I just want to pick up a few more coins and then head back. We'll see."

When Robbie entered Rudy's office, Rudy was at his desk and stood to shake his hand.

"I don't like the way the weather looks, Rudy," said Robbie immediately, "so I'd just as soon pick up some of my coins and head right back."

"I understand completely," replied Rudy.

As Rudy felt for the door latch, he said, "I'll just let you in, and you can go to the treasure room and take whatever you like. I have some business with the Colonel, so I won't come with you. Once you're finished, we'll do a count at my desk, if that's all right with you."

Once Robbie was out of earshot, in a very low voice, Schwarz asked, "Will we be dealing with Mr. McFarland today, sir?"

Rudy hesitated, then replied, "No, not today Claus. I think we should let Little Dog get completely relaxed and at ease."

Seconds later, Robbie pushed the bookcase door open and walked toward Rudy and Schwarz with a handful of Imperial German gold coins.

"I've got fifteen of these," said Robbie, laying the coins out on Rudy's desk and counting them. "I've got to take this thing kinda slow, 'cause if I flood the market with this stuff, it'll raise eyebrows and the next thing ya know, people like the Feds'll be snoopin' around. I think I can sell these in a week or so."

* * *

The next morning after finishing a big breakfast, Lloyd put on his jogging shoes and headed for the beach. Katie watched him for several minutes before she left for tents in Group One.

As Lloyd began his run, he noticed he had to force himself to place one foot in front of the other. It was something he'd never had to do before. His breathing became labored and after only a hundred yards, he slowed to a walk. Then he had to stop and sit on a piece of driftwood to rest while he caught his breath. As he turned back toward the cottage, he muttered to himself, "I guess they were right, I do need a rest."

At the bottom of the long stairs leading to the cottage, Lloyd sat and rested again. He sat on the bottom step for over an hour, just thinking. Finally he began the long climb to the cottage. About halfway up, he began to feel tightness in his chest, but refused to pay any attention to it. The tightness turned to pain and he was forced to stop and sit. In a few minutes, the pain was gone, but Lloyd knew all too well what it was.

* * *

"Where's Bishop Bryan?" asked a man in one of the cots as Katie passed. "I've decided to come clean, and I wanted him to hear my confession before I die. I think I'm getting close. I really need him. He told me he'd hear my confession any time I was ready, and I'm ready now," pleaded the man.

Katie leaned over and wiped the man's brow. "Do you think you'd like another dose of morphine? I can do that for you."

"No," answered the man, who had raised himself up on his elbows to look around the tent. "I want the Bishop. After he hears my confession, then I'll have some more morphine."

"Lie back down, sweetheart," said Katie, "the Bishop is sick. He can't be here today."

"But I need him. I don't want to go to Hell after I die."

"You know you don't have to have Bishop Bryan hear your confession to have your sins forgiven, Jimmy. He told you that himself, remember? I was standing right here just yesterday when he told you that."

"I know that, Miss Katie, but it would make me feel so much better."

"Tell you what," said Katie as she sat on Jimmy Rahn's cot, "why don't you tell me your sins and we'll let God forgive them?"

"But I need a priest!"

"We don't have a priest, and we won't for at least a week. So, why don't you just let go of all your guilt right now? It's only between you and God, anyway. If you're not truly sorry for the things you've done, Bishop Bryan can't make God forgive you."

Jimmy's eyes widened and again he looked around the huge tent in desperation, then back at Katie. "I can't say those things to a lady, it's not right."

"I'm no lady, Jimmy, you know my story. I've probably done things a lot worse than you have, so let it go and be at peace here and now."

Katie's latex-gloved hand patted Jimmy's. She said, "I believe you're truly sorry, Jimmy. I know if Bishop Bryan were here right now, he'd feel the same way. God has forgiven you, Jimmy, and you can die in peace."

"You really believe that, Miss Katie?"

The director of the EO camera crew shadowing Katie as she made her rounds in the tents leaned over to the camera man and whispered, "I hope you got that whole thing, it was good."

* * *

When Katie returned to the cottage that afternoon, she found Lloyd sitting on the deck nursing a drink and watching the gulls ride the winds.

"How are things under the big tents?"

"The same as always," answered Katie, sensing something was wrong. "Everyone who is still lucid asked where you were. Remember Jimmy Rahn?"

"Yeah."

"He wanted you to hear his confession today; he thinks he's gonna die soon and wants to clear decks, so to speak."

"I remember Jimmy when he was a student at Benedictine, before he sold his soul to rock and roll, so to speak. I was wondering when he'd finally break."

"Well, he broke around noon today. I think he came completely clean, at least it seemed that way."

"I wish I could have been there for him."

"Something's wrong, Lloyd, what is it?"

Lloyd nodded and held his glass out to Katie. "Fix me another and I'll tell ya a little secret."

"Lawd God Almighty, I remember when I was young and knocking down a fortune, playing ball for the Redskins. This was my favorite kinda whiskey. I didn't drink nothin' but the finest. Didn't snort nothin' but the best coke, either, and burn nothin' but the strongest weed. Those were some really wild days, Katie. Lookin' back, I don't know why I'm alive today."

Katie didn't say anything for several moments, then finally asked, "OK, Lloyd, what is it?"

Lloyd drew himself up in his chair and looked over at Katie. He was feeling the effects of the Scotch when he said, "You're a beautiful soul in a beautiful body, Katie." Silence again.

"Lloyd, what is going on, tell me!"

Lloyd shrugged, looked back at the ocean. "When I went to run today, I didn't have any energy. I couldn't catch my breath. Then, when I started to climb the stairs back to the cottage, I had a lot of trouble. Less than half the way up, my chest started to tighten, but I ignored it and kept on climbing. It wasn't ten more steps before I had severe pain in my chest. I started sweating real bad and had to stop. After about five minutes, I felt better and started back up again, but the pain came back. It took me half an hour to get to the cottage."

"You need medical help!"

"Not just yet, Katie."

CHAPTER FIFTEEN

KING RAT

"Better to reign in hell than serve in heaven."
—Milton, *Paradise Lost*

By the end of his week at the beach cottage, Lloyd was feeling better. He'd gained some weight, hadn't had any more chest pain, and had been careful not to put his heart to the test again. He'd leave that up to John-Morgan.

With Katie by his side, Lloyd walked down the lines of cots in Group One, speaking to all who were conscious and stopping often to hear a brief confession or offer words of consolation. Finally, after more than two hours under the tents, he and Katie went to the Main House where they had lunch with Rudy and his family. As the meal was ending, Lloyd told Rudy he hadn't visited the Group Two area in over a year and that he'd like go there before he returned to the cottage.

"That's fine, Lloyd," said Rudy, "but you must have a couple of my guards accompany you."

* * *

Lloyd turned to the guards and asked, "Where is everybody?"

The guard who often assisted Lloyd at Mass smiled and answered, "It's a beautiful day, Bishop. Most of these residents are at the beach getting high and playing in the surf. Some are just sitting under a big oak stoned out of their minds. They'll be back when the sun starts to go down, if they're not too messed up to walk. The ones in their cots are probably on their last legs. We generally lose about fifteen a day in this tent."

A little deeper in, Lloyd stopped and focused on something at the far end of the big tent. It appeared to be a walled-off room.

Pointing to it, Lloyd asked, "What's that, Corporal Leary?"

Leary chuckled a little and replied in his thick Irish brogue, "That's King Rat's Castle, Your Excellency."

Lloyd asked in astonishment, "King Rat? Who or what is King Rat?"

"You've got to understand the culture here, Bishop. You see, sir, a lot of people in this group still have some life left in them. They're not at all like the ones you see in Group One. Those residents are too far gone to care about much. In this group, we get a lot of folks who know how to titrate their drug use so they're not completely out of it all the time. We've got people here who are into dominating other residents. They're real control freaks and get off on this domination. That's what King Rat is all about."

"Why does King Rat have his own room?" asked Lloyd, moving closer to King Rat's space.

"It's actually walled off with the wooden crates the supplies come in. I guess the first King Rat built it and the others improved on it. It's sort of a status symbol for them."

"How many King Rats have here been since the colony started?"

"A bunch, Bishop. This present one has been here for about two months."

"Tell me about him, Corporal."

"He's the slickest one I've ever seen, Bishop. He says he comes from Mobile. He acts like he's from high society. He looks like he's in his mid-fifties, in pretty good physical shape, and is quite handsome. Unlike most of the others here, he bathes twice a day and takes great pride in his physical appearance. He seems to be a real charmer. Some of the other guards think he can read their minds."

"Do you believe that, Corporal?"

"I don't know if I exactly believe that, Bishop, but I think he's awfully good at reading body English and facial expressions. And his eyes…"

"What about his eyes?"

"They're scary to me, Bishop. When he looks at me, I feel like I'm starin' into the eyes of a cobra. There's just something really creepy about this fella, Bishop. I'd almost say he's dangerous to be around, if you know what I mean."

Lloyd nodded and looked at Katie. "What do you know about this person?"

"I've heard of the King Rat thing before, but nothing more than that."

Lloyd then asked Leary, "How does a person get to be King Rat and what's in it for them?"

"This guy knows how to manipulate the residents. The women love him and most of the men steer clear of him. I don't know how else to say it." Leary looked at Katie and continued. "He's a sexual sadist. He likes having very rough sex. When he finishes with a women, he literally throws 'em out of his room. I've seen the condition some of them were in…they all have had lacerations and other damage to their…their privates. And, for some reason, after a few days, those women will come back for more. I guess they enjoy it as much as he does."

Lloyd studied King Rat's Castle for a long time, then turned to Leary and said, "I want to meet this King Rat character."

"I'll go see if he's there, Bishop, but just a little warning to you and Miss McFarland, OK?"

"What's that, Corporal?"

"You talk with this guy long enough, and he'll find out something about you that will completely surprise you and maybe even scare you. He's done it to me and the other guards. That's why we stay as far away from him as we can, Bishop. Just be careful. Don't let him get into your head."

* * *

"There're people outside who want to meet you, Doc."

"I've been wondering when Bishop Bryan and Miss McFarland would come calling, Corporal. Please show them in."

"Look, Doc," replied Leary, "no funny business with these folks. Just talk with them and everything will go fine for you, OK?"

King Rat rose from his chair at the far end of the room and walked toward the door saying, "It hurts my feelings, Corporal Leary, to think you believe I could be anything but a complete gentleman. Now, please, escort the Bishop and his friend to my study."

When Lloyd was within twenty-five feet of King Rat's Castle, he stopped to examine the exterior. While it was readily apparent that the wood was rough packing-case grade, the quality of the carpentry used to assemble the structure was very impressive. The room was roughly thirty feet wide, forty feet long and occupied about an eighth of the tent.

King Rat was standing at the far end of the room, in front of the screened porch separating it from the woods behind. When Lloyd entered, he searched first for King Rat; when he found the man, he surveyed the rest of the room. What he saw was another surprise. On the walls were paintings, photographs, and all manner of carvings and other oddities. The workmanship on the interior of the room surpassed that on its exterior.

As Katie slipped in behind Lloyd, she, too, was taken aback. King Rat's lair was nothing like what she'd expected. It was almost as pleasant as her cottage and certainly a lot more interesting.

"Please come in and make yourselves comfortable," said King Rat, coming toward Lloyd and Katie. "I've been waiting for you both with great anticipation. I'd shake your hands, but unless you're wearing gloves, it's not allowed."

Lloyd said nothing and examined the art work on the walls. Finally, without taking his eyes from a half-decent painting of Christ being scourged at the pillar, he asked, "Where did all this come from, and how did this room get here?"

King Rat was trim, about six feet tall with black hair combed back, sprinkled with gray on the sides. His eyes were dark, and Lloyd had trouble deciding where the iris stopped and the pupils began. He understood why Leary said they reminded him of a cobra's.

King Rat smiled warmly at Lloyd and Katie and motioned to the table and chairs in the middle of the room, saying, "Please, come in and make yourselves comfortable, and I'll tell you all I know about King Rat's Castle.

"My friends call me Beau. You can call me anything you like." He waited for several seconds, studying Lloyd and Katie with scrupulous care. Finally he began.

"I'm King Rat the Seventh. I've been here for six weeks." The sweep of his hand encompassed the room. "With the exception of a few pieces of art I was allowed to bring with me and display on these walls, this room is how I found it upon my arrival. It's my understanding the first two

King Rats were quite accomplished carpenters, and this is the fruit of their labor. Executive Outcomes provided the tools and scrap wood and allowed these men to live out their days doing something constructive. I'm told they weren't really drug addicts, just men who knew they were terminally ill with no place to go when the dying process got into high gear. When that time came, they overdosed themselves, leaving this room for those who would follow."

Once again Lloyd's eyes wandered over the room. They finally settled on a large oil painting of the crucifixion. It was an interesting piece, one Lloyd had never seen before. Pointing to it, Lloyd asked, "Where did that painting come from?" King Rat smiled and his eyes lit up when he answered, "That's one of the three I brought with me."

"It's different," said Lloyd, "very real, very brutal, too. I noticed the artist has the nails piercing Jesus's wrists rather than his hands. And his feet are nailed to the sides of the cross through the heels, one nail through each heel. I've always thought that was really the way Our Lord was crucified." Lloyd studied the painting more before asking, "Do you know who the artist is?"

King Rat said nothing until Lloyd spoke to him again, then replied with a smile of great satisfaction, "I am the artist."

Lloyd and Katie looked back at the painting and noticed in the lower left hand corner the signature, "W.B. Bondurant."

"So you're W.B. Bondurant," said Lloyd.

"I am he, Bishop Bryan."

"What does the W.B. stand for?"

"William Beauregard, Your Excellency; Beau for short."

Lloyd gestured at the painting of the scourging at the pillar. "Your work, also?"

"Yes, that's mine, too."

"You're quite an excellent painter, Beau."

"Thank you, I appreciate the compliment."

Katie had said very little since entering King Rat's Castle, content with simply studying Beau. Beau sensed that and said to her, "I watched you and Bishop Bryan on television before I came to the island, and I must tell you how impressed I am by both of you. You're even more magnetic in person."

"You don't appear to be the usual run-of-the-mill Group Two resident," said Lloyd. "Tell us about yourself, if you care to, Beau."

Beau smiled once more and said, "Hold on to your seats, this may be a rough ride for you both." He leaned back in his chair and began.

"I was born and raised in Mobile. I grew up in a house located in the best part of the city, owned by a wealthy and well-established family of

French descent. Both of my parents were devout Catholics and, of course, I was raised in the Church. I'm a graduate of Spring Hill College. After that I attended Emory University School of Medicine and completed my residency training in obstetrics and gynecology at Johns Hopkins. I took a position in Atlanta where I practiced for several years. When I got to Atlanta, I was a young, single physician with money to burn, and I enjoyed the company of many of the loveliest young ladies of Atlanta's society. After a respectable period of time, I decided it would best serve my financial and social status if I married and appeared to settle down. I did just that, but carried on a number of affairs. My wife didn't know of them, but my sexual proclivities soon proved to be too much for her."

Beau stopped for effect and gazed at Katie before continuing with his story.

"You see, I have always been aroused sexually by the infliction of pain, both physical and emotional. In today's jargon, it's simply a 'turn on' for me. Needless to say, it wasn't for my former wife, and she divorced me rather quickly and quietly, not wanting anyone to know the real reason for fear of scandal. However, I did enjoy some rather blissful moments of pure pain with her that I shall never forget. After that, I ran wild through the nursing staff of several Atlanta hospitals. Also, with the money I had at my disposal, I was able to buy women who would submit themselves to whatever I wanted for as long as they could stand it."

Beau stopped and looked again at Katie. With a thin smile he said, "If you were a little older, we probably would have known each other quite well. I was always a high roller who enjoyed coke along with sex."

"I've been abused sexually before, but never for money. That wasn't my thing."

Unfazed, Beau continued, "Finally all my debauchery caught up with me, and I was asked to leave the OB-GYN group I practiced with and lost my privileges at the hospitals. So, I took a position with an abortion mill in Jacksonville. I worked there three days a week and lived in Savannah the rest of the time. It was in Jacksonville that I really came into my proper element. I came to truly love doing abortions, particularly the late-term abortions. You know, the third trimester. I was one of the pioneers of what you probably know as partial-birth abortions. When they were born live, which many were, I'd simply snip through their spinal cords at the base of their necks with some Metzenbaum scissors."

Beau stopped to study Lloyd's and Katie's faces, then looked at his painting of the crucifixion, adding, "Yes, those were moments of supreme power and gratification."

Lloyd's mouth became tight and the furrows on his brow deepened; his eyes bored in on Beau, who saw see the arteries in Lloyd's neck pulsing and noticed his clenched fists.

"I warned you, didn't I? Now, what further questions do you have for King Rat?"

Lloyd cleared his throat and said, "I have several questions for you, Beau."

"I'll be as honest as I possibly can, Bishop."

"The first thing I was wondering about, Beau," said Lloyd, contemplating Beau's painting of the crucifixion, "is what brought you to enjoy inflicting physical pain, especially that associated with sexual activity?"

"Oh, that's an easy one, Lloyd. May I call you Lloyd?"

Lloyd gestured his assent.

"The Roman Catholic Church got me hooked on pain."

"How so?"

"My goodness, Lloyd, everything about the Church exudes pain and suffering. The absolute center of Church doctrine is the crucifixion. Almost all of the great works of religious art center on pain and suffering. I can remember as a young child, when I was an altar boy, how mesmerized I was by the full-size crucifix over the altar with Jesus hanging from it. The nails, the blood, everything about it didn't just speak of physical pain, it *shouted* it! My favorite time in the liturgical calendar was Passion Week. I loved the Stations of the Cross. I can remember becoming sexually aroused while I stood next to the priest on Good Friday as we went through the fourteen stations." Beau laughed and looked at Katie, adding, "I was afraid someone would see my huge erection under my cassock! But don't get me wrong, I realize my attraction to pain and my sexual proclivities aren't exactly mainstream. However, the religious artwork of the Church certainly heightened my deviant interests."

Beau sipped his drink and continued, "I think the emphasis the Church puts on virginity only added fuel to my fires. The thought of painfully penetrating for the first time some young little vagina was a source of great fantasy during my adolescent years. Sexual domination through the infliction of pain during intercourse was at the center of my universe. I yearned for it and sought it out at every opportunity. As I said earlier, it's what caused my former wife to leave me and drink heavily, eventually drinking herself to death. Quite frankly, I even enjoyed that. I'd visit her from time to time just to see how much torment she really was in."

Lloyd glanced at Katie before asking, "Why are you here, and how did you become King Rat?"

"I'm here because I have an incurable malignant brain tumor that will probably be too much to bear within the next six months. Whenever that time arrives, I'll simply drink the hemlock, close my eyes, and fade into nothingness." Beau paused a moment, then continued. "I became King Rat because I was smarter and fitter than anyone else in this group. When I learned about my brain tumor, I did some investigating and discovered that the Ossabaw colony could probably suit the needs of my final days quite well. As things have turned out, I was correct."

"Do you believe in any existence after death?" asked Lloyd.

Beau's face brightened and he quickly answered, "Oh, absolutely, but probably not the kind you're thinking of…but, then again, maybe not."

"Do you believe you have an immortal soul?" asked Katie.

Beau smiled at Katie. "Part of me is immortal. The rest of me, I don't know about and don't really care."

"What do you mean by that?" asked Lloyd, leaning closer to Beau.

"When I die, William Beauregard Bondurant will probably cease to exist. At least I hope he does, because he wants nothing to do with that fire and brimstone mishmash. But I truly know something in the spiritual realm will survive this mortal coil."

"Such as?" asked Lloyd.

"Many years ago, when I was first discovering what a penchant I had for inflicting pain, I began to dabble with a Satanist cult. What a sick bunch of puppies those pitiful people were! Sick, but useful. They started me thinking about the possibility that Satan is real. I had already believed Jesus was real, so it wasn't too much of a stretch." Beau laughed again. "Then presto, I started believing I could tap into that dark side. Before I knew it, I had entered into a pact with the Devil himself. I gave him Beau, and he gave me anything I wanted until I died. That part will live on after Beau is nothing but ashes in Ossabaw's crematorium. If Beau is lucky, there will be nothingness."

Lloyd swallowed and rose to his feet. "Perhaps we could speak once again, maybe tomorrow?"

"You know where to find me, Lloyd. I've enjoyed our little discussion." Looking at Katie, Beau added, "I hope you'll be with the Bishop if he comes tomorrow. It's not often here in the colony that I get to be around such a beautiful woman. The others are such worn-out cokeheads. It's really not much of a challenge."

As Lloyd and Katie reached the Castle door, Beau said, "You know, Lloyd, black males in your age group tend to suffer heavily from essential hypertension and cardio-vascular disease leading to premature myocardial infarction. I hope you're taking your blood pressure meds and don't ignore little signs like tightness in the chest."

* * *

Lloyd stood at the bottom of the steps leading to the door of the ocean cottage, looked up, took a deep breath and started the climb. There were sixty steps, and Katie had climbed them quickly and effortlessly. Now Lloyd held tightly to the railing and used his arms almost as much as his legs. He nearly made it to the top when he began to feel tightness in his chest.

It was late afternoon and a strong thunderstorm was sweeping over the island, pounding it with heavy rains and lightening. When the thunderclaps rolled through, they shook the cottage, and Lloyd went to the screened porch to watch as the storm brought the ocean to an angry boil.

"What do you think about Beau Bondurant?" asked Katie. "Is he simply a man who is quite smart, but terribly sick and twisted? Or, is he a person who is truly evil?"

"I don't quite know, Katie. But, I'm determined to find out."

"What do you mean, Lloyd?"

"I'm set to go to Savannah tomorrow for some tests. Before I go, I'm going to have another visit with King Rat, just to answer that question."

* * *

"I'm so happy you decided to visit again," cooed Beau, opening the door to King Rat's Castle.

Settling into his chair, Beau said, "I thoroughly enjoyed your visit yesterday, Lloyd. I thought about our conversation a lot after you left, and for some reason I was certain you'd return." Beau watched Katie and Lloyd, waiting for a reply.

"I've spoken with a lot a strange and messed-up people in my career as a priest, Beau. A lot of them have been on this island. Some of these people appeared to be possessed by an evil spirit, and I did my best to rid them of it." Lloyd took a deep breath. "I guess what I'm trying to say is that I've never been completely sure any of the people were actually possessed."

"And," interrupted Beau, "you're wondering about me, aren't you?"

"Yes."

"Well," replied Beau, "wonder no more." Leaning back and smiling, he continued, "I can remember as a child in Catholic school being taught how to fight against Satan. One of the things the nuns taught us was that the devil couldn't read our minds, but God could. They said that, while the devil couldn't read our minds, he was always lurking in the shadows of our lives and could surely read our intentions. I was taught it was there the devil had power over us. Do you believe that, Bishop?"

"I might."

"Well, let me tell you something else I was taught," said Beau, shifting his eyes to Katie. "I was taught that Satan had knowledge of everything we'd ever done in our lives and could use those things against us as he bargained for our behavior." With those words, both Lloyd and Katie tensed, and Beau could plainly read that. "I recall how you both responded yesterday when I spoke about the abortions I'd done. Do either of you remember how you reacted?"

Neither Lloyd nor Katie said a word. A smile crept across Beau's lips.

Looking at Katie, Beau said, "I know you've had at least two abortions. You had them when you were turning tricks, didn't you? And you've let it eat at you ever since Bishop Bryan brought you to the foot of the cross, and you realized what a horrible sin it was."

Beau waited a moment as Katie tried to reply, then held his hand up and said, "No need to say anything, Miss McFarland." Fixing his gaze on Lloyd, he continued. "And you, Your Excellency, when you were in the NFL, snorting coke and having unprotected sex with whoever threw herself at you, you paid for several abortions, didn't you?"

Lloyd sighed as his shoulders sank. He looked over at Katie and could see the distress on her face that surely mirrored his. There was silence for a long time as Beau stood, fetched himself a shot of his favorite liquor, and studied his guests with satisfaction.

"So, Bishop, you were wondering if I'm just sick and twisted, or if something much more sinister lives within me?"

"Yeah, that's the bottom line."

"Shame on you, Bishop, for thinking it would be so easy. A man with your training should know better." Beau seemed to shift gears, and said, "You'll have to excuse me, now. I'm expecting some female companionship shortly. We'll be engaging in some rather violent sexual intercourse." He looked at Katie and added, "You're more than welcome to stay."

In silence, Lloyd and Katie stood and went to the door. Just before they went out, Beau said, "You know, Lloyd, that tightness you're having in your chest right now is a bad sign. You really need to do something about it. It could kill you."

On the walk from King Rat's Castle to the Humvee outside the big tent, Lloyd began feel a heaviness in his chest he'd never felt before. When he arrived at Ossabaw's dock where John-Morgan was waiting to take him back to the mainland and medical care, he was feeling better. The long walk down the dock was different. The heaviness came back with a vengeance and the pain in his chest was unbearable. Halfway down the dock, Lloyd collapsed. There was nothing John-Morgan or Katie could do to save him.

CHAPTER SIXTEEN

EVIL

The belief in a supernatural source of
evil is not necessary; men alone are
quite capable of every wickedness.
—Joseph Conrad

Lloyd's death had been national news and all the major broadcast and cable networks covered it. Congressman McQueen delivered the eulogy, which Fox carried live. The impressive and positive coverage pushed Will's approval ratings up three whole points in twenty-four hours. When the Executive Outcomes choir from the Ossabaw colony sang *Non nobis Domine, Domine* and *Panus angelicus,* followed by successive Gregorian chants, even Robbie McFarland was moved.

Lloyd's remains were interred next to the scores of other priests who'd gone before him at the Catholic cemetery on Wheaton Street. Rudy watched as Lloyd's fellow priests carried his casket to the open grave and gently lowered it into the rich, dark earth. Colonel Schwarz was standing next to him and both men searched the multitude that surrounded the burial site. Rudy spotted Robbie standing next to Big Dog and nudged Schwarz.

"If you'll look straight ahead," said Rudy quietly to Schwarz, "you'll spot a problem that needs to be solved."

Schwarz looked across the grave and saw Robbie. "I understand what you mean, sir," he whispered. "I was thinking the same thing only this morning."

* * *

Alone with Rudy in his office, Robbie poured himself his third drink of the evening and settled down in one of the chairs opposite Rudy's desk. In a few minutes, Schwarz entered and took the chair next to Robbie.

"Well," said Robbie, "that was really a first-class send-off for the Bishop, wasn't it?"

Rudy nodded and said, "He deserved it."

"What about my sister, Rudy? What's going to happen with her now?"

"I suppose she'll stay here and function pretty much as she has in the past. I hope she'll be able to carry on with our religious broadcast from the island," answered Rudy.

Robbie cleared his throat and squirmed in his chair. "Whatever, I just don't want any more trouble from her."

Smiling, Rudy replied, "I don't think she'll cause any problems at all, Little Dog." Rudy looked once again at Schwarz and said, "I have the feeling something else is on your mind. Could it be those gold coins?"

"Yeah, Rudy," answered Robbie quickly, "it sure as shit is."

* * *

It rained hard that night on Ossabaw. The next morning dawned clear and cool and Rudy decided to ride his horse to Katie's cottage and check on her. What he saw when he got there was a surprise.

When Katie opened the door, she was wearing a robe pulled tightly around her. There were dark shadows under eyes that were puffy and reddened. Her hair was disheveled and she had no shoes on. It was already ten o'clock, and Katie appeared to have just gotten out of bed. When she greeted Rudy, her voice seemed weak and distant. Rudy's first impression was that Katie was still grieving heavily for Lloyd.

"You don't look well," commented Rudy as he stepped into the cottage.

"I don't feel so hot, Rudy. I haven't since Lloyd died."

"Have you eaten any breakfast, Katie?"

"I don't have any appetite. The thought of food makes me nauseated. Every time I closed my eyes, I thought of Lloyd and how he died. The image of King Rat kept surfacing and scaring me."

Katie wandered out to the screened porch and Rudy followed. They both sat facing the ocean and for several minutes nothing was said. Katie finally spoke.

"I thought about doing some coke to get me up and going, Rudy, but I didn't. It would be like betraying everything that Lloyd did for me, and I just can't do that. I've never felt like this before. Believe me, I've been down before, really down, but this is a different place for me."

Rudy replied, "Tell me about what actually happened when you and Lloyd met with Beau Bondurant that second time."

Katie shook her head ever so slightly as she looked off into the distance and answered, "I've never been so completely frightened in my entire life. Looking into Beau's eyes was like looking into a dark abyss. When he started talking to Lloyd about who he really was, I began to feel the room turn cold. I watched Lloyd and saw him clench his teeth in pain. In a matter of seconds, I saw him age right before my eyes. Everything seemed to move so quickly, and I was so afraid, I couldn't move. I could see the life being drained from Lloyd and could feel it leaving me. If Lloyd hadn't been there, I don't know what would have happened, because I didn't have the strength or the courage to leave that man's presence."

Katie wiped her eyes and looked at Rudy, saying, "I begged Lloyd not to go back there, but he was determined. He wanted to know if Beau really was...was..."

"Really was the personification of true evil, Katie?" asked Rudy.

Katie drew her knees up in her chair, wrapped her arms around them to pull them close, buried her face in them, and began to weep. Rudy said nothing as he watched Katie's body tremble and listened as she heaved with suffering.

Finally, Rudy reached out and placed his hand on Katie's back. She lifted her head and through the tears blurted out, "King Rat killed Lloyd just as sure as we're sitting here, and he stole years off my life!"

"I'll have one of the guards come up and fix something for you to eat. Try to get yourself together, Katie. You've inherited Bishop Bryan's work, and you'll have to be strong for that."

* * *

For about a mile, Rudy rode Blitz at a walk through the deep forest. Everything was green and fresh. Still, Rudy couldn't stop thinking about Katie and what she had told him about King Rat. He couldn't get over how much older Katie looked, and he remembered how beautiful she was when she entered the colony and how attracted he'd been to her. Until now, his thoughts of Katie had been pleasant, licentious fantasies. That seemed to be gone. She wasn't the same person.

The more Rudy thought about King Rat and what he'd done, the deeper his anger became, and he decided to exact a heavy price from Beau Bondurant. When he got to the trail that led to Group Two, he put his spurs to Blitz and raced to the compound's entrance.

"Is King Rat in his castle?"

"Yes, sir."

"Good," replied Rudy, looking down the path to the tent where King Rat lived, then back at Leary. "Come with me, Corporal, I have news for His Majesty."

When Rudy and Corporal Leary got to King Rat's Castle, Rudy stopped at the door and said to Leary, "You wait out here. I'll deal with him, myself.

Without knocking, Rudy forcefully opened the door to the Castle and marched in. Beau was serenely seated at the end of the room under one of the ceiling fans, sipping from a fresh glass of Crown Royal.

"I thought you'd be here sooner, Rudy," said Beau.

Rudy didn't reply as he walked quickly across the room and onto the screened porch where Beau was waiting.

Rudy remained standing, towering over Beau. Then he said coldly "You were warned not to fuck with the Bishop and Miss McFarland, Beau, but you just couldn't help yourself, could you?"

"For goodness sake, Rudy," replied Beau in a condescending tone, "don't be so damn melodramatic. You were that way back when we were residents together at Hopkins. It was unbecoming then, and it's unbecoming now."

Rudy glared at Beau for several seconds as his face reddened with anger.

"This is going to be quick and to the point, Beau," said Rudy, staring directly into Beau's eyes. "It's over for you here in Group Two. You will immediately be moved into Group Three, where you'll find things a whole lot more uncomfortable. If you had heeded instructions and not messed with those people, you'd be staying here. But, true to form, as I recall from our residency program, you had to have it your way. Now you'll pay a very steep price."

Appearing unfazed, Beau smirked at Rudy. "Oh, you mean the place where the gladiators fight those battles. Why, that will probably be delightful! What great fun it will be to kill those cracked-out fools. Scuttlebutt has it there are women there, too, so I won't have to worry about female companionship." Beau stared back at Rudy with great intensity, and Rudy felt the hairs on the back of his neck stand up.

"I guess you're mostly upset about Miss McFarland, aren't you, Rudy? She is a beautiful thing. I could make her scream with pleasure." Beau paused and smiled sardonically. "I'll bet you've thought about fucking that hot little cunt a thousand times, haven't you, Rudy? But I doubt you've done the deed. Now you blame me for messing up her head, and your chance at some really wild pussy. Look in the mirror, Rudy, and you'll see a man who's afraid to use his power for whatever he wants. Don't blame me for your lost pleasures."

Without taking his eyes from Rudy, Beau took a drink from his glass. "Oh, and the Bishop. What a dear little man. So genuine, so sincere and truly religious. I enjoyed looking into his heart and finding out its secrets. His silly guilt about something that happened years ago finally caught up with him. That's what killed him, not I. I don't do guilt, Rudy. I just do pleasure. It's so much more fun!"

Rudy shifted uncomfortably in his chair when Beau set his glass down and leaned forward. "And, you, Rudy. Surely you carry a lot of guilt about what goes on here. Do you ever have nightmares about this island? Have you ever had to take sleeping meds just to block out your thoughts when you place your head on the pillow next to your beautiful wife and can't bring yourself to fuck her because of what goes on under your command?"

Rudy instinctively drew back and forced himself to look away from Beau's gaze. He took a deep breath, stood and called for Corporal Leary, who entered the room with his pistol drawn.

"Take this piece of excrement to Group Three right now."

Just before Rudy left the room, Beau called out to him saying, "Sweet dreams, Rudy, dear!"

* * *

When Rudy and Schwarz ate dinner together that evening with their wives, Rudy seemed somewhat distant, prompting his wife to ask if he were feeling ill. He blamed his remoteness on a long, hard day. As had grown to be the custom, after dinner the men retired to Rudy's office while the women remained in the dining room and talked.

"I heard about Dr. Bondurant being sent to Group Three today, sir," said Schwarz.

"I visited Katie McFarland this morning and she looked awful," answered Rudy, slumped in his chair with his drink.

"She was quite devoted to Bishop Bryan, sir, and one might expect to find her that way," answered Schwarz.

"Not this bad, Claus. She looked years older, as if she'd lost some of her spark."

"What did she tell you about Dr. Bondurant, sir?"

"She blames him for Lloyd's death and the way she feels now."

"And, sir, what do you think about Dr. Bondurant?"

"I'm not sure, but it will be interesting to see how things turn out for him in Group Three."

Schwarz nodded. "Didn't you say, sir, that Mr. McFarland is

returning to the island this weekend?"

"Yeah, he's expected to land at last light on Friday."

"Have you formulated any specific plan of action for his disposal yet, sir?"

"I'm inclined to believe that a quick and clean liquidation of Robbie McFarland would be in the company's best interest."

Schwarz smiled and said, "I believe you've made the right decision, sir. I'll handle this problem myself."

Rudy had trouble falling asleep. Finally, a little after one in the morning, he drifted away. Between three and four his nightmare returned and seemed to last hours. Awaking from his dream at five, Rudy was covered in sweat and felt as if he had the flu. It wasn't the flu, and Rudy knew it.

* * *

For the next week or so, Katie had to force herself to get out of bed and go to Group One. She had an almost constant, dull headache that drained her even more. Rudy hadn't fared much better, but he was good at hiding his discomfort. Occasionally, he and Schwarz watched video clips of Bondurant's actions in Group Three. One thing was clear about Beau; he did, indeed, enjoy beating people to death.

"It's funny, Claus," said Rudy as they sat in his office one evening and watched Beau in action, "Beau told me he'd enjoy himself greatly in Group Three."

"He's certainly King Rat once again, sir, even if it is in Group Three." Schwarz grew silent as he watched Beau kill a man by kicking him in the head, using his martial arts skills.

After Beau finished dispatching another hapless crackhead, Schwarz said to Rudy, "I saw a spot on the news today that Mr. McFarland's Cadillac Escalade was found in Atlanta. The police say they believe Mr. McFarland was robbed and may even have been murdered in the process. His father said the FBI has come in on the case, since it is believed Mr. McFarland may have been kidnapped."

Rudy looked at Schwarz and replied, "Who'd want to kidnap that piece of crap?"

That night, Rudy slept well and awakened feeling refreshed. After a large breakfast, Rudy decided to inspect things in Group One, where he found Katie working with some volunteers from several church groups. She seemed different.

When Katie saw Rudy approaching, she stood and came toward him. She smiled broadly, took Rudy by the hand and led him to a spot away from the rest of the people.

"You won't believe what happened to me last night, Rudy," said Katie excitedly.

"It must have been good, because you look a lot better than the last time I saw you," replied Rudy. He scrutinized Katie's face, taking in each little thing he'd thought was so beautiful about her.

"I may have been only dreaming, Rudy, but it seemed so real." Katie paused to prepare what she was about to say. "You're gonna think I'm crazy, Rudy." Katie hesitated, then quickly said, "Lloyd appeared to me last night. He was as real as you are right now. I woke up in the middle of the night, and Lloyd was standing at the foot of my bed, and he had this radiance about him. He looked like a young man. He told me I was safe and had nothing to fear. Then he told me to lie down and go back to sleep, which I did. When I woke up this morning, I felt so much better. I don't know whether it was all a dream or if Lloyd really was standing in my room last night, but I'll never forget it."

Katie looked down for a moment, then back up at Rudy with tears in her eyes.

"I want to believe he really was in my room, Rudy."

"Whatever it was, Katie, you're looking much better. I was beginning to be concerned for you."

Rudy returned to the Main House where he and Schwarz ate lunch together and discussed the impending population problem on the island. Just as Rudy was about to go to his office, Schwarz added, almost as an afterthought, that Beau Bondurant had been killed the night before.

"I've seen the video, sir. He was mobbed by the members of his own gang."

CHAPTER SEVENTEEN

ANSWERS

Always the beautiful answer who
asks a more beautiful question.
—e. e. cummings

Summer finally hit Ossabaw full bore the last week in June. It was an oppressive heat, laden with humidity and bereft of breezes. In the camps, large fans under the shade of tents were the only solace offered to the residents. In all three groups, those who had been teetering on the brink chose to end their suffering with massive overdoses.

Rudy greeted the heat with enthusiasm, since it relieved some of the overpopulation pressure that was building at Butterbean Beach. While he and Schwarz had discussed thinning the colony again using the modified Spanish flu virus, he was loath to employ such a tactic since it meant evacuating the island and focusing media attention on the colony. Besides, Will McQueen was fast becoming the sure presidential nominee for the Republican Party at its convention that coming August, and Rudy didn't want anything to detract from Will's chances.

* * *

Ann-Marie Hartman really didn't want to open up her home to a bunch of strangers, but she and John-Morgan would do anything to help Will McQueen win the nomination. Ann-Marie decided to step back, enjoy the day, and let the campaign staff do all the heavy lifting.

The guest list for the fund-raiser was impressive. Besides Congressman McQueen and Charlotte, and of course Judah and Hannah, big money from all over South Georgia and the Low Country would be present. Will would deliver a brief speech from the front steps of Driscoll House and take a few questions from the press. Then, one after the other, folks with checkbooks ready would be escorted into John-Morgan's office where favors were sought, deals struck, and money changed hands. It was a practice that had not differed in the thousands of years of political history.

Judah checked the crowd and he immediately saw Rudy and his wife talking it up with the owner of a very large farm in Reidsville. Judah's lips tightened a bit as he watched Rudy. Hannah caught the look on his face, prompting her to say, "You really don't like Rudy very much, do you?"

"No I don't," replied Judah in a whisper. "I still think he had something to do with my getting shot. And, trust me, he's a sixteenth of an inch away from being a goddamn Nazi. His father and grandfather were members of the SS. They helped found Executive Outcomes, and I don't believe that company has ever shed its snake's skin. They're still from that mold."

Judah looked over the crowd once more and said to Hannah, "But successful campaigns require lots of money, and I believe EO is going to pony up quite well for Will. So, my dear and beautiful wife, it is now my duty to be nice to Dr. Hoorst." Holding out his hand, he said with a smile, "Would you care to join me, Hannah, for a visit with Dr. and Mrs. Hoorst?"

Big Dog McFarland and his wife were there, also, and the strain of

Robbie's disappearance clearly showed on both their faces. After Judah and Hannah had visited with the Hoorsts, Rudy approached Big Dog and offered his condolences.

"Do the feds have any idea about what may have happened to Robbie?" asked Rudy with concern.

"The only thing they've found out was that my son was trading in large amounts of gold coins," replied the Dog. "They believe this may have something to do with his disappearance. You know, somebody robbed him for that gold. But that's all they have."

Rudy turned to Robbie's mother and said, "Please know that Carolyn and I both will keep Robbie's safe return at the top of our prayer list. To lose such a wonderful and valuable person, at the same time we lost Bishop Bryan, has been a severe blow to everyone on the island."

Rudy was the last of the guests who met with Will and Judah that day. Their meeting wasn't held in John-Morgan's office, as were the twenty or so others, but in his gun room with the door closed where security and privacy would be absolute.

When Rudy entered the room, he had a very pleasant smile on his face. He was dressed in a well-tailored seersucker suit and, in spite of the record heat and humidity, still appeared crisp and cool. Looking at Judah and Will, he asked, "How can I help you become President of the United States?"

"We need a ground game just like the Dems have, only better. That takes cash and lots of it."

"I understand, Will, and EO is ready with an initial donation of four million."

Judah scratched the back of his neck, pulled his chair a little closer to the table and said, "That's most generous, Rudy. The only thing is, we feel EO money may be a bit of a liability for our campaign. There're still some people out there who don't believe the Ossabaw colony was a good idea, and they're holdin' that against Will no matter how good the stats about crime and drugs have improved. A big chunk of change right from EO could stink things up for us."

Will loosened his tie and unbuttoned his shirt collar. "Judah and I were thinking more along the lines of a super-PAC funded by your company. Something that would be very effective and hard hitting, but would still keep the campaign at arms-length from EO. I hope this doesn't offend you or the company, Rudy, but that's how we feel."

"I'm not offended in the least, Congressman. I deal with the realities of life every day. Simply have someone get in touch with me and I'll write the check."

* * *

Once that summer began in earnest, there was no break in the heat

SPEAK NOTHING OF THE DEAD BUT GOOD | 249

wave. The intensity of the corresponding presidential campaign only served to accent the weather. Will held a commanding lead as the Republican National Convention in Atlanta began to close in. True to his word, Rudy donated $4 million to a PAC that went by the name of Reclaiming America's Values. The PAC produced a series of blistering ads that had the effect of moving the ball a lot closer to Will's goal line.

At the Ossabaw colony, the only problem was the increasing resident population. Rudy and Schwarz had several meetings about the overcrowding during July and early August. Every time, the only workable solutions they could come up with were either to thin the population by massive overdosing of the residents, or another use of the Spanish flu virus. Neither Rudy nor Schwarz regarded those choices as ideal, but both realized something had to be done soon. Reluctantly, Rudy decided to use the Spanish flu virus when Schwarz informed him it had been modified to make it twice as lethal as the one used previously. Three weeks before the beginning of the Republican convention, Rudy gave the orders to infect the general population on Ossabaw with the virus. That evening, while he slept, his nightmare returned with great ferocity.

As before, everyone but essential personnel was evacuated from the island, and EO flew in extra men to help with the collection and disposal of bodies. However, one problem arose that slowed down the disposal process.

Due to an explosion along a pipeline in Texas, a shortage in the availability of propane occurred the day after the liquidation process got underway. Under normal operating conditions, such a shortage wouldn't have adversely affected the crematorium's ability to dispose of the bodies, but a mass die-off like the one Rudy ordered meant all three ovens had to run at full capacity. Soon, bodies began to pile up in the large vacant area behind the crematorium center. The sun literally cooked the bodies in the field, even though they were covered with soil as quickly as possible. It wasn't long before a dozen or more turkey buzzards that roosted on the mainland and searched for carrion over Ossabaw detected the stench of the rotting flesh and descended upon the body pile to pick apart whatever they could.

* * *

Since Will's connection with the Ossabaw colony was common knowledge and considered fair game, his opponents in the press focused their attention on it.

Judah was with Will at a rally in Akron, Ohio, when an aide quietly informed him that *The Washington Post* was going to run a very damning story on the colony. The aide said his sources claimed the information came from a volunteer with one of the local churches that worked in Group One. There would be the assertion that Executive Outcomes was killing people well before their time, to make room for new residents and harvest their body parts. There would also be the implication that Congressman McQueen knew about this policy and approved of it.

As soon as Will had finished his speech and had worked the rope line, Judah pulled him aside.

"You've got a bad case of diarrhea starting right now. You feel like shit," said Judah, "and you're out of here and in bed. You're not making any appearances, and you're not speaking to anybody about anything."

"What's happened, Judah?" asked Will, drawing back in surprise.

"It's about the Ossabaw colony. The *Post* is going to run a nasty one on it that implicates you." Judah looked at the ground, then back at Will. "I'm going to Savannah right away, and I'm going to have a little face-to-face with Rudy Hoorst. Don't say a fuckin' word to anybody and remember, you really don't know shit about what's been happening on that island. I've kept you in the dark to keep you clean. Let me handle this my way. I'll call you when I know more."

As soon as Judah was in his limo and on the way to the Akron airport, he phoned John-Morgan and told him he'd be in Savannah in a few hours.

"I need your help on this one, John-Morgan. I want you to take me to Ossabaw. I've got to have a face-off with fuckin' Hoorst, and I want you by my side, OK?"

When Judah reached the tarmac, the campaign plane was waiting. He looked at it and was glad they'd decided to lease a Gulfstream G-650. With it, Savannah was an hour away. Once aboard, Judah called Rudy and told him he urgently needed to meet with him.

"That's fine, Judah," replied Rudy, "will you be staying for dinner?"

"This ain't about food, Rudy," was Judah's terse reply.

By four in the afternoon, John-Morgan and Judah were aboard *Graf Spee* speeding toward Ossabaw Island while Judah told John-Morgan about the *Washington Post* story.

"You two boys look like you could use a nice cold drink," drawled Carolyn Hoorst as she showed Judah and John-Morgan to the door of Rudy's office. She knocked and said, "It's Judah and John-Morgan here to see you, honey." She opened the door saying, "I'll be right back with two big glasses of tea."

"Y'all look like you've been in a steam bath," said Rudy with a little smile.

"We have been," answered Judah who looked down at his navy blue slacks and realized he still had on the coat that went with it. His hand went to his collar, and he found he hadn't even loosened his tie.

"My goodness," remarked Rudy, "you're so wrapped up in all this political stuff, you didn't even think to remove your coat and tie for the trip across the sound, Judah. It must be something serious, so have a seat and let's wait until Carolyn returns with some refreshments before we get down to business, shall we?"

It wasn't long before Carolyn returned with the iced tea, but Judah and Rudy used it to size each other up. Rudy could easily see how agitated Judah was, prompting him to lean back in his chair and give him that clever smile Judah had come to despise so much.

"If y'all need anything else, just holler," said Carolyn, closing the door behind her. John-Morgan and Judah drank Carolyn's iced tea quickly and gratefully. Rudy clasped his hands beneath his chin, and when they had finished, he asked, "What brings you gentlemen to the Ossabaw colony in the middle of such an exciting campaign and on a day as hot as this one?"

Judah looked sternly at Rudy and said, "I've been informed by good sources that *The Washington Post* is going to run a story about this place that puts Will in a very bad light.

"My source says the information comes from an informant who worked for one of the church groups that helped Bishop Bryan with the residents in Group One. This informant claims the epidemics that wiped out the island's population three different times weren't a random act of nature, but were done intentionally by those who run the colony as a method of population control. The *Post* is going to try to hang this around Will's neck and sink him with it."

Judah paused to let what he'd said sink in. Rudy glanced over at Schwarz who, with a nod of his head and a gesture, seemed to be saying, "I told you so."

Judah continued, "When I first realized the operation of this island wasn't what the board of directors initially thought it was, I immediately moved to cut Will off from any information that would indicate otherwise. As best I know, he has no knowledge about the dirty little secrets that take place here, Rudy."

"Then he has nothing to worry about, Judah," said Rudy. "He's an innocent lamb."

"Major league hard-ball politics doesn't work that way, Rudy, and you damn well know it!"

"Well, if he's clean, then what's the worry? Why come all the way down here just to tell me somebody's going to write a less than flattering story about this place?"

Judah leaned forward in his chair and said, "It's not that fuckin' simple, Rudy. I need to know the truth about this place if I'm going to defend my man."

"It sounds to me as if you already know the truth about this colony."

John-Morgan could tell Judah had started a slow burn just by the way his hands were gripping his knees. Then Judah let the other shoe fall.

"I have friends at the FBI who have been keeping me up to speed on their investigation of Robbie McFarland's disappearance. What they're telling me is even more unsettling."

Rudy had moved from borderline sarcasm to full blown when he asked, "And what does the FBI have to say about that?"

"They say they have Robbie's cell phone records that show him making calls from some property that EO owns in Forsythe three weekends in a row. They also have records of calls made between Forsythe and Savannah that had to be made from something that was moving faster than any car can go. They also say the coins Robbie was selling were all minted before World War II, most of them before the First World War. They claim these coins were most likely stolen from Jews and others deemed undesirables when the Nazis came to power."

Rudy slowly dropped his hands from his chin and leaned forward.

"What has Robbie McFarland's disappearance got to do with bad blow-back from this colony on Will McQueen," asked Rudy, glaring at Judah without a single blink.

"It sends me the signal that there's a whole lot of shit happening on this island that is orchestrated personally by you, that could blow up in the congressman's face and cost him the election," answered Judah, returning Rudy's cold stare.

Rudy turned to Schwarz. "What is your impression of all this, Claus?"

"It appears to me, sir, that Mr. Benjamin is quite intent on getting answers. However, those answers may not be exactly what he is ready for, Dr. Hoorst."

Rudy pursed his lips as he looked at Schwarz, then nodded slightly in agreement and turned back to Judah. "I believe you have the best interests of Congressman McQueen at heart, Judah. I also have his best interests at heart. I think my contribution to his campaign speaks much louder than any words I might utter." Rudy was silent for several seconds as he studied Judah. Then he walked to the front of his desk and leaned against it.

"You've most certainly heard the old saying, 'In for a penny, in for a pound,' haven't you, Judah?"

"I know more than I'm comfortable with, yeah."

"So you want no surprises from this island. Nothing that could catch you off guard, Judah?"

"Quit fuckin' with me, Rudy, and get to your point."

"Fine, I will." Rudy stood and looked at Schwarz who rose from his chair.

"You and Dr. Hartman are about to be in for a lot," said Rudy, walking toward the bookcase at the far end of his office. John-Morgan glanced at Judah with a 'what-the-fuck' expression. He watched as Rudy slipped his hand behind the bookcase and tripped the latch.

"If you gentlemen will follow me, you will learn all the secrets of this island," said Rudy, stepping into the passage way.

Rudy entered the room where the coins were stored and turned on the lights. Judah and John-Morgan were only a few feet behind, with Schwarz in the rear. When Judah stepped into the little room and saw the gold coins stacked on a pallet in the center of the floor, he couldn't help his slight gasp.

With satisfaction, Rudy watched as Judah knelt and examined the coins, then the precious jewels and works of art that filled the room. Finally, after several long minutes, Judah stood. His face was ashen and he appeared shaken by what he was seeing.

"This is all stolen property taken by the Nazis mostly from European Jews isn't it, Rudy?"

"Mostly Jews," answered Rudy in a flippant tone. "But some of this came from Gypsies, homosexuals, and other miscreants. It doesn't really matter where it came from. What matters is that it's here."

Rudy didn't say anything more as he watched Judah's eyes roam the room. Finally, Judah looked at Rudy and said, "This is where the gold coins Robbie was selling came from, isn't it?"

"You're a smart boy, Judah. I knew you'd catch on quickly."

"So," said Judah, "why did Robbie have any of these coins?"

"As payment for services rendered, Judah. Little Dog got the bill passed that gave EO the exclusive rights to funeral homes that could harvest artificial joints. We've made a fortune from that."

"OK, so what happened to him?"

"Robbie McFarland was a pig of a man. What he did to his sister was despicable. But his ultimate downfall was his greed. The world is a better place without Robbie sucking up precious oxygen."

"Did you have him killed, Hoorst?"

Rudy didn't reply; he only smiled slightly as the air in the little room thickened.

"Your silence speaks volumes, Hoorst."

"Let me tell you what speaks volumes," said Rudy with a cold stare. "Both you and Dr. Hartman are now in as deep as it gets on Ossabaw Island. I admit to nothing, but the two of you are free to imagine whatever you'd like, and maybe it would be true. Colonel Schwarz and I work for an international corporation so powerful that I had no fear of bringing you to this room and showing you what amounts to a minor portion of its assets. If this *Washington Post* story happens, I predict it will come to nothing. E.O. has that kind of power. I suggest that, if you are asked about the colony, you simply say things are as they appear here on Ossabaw. The press won't get anything different from me, and no evidence exists that will prove otherwise. So, relax and enjoy the moment. Will McQueen is going to be the next president of the United States."

Judah looked quickly at John-Morgan, who simply shook his head and said, "This is deep serious shit." Judah looked at Rudy. "You're slick, Rudy, you're really slick, and you're right. John-Morgan and I are now up to our ears in all of this, thank you very much. Of course, it wouldn't serve any purpose for either of us to crap all over the place about what actually happens here. If the worst still somehow happens, and the truth about the colony gets out, I'll take the bullet and say I kept Will in the dark. At least that would be the truth, and it would be nice to wallow in the truth a little, especially after rolling around like a dung beetle in this cesspool with you."

Just before Rudy turned off the lights, Judah said, pointing to the coins, "You aren't any different from the thieves who stole this stuff."

Glancing at Schwarz, then looking hard at Judah, Rudy replied, "If you only knew the half of it."

* * *

Will was the speaker at the National Press Club luncheon in Washington the day *The Washington Post* broke the story about the Ossabaw colony. Will's appearance before that group and been much anticipated and well-hyped by the national media, and Judah was fuming about the timing of the piece. Whatever the reason, Judah knew this appearance could be a make-or-break opportunity for Will's campaign. That morning as Judah prepped Will for his answers to the questions that would follow his speech, at the end he leaned in close to Will and whispered so no one else could hear, "When they ask you about that island, you can honestly say you don't know shit, because it's the truth. I'll handle everything else that follows."

While the questions were direct and sometimes very pointed, Will did exactly as he'd been advised, and most of the reporters walked away with the feeling that Will was probably telling the truth. But the firestorm started by the *Post* story caused the national media to focus its attention on the Ossabaw colony. There were calls for impartial inspections of the colony and Big Dog McFarland buckled and let a group of twelve people chosen by the state legislature do a thorough and unfettered inspection of the colony. While what the inspectors saw horrified them, nothing was found to substantiate the story in *The Washington Post* that residents were being killed in order to harvest their organs, or that mass murder was being carried out to control the population. It appeared that the storm had passed over the island.

CHAPTER EIGHTEEN

THE GHOST

Look like the innocent flower,
But be the serpent under it.
—William Shakespeare, *MacBeth,* Act I, Scene V

Just as Rudy had predicted, the *Washington Post* story fell flat on its face, and Will won the Republican nomination in overwhelming fashion. As the political season went full bore after Labor Day, all the polls indicated Will would win in November.

On Ossabaw, the heat was still intense, but the population was stable. Katie had taken over Lloyd's position as the spiritual leader of the colony and had done an admirable job. And, at long last, Rudy thought he could relax some and enjoy this last assignment with the company before he and Carolyn moved into the house they'd bought on the Isle of Hope and raise their boys in a normal environment.

On the mainland, near Richmond Hill in Bryan County, the turkey buzzards that had eaten the infected flesh of the corpses rotting in the sun outside the crematoriums began to surrender to the virus infecting them. One by one, their bodies were consumed by a number of different scavengers, but most frequently by the feral hogs populating the forests in that area. The animals that came in contact with the buzzards became infected as well and soon died.

The hunting of large feral hogs in South Georgia is a sport relished by the locals, and the hunters around the Richmond Hill area were no exception. In the beginning of October, a hunter and his twelve-year-old son brought down a hog infected with the virus. During the dressing-out of the carcass, both the hunter and his son inhaled the virus as the hog's lungs were removed, and they became infected. They, in turn, infected other family and community members.

Rudy's older son, Rudolph Jr., had taken a keen interest in the American Civil War and his father had encouraged him to visit the many Civil War forts around Savannah. One of the most interesting to little Rudy was Fort McAllister, an earthwork fortification on the Ogeechee River, only a few miles from Richmond Hill. His Boy Scout troop from St. James School left for the fort on a Friday afternoon to camp out there for the weekend. Late that afternoon, little Rudy came in contact with another child his age who had a bad cough. They happened to be in a small restroom at the fort, where the infected child sprayed tiny droplets of his contaminated sputum each time he coughed or sneezed. In the confines of such a small space, it was inevitable that Rudy Jr. would become infected with his father's killer virus.

Friday evening, as he sat around the campfire after dinner, little Rudy began to feel as if he were getting a cold and was angry with himself because he was looking forward to the next day when the troop would tour the fort and study it in great detail. As the evening wore on, Rudy began to feel worse and went to his tent, where he fell asleep. Later, the two boys who were his bunk mates finally turned in, and they were soon sleeping soundly.

Around one in the morning, Rudy was awakened by a strange feeling in his chest and began to cough. In no time the tent was filled with contaminated air the other two boys inhaled, and in a matter of minutes they had been infected. By six in the morning, young Rudy was starting to hemorrhage from his nose. By seven he had severe and bloody diarrhea and was so weak, he was forced to lie in his sleeping bag and endure it. When Rudy and the other boys didn't show for reveille, the scoutmaster came to their tent looking for them. Sticking his head inside, he found Rudy barely conscious and the other boys hacking their heads off. Three full breaths of the air inside the tent, and the scoutmaster was infected.

Young Rudy and other Boy Scouts weren't the only people staying near Fort McAllister demonstrating signs of severe influenza. Half of the fifty Civil War re-enactors on hand that weekend for an artillery demonstration were also showing signs of the infection. That, however, was nothing compared to what was happening at Richmond Hill. The two immediate-med offices there were overwhelmed by locals, some of whom showed signs of bleeding from the ears as well as bleeding under the skin, along with edema of the lungs.

One of the physicians who saw those people was also a member of the United States Army, moonlighting for extra money. His specialty was infectious diseases and he was able, in rapid fashion, to diagnose the problem. He thought it was a mutated form of swine flu and, when he learned about the cases at Fort McAllister as well as those at the other clinic in town, he called his commanding officer at Fort Stewart.

"There's one thing I'm sure about," said Colonel Jurgensen, "this isn't some run-of-the-mill flu, Dr. McGlamry, it's taking this community by storm. I've never seen anything move this fast. My first impression is that we could have a case of bio-engineering on our hands. If that's true, this could be an attack by bio-terrorists. In any event, I recommend you institute Special Order Medical Alpha-Two and have this whole county sealed off. If this gets into the general population, as fast as it's moving and as virulent as it appears, we could have a disaster on our hands in a matter of hours."

Special Order Medical Alpha-Two had been put in place by the Department of Defense and honed to a sharp point after 9-11. It was meant to deal with a biological event similar to what was happening in Bryan County. In short, martial law would be declared, and the infected area sealed off by the military. Medical teams would enter the restricted area and assess the situation. Within three hours of Dr. Jurgensen's call, military police units from the Third Infantry Division at Fort Stewart had blocked every road that led into Bryan County. The only exception was I-95, and no one could enter or exit the interstate as it ran through the county.

At Fort McAllister, young Rudy's scoutmaster was overwhelmed. He had planned to call Dr. Hoorst and tell him he needed to come and take his son home, but more of his troop began to show signs of the illness. By time the scoutmaster was able to call his father, Rudy Jr. had slipped into unconsciousness. Just after that, he was informed that three other boys from his troop were demonstrating the same symptoms as Rudy; it was then the scoutmaster called Dr. Hoorst and informed him of his son's malady.

When Rudy received the scoutmaster's phone call, he was preparing to have lunch with his wife. "How bad is he?" asked Rudy.

"He's unconscious, and we can't get an ambulance to take him to the hospital. The 911 operator says something's happened in Richmond Hill and half of the troop's getting sick just like Rudy. I think I'm coming down with it too, Dr. Hoorst. There's no way I can drive your boy to the hospital."

"I'll come by helicopter. I should be there in about thirty minutes."

Rudy looked quickly at Carolyn, saying, "Rudy is very sick. I'll fly to Fort McAllister and get him. I'll let you know something as soon as I find out."

As Rudy turned to leave the dining room, Colonel Schwarz entered with a concerned look on his face.

"What is it, Claus?"

"I've been watching the TV, Dr. Hoorst. Martial law has been declared in the Richmond Hill area. The reports are that a plague has broken out there, and the authorities are saying it could be a modified version of the H1N1 virus, you know, the swine flu. Only now they're calling it the H7N9 virus. The same virus that wiped out this colony a month ago."

That news staggered Rudy and he had to grab the back of his chair to steady himself. Slowly he sat back down as what he'd been told began to sink in with all its implications.

"Is it bad?" faltered Carolyn, terrified. "Is our son gonna be OK?"

For several seconds Rudy didn't move, he simply stared at the floor. He quickly stood again and turned to Carolyn. "Rudy will be fine. Schwarz and I are leaving immediately to retrieve him."

As Rudy and Schwarz left the Main House and got into the waiting Humvee, Schwarz told Rudy the rest of the story. "The military police have cordoned off all of Bryan County. No one goes in or out. I don't know if we'll be able to get to Master Hoorst, sir."

"We'll fly in," was all Rudy said as they climbed into the Humvee and headed for the landing zone.

The Army had established the Florida Passage and parts of the Ogeechee River as the eastern boundary for the quarantine of Bryan County and had Apache helicopter gunships patrolling the area. As soon EO's Huey was seen approaching, two Apaches converged on it at the confluence of those rivers. Heated words were exchanged over the radio between Hoorst and the Apache pilots when the Huey was denied entry, but it quickly became apparent to Rudy they weren't going any further, and he asked to be guided to the perimeter of the blockade on US-17.

The Army's roadblock on Highway 17 was on the north side of the Ogeechee River at the King's Ferry Bridge. A command center had been established there, and when EO's Huey landed in the parking lot, a Humvee was waiting to take Rudy to the center.

As the Humvee wound its way through the throngs of people waiting at the river, Rudy asked the driver who was in charge of the quarantine operation.

"That would be Colonel McGlamry, sir," came the reply, and, for the first time that day, Rudy felt he had been given good news. He knew McGlamry well.

* * *

"I'm so sorry about your son, Rudy. I'll do all I can to help."

"Thanks, Dalton, 'cause I'm gonna take you up on your offer. I want to go into the restricted zone and get my boy out."

McGlamry shook his head as he looked sadly at Rudy and said, "I was afraid you'd want to do that, Rudy, but it's simply impossible. I have to follow the protocol spelled out in my special orders. Nobody leaves until it's safe, and I don't know when that'll be."

Rudy put his hands on his hips, rolled his lower lip between his teeth and bit down as he thought. "OK, I can accept that," replied Rudy, "but you can at least let me in. I know you've got personnel inside that perimeter dressed in hazmat gear checking the situation out. I'm a medical doctor, I can help. Let me dress out and go in, too, so I can at least find out if my son is dead or alive. Please do that for me, Dalton."

McGlamry let out a long breath and nodded in approval, saying, "Just don't do anything stupid like trying to smuggle your son out, OK?"

"Not a problem, Dalton. Just one more thing, though. I want Colonel Schwarz to come with me."

The ride down Highway 17 to State Route 144 seemed to take forever. Being dressed out in a full hazmat suit didn't help. When Rudy's Humvee got to the crossroads of 17 and 144, what normally would have been a bustling intersection looked like a ghost town. A few military vehicles and personnel were all that could be seen. At the intersection, the Humvee turned left on 144 and headed for Fort McAllister.

When the Humvee got to the camping area outside the walls of the fort, it stopped. Rudy and Schwarz climbed out and quickly scanned the area. What they saw was terrifying.

The bodies of at least a dozen boys were sprawled out on the ground. Almost all had blood coming from their noses and mouths. The scoutmaster was on the ground in front of his tent, alive but unconscious. Rudy looked around the campsite as he quickly tried to identify his son's tent. When Rudy pulled back the flap covering the entrance to one of the tents, he saw his son.

Little Rudy's body rested on his sleeping bag. Blood that had trickled out of his nose and mouth was now dried and caked on his cheeks and chin. His eyes were fully open and had a look of terror in them that his death couldn't erase. His mouth was open, too, as if his lifeless body were still gasping for air. His face was cyanotic, and his beautiful blond hair twisted and matted from the perspiration that had poured out of him while he was still alive. Colonel Schwarz stood behind Rudy and looked over his shoulder as Rudy reached into the tent and pulled back the rest of the sleeping bag. What they saw was a child covered in his own bloody diarrhea.

At the tent's entrance, Rudy crumpled to one knee, dropped his head and gave a great, agonized scream. It was like the shriek of wounded animal. After a few seconds, Schwarz gently reached out and put his hand on Rudy's shoulder, saying, "Come on, sir, it's time to leave. I'll find a blanket and cover Master Hoorst."

Rudy didn't budge. When Schwarz tugged a little, Rudy violently pulled his shoulder away and shouted, "Leave me alone. I'm staying with him. I won't leave him here like this!"

"You have another son and a wife who are going to need you terribly now, Dr. Hoorst. Don't you think it's best we leave now, sir?"

Rudy didn't say anything. Finally he nodded slightly, then slowly stood. He turned to Schwarz and whispered, "I've killed my own son, Claus. How will I ever live with that?"

"No, no, sir, you did not," responded Schwarz forcefully. "This is an unforeseeable accident, an act of nature. You're not responsible for any of this!"

Rudy looked at Schwarz through the clear plastic of the hazmat suit and slowly shook his head from side to side. "I've been playing God for too long on that island, Claus, we both have. Now it's God's turn to play Himself, and He's done it with great vengeance."

* * *

The news about Richmond Hill instantly became huge. It was big not only from a medical standpoint, but from a political one as well. When it broke, Will and his wife were spending the last weekend he'd have free for a long time with Judah and Hannah at their beach cottage on Tybee Island.

"This sure as hell ain't gonna help things any, Will," said Judah between bites of his hotdog and swigs of beer, "but I don't see how it's a game-changer. You've already weathered the worst part of the Ossabaw storm, and they didn't lay a glove on you. All you have to do is keep tellin' the fuckin' truth."

Will fished around in the cooler next to his rocking chair and pulled out another beer. He stopped rocking and asked, "Just what is the truth, Judah?"

Judah sighed and wiped his hands off on his jeans. "I advise you to never to ask that question again. The truth could sink this campaign. Plus, you don't want to know. Just remember this, though." He faced Will and said slowly, "If the shit hits the fan and it gets to that fallin'-on-your-sword time, I'll do the fallin' and you'll be just fine."

* * *

On the brief flight back to Ossabaw, Rudy had very little to say. He could only look out the door of the Huey. When the chopper finally settled on the landing pad, Schwarz said, "You must be strong, sir. Both my wife and I will be with you during all of this, and we'll help with Mrs. Hoorst and your other son."

Rudy was able to manage a slight nod in acknowledgement and, before he stepped from the door of the Huey, he turned to Schwarz and said, "We'll have to return to the mainland and retrieve Rudy's body as soon as the quarantine is lifted."

Schwarz waited for the helicopter's engines to spool down completely before answering, "No, sir, that won't be possible."

"But why not, Claus?"

"I was informed by Dr. McGlamry that all bodies were being collected and burned in an open pit. The ashes will be buried in a common grave. It's one of the central parts in the plan to contain the epidemic."

"Oh my God, no," said Rudy, slumping back in his seat. "My son is disposed of in the same way we dispose of the residents in this colony. What a paradox; what perfect poetic justice has been meted out to me!"

The next couple of weeks were difficult for the Hoorst family. With no body to bury and no grave to visit, closure was elusive for Rudy and Carolyn, but they both exhibited a type of Teutonic stoicism and put on their best face for their surviving son.

At first, the days passed well enough for Rudy, but it was the nights that took a toll. His nightmares had returned, except now they were a regular occurrence; the only way he could sleep was with the aid of ever-increasing medications. He began to drink not only in the evening, but during the day as well, and he was not holding his liquor. Colonel Schwarz had assumed almost all responsibilities for day-to-day business of the colony, believing it would give Rudy a chance to heal and regain his emotional stability; but as time passed, Schwarz could tell things were not improving. Carolyn could see her husband was in a downward spiral, but what was worse, the guards could see it, also, and faith in his leadership was very important for the colony's smooth operation.

A week before the presidential election, Schwarz found Rudy in his office late at night. Rudy had been drinking and when Schwarz entered the room, he found him seated at his desk staring at a picture of little Rudy. Without saying a word, Schwarz sat in one of the chairs opposite the desk. After a minute of thick silence, Rudy finally spoke.

"I was just thinking about my little boy, Claus," said Rudy slowly and deliberately. "He would have been thirteen years old next month and beginning to grow into a man. But that won't happen because of what I did."

Schwarz shifted in his chair and replied gently, "You are not the reason Master Hoorst died, sir."

Without taking his eyes off the photo, Rudy answered, "Oh, but I am. I gave the order to use the virus." Rudy slowly lifted his head and looked directly at Schwarz. "God has punished me for what's been done on this island, I'm sure of it."

"Our Lord only punishes sinful actions, sir. What has happened here is not sinful."

Rudy snorted, raised his voice and said, "Not sinful! If what I've done here is not sinful, then what is it?"

"What you've done here, what we've both done here, is an act of mercy, Dr. Hoorst. You've said that many times. The residents who came here did so to die without pain, and we've jolly well seen to that, sir. No one has been mistreated."

"Killing people before their time isn't mistreatment, Claus? Using their depravities to make money with television shows isn't sinful? How can you, of all people, take me for such a damn fool, Oberst Schwarz?"

"Sir," replied Schwarz calmly, "we both were born and raised as Roman Catholics, and we've both been taught that mercy is the greatest of all Christian acts. The good this colony does is immense. These residents don't have to kill and steal or prostitute themselves to get the drugs they need. They knew they'd never leave this place. When the suffering at Butterbean Beach became so great because of the overcrowding, someone had to have mercy on those people. Someone had to do what was necessary to alleviate that terrible suffering and, to your credit, you did that."

Rudy didn't say anything as he pushed his chair back from his desk and started toward the bar for another drink. With glass in hand, he took a seat in the other chair in front of his desk and turned it to face Schwarz.

"You'd have made a good lawyer, Claus," said Rudy, taking a long drink from his glass, "but you can't make chicken salad out of chicken shit."

Schwarz made no reply as he looked at Rudy.

"And what about killing Robbie McFarland," slurred Rudy. "Was that an act of mercy, also?'

"Knowing Mr. McFarland as I did, sir, I look upon his elimination as the sword of justice being wielded."

Rudy didn't reply; he just took another long swallow from his glass as Schwarz studied him.

In all the time that Schwarz had been associated with Rudy, there was never a moment when Schwarz had ever been familiar with his superior. He had always been formal and proper, so what Schwarz did next came as a complete shock and surprise to Rudy.

Placing his right hand on Rudy's knee, Schwarz said tenderly, "Rudy you've been with the company for many years now; have you ever heard stories about The Ghost?"

Immediately Rudy's head snapped up and he looked right at Schwarz. His mouth opened, but Rudy couldn't find the words. He was flabbergasted that Schwarz had addressed him by his first name and that he'd put his hand on him. Rudy was speechless. Then, with a kind, fatherly smile, Schwarz rephrased his question.

"Certainly, Rudy, you've heard company stories about The Ghost, haven't you?"

Dazedly, Rudy nodded and said, "Yeah, he's supposed to be one of the big shots in the company who goes undercover and spies on how things are being done in the colonies. Nobody really knows who he is, and it's been going on from the beginning."

Schwarz patted Rudy softly on his knee and replied, "That's very good. I am The Ghost, Rudy."

Rudy leaned back in his chair and simply blinked as he looked in astonishment at Schwarz. Then Schwarz spoke again.

"You've done an excellent job here at the Ossabaw colony, Rudy, and the company will reward you handsomely. But, sadly, the tragedy of Little Rudy's death has rendered you ineffective and I must relieve you of your command immediately."

* * *

A week later, on election night, Katie watched the results in the Main House with Colonel Schwarz and Eva. At nine-thirty, CNN called the election for Will McQueen. A few minutes later, the other networks followed suit, and around eleven Katie and the Schwarzes watched Will give his victory speech. Standing to his right were Judah and John-Morgan When Will acknowledged Judah as the architect of his successful campaign and John-Morgan as his lifelong friend, Schwarz was unable to suppress a giant smile. When Eva saw this, she reached over and patted Claus's hand, saying, "You've done well once more, my darling."

At the same time, Rudy sat with Carolyn in the den of their new house on the Isle of Hope. Rudy wasn't drunk, not yet, just a little tight. When he saw Judah come to the podium and embrace Will, he thought back to the treasure room at the Main House on Ossabaw, and the time Judah was brought there, and the last words he'd spoken to Judah in that room filled with gold: "If you only knew the half of it."

CHAPTER NINETEEN

THE CLEANSING

Purge me with hyssop, and I shall be clean:
wash me and I shall be whiter than snow.
—*The Holy Bible*, King James Version, Psalms 51:7

After Colonel Schwarz removed Rudy from the colony, he took complete control of EO's American operations and, following the success of the funeral home legislation and its joint-harvesting program, the company began to eye a cut-rate nursing home plan that would offer Spartan, but agreeable, care for seniors. The new nursing home business was Schwartz's brainchild and he modeled not only its business plan after the Osssabaw Colony, but also its enhanced joint-harvesting program. There were quantities of surplus dated food and medical supplies, the bulk of which were still usable, as well as repossessed real estate bought on the cheap. And Georgia was rife with low-skilled labor willing to work for minimum wage. The company hired them by the hundreds, trained them, and put them to work caring for the elderly in six different facilities scattered over the southern part of the state. As with its other endeavors, EO started making money almost from the start.

At each of its nursing homes, a loyal EO employee was the administrator. Usually, they were older physicians from Europe looking to retire in a few years and willing to go along with just about anything. They knew which residents had usable implants and, when notified there was a need on the world market for that device, were willing to ease those residents along a little more quickly. At death, one of the company's funeral homes would take the remains and, before cremation, harvest the implant and complete the deal. It was almost a vertical business, diabolical, but efficient and profitable. What the company hadn't anticipated was the diligence and honesty of a fifty-year-old black woman from Valdosta who worked at the company's Pleasant Park Nursing Home.

* * *

Queen Esther Pelote knew she had to go back to work after her second daughter showed up one day and dumped her two children on her parents, then entered the Ossabaw colony. The girls were only nine and eleven, and Queenie couldn't bear seeing them in foster care. Her husband was retired on disability, and the only way things could work was if Queenie took a job. When the opening at Pleasant Park came around, she regarded it as an answer to her prayers. She'd done that type of work before and was good at it. She was a kind and compassionate soul who enjoyed being around the elderly, took her Baptist faith seriously, and used it to guide her life.

At first, things at Pleasant Park appeared normal to Queenie, and soon she was a trusted member of the nursing staff. Then little things started to trouble her.

From the beginning, Queenie wasn't particularly comfortable around the administrator, an older female physician from Germany who treated her with little respect and spoke heavily accented, broken English. Needing the work, Queenie wrote that off and forged ahead. It took a few months, but Queenie started to notice patients dying suddenly. One day a resident would be full of life, and the next day he or she would be gone. Queenie had no formal medical training, but she had spent a lot of time around such people and, after a while, things just didn't add up to her. She could read old people well and soon began to make mental notes about visits by the administrator to a patient's room and the rapidity and regularity of their deaths. What really made Queenie suspicious was when her Aunt Pearl passed away. It was all too quick and convenient. Then, two days later, another resident was gone.

One of the local TV stations out of Savannah had a program that asked the viewers to call them about unscrupulous activities and, if the station deemed the call credible, an investigative reporter would be sent for an interview. Queenie did just that, and a discreet investigation was launched. In a matter of weeks, things at Pleasant Park Nursing Home started to unravel after the station passed the story on to CNN.

In very short fashion, Executive Outcomes became the center of a national news story when it was revealed that EO owned both the nursing facility and the funeral home that took the remains. Then it was discovered that the company owned five other nursing homes with ties to other funeral homes owned by EO. The final nail was driven in when it was revealed that a super-PAC funded by Executive Outcomes had spent millions on campaign ads favorable to Will McQueen. Things began hitting the fan in rapid succession, and Will's political enemies in Congress were howling for an investigation. The mainstream media latched onto that and went with it full-bore.

While President McQueen and his chief of staff Judah Benjamin were somewhat insulated by the security bubble surrounding them, Rudy Hoorst wasn't. As soon as it was learned that Rudy wasn't living on Ossabaw anymore, but in his home on Isle of Hope, a small army of television and print reporters laid siege to the house.

To his credit, Rudy had come to grips with his son's death and ultimately his abuse of alcohol and sedatives. However, what was transpiring in front of his home almost drove him back to those things. Neither he nor his wife could leave the house without being harassed by reporters shouting questions and photographers poking cameras in their faces. They even followed as Carolyn took their remaining son to St. James School and were in the parking lot as she waited to pick him up in the afternoon.

President McQueen's political enemies sensed a way perhaps to bring down Will's fledgling presidency and were calling for a full-blown investigation of Executive Outcomes. This was of particular concern to Rudy, since he was certain he'd be subpoenaed. However, if he were back on Ossabaw Island again, there would be no more reporters and cameras, and

EO's agreement with the State of Georgia might protect him.

* * *

Schwarz was sitting behind what used to be Rudy's desk in Rudy's old office when he heard a knock on the door. "Enter," called out Schwarz. When the door was flung open, in stepped Rudy, wearing his EO dress black uniform. He approached the front of the desk, stopped and looked directly at Schwarz. "I am my old self again, Colonel Schwarz. If you will allow me, I would very much like to return to the colony in some capacity. I understand that I will be subordinate to you, and I am fine with that."

Schwarz looked at Rudy, sizing him up from head to toe. His color was good, his fine blond hair well-groomed, and his blue eyes bright and clear again. Soon a warm smile crept across Schwarz's face. He stood and walked around the desk to Rudy. He extended his right hand and Rudy took it in a firm grip.

"I always believed you would overcome your sorrow, Rudy," said Schwarz. "You have it in your genes. I could see so much of your wonderful father in you, and he was such a strong man. Of course you can come back to the island."

Standing back, Schwarz gestured around the office saying, "Everything is still here, just as you left it. Nothing has changed, this will be your office once more, and you will be the commandant. Eva and I are planning to retire soon, and I was searching for someone to run the colony. I'm thrilled for you and Carolyn and your little boy."

Rudy smiled and he softly said, "Thank you, Claus." He began to relax as he looked around the office he'd taken such great care to design and furnish.

"Come on, Rudy," said Schwarz, "go, take your old seat behind your desk and fill me in on things. By all the news reports, I understand the company may have some problems. I thank God I have someone like you to be here with me during these times."

* * *

As the summer dragged on, so did the controversy surrounding Will McQueen and Executive Outcomes. It had been Judah's strategy to pull a "rope-a-dope" with the press, but by mid-August, it became clear that strategy wouldn't work when two more EO employees came forward to say they also believed nursing home residents were being overdosed by EO administrators. When the Republican Speaker of the House called Judah and told him many members of his own party were getting weak in the knees over the scandal, and that much of the reform legislation Will had run on and won with was in jeopardy, Judah decided it was time to act and he called a press conference for the next day.

That afternoon, Judah stood at the podium in the White House pressroom. He took a sip of water, cleared his throat and said, "I'm going to make a brief statement, then open things up for questions.

"Now, I don't see any need for me to rehash all that's been said about Executive Outcomes and the charges against that company. What I do want to address are the accusations some of you in the press have been making about the president's relationship with that company and his knowledge about what EO has or has not been doing with residents in the nursing homes they own. The Ossabaw colony has been the success the people of Georgia hoped for. Everyone here knows that I, as well as President McQueen, served on the board of directors of the Ossabaw colony."

"For many months, the colony seemed to be functioning properly. Then I began to get suspicious of little things and decided to do my own discreet investigation. What I found out seemed to indicate that certain residents with joint implants were dying more quickly than one would think. I had no concrete evidence, none that I could hold in my hand and show you, but I had my suspicions that the State of Georgia wasn't getting what it bargained for. About this same time, President McQueen decided to run for the office he now holds and asked me to help him. I agreed, but I also realized that the Ossabaw colony was a potential time bomb for him and urged him to resign immediately, which is what happened."

Judah paused. "At no time did I tell President McQueen about any of my suspicions. I wanted him to be able to say, truthfully, he knew nothing at all about this entire situation. The President is watching this in the Oval Office and, as my words reach his ears, this is the first time he has heard me speak of this. He is innocent of any and all accusations that have been leveled against him."

Judah waited for several moments. Then he raised his chin and said, "OK, now I'll take your questions."

The room erupted in voices and shouts as reporters tried to get Judah's attention.

"So, you're taking the fall for the President, Mr. Benjamin?"

"If you want to call it that."

"Are you going to resign?"

"My letter of resignation is being delivered to President McQueen right now."

"Do you believe there'll be a Congressional investigation of Executive Outcomes?

"Yes, and I think the first people called to testify under oath should be Dr. Rudolph Hoorst and Colonel Claus Schwarz."

* * *

Rudy and Schwarz sat together in the Great Room of the Main House and watched Judah's press conference. Neither was surprised by what Judah said, and after the conference ended, Schwarz looked at Rudy and remarked, "Remember when I told you to beware of the Jude?"

"How well I do, Claus, but what do we do now?"

"We wait and see how things shake out. We're probably well-insulated from having to testify before any Congressional committee. Besides, we can always leave the country," added Schwarz, standing to go to the windows. Rudy followed him and stood by his side as both men's eyes fell on the newly-erected twenty-foot-tall cross in the distance. It was a crucifix carved from white Italian marble, which Rudy had ordered as a monument to Lloyd Bryan's work in the colony. Rudy had it carved just as Lloyd had told him he thought Jesus had actually been crucified, nails through the wrists, not the hands, and feet nailed to the cross through the sides of each heel. The way the afternoon sun caught it made the giant cross almost glow as the head of Jesus, crowned with thorns, looked skyward with what appeared to be a plea for mercy from His Father. Both men were lost in their thoughts when something on the TV got their attention.

It was Neil Cavuto on Fox, saying a tropical storm in the Caribbean had strengthened to hurricane force and that forecasts had it tracking toward the southeastern coast of the U.S. Landfall was expected in about five days, and the cone of projection was centered directly on Ossabaw Island. The name of the storm was George. Later that day, one of the people at the Weather Channel mused about the possibility of George's making a direct hit on the drug colony at Ossabaw and began referring to the storm as "Saint George the Dragon Slayer."

"I guess we should start making plans for evacuating the island," said Rudy, moving closer to the TV screen to study the projected path of Hurricane George.

Watching the storm's path, Schwarz replied, "We evacuate only the guards and their dependents, Rudy."

"Do you mean all of our people will be removed from the island and the residents will be left on their own, Colonel?"

"Not completely, Rudy. Company policy is that the colony's commanding officer remains on the island. If the company completely abandons the colony, then, according to our contract with the State of Georgia, it has broken its terms with the state, and EO will lose any remaining funds due it."

Astonished, Rudy said, "So, Claus, you're saying you're going to ride this storm out? You're not leaving?"

Calmly Schwarz replied, "That's company policy, Rudy." He turned away from the television and admired the construction of the Great Room. "This old place has ridden out many hurricanes in its long life. Look at it, it's a fortress! I have no doubt I'll be safe here. I'll have everything I could need for seventy-two hours or so—emergency power, food and water, guns and ammunition. And, even if the storm surge reaches this structure, there's always the second floor and then the roof. The winds can't take out this great lady!"

Rudy nodded slightly and walked over to the bar to pour himself a vodka over ice. Schwarz went again to the windows and looked at the sky. After several seconds of silence, Rudy said, "I'm staying with you, Colonel."

Schwarz looked back over his shoulder, smiled at Rudy. "That's not necessary, Rudy, but I do appreciate the gesture. You still have a wife and son. There's always the outside chance that things won't play out as I believe."

As a matter of personal honor, Rudy felt it imperative that he show no signs of weakness and shot back, "I insist, Colonel!"

Schwarz turned to face Rudy directly. "You're a loyal man, Dr. Hoorst. The company appreciates such behavior; you may stay if you so desire." Turning back to the window, Schwarz added, "Riding out this storm will be a once-in-a-lifetime happenstance, something you'll be able to tell your grandchildren about." He walked to the door and told the guard to summon Sergeant Leary. When Leary appeared, Schwarz instructed him to begin preparations to evacuate all personnel from the island within forty-eight hours.

Among those leaving would be Katie McFarland. When Rudy asked Sergeant Leary where she was, he said she was probably at the monument to Bishop Bryan, where she left a bouquet of cut wildflowers around this time each day.

Rudy hadn't spoken alone with Katie since his return and, when he approached her standing at the foot of the cross, she smiled warmly and told him how happy she was that he was better and able to be back on the island again. Rudy nodded and thanked her, then looked at the inscription on the base of the monument. It read, THE ONLY MAN-MADE THINGS IN HEAVEN. Under that was Lloyd's name. Rudy read the inscription once more and looked up at the crucified Christ. Finally he turned to Katie. "A hurricane is expected to hit the island within five days. Colonel Schwarz has directed that everyone except the residents is to leave here within forty-eight hours. That includes you, Katie."

"A hurricane? How big is it?"

"Right now, a Category Two, but it's expected to strengthen by the time it gets here," replied Rudy. He looked into Katie's beautiful eyes and felt that little twinge of excitement.

"But what about the residents, Rudy?"

"They'll be left here alone. That's just the way it is. What you need to do right now is report back to the Main House in an hour. Schwarz wants you to be in the first boat that leaves for the mainland."

"What about you, Rudy? Will you be on that boat with me?"

"No, Schwarz and I are staying. It's company policy."

For a long moment they held each other's gaze. Katie turned to the crucifix, reached to run her hands gently over Jesus' marble feet and looked up at His face. "I think He just wanted it all to be over with, don't you, Rudy? Just like the people on this island. They all just want the pain to stop." Katie came close to Rudy. Tenderly, she hugged him, resting her head against his chest briefly, then stepped back and said, "Please take care of yourself." Without another word, Katie quickly turned and walked away.

When Rudy returned to the Main House, he found Schwarz in his office, speaking on the phone with Governor McFarland. By the look on Schwarz's face, Rudy could tell Big Dog was raising hell about Judah's press conference only hours earlier. Rudy sat silently and listened as Schwarz brought the conversation to a close, hung up the phone and leaned back in his chair. Schwarz looked at Rudy and said, "Among other things, the governor believes we are responsible for Robbie's disappearance. He's also thinks the company engineered the infections that wiped out our population and killed your son. He's very angry and says he's sending the National Guard to the island to take the two of us into custody. When I reminded the governor that the situation here on the island will dwarf every other distasteful thing that has surfaced about the colony, I believe that gave him pause for reflection."

"It appears the situation here at the colony could become untenable for the company. Perhaps leaving the country is the only way out for us, Claus."

"Executive Outcomes has been in worse situations before, Dr. Hoorst. The company always has a back-up plan or two. Just remember, the money trail will lead directly to the governor's front door. When he's been adequately educated on the subject, I believe Big Dog McFarland will have a different perspective when it comes to sending in the Guard. Besides, we have a hurricane headed our way, and both we and the governor have more pressing things than some silly notion the company is doing anything improper on this island."

* * *

The evacuation of the Ossabaw colony went smoothly and was completed ahead of schedule. As the last boat for the mainland left from the Ossabaw dock, Rudy and Schwarz were there. Eva Schwarz was the last one to step on board. She would be staying with Carolyn at Rudy's house, and Rudy was grateful for that.

On Schwarz's orders, before the last guards were withdrawn, they left a week's worth of food, water, and drugs at the distribution points for each of the three groups. The residents were informed about the pending hurricane and that they were all now on their own. The electronic fencing at Group Three was left up and running, but it depended on the back-up generators once power from the mainland was severed. When that happened, Schwarz hoped the winds and rising waters would be able to contain the almost two hundred members of Group Three until order could be re-established. If it couldn't, he was sure maniacs would roam the island and prey upon the other residents like wolves on defenseless lambs.

Once back at the Main House, Rudy and Schwarz settled into Rudy's office where they monitored the progress of the storm. Nothing had changed about the storm's predicted course; it seemed to bear down on their island with some kind of meteorological intelligence, hell-bent on destruction. When the sun began to set on a pristine day, Rudy and Schwarz started securing the Main House from George and anything else that might be lurking in the dark..

* * *

Brittany Habersham was a rising star at WTOC Channel 11, the CBS affiliate in Savannah. She'd covered a number of hard-hitting stories for the station, had done well, and the scuttlebutt around the newsroom was that she'd probably be scooped up by another station in a much larger market. So, when the chance to cover the shut-down of the Ossabaw colony presented itself early Saturday morning, she knew it would be big and jumped on it. What greeted Brittany at Butterbean Beach was startling.

Even though a hurricane was headed for the area and expected to hit within days, Brittany found almost three hundred people waiting outside the fences at Butterbean Beach, with another two hundred fifty already inside the enclosure. She detected an air of desperation in the throng of people gathered outside the fences as she exited the SUV, plastered with large WTOC logos. She was frightened by the way the crowd was behaving and told the driver to pull back farther from the crowd. Moving to the other side of the Diamond Causeway, Brittany and her cameraman set up their equipment and prepared for a live feed to the station at noon.

Sonny Dixon was the long-time anchor at Channel 11 and, as he looked into the camera, he said in his soft Southern accent, "Now we go live to our own Brittany Habersham at Butterbean Beach."

The panorama of the embarkation point at Butterbean Beach was just over Brittany's left shoulder as she lifted her microphone to speak. Before she could utter a word, a fight started among some of those on the outside of the enclosure, and the camera focused on it.

"Yeah, Sonny," replied Brittany, "what you're seeing over there has been happening most of the morning. As you already know, the Ossabaw colony has stopped all admissions, but new people hoping to be admitted to the colony continue to arrive here in large numbers. As you can see, it's pretty much a state of chaos among those outside the wire. I've been told that all guards on Ossabaw have been evacuated and that, by six this afternoon, the guards who run things here at Butterbean Beach will also be pulled out as George continues to take aim at Savannah."

"Well," asked Sonny, who appeared genuinely concerned, "what's going to happen to all those people? Is there any police presence at all?"

"No. As you are aware, a mandatory evacuation order has been issued for the whole Savannah area, and there is no police protection. To be truthful, my cameraman, Doug, and I are beginning to feel very uncomfortable, and I don't think we'll stay around much longer. From what I can see, things are going to get very, very ugly in a short time."

* * *

Rudy and Schwarz had just finished lunch in the Great Room and watched Brittany Habersham's report with a feeling of satisfaction. "I hope Big Dog McFarland gets to see this," said Rudy. "It will make him think twice."

"The Governor doesn't think, Rudy," answered Schwarz, pointing the remote at the TV to switch to the Weather Channel, "he only reacts. When this has passed, we'll have a firm understanding with him. We'll take him to the mountaintop and show him the valley below."

"This isn't a big storm, it doesn't cover a wide area," said the announcer, "but it does pack a wallop. Winds at the center are sustained at 105 mph. We still show the track taking it over the Georgia coast, probably making landfall at Ossabaw Island. The bad thing about the timing of George's arrival over land is, we think it will hit right at high tide, and that tide will be a very high 10.1 feet at 7:35 in the morning. We're already predicting a storm surge of around twenty feet or more and, with the winds keeping that surge in place for hours, the National Weather Service is predicting Ossabaw and the other barrier islands along the Georgia coast will be under as much as fifteen feet of water, perhaps even more."

Rudy looked at Schwarz and said, "We can still leave, Claus. We've got time. We can easily get back to the mainland in the launch. Are you sure you want to stay?"

Schwarz turned to Rudy saying, "Steady, Rudy, steady! As I told you before, this old fort has ridden out many a storm the equal of our George, and here it still stands. We'll be tossed and turned a little, but we'll be fine. However, Dr. Hoorst, if you feel compelled to evacuate, I'll completely understand."

Rudy's face turned crimson with embarrassment, and he quickly replied, "No! I said I'd ride it out with you, and that's what I'll do."

Schwarz smiled. "I knew you weren't leaving."

Schwarz was right about the Main House's surviving hurricanes. However, he was only partially right. He'd searched the hundred-year weather history of the Savannah area and found almost half a dozen hurricanes had hit there. The worst of them were all Category Two events and, while causing significant damage, none had put any of the barrier islands under water. He should have gone back a little further and learned about the storms in the 1890s that buried those islands and killed thousands of people living on them. The Main House was built in the 1920s and had never experienced a storm like George.

* * *

George was now about twenty-four hours from making landfall, and Ossabaw Island remained its projected target. All the barrier islands along the Georgia coast had been evacuated, as had Chatham, Bryan, Liberty, and McIntosh counties. As George approached, the eyes of the nation became focused on the area, but Ossabaw and its drug colony were the focus of attention. TV and radio talk shows bubbled with speculation about the fate of the island's residents, and all the mystery and scandal involving Executive Outcomes only served to heighten the interest.

On Sunday morning, Colonel Schwarz told Rudy he thought a final inspection of the island was in order before the storm hit. They took Rudy's black Hummer and went first to the barn, where they opened the doors and let their horses go free. After that, they went to Group I.

Rudy drove the Hummer right up to the entrance of the first big tent and stopped. Neither man chose to get out. Rudy nudged the Hummer into the tent and turned on his bright lights. Most of the cots were filled with dead or dying. In the back of the tent, a few residents could be seen walking, in most cases staggering, around. Then they noticed some in the tent caring for those who couldn't help themselves. Schwarz recognized them as Group II long-timers.

"I'm surprised," said Rudy as he watched a woman in her thirties hold up the head of a man lying in a cot and help him drink, as another resident went from cot to cot and handed out drugs from the stockpile left by the guards.

"Even drug addicts can show compassion," responded Schwarz quietly.

Rudy and Schwarz drove deeper into the island to inspect Group II. Schwarz and Rudy were surprised by how few residents were there. When they saw someone walking nearby, they got out and approached him.

"Where is everybody?" asked Rudy of a man in his forties, high on coke.

"They've all grabbed up their shit and headed for the dunes," he replied. "That's the highest place on the island. They think the water won't get over the dunes." Pointing to a large oak tree, the man continued, "See that tree over there, that's my high ground. I'm gonna climb that thing and get up real high, and tie myself to it. I'll ride it out there."

Back in the Hummer, Rudy pointed it toward the deepest part of the forest and Group III. As they drove through the tunnel of trees, Rudy became quiet, reflecting. He liked Wagner and had *The Ride of the Valkyries* playing on the stereo. After several minutes of silence between them, Schwarz looked over at Rudy and asked, "What's on your mind, Dr. Hoorst?"

"I don't have a good feeling about this, Claus. I suspect we both could die here tomorrow."

"Are you afraid of dying, Rudy?"

"I'm afraid there'll be something on the other side that will be most unpleasant."

"That's normal. You've never faced the real prospect of your own death, have you? Well, I have, several times, and it lends an entirely different perspective to the question."

"After my son died, I started thinking about all this company has done, and my part in it. I started looking deeply into my actions, compared to how I was raised and what I profess to believe. And now I'm afraid of what I've done."

"Rudy," said Claus in a soft tone, "the two of us have done those things to protect ourselves and our families. To make them prosper and continue on after we're gone. The company is our lives. Executive Outcomes is what we are. We are like soldiers. We fight and sometimes kill to keep it alive and strong. There are thousands who depend on the fight we make."

"I don't know, Claus."

In a sterner voice, Schwarz replied, "I was raised as a Catholic just as you were, and I still believe. But this is a brutal and harsh world, and to survive, sometimes brutality must be met with even more brutality, or our people perish. The important thing I learned on my journey in life is that, while I've killed a number of people, I never did it for pleasure. I never took another life for the fun of it. I never did anything in our colonies for purely personal gain. It was always for the greater good of the company."

Schwarz waited for a few moments, then continued, "I believe you're the same. I know what a great temptation Katie McFarland was for you. You could have had her, but you didn't. Taking her would have been for your pleasure, and it would have been sinful. You would have violated your sacred marriage vows. Helping wretched souls die a little earlier rather than linger in their own self-imposed hell isn't. That, my dear Rudy, is what you must focus on."

The first thing people approaching Group III noticed were the day-glo orange markers every twenty feet that announced an electronic fence was just a foot farther in and that attempting to cross from either side would be fatal. Rudy stopped the Hummer at the now abandoned guard tower, where he and Schwarz got out and surveyed the perimeter.

The enclosure was large, measuring more than 1-1/2 square miles. At first they couldn't see any residents; then a white man in his thirties, well-developed with tattoos on his arms, chest, and even his head, emerged from the shadows and walked as close to the wire as he could, only fifteen feet from Rudy and Schwarz. He was obviously high, probably on the methamphetamines provided, and very angry and agitated. He stared at Schwarz for several seconds in a most menacing manner, then quickly coughed up a large amount of phlegm and spit it at Schwarz. When the sputum hit the invisible line, it was vaporized in a flash of steam.

Rudy was startled and drew back, but Schwarz stood calmly and smiled as the man spit at him once more. The man screamed at Schwarz saying, "You fuckin' bastard, you put me in this place, and I've had to fight for my life every day. When I signed up for this island, I thought I was gonna be able to get high and chill, but you sent me here. You bettah hope that fuckin' storm kills me, cause if I get outta here, I'm comin' to cut your fuckin' head off, Schwarz!"

Schwarz had spotted this person when he checked into the colony, rightly figured he'd become a big draw for EO's *Ultimate Gladiator* series, and had him placed in Group III. "Alex the Exterminator" moved that program to the number one spot, and Schwarz had no intentions of severing that up-link during the storm. He figured it would draw an audience in the millions.

Schwarz turned to Rudy, who had retreated behind the Hummer. Without emotion, Schwarz said, "Pray the generator that powers this fence doesn't fail, Rudy. If it does, either I or you may be obliged to shoot this individual. Are you up for that?"

Rudy's cheeks puffed out as he exhaled, blinked at Schwarz and looked back at the man on the other side of the wire. "I've seen enough, Claus. It's time to head back."

Rudy and Schwarz returned to the Main House in time for lunch and watched the progress of the storm as well as all the commentary about Executive Outcomes and its involvement with Will McQueen, and what the chances were that it would bring down the McQueen administration. Fox even did a biography on Rudy, complete with his high school yearbook photos as well as pictures of his wife and sons. Judah was featured on the show, and the former chief of staff to the president didn't mince words when it came to painting Rudy and Schwarz as cold-blooded killers.

Hurricane George had picked up speed in its forward movement and was now traveling at twenty-five miles an hour. Changes in the weather over Ossabaw Island became evident around two that afternoon, when the first of George's feeder bands began to move in. The winds from the northeast picked up dramatically, and soon rain began slicing in from Ossabaw Sound, pelting the Main House and rustling the big oaks surrounding it. The temperature dropped, too, as did the barometric pressure, and Rudy could feel the change as he'd never felt it before. The clouds became darker and by four, Rudy had to squint to see the white marble crucifix in the distance.

By six, the winds began to howl, and they would not let up for the rest of the night. Sunset was at eight-thirty that evening, but by seven, it was completely dark with the blackness interrupted by flashes of lightening and the crashing of thunder. At nine, the power from the mainland failed, and the emergency generator for the Main House kicked in as its diesel roared to life. Rudy and Schwarz sat in Rudy's office, where they watched the screens that monitored every place on the island. One by one the monitors went dead as the wind began ripping them from their attachments. When this started happening, Schwarz brought up the video feed from Group III and was relieved to discover that the emergency generator there had activated as planned, and the electronic fencing was still up and running. Then, the video feed went blank.

By midnight, the tide was coming back in, and the low-lying areas on the southern part of the island were the first to be affected. As the water rose, the animals on Ossabaw began to move to higher ground as water pushed them further and further to the north end. The island had an abundance of deer, feral hogs, snakes, rabbits, rats, squirrels, raccoons, opossums, even bobcats, and a large alligator population. As the water claimed more and more dry land, these creatures became concentrated on less and less.

The residents of Group III were the first inhabitants to feel the effects of George and, because of the electronic fencing, had no option other than climbing into the trees to escape the water, now two feet deep in their area. When that water finally reached the intake manifolds of the emergency generator powering the fence, those in Group III who hadn't drowned or purposely overdosed were free, and they joined the great exodus of the wild things seeking higher ground.

Because of the tree cover on Ossabaw, those areas in the interior didn't suffer as much from the winds as did the island's periphery. Soon, those trees would fill with thousands of creatures able to climb into them and find safety from the waters. As the storm intensified and the water relentlessly claimed more land, the branches of those great oaks were transformed into battlegrounds where people and wild animals fought with each other over a dry spot on a limb. There was no light other than flashes of lightening, and the fighting was fierce between men and animals with much biting and clawing, but thirty-eight Group III residents were able to prevail and would live through the night.

In Group II, those who had chosen to seek high ground in the dunes found the same problems as those who took to the trees, only they had to contend with three-hundred-pound wild boar and eight-hundred-pound alligators. They did not fare as well as the tree people.

As the night wore on, this mass of people and animals were driven closer and closer to the Main House. Sunrise that morning was at 5:50 and, when the sun rose, little light shone through George's thick gunmetal-blue clouds, but it was enough for Schwarz and Rudy to see a thin line in the distance the distance moving their way.

The few residents of Group II who made it to the high dunes were forced to contend with the wild hogs, with nothing more than sticks to defend themselves. Exhaustion finally overcame those who had made it to the dunes, and they fell prey to the hogs that slashed them with their tusks, while the bodies of the already dead were snatched away by alligators to be consumed when the storm had passed.

At nine-thirty in the morning, the eye of George passed over the island and an eerie calm was cast over Ossabaw, as blue skies and sunlight revealed to Rudy and Schwarz the total devastation brought by the storm. The surge had flooded the first floor of the Main House, and they had moved to the second floor, thinking they had survived the worst of George. From that vantage point, Rudy and Schwarz could see hundreds of deer and hogs fighting their way to the high ground surrounding the Main House. They could also see more than two dozen men, most from Group III, methodically heading their way.

With the big swastika tattoo in the center of his chest, Alex the Exterminator was hard to miss, and Schwarz smiled slightly as he brought the H&K model 91 assault rifle to his shoulder, took careful aim through the telescopic sight and fired. The Exterminator's head exploded in a pink mist. Then Schwarz held the rifle out to Rudy, saying, "Your turn." The desperate residents trying to make it to the Main House never stood a chance, as Rudy expertly and methodically picked them off until none were left.

When the trailing portion of the eye wall passed over the island, the storm was just as intense as ever, spawning small tornadoes that licked and ripped at the trees and the people hiding in them, tearing them out and sending them thousands of feet into the air, only to be dropped into the marshes and rivers around the island. One of those tornadoes bore down on the Main House while Rudy and Schwarz watched it move toward them, transfixed by its funnel twisting and jerking like a rat's tail. When Rudy pulled back from the open window, Schwarz could see he was terrorized.

Grabbing him by the collar, Schwarz pulled Rudy in close and shouted above the roar of the storm, "If you must die, boy, die without fear. Make your ancestors proud!"

Rudy was unable to speak. As the wail of the tornado intensified, he turned back to the window and watched its approach. Suddenly both men felt the air being sucked from their lungs and cried out in pain as their eardrums burst from the sudden drop in air pressure, also causing their bowels to evacuate. Suddenly, the pressure dropped again, and the pain of their eyes bulging from their sockets became unbearable. At that moment, as if some invisible hand had reached into that room, Rudy and Schwarz were snatched from it through the window and sent hurtling skyward to ride along with the bricks and timber of the Main House as the tornado swept them into Ossabaw Sound.

Their bodies were never recovered. The same tornado that killed them also erased the Main House and docks from Ossabaw. When George the Dragon Slayer had finally passed over the island, no person was left alive, and all vestiges of humans and their work, whether good or evil, save one, had been cleansed from Ossabaw Island.

Two days later, Governor McFarland and President McQueen toured the Savannah area from the air, assessing the storm damage. The last place they visited was Ossabaw and, when they passed over the island, they noticed the paths of five tornados that had plowed their way through it, cutting long scars a hundred yards wide, leaving nothing but bare earth. Their chopper flew low over the north end, where the Main House and docks had stood for almost a hundred years, and they could see no signs of anything except the large marble cross out in the open in memory of Lloyd Bryan and the only man-made things in heaven.

End